Known to millions as the agony aunt from [illegible] Television's *This Morning* programme, Denise Robertson has worked extensively on television and radio and as a national newspaper journalist. Beginning with *The Land of Lost Content* in 1984, which won the Constable Trophy for Fiction, she has published 18 successful novels. She lives near Sunderland with her husband and an assortment of dogs.

Other titles in
The Beloved People trilogy:

Strength for the Morning
Towards Jerusalem

DENISE ROBERTSON

The Beloved People

This edition published in the United Kingdom in 2004 by Little Books Ltd,
48 Catherine Place, London SW1E 6HL

First published by Constable 1992
Published by the Penguin Group in Signet 1993
This edition published by Robertson Books 2004

A CIP catalogue record for this book is available from the British Library.

ISBN: 1 904435 34 3

BOOK ONE

1922

1

It began with a death. Afterwards, Howard Brenton would see it as the moment when the careful mould of years was broken and his life spilled out, for better or worse. But there was no thought of death or breakage in his mind that October afternoon, as he drove the green Hispano Suiza towards the village of Belgate and the hill they called the Scar.

On the western slope they were building a house, a long, stone mansion with wide windows and a roof of green Westmorland slate. He glanced at his wife, Diana, sitting forward in her seat, lips parted in anticipation, kid-gloved hands folded on her knees. Her grey dust-coat was buttoned to the neck, her scarlet tam o'shanter secured against the wind by a long chiffon scarf. A sudden gust whipped round the front shield of the open car and she put up her hands to wipe the black hair from her eyes. Suddenly she realized Howard was looking at her and she smiled, the smile of a child who knows there are treats in store.

Howard nodded towards the blaze of limestone that gave the Scar its name. 'Not much further now.' The wind caught his words and carried them away, and Diana shook her head in happy incomprehension before turning her gaze once more towards the huddle of houses that lay ahead, and the hill behind them. On either side the Durham countryside was turning to gold and brown with the approach of autumn but to Diana, used to the lush green of Berkshire, it looked bleak. She shuddered a little, until she remembered the new house and her spirits lifted again.

The gusts were getting stronger, sending clouds scudding across the sky, causing the wheel of the Suiza to buck in Howard's hands. It was not the car he would have chosen, but Diana had gasped with delight at the sight of it in a London street and he had bought it the same day. It was the first time his wealth had given him conscious pleasure.

They were entering Belgate now, passing the Methodist Church and the Institute, shuddering over the cobbles of the main street. Home-going colliers turned at the noise, for a motor car was a rare sight. A thin dog leaped for safety across a water-filled gutter, and a child stopped bowling an iron hoop and stood, open-mouthed. As for the women, they stared unashamed, moving nearer to the pavement's edge to get a better view.

'So that's the new bride,' one woman said, easing her sleeping child on her hip. 'She's bonny enough, but nowt special, for all her father's fancy title.' She sniffed to imply a deep contempt for all aristocrats, and southern-born aristocrats in particular.

If Diana was aware of their scrutiny she gave no sign. Her eyes, narrowed against the wind, were fixed on the hill where they were building the house that would enable her to escape the gloomy disapproval of her mother-in-law and do as she pleased for the first time in her life.

Howard changed gear to negotiate the Half Moon corner, causing the engine to roar fiercely. In the back yard behind her father's drapery store, fifteen-year-old Esther Gulliver heard the noise and stopped her pegging out It would be Dr Lauder or Mr Howard, for no one else in the neighbourhood owned a car. She left the wet sheets and ran to the gate, wiping her hands on her gingham pinafore, to be rewarded with her first glimpse of the Brenton bride, Diana Carteret, a society beauty from the other end of

England, only daughter of a baronet, sitting high in the green car, a red tam o'shanter on her head.

Howard saw the child at the half-open gate, her hair tied back now that she was growing up, her dress covered by a frilled apron, her eyes like saucers. He knew little of the Gulliver family, but the widowed father was rumoured to be a dreamer and a drunkard. He tipped his hat to the child and was pleased to receive an answering smile: not all the people they had passed had responded so pleasantly. He was glad when the car was out of Belgate, away from the clustering roofs, the unmade streets and the general air of desolation that surrounded the colliery. Charles Brenton, his father, was certain that the workers of England preferred to live close to their livelihood, but Howard had an uneasy feeling that most men, given the chance, would choose to live away from the grime of the pit. Their houses were mostly hovels, the unmade streets with their open sewers hotbeds of disease. And he was building a house set high on a hill fitted with every conceivable luxury. Not for the first time, his conscience stirred.

Watching her husband, Diana saw his brows come together in a frown. She could seldom tell what lay behind that watchful face, and it irked her. The thin, white scar beneath his left eye twitched as though he realized she was scrutinizing him and resented it, and she turned away, anxious for the first glimpse of her new home. She had the rest of her life to understand her husband.

Above, on the hill, the men tried to ignore a wind that plucked at their clothes and snatched words from their open mouths. They were all Brenton workmen, drawn from pit and factory to build a house for Mr Howard's new wife. There was the chance of a bonus if the house was finished on time, so they worked with a will. The money they earned in the pit was committed before it was earned. A bonus was uncommitted money, a godsend, to be used for getting out of debt or buying the wife a long-desired trinket for the home. They would work for it until they dropped. They were all colliers but some were tradesmen, skilled in bricklaying or stonework or carpentry. Only hewers ranked alongside them.

The blacksmith, Stephen Hardman, stood head and shoulders above the rest. He worked naked to the waist in spite of the wind; his chest crested with curling black hair and pitted with the blue scars that mark a collier. He had come to the Scar today to hang the wrought-iron gates.

He looked at them now, admiring his handiwork. The gate was massive, its tracery a blend of tendrils and twisted columns with a central monogram of 'H. B.' for Howard Brenton. They would have to go a long way to find better. Suddenly he heard the outraged call of a ring-ousel, perched in the lee of a rocky outcrop. 'Listen to that little bugger,' he shouted. 'He's put out, an' no mistake!'

No one heard him and he turned back to the bird. 'Dinnat fret, bonny lad. We'll be out of here afore long and you can have the place to yersel.'

He put up a hand to his shoulder, feeling the scar. It had happened in his second week in the pit. An injured putter had been carried out-bye and the harassed deputy had put Stephen in charge of his pony. 'Can y'manage, lad?' The boy had fallen over himself to agree: 'Aye, marrer. I can manage.'

The galloway had pricked up its ears. The hands on the traces were young and inexperienced, and it was in the mood for fun. It arched its neck and broke wind as it waited for the deputy's lamp to disappear. Alone with the boy, it let off another foul gust, and then raced in-bye. Stephen lost the reins but clung to the limbers, shouting 'Baa!' and 'Ha'ad up!' as he had heard the men do. One soft 'Gee baa' from the putter would have done the trick, but the boy had not yet learned the knack. His foot caught in the traces and he fell, the pony dragging him along while the broken stone that littered the ground tore into his back.

All that had been ten years ago, but the shoulder, with its puckered, ingrained scar, pained him still.

Stephen looked around at a landscape washed with the soft grey that marks the northern counties. No wonder the bird resented its dispossession, he thought. To the east he could see the sea; to the west the Pennines, a scattering of pit-heads, and the cathedral towers of Durham in the distance. This was a good place for a house. One day he would get his family away from the Shacks, out somewhere where the air was clean.

He looked down on Belgate, seeing the squalor and the dirt. He had a wife and bairns down there, breathing in muck, playing in the stinking gutters. Most days he never thought of his environment. Today it troubled him. He glanced at the almost completed house a few hundred yards behind him. It was bonny all right, its dozen windows twinkling in the sun, men swarming here and there with hods and ladders and lats of wood. For a moment Stephen was seized with resentment towards the Brentons and all their works; and then he remembered his blessings, a wife and bairns against the world and a broad enough back to work for them. There was nowt Mr Howard had to put against that.

He flexed his shoulders and stretched his arms skyward. 'Any chance of a brew?' he shouted, and saw the tea-lad scurry towards the open fire to obey. A nice brew, and then a few more hours' effort and he could go home.

He was thinking of his wife, as he hauled the great gate upright and held it against the wind. There had been other women, but never one like Mary. He thought of her eyes, blue and steady beneath her fair hair. She had smiled when he planted heart's-ease for her in an old, cracked sink. On Saturday he would buy a tub, a proper tub, and fill it with bulbs for the spring. That would make her smile, all right! She was twenty-three in a month or little more. If he got this gate hung, there would be plenty of money left over for a well-deserved birthday gift.

It would have taken any other two men to lift the gate but Stephen held it, bracing his thighs to take the weight. His forearms were corded with effort, and sweat broke out on his brow. He licked his lips and shifted his grip as the sound of the car drifted in on the wind.

Men turned at the noise, downing tools. Stephen, momentarily distracted, relaxed his grip on the gate and the wind seized its chance. If the blacksmith made a sound the gust carried it away. When the men turned back they saw him on the ground beneath the mass of wrought iron. The wind, having obtained its sacrifice, abated. The angry bird stopped its complaining. The men stood, open-mouthed.

At first there seemed to be no harm done to the body. Then blood leaped upward from the ruptured lungs and gurgled from the mouth. Men moved forward to lift the gate but the foreman stood still. He had seen such things before, and knew there was nothing to be done. The ousel started up again, an angry tac-tac of alarm, and a tear formed in the dead man's eye. One man, stunned, put out a hand as though to rouse the inert figure, but then drew back.

'Better fetch his wife,' the foreman said at last. 'He lived in the Shacks.' He used the past tense deliberately, and it had its effect. The tea-boy went scudding down the hill in search of the dead man's wife. Another man, fearing he might vomit his dismay, ran after him.

The green car did not falter as they passed. Diana was unaware of them and Howard, seeing them, thought they were off to fetch something and was glad his men were going smartly about their work. They had almost reached the stone gateposts before he realized something was wrong. He pulled on the hand-brake and turned off the engine. 'Stay here,' he said curtly and stepped from the car.

Diana watched as he walked away. He still limped slightly from the shrapnel that had entered his knee at Ypres but he cut a good figure. That was what had first attracted her; the way he carried himself. She looked from Howard to the men, and then saw the body, knowing at once it was dead. No one could be so motionless and still have life.

She felt a sudden stab of anger. Why die here, at the new house, spoiling everything? She felt afraid in her anger, and then ashamed. She put out a hand to the door and withdrew it, knowing there was nothing she could do. Instead, she began to examine the seams of her grey kid gloves, counting the minute stitches that patterned the gauntlets, wishing all the time that they had never come.

Howard looked down at the blacksmith, magnificent still in death. He had seen him about the pit and nodded the time of day, but they had never spoken. Now they never would.

'Was he a married man?' he asked.

The foreman's voice was sombre. 'Aye, Mr Howard. He was wed to Maguire's lass. I've sent to the Shacks to fetch her'

Howard's heart sank. Of all the places for the man to live, it would have to be the Shacks, tumbledown houses that should have been razed before the War!

He looked back at the body, seeing the blue scars that studded the torso. His hand strayed to his own scar and suddenly he could smell it again, that queer, warm smell of the trenches... glowing coke and frying bacon, dampness and the eternal odour of sweat.

He had seen death in battle a hundred times. Why, then, did death on this peaceful hillside seem so much more obscene?

The next moment, or so it seemed, the young woman was there, pushing past him as though he did not exist. She was breathing heavily and her breasts heaved at the buttons on her dress as she kneeled down to stroke the bare chest, her fingers moving easily over the curling hair. She stayed like that for a moment, then she put out a finger and wiped the tear from the dead cheek. Howard watched as she lifted her finger and licked the tear into her mouth. He felt at once revolted and stirred by the sight of such intimacy.

After a moment's stillness, she rose to her feet and turned. Her shabby brown dress was covered by a ticking apron; the skin of her throat was burned by wind and sun. Howard cleared his throat. 'I'm sorry, Mrs . . .' In that second he realized he didn't know the dead man's name, and cursed his ignorance. His discomfiture increased as another woman came pushing through the ranks of men, to stand beside the widow.

'Would you stay with her... ?' Howard began but there was such resentment in the woman's eyes when they met his that the words died on his lips. He turned instead to the foreman. 'I'll come to her later. See to everything, will you?' Then he put out a hand and touched the widow's forearm. 'I'm sorry.'

Her arm stayed motionless, and Howard took his hand away.

All eyes followed him as he walked back to the car, with its elegant passenger, but no one spoke until a man said: 'She did this. Her... wanting everything done yesterday!' As if she had overheard, Diana shrank down in her seat. The car roared to life and the men looked away as Howard turned it downhill, all thought of visiting the house abandoned.

A workman appeared, dragging a piece of wooden shuttering, and they lifted the dead man on to it. The two women linked arms and waited for the men to fall in behind them. Then the foreman nodded and the grim little procession began to descend the hill. Below, the Hispano Suiza gathered speed until it was a speck on the road. When they were all gone, the ring-ousel repossessed the hillside and shouted its triumph to east and west.

Esther Gulliver had long since finished the pegging-out and was back behind the counter of her father's drapery when the cortege reached the main street. 'There's been a death at the Scar,' a woman said, opening the shop door with such eagerness that the bell went on jangling, almost drowning her words.

Anne Gulliver, Esther's older sister, was cutting remnants into lengths at the opposite counter. 'Who was it?' she asked.

The woman clutched her shawl closer to her chin. 'Mary Maguire's man... Hardman, the blacksmith. Flattened, they say. Clean flattened. A wall blew down in the wind and finished him.' By nightfall the story would have escalated to total collapse of the whole house, but Anne Gulliver was not interested in the weapon, merely the victim.

'Mary Maguire... Frank Maguire's sister?' she asked. Esther went on folding modesty vests into their cedar-lined drawer, trying not to catch her sister's eye as they waited to hear the woman's reply. Frank Maguire was sweet on Anne, and although Anne pretended to scorn his attentions, Esther was never sure.

'She's Frank's sister, all right,' the woman said. 'He'll be foaming when he hears. He doesn't like the Brentons at the best of times.'

'Why not?' Esther asked, intrigued, but Anne was sweeping round the counter. The messenger had served her purpose; now she must be got rid of before she started gossiping.

'Did you want serving?' she asked tartly.

'I only came in to tell you what was going on,' the woman said, crestfallen.

'Thank you,' Anne said firmly. 'Don't forget to close the door as you go out. It's not easy in this wind.'

The woman went out, clashing the door behind her, and Anne returned to her counter. Esther would have liked to discuss the death, but she knew better than to push Anne in this mood.

'Do you think it's true?' she asked tentatively.

'How do I know?' Anne said. 'They say anything round here, you know that.'

'Perhaps Frank'll come by later on,' Esther said, suddenly feeling impish.

'And perhaps he won't,' Anne said. 'And p'raps he'll find you working if he does, but I doubt it.' There were twin spots of colour on her pale cheeks now and her dark lashes veiled her eyes. She put up a hand to smooth the dark hair that was swept back from a centre parting and coiled at the nape of her neck. Her fingers were slim, her nails perfect white-rimmed ovals, and Esther sighed with envy, thinking of her own chewed cuticles. It wasn't fair that Anne should have so much.

As if she sensed her sister's thoughts, Anne reached out and grabbed Esther's hands. 'Look at that! You look as though you've been navvying. Finish that drawer and then get washed. What will the customers think?'

'A pity about her,' Esther thought, as she eased the drawer into its bed. 'She's only four years older-than me and you'd think she was fifty, never mind nineteen.' But her resentment of Anne dwindled as the shop bell jangled and her father entered, weaving unsteadily although it was not yet two in the afternoon.

Esther could not remember a time when her father had not come home mid-day and midnight with drink on him, but it had got worse lately. Much worse. She tried to recall the time before her mother died, before Anne had become boss of the house and shop and her father begun staying out as long as he possibly could. But it was too long ago; almost half of her fifteen years. All she could remember was that her mother had been kind and soft-voiced, and that Anne had seemed to know everything, even then.

'Hallo, dadda,' she said as her father closed the door. 'Have you heard the news?' But he was already moving past her, the dark hair he had passed to Anne rumpled untidily, his eyes unfocused. He reached to pat her arm. 'There's a good girl,' he said vaguely. 'There's a good girl,' and he was gone from the shop.

They carried the blacksmith's body up to the single bedroom of his house, stumbling awkwardly on the narrow stairs. Once the body was laid on the bed Mary Hardman refused all offers of help. Each day, when Stephen had come home from the pit, she had bathed him before the fire. Washing him now would be one last duty.

The limbs were already stiffening and she struggled in vain to strip off the trousers. In the end she fetched scissors and cut them away. When he was naked love welled up in her for the great body, more helpless now than a new-born baby's. Again and again, as she washed him, she put out a hand to the rounded belly and down into the groin, half expecting the flesh to come to life under her hand. But the flesh was turning to marble in spite of her, and she gave it rest.

Tears sprang up in her eyes as she thought of their two children, hustled away to a neighbour's house. What would become of them now? She was suddenly struck by the thought that Stephen would never again come whistling up the street, stooping through the doorway, holding out his arms to the first comer. 'Oh God,' she said aloud, 'why have you done this to me?'

When Stephen was washed, Mary folded his hands and settled the dark hair upon his brow, then she wound the sheet around him as she might have swaddled a child. The smell of his work clothes, soiled at the moment of death, pervaded the room. She carried them downstairs, folded them neatly and cast them into the heart of the fire, before drawing every curtain in the house.

Once seated in her chair, she wondered again how she was going to manage. Life had been hard enough with a man to work for them: how would she manage alone? And how would she live without him? Pain welled up in her, threatening to cut off her breath, so that she sank to her knees on the hearth rug, burying her face in the seat of the chair that Stephen had made his own. Someone was knocking at the door, but she had bolted it, and at last whoever it was went away. Mary let her tears come, then, her sobs sometimes escalating as she remembered Stephen's face, his hands, the way he had carried her to bed on their wedding night. 'I love you, Stephen,' she said aloud into the quiet room and then, as the reality of his death came home to her: 'Oh, God! How can I live without you?'

At last, worn out with weeping, she dozed, only waking when she heard her brother's voice at the door and knew he would not be refused admittance.

'Come here, our Mary,' Frank said, as he walked in. His normally cheerful face was thunderous, his fair curly hair stood up in an angry halo. 'Someone'll pay for this,' he vowed as he held her close. 'I'll see to that.'

'How did it happen?' Mary asked, knowing Frank would know and would tell her the truth. 'Was it the wind that did it?'

'It was and it wasn't,' Frank said angrily. 'The wind did catch the gate, but the work could have waited till the wind died. They were pushed, all of them, not just Stephen. Pushed to do the impossible... and all for a slip of a girl with fancy ideas.' He held his sister away from him and looked into her eyes. 'Cry if you want to, our Mary – scream, come to that. It's about all we can do against the Brentons. But our day will come.'

It was four o'clock when Howard Brenton drove back into Belgate. The squalid streets always depressed him but today he looked at them with a new revulsion. Men should not have to live like this! Roofs undulated with subsidence, earth closets stood sentry-like between houses, dogs sniffed at open drains. The state of the village was a reproach to him, a reminder of vows unfulfilled.

He had been eighteen when he went to France; twenty when the last shot rang out at Erquellines and it was over. When the Armistice was announced Howard could scarcelybelieve he had been spared in a conflict that had claimed so many of his contemporaries. All those men who came through it felt there must be some reason why they had survived. For some, the pursuit of pleasure was sufficient reason. They danced the nights away as though to shake off the filth and stench of the trenches, and as it became apparent that 'a land fit for heroes' was just a pretty phrase the frenzy of their dance increased until at last they fell, exhausted, into the uneasy ways of peace.

Other young men came home with their eye upon a star. Howard Brenton was one of them. The war had made him see the need for change. The Brenton empire had fattened itself upon the conflict; now, he thought, it should distribute some of its profits. He outlined his plans for decent houses and made-up streets in Belgate and his father, the colliery owner Charles Brenton, promised to give them consideration. But by the time Howard was demanding action Charles could point to signs that the brief post-war boom was over. The unmade streets stayed as they were, the shabby houses remained, and the men took a cut in wages.

Howard reflected on it all as he rounded the Half Moon corner. A light burned in the public house in spite of daylight, but the pawnbroker's shop was closed and shuttered. Twice a week the Jew, Emmanuel Lansky, would drive over from Sunderland where he lived, Gladstone bag in hand. On Fridays, pay day, the pledges in his shop were redeemed. On Mondays they were bought in again to see families through the week.

Once Howard had viewed the old Jew with some scorn, seeing him as a leech upon the body of Belgate. But Lansky was fair in his dealings, and nowadays Howard wondered whether the pawnbroker's function was not less parasitic than his own.

He turned into a narrow side street and slowed down as the Suiza began to bump and rattle over the unmade track. A woman emerged from one of the houses, a bowl of greasy water in her arms. She made to throw it into the open drain that ran the length of the street and then, seeing the car, hesitated. Howard smiled as he passed, but her face was stony. He saw her arms come up as he drew level and then he heard the spatter of water on the body-work.

The small gesture of defiance filled Howard with unease. If the coalfield was any example, the country was in a ferment. No wonder the Labour Party was gaining ground. As the car rattled on, he wondered what he would find to say to the blacksmith's widow and whether she, too, would be disposed to hate him.

He felt a deep unease at the manner of the man's death. He had not been killed in the pursuit of coal, which would have been tragic but bearable. He had been killed because of Charles Brenton's relentless determination to indulge his new daughter-in-law wherever possible. Diana's family, the Carterets, might have a bloodline going back to the Flood but they were chronically short of cash. In this, at least, his father could claim superiority – and he meant to prove it.

The Brentons had not always had money: a long-dead Brenton had dug out a drift-mine in his single field, harnessing himself to the tubs until he could afford a pony. But by 1914 the Brentons owned three pits: the Venture, the Dorothea and Belgate, the richest and deepest of them all. At the end of the war Charles Brenton owned a bottle-works, a coking plant, and several small factories, and never referred to his harnessed forebear. His son's union with a woman from a titled family had set the seal on Charles Brenton's ambitions.

Howard thought of Diana's face an hour ago, petulant yet appealing. 'I can't come with you, Howard. Don't ask me. I know I should come, but I can't. Besides, I should be useless, quite useless. You don't need me. You'll say the right thing – you always do.' Her tone made the words seem more like a reproach than a compliment, and Howard had turned away, defeated. And then, as he was preparing to leave, Diana had announced her intention of going to London instead. Shopping was her excuse, but he had an uneasy feeling that she was really running away.

He steered to a halt, the Shacks ahead of him, rubble-walled houses with leaning chimneys. His eye fell on a begrimed nameplate: Rosemary Row. He had forgotten that was the proper name for the Shacks. The irony brought a smile to his face. At the end of Rosemary Row the vast, steaming bulk of the pit-heap shut out the sky.

The doors were not numbered but a house of death would have drawn curtains, surely? Howard looked along the row. Every window was shrouded in sympathy, so there was no help there. The gardens were full of ragged cabbages and soot-stained Michaelmas daisies. While he watched a small dog of indeterminate breed lifted a leg to anoint the cabbages and went on its way.

Howard stood, remembering how the young widow had run up the hill yesterday, hampered by her coarse brown skirts, running and dropping to kneel panting beside her husband. She had not spoken to him then, and he wondered apprehensively what she would say today. 'There's no need to see her yourself,' his father had said. 'Gallagher deals more efficiently with that sort of thing.' But Howard had no intention of leaving it to his father's agent, a man whose unctuous expression and mean ways sickened him. He put out a hand to open the nearest gate.

'Not there, mister.' The voice was sharp but kindly, and Howard turned. Without waiting for an answer the old woman pushed open a nearby gate and beckoned him through. He murmured his thanks as she turned away, adjusting the black shawl over her head.

There was no answer to his knock, and after a moment Howard mounted the step and turned the handle. His first impression was of heat. The fire was piled high and the fender glowed. The widow stood with one hand on the mantel, a baby cradled in her other arm, a small child clinging to her skirt. Dear God, no one had mentioned children!

To cover his embarrassment Howard held out a hand to the child, but it shrank from him. The woman made no attempt to force it forward and he was glad. Instead she moved away from the fire, swinging the baby easily from one arm to the other. 'Will you sit down?' Her tone implied doubt, as though she felt he was merely passing through.

Nettled, Howard pulled off his gloves and shrugged out of his dust-coat. 'Thank you.'

'I'll take the bairns next door,' she said. He nodded and she was gone, the child staring at him suspiciously before following her.

Howard looked around. Washing was airing on a thin line above the fire. A crucifix with a drooping Christ stood on the mantelpiece between two pottery dogs. There was a red plush cloth on the table and some of the sooty Michaelmas daisies in a jar. From the corner of the room the stairs rose up into darkness, and Howard wondered if the body lay up there. Remembering the massive frame of the dead man, he marvelled that the blacksmith had managed to exist in this cramped room. If he put out his arms he could touch the walls... The next moment Mary Hardman came back into the room.

As Howard watched, she put her hands to the opened neck of her dress and began to force the buttons back through the holes, one by one. He wanted to look away but the action of that strong hand fascinated him. She was young, surely no more than twenty-four or five, but there was a steadiness about the wide brow and the blue eyes that were almost on a level with his own.

Looking at Howard, Mary decided he was not like the old man, his father. There had been shock on his face when he saw the children, as though that was more than he could bear. She had expected many things of him but not that he was soft. He was handsome. Pale... a bit bookish even, like a teacher or a parson. The scar on his cheek was a queer puckered affair, but he had been blown up in the war so that would explain it.

She moved over to the fire and lifted the kettle from the hob on to the glowing coals. 'Will you take a cup of tea? I'll be mashing one anyway.' She reached for the caddy and began to spoon tea into the pot, adding one extra because she had company.

'Is there anything you need?' Howard asked, with difficulty, as she got out cups. 'The usual compensation will obtain... but I wanted to be sure you were all right for the present.' The kettle began to sing, faintly at first and then with gusto.

'I'll manage, Mr Howard, never fear.' Mary took down a pad from the mantel and lifted the kettle, swishing the tea round in the brown pot, letting it brew, trying to remember that he was the cause of her misery. The trouble was that Howard Brenton cared, and it showed – and she had not been prepared for that. 'Bloody Brentons!' her brother Frank had said. 'Must have this and must have that. There'll be a day of reckoning for their sort.' When Frank had gone, Mary had taken down the Bible and looked for the passage that spoke of an eye for an eye. But the Bible had opened at John 14: 'Let not your heart be troubled...

'Are you all right, Mrs Hardman?' The anxiety in Howard's voice brought her back to the present. He was out of his depth, poor bugger. In spite of his class and his money and his fancy education, he was no more capable than a trapper lad fresh out of the pit. Suddenly Mary was confused. This morning she had known where she stood and it was them and us, oppressors and victims. Now she was not so sure.

'It's been a long day,' she said, and Howard nodded as though he understood and did not find the remark inconsequential.

'Would you like to see him?' Mary's invitation seemed half-hearted, and Howard was about to decline when he saw the beginnings of contempt in her eyes.

'Yes, thank you. I'd like to pay my respects.'

She turned towards the stairs. 'You'll have to mind your head.'

He followed her up the boxed-in stairs to the tiny landing and she stood back as he stooped over the threshold; There was a dreadful smell in the room, an intense cleanliness that reminded Howard of the field hospital at Ypres.

The blacksmith lay on the bed, somehow diminished under the white sheet. Howard moved forward. There was no bandage around the jaw, and the rictus of death looked almost pleasant in the gloom. He heard the woman's breath catch in her throat. 'I'm so sorry, Mrs Hardman. He was a fine man.'

Her eyes glittered in the half-light, but she didn't reply.

They didn't speak again until they were back in the kitchen and she was pouring the tea. Then Howard began carefully: 'I admire your spirit, Mrs Hardman. You say you'll manage and I have no doubt you will. However, I hope you'll allow me to help? There'll be compensation eventually, but in the meantime you'll have expenses.' He took a sovereign case from his waistcoat pocket and began to slip free the coins.

'I'll get work,' Mary said.

She was holding her cup, fondling it between her hands, and Howard tried to keep the conversation going. 'There's not much work around here.'

She nodded, her eyes on the cup. 'Only service. I was in service at the vicarage until I wed. They don't let you stay once you're wed.'

'And they won't be too keen on taking you back,' Howard thought. 'Not with their pick of pliant young girls fresh out of school.' He cleared his throat. 'We'll be wanting help up at the new house, my wife and I.'

Mary kept her eyelids lowered, but her mind raced. 'My wife and I' – nice round words. 'My man and I,' she used to say – but not any more. When she raised her eyes there was a hardness in them that took Howard by surprise. 'I need work, wherever it is.'

Howard felt the implied insult in the words, but he let it go. She had every right to feel bitter: the men should not have worked on in that wind. He wondered if he should try to explain Diana's youth, her impatience for the house, his father's indulgence ... but he decided against it. 'I'll ask my wife to get in touch with you later. She has to go up to London, on family business…' Mary sensed his embarrassment but couldn't understand it. He was looking around for his hat and coat and once more she felt sorry for him. They said he had been brave in the war, but there wasn't much of the hero about him now. She would have to ease him out of her house or he would be stuck there forever, floundering like a beached cod.

She handed him his coat and watched as he shrugged into it. She could remember him as a boy, riding in his father's carriage and looking eagerly around. She had been a child then, peeping round her mother's skirts at the Brentons, the lords of the coalfield. And Stephen had been a child, too, growing up in Pelton Fell, each of them unaware of how sweet their meeting would be. If she had known then, known what the Brentons and their fancy ways would do to her happiness, would she have smiled at the carriage and the little lad in his sailor suit?

She looked now at the man he had become. He had not inherited his father's bulk; his hawk nose and straight brows came from his mother. He fastened the last button of his coat and gestured towards the crucifix. 'You're Catholic, Mrs Hardman?' She nodded. 'The funeral… I'd like to be there,' he went on. His father had told him to send Gallagher, but it wouldn't do.

Mary had folded her arms across her chest and Howard wondered if she would expect to shake hands. Suddenly she spoke. 'Will I have to go from here? From this house, I mean?'

The flatness of her tone could not disguise her desperation and Howard's reply was gentle. 'Not unless you wish to go. Wait and see how things turn out. You might find a better house.'

She seemed satisfied, but Howard's mind was racing over the possibilities. He must try and get her out of here, away from this dreadful place. As he walked down the path he saw that someone had planted a clump of pansies in an old stone sink.

When Howard had gone, Mary Hardman subsided onto the fender. The supply of coal that had been part of Stephen's wage would stop now, so she might as well enjoy it while it lasted. She put up a hand and unbuttoned the neck of her dress, then she leaned her head against the mantel and gave herself up to memories.

2

Diana was surrounded by cases and piles of clothing, handing garments to a maid, who was putting them into the big leather portmanteaux. She felt better now that she was actually going to London, away from this gloomy house and her mother-in-law's disapproving eye and the dreadful fuss about the blacksmith's death. And besides, she needed time to hug her secret to herself for a little while, just to be sure it was true.

'I'm almost ready, darling. Do talk, but I must get on with this,' she said when Howard entered the room. She waved a hand at the disarray and pulled an apologetic face. Howard moved to the window to look out on to the green lawns and tall hedges of Sunderland's most exclusive suburb while his wife saw to the completion of her packing.

This was where the rich built their homes, the Croxfords, the Greenwoods, the Hardings, the Brentons – coal-owners and shipbuilders, people of wealth and power. Like all large species, they had their satellites, the Pratts and the Grays, the Darnleys and the Dunnings. Howard could glimpse some of their houses in the distance, stone-built, set among trees, widely spaced... unlike the cramped brick or rubble-walled houses of Belgate. He closed his eyes, smelling the pit until the odour changed to that of the trenches, sweat and fear, the cries of wounded men and the whinnying of frightened horses. The railway wagons had all had stencilled signs: '40 men or 8 horses'. Now the Brentons and their ilk lived like horses, and their colliers were crowded like men.

He turned back into the room. 'How long do you intend to stay in London?'

Diana laughed, evading his eyes, holding a grey dress against her and twirling before the mirror. 'Not long, darling. Only a few days. Time to see Loelia and tell her about the house, that's all.' She threw the grey dress on the discard pile and put her hands on her hips. 'I can't decide, so I shall just say "no more". Close the bags, Jane, and ring for someone to take them.' She went to stand beside Howard at the window. 'You will chivvy them about the house, won't you, Howard? I know it's sad about that poor man, but it won't help him if we delay, will it?' She slipped her hand into her husband's arm, suddenly contrite. 'I know I should have gone with you to see his widow yesterday. I'm sorry. I was cowardly and childish, and I will do better. As soon as I come back I'll go to see her.'

She leaned her head against his upper arm and Howard would have turned to embrace her if it had not been for the presence of the maid. Instead he murmured something about nothing mattering too much, and went on staring out over the garden.

'Are you sure you won't wait until I can go to London with you?' he said at last.

Diana shook her head. 'I'll be perfectly all right on my own, darling. I haven't seen Lee for ages – not since our wedding. We'll have a thousand and one things to talk about.'

The Hon. Loelia Dunane was a strange but rather appealing young woman, with a dumpy figure and a disarming frankness. She had followed Diana and Howard down the aisle of St Martin-in-the-Fields, clad in a gold-lace bridesmaid's dress that made her resemble nothing so much as a Fabergé egg. But she was a true friend to Diana. Diana would be safe with Loelia, Howard reflected, and a visit to London might do her good. He knew the death at the Scar had disturbed her. Last night, as she sat up in bed and wept that she could not stay in Durham another day, he had reminded himself that she was only nineteen years old. There would be time enough to face the realities of life.

But Howard's concern for his wife had made him think more of the blacksmith's widow. For Mary Hardman there would be no luxury of escape to London. In her whole life she would probably never travel beyond the Cleveland Hills. The thought preoccupied him as he went down the wide stair and across the hall to the dining-room.

His father was seated at the breakfast table, his plate piled high with kedgeree, his *Times* folded at the financial pages and anchored with the heavy cruet.

'She's still going to London, then?'

'Yes,' Howard said, turning from the sideboard with a laden plate. 'She hasn't changed her mind.'

'Well,' Charles said ungraciously, 'I think your place is with your wife.'

Howard speared a morsel of kidney, marshalling his words before he spoke.

'I'll follow Diana to London,' he said at last, 'but I'm not able to go with her today.' Charles grunted disapproval before returning to his paper, a grunt that once would have affected Howard. When he was a child, his father had seemed to him the epitome of power, a god-like figure who ruled as far as the eye could see. But as Howard's horizons had broadened so his father had slipped into perspective. The huge nose set off by beetling brows, the curious purple shadows round the eyes, the massive bulk of the shoulders these things were still commanding, but they belonged to a man, not a deity.

'I'll go straight to the Dorothea from the station, and then I've business in town. I should be at the office by eleven. Gallagher knows I'll be in late this morning.'

His father didn't look up from his reading and Howard sighed. Though he no longer feared his father's displeasure, it still irked him – particularly when it concerned his relationship with Diana. Sooner or later he would have to remind his father that Diana was his wife and not another Brenton possession.

Frank Maguire drained his mug and put it down in the hearth, as his sister rocked slowly backwards and forwards in her chair. He looked at her, wondering what he could usefully say, wishing he was out of a house of death and up on the hill above Belgate, in the clean, clear sunlight – or, better still, in the Half Moon with a pint tankard in his hand. A shift down the pit would be better than this! But even as he thought it, his conscience pricked him.

'Hold on there a minute, our Mary. You'll have the drugget worn through.'

Mary smiled, a brief uplift of the corners of her mouth, and then went back to rocking. She was grateful to Frank but, all the same, she wished he would go and leave her. The neighbours had thronged round her, anxious, attentive, urging her to eat and drink or talk or cry, shirking mention of the corpse – as though, by dying, Stephen had disgraced himself. One or two had cursed the Brentons, sure that was what Mary would want. She ought to feel bitter, but she felt nothing now. Nothing at all, not even fear about how she would manage without a man's wage coming in.

She went on rocking, and Frank put up a hand to rub his chin in perplexity. 'So he came yesterday?' he said at last. They both knew who he meant. 'What did he want?' He moved to the table and felt the teapot. It was still warm, and he reached for a cup.

Mary shrugged. 'He's sorry. He'll do what he can. The usual.'

Frank grimaced at the stewed tea. 'I hope you told him! They never should have been working up there in that wind. Everybody says it was murder.'

Mary shrugged. 'There's no point in rubbing his nose in it. It's done, now.'

Frank's face tightened in disapproval. 'That's how they get away with it. It's "done" until next time, and then it's too late again.' He sank back into the chair on the opposite side of the fire. Mary could not remember her brother sitting in that chair before; it had been Stephen's chair and sacrosanct. Now it was open to all, and Frank looked out of place with his baby face puckered in misery beneath the fair curls. He was two years her junior, and as children they had been inseparable.

'What's he going to do for you?' Frank asked.

She nodded towards the mantel. 'He's left a few pound and he says there'll be compensation.'

'Only right,' Frank said stoutly but secretly he was relieved. He knew the agent's capacity for finding let-out clauses, but if the owners said there would be compensation then Gallagher could not gainsay it. He leaned to touch his sister's knee. 'Hold on, our lass. Things'll work out, you'll see.'

Mary covered his hand with her own, feeling the bumps and callouses of a collier's hand. 'I know,' she said, 'I know,' all the while remembering Stephen's hands upon her and the tenderness they could arouse.

Frank saw her face cloud over and his heart sank. Should he put his arms around her, or would that make things worse? Bloody Brentons! They had him working for a pittance, and now they had left his sister a widow with a houseful of bairns. Cockcroft had said it was the wind to blame, but everyone knew it was the Brentons' pride, and greed, and impatience. He sighed, thinking of the unfairness of it; and Mary ceased to rock and took her hands from the arms of her chair.

'For God's sake, our Francis, get to hell out of here. I'm all right. I'll have to be all right on me own; I don't expect even you intend to sit here for the rest of time. I want you out, and I want my bairns back.'

Frank knew she was serious. She never called him by his given name of Francis unless she was annoyed with him. Now, though, her face softened and she leaned forward to touch his knee. 'Don't look like a whipped pup. You're ower big for a pet-lip. Get off and make sheep's eyes at Gulliver's lass. You've got nee chance with a stuck-up madam like that, but at least it'll get you from under my feet.'

Frank was embarrassed at her words. He had been careful not to tell anyone how he felt about Anne Gulliver, and yet Mary had guessed. How many more had noticed?

He let her bundle him out into the fresh air and then set off towards the main street, where Gulliver's drapery shop stood, straightening his jacket and smoothing his hair as he went. He always walked with his chin up, so that everyone would see that now he was afraid of nothing.

It had begun on his first day in the pit. Thirteen years old, he was left alone to lift the leather trap each time a pony and tub came through. The overman had left him a lamp, a small circle of comfort in the gloom, but before long a putter stumbled out of the darkness and took it from him. The man's own lamp had failed and he was on piecework. He must have a lamp, if he was to make up his money.

The shivering new boy had been left alone in the dark. It was the first time he had seen total blackness and it terrified him. There were strange creakings as layers of earth moved and compacted. Mice, brought down in the ponies' feed, ran scuttling along the tunnels. The heat was stifling. He reached for his can of cold tea, and as his fingers touched it a tub came rattling along. Light flared and he saw that his bait can was swarming with blacklocks that gleamed obscenely as the light passed. He spent the rest of the time waiting for them to infiltrate his clothes. At the end of the shift he stumbled out-bye to the landing. Never again, he vowed, would he let anyone take away his lamp. He would fight if he must, but he would not be left alone in the dark.

The next day a grinning driver offered him a ride to the face on the shafts of a tub. He sat hunched on the limbers as the pony rattled along. Its tail had been docked for the summer and when it suddenly came erect the stubby bristles scored his bare arm.

He winced with pain and then he heard a rumble from the beast's belly. The next moment its bowel emptied, the bright green slime erupting red-hot and stinking into the boy's eyes and mouth. The smell was vile, the excrement stung, but the worst thing was the laughter of the men. It was common practice to physic the ponies when their tails were docked and then stick an unsuspecting lad within range.

He had stood at the cistern while a less unkind putter swilled him down, and wondered how much worse things could get. But he had not run. When his mother asked how his day had gone he told her it had been easy. Within a year he had thrashed the man who played the trick, and felled another for taking his lamp. After that he never allowed a trapper lad to be tormented while he was within range.

The men had come to respect the power of Frank's fists and the length of his tongue. He was ardent for the union, the Labour Party and the Catholic Church. No one knew that he feared the pit, rehearsed his death a thousand times. He was always first into the narrow seam, the last to leave when water rose. He lived with the knowledge of his own mortality, and he walked with his head in the air as though to defy it.

There were no customers in the shop but Anne and Esther kept themselves busy, dusting, tidying, putting tickets on the small amount of new stock they carried in from the back shop. Esther had known the shop all her life, had been carried behind the counter in her mother's arms as she served threads and lace edgings, corset-laces and packets of needles for everything from crewel-work to the finest stitching. It worried her that she could remember less and less of her mother, and now, as she struggled to untangle a web of wool, Esther tried to summon her to mind. She had been small and fair and pretty. Or had she?

Suddenly Esther caught sight of herself reflected in the glass doors of the cabinets – ridiculously gawky, with awful fair hair frizzing on her forehead, and pop eyes. 'You are lucky,' she said to Anne, before she could stop herself.

'Me?' Anne said, for once taken aback. 'Lucky? How?'

Esther tried hard to think of a way out but there was only one way: the truth. 'You're good-looking,' she said grudgingly.

'Ha!' Anne tossed her head. 'That's as may be and a lot of good it does me. But if you thought a bit more about washing behind your ears and using a hairbrush you'd look no end better.' Esther felt her eyes sting and bent her head to her work. Anne was a beast! She was filled with rage until she thought how hard her sister had to work, running a home and shop and endlessly worrying about money.

She remembered the night that she had learned of her father's drinking. She had moved towards Anne in the double bed as she heard her father's furtive entrance below. 'Is he all right?' she had asked, her mouth close to Anne's unyielding back.

'He's drunk,' Anne had said shortly, but Esther could sense the despair in her.

'He's not!' she said automatically, feeling a wave of loyalty for the father who had never said a cross word to her, not in the whole of her life.

'He *is* drunk,' Anne said. 'He drinks every penny we slave for in that shop, and one of these days he'll drink us all into the street. Now go to sleep!'

Esther had fumbled under the pillow for the worn rag doll she hid there from Anne's prying eyes, and had tried to sleep, but her eyes burned when she shut them and her ears had stayed alert.

'What if he can't get upstairs?' she asked as the fumblings below continued.

'So?' Even in the dark it was as though Anne tossed her head. 'Let him stop down there – and I hope he rots.'

So Esther had lain, dry-eyed, while her father hauled himself up the stairs, and then she had turned her face into the pillow and wept, all the while aware of Anne, rigid and disapproving beside her in the darkness.

Now she sniffed as the smell of cooking invaded the shop. 'Mutton again,' Anne said, also wrinkling her nose. 'When I have a home of my own I won't have a piece of mutton or a ham shank across my step.' She clattered a drawer of corset-laces home and threw back her head. 'Or butter beans, or tripe, or sheep-head's broth.'

Privately Esther was as fed up with their daily fare as her sister, but to say it aloud would only make Anne mad. 'What will you cook, then?' she said instead.

'Nothing, if I can help it.' Anne smoothed her hands over her grey worsted bodice and pinched in her waist. 'I've had enough. I'm going to have someone else for the drudgery...' Her eyes flicked upwards as the unmistakable sound of her father's tread came from the stairs. 'Up at last!' she said bitterly. 'He'll need to hurry if he's going to make the Half Moon by his usual.'

Esther's heart sank. There was going to be another row.

'Just look,' Anne said, turning to the sparsely filled shelves. 'We've next to no stock, and what we have got is twice the price of the Co-op – and all he can do is soak himself!'

'He's lonely,' Esther said defensively. 'And all men drink a bit.'

'Maybe, maybe not,' Anne said. 'But I'll tell you this, Esther Gulliver: when I get married it won't be to a sot.'

She spun round as a soft tap came on the shop window.

'It's Frank Maguire,' Esther said, trying not to grin. 'I think he wants you, Anne.'

'Well, want will have to be his master,' Anne said, scooping up discarded wrappings and sweeping round the counter. But Esther noticed that she gave an extra toss of her head as she passed Frank, his hands and nose pressed against the glass. And she saw from his satisfied grin that Frank had noticed it, too.

Frank had loved Anne since he had been sent into the Gulliver shop on an errand, no more than twelve years old. He had seen the little girl seated solemnly at the counter tidying bobbins. He had grinned at her, and she had tossed her head and scorned him. He had gone home, clutching the paper poke of elastic, determined that one day he would make her smile. And now he had. Nor was making her smile all he meant to do. If he played his cards right, there might be a job with the Miners' Federation one day, a job with status and a union house well away from the pit – even in Durham city.

Last night he had gone to a meeting to hear a talk by the syndicalist, A. J. Cook, one of the founders of the Unofficial Reform Committee. He had a well-worn copy of their pamphlet, *The Miners' Next Step*, which advocated one all-inclusive union for mineworkers and a gradual assumption of power, until the workers finally controlled their own industry. Their demand for nationalization had already forced the government to set up the Sankey Commission, which had led to the seven-hour day.

Because of the export-market collapse, the Miners' Federation had been forced to go slow on their demands, but the right men now had control of the Federation, militant men who would not take no for an answer. Before leaving, A. J. Cook had clapped Frank on the shoulder and called him a good man. It was heady stuff.

When he took his bottle of water and his jam sandwiches from his snap tin now, he would settle down with a sigh of contentment. In the shadows Blossom, the pony, would fret, hoping for a bite of something, and he would let her nuzzle crusts from his palm, all the while dreaming of the day when he would share a platform at the Durham Gala with A. J. Cook – and Anne would be there in the crowd, gazing up at him with pride. Now he pressed his nose to the window, until, affronted, Anne pulled down the blind.

As Howard handed Diana into the train she smiled up at him. 'Will you miss me while I'm away?'

He leaned forward and kissed her cheek. It smelled deliciously of *papier poudré* or some such preparation. 'Yes,' he said, straightening up. 'Yes, you know I'll miss you.'

It was true. He would miss her: miss her coming to him so easily when he turned down the lights, coming behind him and imprisoning him in her arms, driving her chin into the space between his shoulder blades, her breath warm and sweet upon his spine. But sometimes he caught her watching him as though he was merely a stranger who had aroused her curiosity.

Diana was pulling at his arm. 'It's time, Howard darling. Do close the door.' She waved through the carriage window as the train moved jerkily away.

'I'll miss you,' Howard mouthed, and went on waving until she was out of sight. Did he love her? He would miss her, but did he love her? They had been married for five months, but still Howard held back a part of himself; still he wondered if this was love he felt. It was pleasurable, certainly, but *was it love*?

He was an only son and the Brenton heir. He had known the subject of marriage would be raised one day, and it had scuttered around the edges of his mind, a dim but not unwelcome prospect.

His first sexual encounter had been a business transaction in the chenille-hung bedroom of a French brothel, arranged by his brother officers. Nothing had prepared Howard for the ferocity of his feelings. Afterwards, he sat huddled over his knees, the tart slumbering contentedly beside him, and came to terms with the discovery that he had not enjoyed it. If this was the thing his fellows prized above all else, it was a great disappointment.

When his friends suggested further sorties into the sleazy underworld of war-torn France, he was ready with his excuses. And then the war was over. There were daughters of family friends to be escorted and cherished and handed into chauffeur-driven cars, but he did not see in them the possibility of sexual conquest. It never crossed his mind. It was his father's ambition that bore him forward into marriage.

He had thought Diana Carteret beautiful but beyond him until Charles raised the subject of a union. The Carterets, an ancient line of baronets, had acres galore in Berkshire, but Diana's brother had fallen in the Battle of the Somme, and the estate was entailed to a cousin. Diana would inherit nothing but a fine pedigree. When Howard suggested that Diana might not be willing to marry him, his father dismissed the idea of a Brenton needing to woo a bride. Arrangements would be made and honoured, and that was all that was necessary. Old blood would sweeten new money, as it had done since the Flood and would do again.

At his father's prompting Howard had stayed in London paying court to Diana. He had derived great pleasure from contemplating her beauty, and mild amusement at her pretensions to be a woman of the world – and then he had found himself proposing. Diana had pouted and lowered her eyes and demanded time to think. Twenty-four hours later they were engaged.

'You're a lucky man,' Charles had said, and now that they were married Charles continued to gloat over the union. The house at the Scar was his latest gift. Perhaps he and Diana would be happier at the Scar, away from his father's over-indulgence and his mother's unspoken disapproval of any show of affection between them.

Diana had come to him on their wedding night, sliding her arms around his neck and locking them in place. 'I've never done it before, Howard.' He had wanted to turn away in his embarrassment but she would not let him go. 'I hope you know all about it. You do, don't you?'

Howard had nodded with an assurance he was far from feeling.

She cried out when he took her for the first time, and he flinched at the thought that he had hurt her. It was only later he realized it had been a cry of triumph!

Since then Diana had initiated and directed their lovemaking, showing a naive delight in her new-found accomplishments. If only he could respond as freely!

As he watched the departing train, Howard vowed to do better when she came back, and by the time he replaced his Homburg and turned back to the car he was smiling.

Alone in her first-class compartment Diana laid her magazines on the opposite seat and sat back to take stock. It was a relief to get away from Durham. Howard had been sweet at the station but she couldn't forget the way he had looked at her after the blacksmith's death, eyes bleak and accusing as though the whole beastly accident had been her fault. She hadn't wanted anyone to die. It was perfectly awful that it had happened – and she *had* wanted to visit the man's wife. Besides, it had spoiled what should have been an exciting time, the moment when she would really prove herself as Howard's wife.

As the train moved into open country, Diana made a decision. As soon as she got back from London she would keep her promise to go to see the woman. By then she would be sure she was pregnant, and Howard would forgive her anything – but she would visit the widow all the same. It was the least she could do.

Her monthly period was more than a week late, and she felt decidedly strange into the bargain. She had been tempted to tell Howard yesterday but had kept silence for fear he might forbid the London visit. She was so dying to see Loelia again! Yes, she did feel strange. Quite *enceinte*! She rolled the French word for pregnant around her mind, liking it better each time. They had found it in a French dictionary years ago at school and giggled over it for a week. *Enceinte*! She would be hugely and beautifully with child, and kind to the blacksmith's widow, and Howard would love her for it. But first she would visit Loelia, dearest Lee who was always such fun. Diana wriggled in her seat at the very prospect.

Carteret land adjoined Dunane land in Berkshire, and visits to each other's homes had been the girls' only relief from dull nursery days. They had gone away to school together, but for Loelia there had been a finishing year in Paris while Diana cooled her heels at Barthorpe, her own family home.

On Loelia's return they had been presented at Court together, journeying down the Mall in the Dunanes' stately Delaunay-Belleville while curious Cockney faces pressed up against the windows. One woman pronounced Diana 'a peach' but was less taken with Loelia, upholstered in regulation white slipper satin. 'Ow, ain't she funny!' she had mouthed through the glass and Loelia put out her tongue in reply. Afterwards they had consoled one another on the terrible anti-climax of their presentation, and had settled down to enjoy their first season.

First, however, Diana had been summoned to her mother's bedroom to learn 'about life'. Her mother's solemn face and funereal tones were funny but Diana dared not laugh. Loelia had already imparted all she had learned in Paris, so Lady Carteret might have saved her breath, but Diana sat dutifully while her mother gave her the grisly details. Exhausted by the ordeal, Eleanor Carteret took a *cachet faivre* and retired to her room while Diana tried to reconcile her mother's version with the version Loelia had given her. They did not tally.

The flower-banked ballrooms and noon luncheons of their season soon palled. The girls were unbearably eager to please, the boys tediously sophisticated. There were garden parties at Hurlingham, and polo at Ranelagh, and Diana had more than her fair share of admirers, but she found most of them boring.

As the season drew to a close the prospect of a return to Barthorpe and the dull country routine loomed ominously close. Howard's proposal of marriage had not surprised her: she had known she had the power to provoke it. But did she want it? She took the problem to her father.

'They're money,' Sir Neville had said, implying that that was the only thing of which the Brentons could boast. Diana went back to her room and considered. She had been trained for nothing else but marriage. She had been taught the proper way to treat animals and servants, and how to observe the social code. She could speak French and add up three figures before getting muddled. Who would pay for such small skills? As a Carteret, her social station was exalted, but without money it meant nothing. As Howard Brenton's wife, she might be dependent on industry but she would be rich enough not to mind. Besides, Howard was handsome and kind and blissfully unostentatious. When she told her father her answer was 'Yes', he grunted relief and turned back to his *Times*.

So the bargain was struck. The fathers were discreet but thorough, and draft settlements were speedily drawn up.

Diana was immersed in wedding preparations: endless fittings for the white lace bridal gown and gold-lace bridesmaids' dresses, wedding gifts to be unpacked and admired as rooms filled up with tissue paper. Haltingly Howard asked if she was sure of her feelings for him and Diana cut him short with a decided 'Yes'. She liked Howard. His only failing was a lack of fervour, but surely that would come with time?

Now, as the train carried her towards London and reunion with Loelia, she thought only of the pleasures ahead. For the first time in her life she was her own mistress. Charles Brenton had arranged unlimited credit for her at his London bank, and as a married woman she no longer needed a chaperon. She was still exulting when the cab drew up before the white pillars of Scotland Gate and she saw Loelia at the door.

Loelia's dark-red hair was cut fashionably short in front and gleamed above a vivid dress of peacock blue; her ugly monkey face was creased in a grin. Best of all, her arms, when she folded them about Diana, were as welcoming as ever. 'You look marvellous, Di,' she said and drew her into the house.

She made for the stairs, throwing instructions to the hovering maids as she went. On the first landing she turned to Diana. 'I'm here alone, darling, so it couldn't be better. Nanny is with me, of course, but she's utterly gaga now. You'll see her later. And Max is floating around, God knows where. Let's get comfortable and have tea and you can tell me *everything*.'

As they settled in Loelia's sitting-room, Diana thought gratefully how good it was to get back to the shabby elegance of Scotland Gate. Charlotte Brenton's home was like the woman herself: handsome and well-upholstered, but dull. Here the fine carpets were worn, the deep chairs sagging, and yet the whole effect was distinguished. A maid came in with tea, the tweeny behind her with muffins in a silver basket. Dunane muffins were famous, eaten with oodles of butter and home-made preserves.

'Ooh, scrumptious,' Diana said, and fell upon the feast.

They talked as they ate, wiping melted butter from their chins and licking their fingers. For a little while they were back in the realms of nursery tea and it was a good feeling.

'How was Paris?' Loelia asked, nostalgia in her voice. Agreement that Paris was divine and French chic unparalleled lasted until tea was over and Loelia produced a box of cigarettes and two ivory holders. 'Do have one, Di. Everyone smokes now, absolutely everyone.' They lit up and puffed frantically, filling the air with smoke and tapping off the ash between each puff.

At last Loelia swung her short legs on to the arm of her chair and looked expectantly at Diana. 'Well?' she said. 'What's it like, being Howard's wife? Is it marvellous?' Privately Loelia found Howard almost unbearably attractive. Unlike most of the men she knew, he did not make inane conversation, and his dark eyes were questioning; he looked like a man of consequence. If he ever got away from that odious father he probably should be. Now she repeated her question, but more lightheartedly: 'Do tell! I'm dying to know what it's like to be married.'

Privately Diana was disappointed in sex, finding it much less exciting than she had been led to believe. And it was over so quickly, and Howard was so restrained, that she sometimes wondered if it was worth the effort. Now, though, she made herself meet Loelia's eyes. 'It's divine – didn't I always say it would be? I miss Barthorpe sometimes, and the dogs, but otherwise it's splendid.'

For a moment Loelia looked at Diana shrewdly, and then she nodded. 'Good,' she said, as though to dismiss the subject. Diana sat back in her chair, hoping her relief did not show in her face.

They talked of Durham, then, and the new house on the Scar. Loelia was sympathetic when Diana told her about the blacksmith's death. 'Horrid for you,' she said, adding: 'But much worse for his wife. Was he old?'

Diana nodded. 'Yes. At least thirty. And his wife looked even older.'

A picture of the widow came into her mind, running past the Suiza and pushing her way through the knot of men. 'I should have gone to see her, shouldn't I? Instead I ran away. It's too shame-making.'

Loelia Dunane, wise as well as kind, turned the conversation to other things. 'What about the Brenton *mère* and *père*? Are they as fierce as they look?'

Diana sought for words to describe her parents-in-law. 'He's not too bad,' she said at last, remembering the bank draft in her bag. 'She's rather starchy, but I expect she means well. I always feel she is weighing up my breeding possibilities. Her own showing was rather poor: two dead babies before Howard, and then a threatened miscarriage before Caroline. I shall litter much better. And they will pay me for it.'

Loelia's face creased in horror and Diana laughed. 'They're fearfully keen on perpetuating the Brenton line, Lee, and I am a good catch, after all – not quite the blood royal, but indubitably blue.' The mild disapproval in Loelia's eyes only served to make Diana more defiant. 'They wanted me for my breeding properties; well, if they want me they must pay for me. It's perfectly logical. If you want to improve your stock you buy in a good brood mare. And they like to own things – not land, like our respective pas. They own factories and collieries, things that create wealth.'

There was grudging respect in Diana's voice and Loelia nodded resignedly. 'I know. Money is the only thing that counts now. The Old Medieval says land prices have halved since the Armistice. Sales are announced in the papers every day… and not just land, but houses, too. The 0. M. says they're all being bought by horrid little men who were made by the War – and of course he blames it all on L. G.' Loelia always referred to her father as the Old Medieval, and was proud of his reputation as a scourge of poachers and the Liberal Party.

Diana knew what Loelia must be thinking. Once the Brentons would not have aspired to marriage with a Carteret; now they could almost demand it. Once Diana would have had her pick of neighbouring landowners, but half of them had perished in France and the other half were looking for heiresses from trade or the United States of America. As if Loelia read her thoughts she spoke: 'You're all right, Di, you've married into the new aristocracy. The Brentons are sick-makingly rich, aren't they?' Before Diana could reply, she sat erect. 'Oh Lord, that sounded horribly patronizing... I didn't mean it to come out like that.'

Diana shook her head. 'It doesn't matter, Lee. I don't think about it – about class, I mean. But *they* do! Old man Brenton is obsessed with it. Yesterday he was talking about some knight in the next county and he said, "He'll agree, of course. We're of the same class, he and I." She raised her eyebrows to punctuate her words and Loelia grinned in sympathy.

'All the same, Di, the money must be delicious. We're terribly blue-blooded, you and I, but beastly hard up.'

Suddenly Diana felt joyous. 'Not any more, Lee darling. Not any more!' Charles Brenton's bank draft was produced and gloated upon, and they spent the next half hour in happy contemplation of a spending spree.

They were still making plans when Loelia's brother arrived, with a friend in tow. Max Dunane had all of his sister's panache but in him it was allied to a handsome face and an arrogant nature. He had spent the last three years at Oxford, reading Greats, and he was taller and broader and much more handsome than Diana remembered. His red hair curled like a Greek god's, he wore a grey flannel lounge suit with the revolutionary turn-ups and front creases preferred by the Prince of Wales, and there was a blue silk tie at his neck. He introduced the other man as Henry Colville, an Oxford friend, and directed him to sit by Loelia. Max settled himself at Diana's feet.

'Be a chum and ring for more tea, Lee. I want to get to know this delightful creature.' Diana protested that he had known her all her life, but she was flattered by his attention. His red head was up-tilted to catch her every word, his brown eyes narrowed in concentration.

'You've changed, Diana,' he whispered over the teacups. 'You were always stunning but now there's something else. You look...fulfilled. Yes: that's it. You've ripened.' His words were innocuous enough but the way he said them was not, and Diana was relieved when he began to talk about London, rattling off the names of exclusive clubs as though he owned them.

She hung on his every word. Cabinet ministers might refer to the nightclubs of London as 'social sewers' but she found them irresistibly attractive. As an adolescent she had drunk in tales of the Coterie, the pre-war set that had scandalized society, and had tried to model herself on Lady Diana Manners, now married to Duff Cooper but still a brilliant rebel.

Watching Diana as she quizzed him about the Duff Coopers, Max decided that this Diana had much in common with her famous namesake. Both women had those large and luminous eyes that spoke of innocence but held at least a prospect of wickedness. He had always thought her a good sport but he had never realized how absolutely stunning she was – and now she had married some Northern nobody. Shame!

At last he issued an invitation. 'Get ready, both of you, and Henry and I will take you dancing, won't we, old chap?

We'll go to the 43: Kate Merrick's place in Gerrard Street. How soon can you be ready?'

The girls ran gleefully up the stairs to change. 'You're in the night nursery,' Loelia said. 'I know you like to sleep there. Ma is always threatening to make it into another guestroom, but then she has terrible thoughts about grand-children and nothing gets done. And then, of course, there's Nanny; she'd never let her precious nursery go.'

As if at the mention of her name, Nanny Dunane appeared. She looked smaller and more wizened than Diana remembered but the hawk-eyes still gleamed. There was a huge drip on the end of her nose and she wiped it away with a lumpy forefinger.

'Hallo Nanny,' Diana said, bending to kiss the leather cheek.

The black eyes raked her face. 'Yes,' the old woman said. 'Yes, indeed, miss. Mind your Ps and Qs.'

Diana's eyes met Loelia's. 'I told you so,' Loelia mouthed and put an affectionate hand on the old woman's arm. 'You remember Diana, Nanny? Diana Carteret?'

The old eyes filled with outrage. 'Of course I do, Miss know-it-all. Carteret that was; Brenton now.'

Loelia pulled a rueful face. 'Sorry, Nanny.'

The old woman nodded, honour satisfied. 'I should hope so. You're in the nursery, Diana. Bed aired and turned down.' As she shuffled away she spoke again. 'Bugger Balfour.' It was quite distinct.

Diana's clothes, newly unpacked, were hanging out to shed their creases and she cast a critical eye over them. Her trousseau had been bought from the grey-and-pink salon of Madame Lucille in Hanover Square. Madame Lucille, Lady Duff Gordon in private life, was the sister of Elinor Glyn the passionate novelist, but her clothes, unlike the novels, were dull – especially compared to Loelia's chic. What did one wear for the 43? It had a terrible reputation but everybody who was anybody went there.

Diana chose a pink slipper-satin dress with matching shoes and stockings and a beaded bag. It had seemed the height of elegance when it was delivered to Barthorpe in swathes of tissue, but now she was not so sure. As she stepped out of her travelling clothes Nanny appeared, a flannel-wrapped earthenware bottle in her hands. She didn't speak as she thrust the bottle into the bed but as she moved back to the door Diana heard her say, 'It's no way to run a country. No way at all!' As the door closed behind the old woman Diana hooted with laughter. Life at Scotland Gate was such delicious fun! She peeled off her stockings and began to unpin her hair.

When she was ready she sat down at the dressing-table and took a last look at herself. Her eyes looked back, wide and innocent and bland. She tried narrowing them but it was no use. She looked what she was: a well-bred, well-groomed gentlewoman.

Her eyes dropped to her bosom. Her breasts were well-shaped, but the bulky slipper satin blurred their outline. She pursed her lips and then slipped out of the frock. The bodice was lined with row upon row of narrow lace, and she took the scissors from her *nécessaire* to cut the stitches. When the offending padding was ripped away she put the dress on again. The lines of her breasts were visible now, especially when she raised her arms above her head. If only she had protruding nipples instead of the tiny, in-curving dimples God or Nature had given her. It was too annoying. Her mood of self-deprecation was not helped by Loelia's arrival.

'You look ravishing,' she said and meant it. Loelia wore a beige gown of simple cut with a transparent overskirt that dipped at the back and was daringly high in front. But it was her hair that fascinated Diana. It was brought forward over her cheeks now, in spit curls.

Loelia saw Diana's eyes widen and put a hand to her temple. 'Do you like the *croche-coeurs*? They're all the rage.'

Tomorrow, Diana decided, she would have her own hair bobbed and buy some half-decent clothes. Tonight must be endured.

The look on Max's face as she came down the stairs did something to restore her spirits. 'Oh Lord,' he said simply. As they climbed into his ancient Napier, Diana thought briefly and guiltily of Howard. He would be sitting down to dinner now, discussing share prices and the coal trade. Poor Howard! The next time they came to town she would introduce him to the seamier and more exciting side of life. But first she must discover it for herself.

As soon as they entered the 43, a damp, ill-lit basement, it was obvious that Max intended to monopolize Diana. He talked to her exclusively, as though the others were not there. Soon the air above their table was thick with smoke from their Abdullahs and awash with small talk. They drank cocktails with improbable names like Widow's Kiss and Between the Sheets, and Diana talked about her new life in rather grand terms until Max urged her to her feet.

They danced cheek to cheek on the tiny floor as the night blurred into a haze of smoke and half-light and winking glasses. The moaning clarinets made London seem a world away from Durham, and Max's hand was firm against her spine. When she danced with Howard he held her so tentatively that once she had whispered, 'Hold me closer,' but his hand had continued to hover until she had been forced to take it in her own small, determined hand and clamp it in place. There was no need to tell Max to hold her close. Diana looked to see if Loelia was disapproving, but the faces at the tables were indistinguishable in the dark, and she let Max draw her closer still.

As the night wore on Max became more than a little drunk and more than a little amorous. At last Diana decided the time for discretion had come and threaded her way back to Loelia and safety.

It was after midnight when they got back to Scotland Gate, and Loelia vetoed Max's suggestion that they all have a nightcap. Brother and sister were arguing when a querulous voice sounded from above: 'Loelia? Is that you?'

'Oh Lord – Nanny!' Max said in genuine horror. The nightcap was forgotten, and the four young people tiptoed upstairs like guilty schoolchildren. Nanny, a shawl over her nightgown, stood on the landing and counted them into their respective rooms, and not one of them gave her more than a meek 'Goodnight, Nanny,' for her pains.

In bed, her feet on the still-warm bottle, Diana folded her hands in prayer. For years she had wondered whether or not it was necessary to kneel to pray. At sixteen she had decided God was much too sensible to demand anything so useless and painful, and now she said her prayers flat on her back. Tonight her head was swimming, but she prayed anyway, beginning with apologies for her sins and promises of better behaviour in future. When all the necessary people had been God-blessed, she gave a sigh of satisfaction and settled down to take stock of the evening. She would have to careful about Max. She wriggled under the linen sheets, remembering how he had held her. Men had wanted her before and she had been aware of it, but the rigid code of proper behaviour had shielded her then. There had always been someone's mama there, ready to cluck at the first sign of impropriety. Now she must look after herself.

It was bliss being married and she was probably pregnant, which meant she was a proper woman. Diana slid her hands under the sheet, probing her belly for signs of change. It was still flat, and she was glad. She needed a little time to be gay, to have fun, to spend money. She would have her hair bobbed like Loelia's and buy some clothes. The women in the club tonight had looked different: daring, with skirts creeping up towards their knees and flesh-coloured stockings that made their legs look naked. Their backs had been bare, too, and one or two had had dyed hair, and they all looked flat-chested. But the thing that had most impressed Diana was their painted faces: not colourless lip-salve and *papier poudré* but rouged lips and plucked eyebrows and black-rimmed eyes. Tomorrow she would buy some cosmetics, and she and Loelia could experiment.

She would have to tell Lee about the baby but not yet. Lee would expect her to become all broody and sedate, and it was too soon for that. Before long she would be huge and misshapen and marooned in Durham, but for the next two weeks she could be a free spirit. After that she would be the dutiful wife of a coal-owner. She would be good. She *must* be good! Diana screwed up her eyes and offered up another prayer for rectitude.

When she opened them again she saw Loelia' s battered teddy regarding her with its one good eye. Suddenly missing the comforting bulk of Howard beside her in the bed, she reached for the teddy and tucked it in beside her. The nursery fire glowed behind its guard and flickered on the walls with their pictures of flower fairies. There was always a fire in the Dunane nursery, winter or summer. When she had the baby, Diana thought, she would make sure it always had a fire to glow in the dark. A few moments later she was asleep, the smile of a contented child upon her face.

3

Mary Hardman was glad when the day of the funeral arrived. Since Stephen had been carried down from the Scar she had spent every spare moment beside her husband's bier, refusing all offers of adult company. But the body was taking on the odour of corruption now, the sick, sweet smell of decay which mingled with the scent of the chrysanthemums she had placed in the curtained room. If her husband had stayed as he was in the immediate aftermath of death, seeming just to sleep, she could not have let him go. Now she knew it was time.

She was up before daybreak to check on her sleeping children, tucked in their box-beds either side of the fire. John slept on his side, one sturdy arm under his head. He would be a big man one day, like his father. Catherine, the baby, lay on her back, her hands thrown up behind her head. Mary bent to kiss the broad infant brow and then retrieved John's toy gun from the floor, where it had fallen. Stephen had carved it for him from a piece of wood. Stephen! She pressed the carving to her lips, then she laid it on the bed and went upstairs to stand for a moment in the silent room, before she let herself out of the house into the sleeping back garden of the Shacks.

She smiled as she passed the stone sink in which Stephen had planted the heartsease, remembering his triumph when they had bloomed. They were dying now, but they would seed themselves and come again, if she cared for them: an annual reminder that once she had been loved.

Mary slipped through the Belgate streets, making for the Scar, its white blaze a beacon in the semi-darkness. The sun came up as she climbed the hill, lending a radiance to the pit village so that it looked almost a place of legend and not one of squalor. She was panting as she reached the lee of the half-built house, and paused to look back on Belgate, marvelling that men and women could live and love and give birth and rear children in those tiny boxes; marvelling still more that one man and one woman could need the vastness of the house on the Scar, the house she could not bear to look at today because it had robbed her of happiness.

Unable to make sense of it, Mary sank first to her knees and then lay full length on the turf of the hillside, seeing in the distance the green fields and woods of the county, the towers of Durham a faint blur in the distance. She had always feared that one day Stephen would die in the pit, but here, where he had in fact died, the grass was soft, the air was clean – if you closed your eyes and did not let the bulk of the house, with its stonework and chimneys and ugly brick, intrude. It was hard to make sense of it all, harder still to apportion blame. Cockcroft had said it was the wind; Frank blamed the Brentons' haste… but Mary was not sure. In the end she laid her face against the cold, Durham earth and tried to let all thoughts of blame slip from her mind as she remembered the happiness she and Stephen had shared. She had loved him since she was fifteen and he a seventeen-year-old datal hand, proud of his strength. He could pick her up and carry her as though she were a feather, even when she was eight months gone.

Mary stayed on the hill till the sun was fully up and Belgate began to stir. She was tidying her hair and preparing to go down again when she saw a knot of men emerging from the pit. They were young men, but their heads drooped and their arms hung limp with fatigue at the shift's end. She looked down on them as they trudged down the lonnen towards the pit pond and then halted, seeming to argue. Suddenly they came to a decision. With one accord they dropped their bait cans and began to shed their pit clothes, tossing soiled garments aside until, white and naked, they ran shrieking into the cold water of the pond. There was something joyous in their abandon, a celebration of light and air after the darkness of the pit. Mary smiled as she watched them. Then, as they stepped, naked and proud, but shivering, from the water, she turned away and began to descend the hill.

The money Howard had given her had paid for a black dress and left enough for funeral expenses. Back in the house, she put it on, kissed Stephen's marble face one last time, and let his fellow-miners take him. Noses wrinkled against the mingled odours of flowers and death, they struggled down the narrow stairs, sometimes bumping against the wall, causing the balustrade to groan and tremble. The women had been busy since dawn, and the smell of the boiled ham and pease pudding and new-baked bread they had brought filled the house. Mary smiled her thanks; then she covered her head with a black shawl and fell in behind the coffin for the journey to the grey stone church.

As they passed the pawnbroker's shop she saw the old Jew, Lansky, standing beside the kerb. He didn't remove his hat as the other men did, but there was something in his down-bent head that suggested reverence. A woman stood near to him, dressed in a grey cloth coat, a small child clutching her skirt. Their eyes met, and Mary was taken aback by the other woman's expression. It was not grief or sympathy – more a kind of hostility, as though she was defying death to touch her or her family. And then Frank was tugging her arm, and Mary saw the long, green car parked by the church wall. So young Brenton had come after all!

The priest's voice droned through the comforting Latin incantations. Mary was aware of someone sobbing noisily beside her and Frank making his responses loudly, as a principal mourner should, but all she was longing for was the moment when it would be over and she could gather her children to her and bar the door again.

At the back of the church the Gulliver girls did their best with the unfamiliar service and the strange smell of the church. It had been Anne's idea that she and Esther should go to the funeral, and the suggestion had taken Esther by surprise. 'We don't know them,' she objected.

'Yes, we do,' Anne responded, huffily. 'We know everyone in Belgate.'

'We don't go to everyone's funeral,' Esther said pertly.

'Everyone doesn't die in a tragedy.' At the note of finality in Anne's voice Esther gave in. Besides, it was good to get out, even to a Catholic church. Esther would not have admitted it to outsiders but the atmosphere behind the shop door these days was far from congenial.

As they walked back from the funeral in their sombre Sunday best, she wondered if she dared raise the subject with Anne. This morning her father had pushed aside his plate of bacon and black pudding without touching it. She had looked at Anne to see if she needed to worry that he was ill, but Anne's eyes had merely signalled, 'Serve him right.'

Now Esther shivered, in spite of the sunshine, and Anne looked at her sharply. 'I hope you're not coming down with anything?

Esther braced her shoulders and tried to look healthy. 'No, I'm all right. I think it was just the church. That poor woman...

'We all die some time,' Anne said, as if that made everything all right. 'All the same, those Brentons have a nerve.' Behind them, the pit loomed. The Gullivers seldom talked about the colliery, feeling it was a world apart from their world. Today, though, the pit could not be ignored.

'Well, I'm glad we went,' Esther said. 'The church was full. Did you see Frank Maguire? I thought he was being good to his sister.' She sneaked a glance at Anne to see if she dared to go on. 'And he's very handsome.'

'Handsome is as handsome does,' Anne said and set the shop bell jangling to signal their return.

They crowded around the groaning table in Mary's living-room, curtains half-drawn, family and friends seated, while neighbouring women waited on them, clucking like anxious hens as they poured from vast aluminium tea-pots borrowed from the priest.

'He got a full church,' Frank said as they ate the funeral meats. There was satisfaction in his voice. 'Cockcroft missed a shift to come, and so did Mellors. And did you see the Sheeny standing still till we got past? Time's money to him, you know.' This last was delivered in what he considered to be a Hebrew accent.

'Yes, I saw him,' Mary said. 'I thought it was good of him.'

'Did you see the Gulliver girls?' a woman asked. 'At the back of the church – all dolled up, gloves and hats, the lot.' Mary was surprised. She knew the Gulliver family; she had bought odds and ends in the shop, and once a petticoat with a *broderie anglais* flounce. But she wouldn't have expected them to come to the funeral. Unless there was something really going on between Frank and the older sister, which heaven forbid!

'Frank knows why they were there,' someone said slyly. 'Don't you, Frank?'

Mary saw the flush run lip her hrnther's neck and stain his cheeks. 'They're not Catholics,' she said, automatically.

There was a muted guffaw from around the room.

'I expect they came to pay their respects,' Frank said, 'like everyone else. Anyroad, our Mary doesn't want to be entertained by gossip.' There was reproof in his tone, a reminder of the solemnity of the occasion, but there was a note of gratification, too. Mary sighed to herself. One of the Gulliver girls was still a bairn and the other one was a faggot by all accounts. She stood up to reach for the kettle to top up the tea, but a score of hands were there to stop her. 'Sit still, hinny. There's plenty of us to see to that.'

When the last one left Mary wanted to sink to her knees with relief. All the week her neighbours had swarmed around. The women had baked for her, the men had taken turns to draw her water. But she knew it couldn't last. The Belgate pit, cheated of Stephen, would take another man into its maw and leave a new widow to cherish. That was the pattern in a community accustomed to loss.

She glanced at the clock. It would be an hour or more before her neighbours returned the bairns. Half of her wanted to feel her children in her arms; the other half relished the peace, the freedom from responsibility, the chance to mourn. She mounted the stairs and sank to her knees beside the hope-chest she had brought to this house as a bride. Inside were her souvenirs. The shell box from their day at Redcar, when Stephen had kissed her in the street for all to see. The shawl he had won for her at Houghton Feast, so flimsy that she had never dared to wear it for fear of its disintegration. She fingered the book of collects she had been given at her confirmation, the yellowing celluloid orange-blossom that had crowned her hair on her wedding day, and the veil, gone grey, that Stephen had lifted for their first married kiss. She cried again, then, and blessed the tears because they brought relief.

After he left St Benedict's, Howard drove into Sunderland. As the Suiza crested the western outskirts he looked down on the slate roofs, the dozen spires, the derricks and cranes that marked the dockside. Sunderland was a shipbuilding town, proud of its skills; but the post-war boom had given way here, as everywhere else, to a monumental slump. A million and a half were out of work. Prices had soared in the boom; the shipyard workers had struck, and been driven back to work after two months. No wonder there were sullen faces on the streets of Sunderland. Howard thought of the Belgate woman and the basin of slops she'd thrown at his car. Everywhere men were flocking to join the Plebs League or the Communist Party, and it was difficult to blame them.

But one particular unfairness he could redress, and he meant to do so. He intended to give Mary Hardman £200 from his own pocket. It would have to be given quietly, for if his father or Gallagher heard about it they were quite capable of docking her compensation.

From the corner of his eye Howard saw a man emerge from a gate. There was something familiar about the figure, and he looked again. The next moment he was bringing the car to a halt and hurling himself onto the pavement!

'Trenchard?'

The man turned, but there was no answering smile on his face, only a deepening embarrassment.

Michael Trenchard had fought beside Howard in France. In the last days of the war they had dreamed and planned together with their brother officers, faces alight with expectations of peace. Now, looking at Trenchard, Howard was shocked. The man looked tired and shabby. He was dressed in clothes that appeared not to fit, and was carrying the cardboard suitcase of the travelling salesman.

'Trenchard: is it really you?'

The other man held out his hand. 'Brenton! It's been a long time.' His words were stilted.

Howard seized his hand and shook it vigorously. 'It's good to see you again. We meant to keep in touch. Why do things slip away as they do? But never mind, we've met again.' He turned and gestured towards the Suiza. 'Get in, and we'll go into town. I've an appointment but it won't take long . . . then we can talk. I've so much to tell you.'

Trenchard smiled. 'Sorry, old man, but I have business, too.' He gestured at the suitcase. 'I have here the wonders of the Aztec Brush Co, which I am about to reveal to the astonished ladies of Tunstall Road. This is a prosperous street. Rich pickings.' He leaned back a little and squinted at Howard. 'You look like a carpet job. Wilton, or Chinese I could do you a nice line in pure bristle?'

His self-mockery was painful to Howard. Together they had cowered in water-filled trenches, and marched grimly on. Trenchard had been commissioned in the field for an act of conspicuous bravery, and now he was a brush salesman. He must do something for him.

Howard was about to voice his thoughts when reason prevailed. Instead he smiled and nodded. 'Of course. Foolish of me. I'm still impetuous, you see. Remember Hooge Wood?' They both smiled, remembering Trenchard's repeated injunctions to Howard to keep his head down.

'Give me your address,' Howard went on. 'We must meet soon. Let me know where I can reach you.'

Trenchard drew out a leather card-case. The pasteboard oblong he handed to Howard bore the name of the Aztec Brush Co in large letters, and underneath, in minute type: *M. R. Trenchard, Representative, 26, Paton Street, Sunderland*. Howard put the card carefully inside his own case. 'I thought you came from York?' he said. 'You never mentioned Sunderland.'

Trenchard was already moving towards another gate. 'I don't belong here. I came to find work.' His final words were low but Howard caught them. 'It's a dirty bird that fouls its own nest.'

As he climbed into the Suiza. Howard felt sick at heart. Trenchard had been a man of action; he would never make a salesman. The idea was ludicrous. As the car roared to life he looked back at the shabby figure, waiting patiently for a door to open. He had a sudden, odd feeling that something momentous had happened, a clicking of cogs in the wheel of fate – and then the car was moving forward towards the town, and Trenchard was lost to view.

While Howard was encountering Michael Trenchard, Diana, in London, was surrendering herself to the discreet temples of beauty culture. She chose the exclusive salon of Madame Iris on Loelia's recommendation. 'She trained in Paris,' Loelia said, as if that, in itself meant expertise. 'And she's been to America. She's frightfully chic, but a tyrant and her charges are exorbitant.' Diana merely smiled at this, confident that Charles Brenton could afford a dozen Mesdames Iris, but Loelia shook her head. 'You'll have to do what she tells you ... whatever she tells you. Even if it's a shingle!' She invested the latter word with a dreadful significance, and put up a hand to the nape of her neck, where a coil of hair remained. 'I can't go back because she'll shear me and the 0. M. will get in a wax. Also she said I should fast for three days once a month and drink only water and lemon – and I simply haven't the strength of will.'

Diana's heart beat faster when she entered the eau-de-Nil splendour of Madame Iris's salon. She was enveloped in an eau-de-Nil gown that felt suspiciously like silk and then conducted to a throne in the centre of an oval eau-de-Nil chamber. Madame Iris appeared, dressed from head to foot in starkest black, the only relief a huge pearl pin in her black turban and a rope of pigeon's egg-sized pearls that fell almost to her knees.

She put out a hand and grasped Diana's chin, turning her face this way and that. 'And what am I expected to do with this?' she asked. Diana was lost for words but Madame did not seem to need an answer. An army of acolytes appeared, all clad in eau-de-Nil, and the transformation began. Madame Iris moved to a second throne and kept a critical eye on proceedings, all the while flourishing a foot-long cigarette-holder and issuing a burst of instructions whenever an acolyte slowed down.

Diana's hair was cut short, but mercifully not shingled, brushed back from her forehead and then brought forward into half curls against her cheeks. Her face was anointed with lotions made from a dozen sweet-smelling jars with strange names, like milk of almonds and tincture of myrrh and Seville Orange skin food. Her eyebrows were plucked almost out of existence and then drawn in again with a special pencil, and her eyes were defined with kohl, the initial application being expertly smudged until it looked for all the world as though she had a double set of sooty lashes. The upper half of her face was powdered with a dark powder, Spanish Rachel, and the lower half with a lighter shade, Orchid. This, Diana was informed, was to give brilliance to the eyes. Her cheeks were rouged with powdered Carmine Blush, blended with a camel-hair brush, and her chin was rouged, too. She was told she might apply rouge to the lobes of her ears, but only in the evenings.

'Never,' said Madame, 'never dye the hair. It is a crime – the hallmark of vulgarity.'

Diana's lips and nails were painted in identical purplish red, and the final touch was an all-over spray of perfume from an opaque eau-de-Nil bottle with a tasseled bulb and the single word *Iris* embossed upon it in gold.

Madame said 'Good,' and made her exit. One eau-de-Nil overall fetched a gold mirror, and Diana looked into it and saw a stranger. Another eau-de-Nil overall appeared with an eau-de-Nil box, again embossed in gold, this time *Iris Wigmore St, London New York Paris*.

'*Votre maquillage, madame*,' she said and presented a bill for twenty-seven guineas.

The look on Max's face when he sprang open the door of his Napier told Diana the transformation had been a success. She was tempted to ask for his approval but decided against it. She was her own woman now and needed no approval but her own.

It was late afternoon when Howard came again to the Shacks. Mary opened the door to him, still wearing the good black dress, unbuttoned now at the neck and shrouded from the waist in a sacking apron. She pulled off the apron with one hand and began to button the neck with the other. Howard recognized the familiar gesture as he followed her into the dark living-room, aware once more of the huge fire and the scent of chrysanthemums. There was no sound nor sign of her children, and he guessed they had been taken away to give her peace.

He laid an envelope of Treasury notes on the red table-cover. 'I want you to accept this from my wife and me. It has nothing to do with your compensation from the company. That will come to you through Mr Gallagher.'

He did not mention that the official compensation had been won only after a bitter wrangle. Gallagher had suggested that the usual terms, agreed with the Miners' Union, need not apply to a man killed outside the pit. Howard had waited for his father to dismiss the suggestion but Charles had merely puckered his lips. 'There's no real liability, sir,' Gallagher had said, sensing his opportunity. 'Wind is an act of God. An *ex gratia* payment would be more than generous.'

The row between father and son had erupted when Gallagher had left and continued when they reached home that evening. Charlotte had pleaded a headache and sought refuge in her room, but Howard had stood firm, and when the harsh words subsided it had been agreed that Mary Hardman would receive the proper compensation.

Now Howard tried to convey to her his concern for her future. 'The money you receive from the Fund should help, and I'm glad of that. But I want you to take this money, too.'

Mary inclined her head, knowing it was expected of her; but the days she had spent alone had made up her mind about the future. She wanted work: that would be her only real security. She raised her eyes as Howard continued.

'I've told Gallagher you may keep this house, if that is your wish, but I hope you'll be able to leave it. These hovels should have been razed long ago. They're unfit. That's why I wanted to do this myself...' He tapped the envelope and she sensed he was embarrassed. 'Which brings me to another point...' He paused again and she knew he was seeking the right words. She waited.

'Because it's not part of the agreement we have with our men I would be grateful – that is...' He faltered again and this time she finished for him.

'I'll tell no one, Mr Howard, if that's what you want.'

Howard looked at her gratefully. He had felt drawn to her on that first visit, and now the feeling was reinforced. There was intelligence in her eyes and the prospect of warmth in the mouth compressed now in resignation.

He pushed back his chair and rose to his feet. 'I'll say goodbye, then, Mrs Hardman.' He held out his hand and she put hers into it. Her skin was rough, but her hand felt surprisingly small. 'Remember you can turn to me at any time. Don't go through Gallagher. Speak directly to me... or my wife. I expect she'll be contacting you before long.' There was tenderness in his voice when he spoke of Diana, and Mary noticed it.

'There is one thing, Mr Howard.' He smiled encouragement and she went on. 'I do need work. Oh, I'm glad of your money and I'll take it – and the compen – but I want work. You mentioned needing someone? I can't be away all day, but I've got good neighbours who'll see to the bairns for a few hours a week ... if I could get some scrubbing work.'

Howard nodded and then bit the side of his lower lip. 'The house will be my wife's province,' he said, 'but we'll be needing staff. Staff to live in, and other help. I don't know how you'd feel about working at the Scar?'

Mary remembered how she could not bear to even look at the house on the day of the funeral, and waited for anguish to follow his words, but it did not come. Instead she felt oddly peaceful.

'I'd like to work there,' she said.

When Howard had made his goodbyes she shut the door after him and crossed to the window, standing there, her breath misting the glass, until the big green car moved away from her home.

Howard was dressed before the gong rang to signal dinner. He met his mother on the landing and proffered an arm. 'You look nice,' he said, smiling.

His mother had not altered her mode of dress for twenty-five years, when she had decided to model herself on her beloved Princess May. The post-war craze for beige had passed her by; mauve remained her favourite colour and her dresses hung long and loose from her ample bosom. Howard knew that she must buy new clothes, for she never looked shabby, but he was seldom able to detect a change. Tonight she wore lavender moire taffeta, tucked at the shoulders and inlet with matching lace. Pearls swung from her bosom and fell to below her waist, and there were matching pearls in her fleshy ear lobes.

'Have you heard from Diana?' she asked, as they moved together down the stairs.

'Not yet,' Howard answered. 'She may telephone me later, but you know how she is with Loelia. They love to gossip.'

His mother's sniff was full of meaning but he ignored it.

He needed a pleasant atmosphere tonight if he was to obtain help for Trenchard. Everything else was of secondary importance. He himself could give the man a menial job, but if he was to find a position suited to Trenchard's stature he needed his father's approval. So he opened the drawing-room door for his mother, resolving as he did so to keep the conversation over the dinner-table as pleasant as he could.

Charlotte Brenton had been twenty-nine when she married Charles. As Charlotte Fletcher she had been the plain daughter of a minor bishop of the Church of England. When Charles Brenton came courting he made no secret of his motives: as a daughter of the church she would lend an air of gentility to his home. Furthermore, she came from a family that bred well. The eldest of nine children, she had three younger sisters, each producing a baby a year. It was Charles's confident expectation that Charlotte would do the same, and his wedding-night assault upon her was silent and clinical, a means rather than an end.

After three barren years, during which Charles made his disappointment plain, Charlotte suffered two miscarriages in swift succession. Howard's birth had turned her husband's cold fury to jubilation. Two years later she gave birth again to a girl, Caroline, after a protracted labour that ended with the doctor's announcement that there would be no more children.

'You've failed me,' Charles told her with every gesture of his hands, every inflection of his voice. When his precious son was taken off to war in 1915, he had put his disgust into words. 'There should have been others,' he said. 'If the boy dies it will all be for nothing.' That night he had had Charlotte's possessions moved to another room, and had made it clear she should leave the double bed they had shared in icy discomfort for the past twenty-three years.

Now, as Howard led her into the drawing-room for the ritual aperitif, Charles nodded at his son and ignored the woman on his arm as though she were a mere accessory.

When they were summoned to the dining-room, it was Howard who settled her in her chair and smiled at her as he took his own seat. When she bowed her head to murmur grace, it was a prayer for deliverance and not a thanksgiving for the food.

As soon as the asparagus soup had been cleared and the maids were moving about with the fish course, Howard brought up the subject of Trenchard.

'I met an old friend today, Michael Trenchard. Do you remember him from my letters? We were together in France.'

Charlotte nodded. Charles looked up from his plate. 'I can't say I remember the name. Still, what's he doing now?'

Howard pretended to have difficulty with a bone while he sought the right answer. 'He's in manufacturing. Something to do with brushes, I think. Industrial. Only in Sunderland to discuss business.' He chewed for a moment. 'He has a lot to offer, father. I never saw anyone like him for managing men. He was promoted in the field. I was wondering...

He never completed his sentence. Charles licked in a stray drop of Hollandaise sauce and stated his position.

'So the fellow was promoted in the field, was he? No experience except the trenches, and no qualifications, I'll be bound. The whole of English industry is awash with exofficers, all of them thinking they have a right to an easy sitting-down.' His tone implied that the holding of a King's commission had positively unfitted some men for work.

'Trenchard's not like that, sir.'

But Charles was not disposed to listen. 'Has he qualifications or experience, or has he not? Relevant experience, that is? We need experts in the coalfield now, Howard, not amateurs.' He waited, enjoying Howard's discomfiture. 'No? Well, let's hear no more of it. These ex-officers must make their own way, like the rest of us. I want to talk about the house at the Scar. They're making damned slow progress now. I've put Gallagher on to it. The sooner that house is up the better.'

When he married, Howard had taken it for granted that they would live under his father's roof, and Diana had been too taken up with wedding preparations to demur. The Brenton house had twelve bedrooms and seven reception rooms, but the 1906 carved above the fireplace was less than impressive to someone accustomed to the Elizabethan splendour of Barthorpe. It had taken Diana two days to conceive the idea of a new house, and two minutes to persuade Charles Brenton to give it to her. She had looked from his study window and seen a white blaze in the far distance. 'It would be heaven to live there,' she had said. A week later, Charles owned the land around the Scar and his architect was transmitting Diana's whims to paper.

When the plan was costed it had made even Charles gasp. 'It's too much,' Diana had said in a small voice, and her air of resignation tipped the scale.

'Nonsense,' Charles had said. 'If we use our own men, it could easily be done.'

People who knew Charles Brenton slightly marvelled at the ease with which his new daughter-in-law manipulated him. Charles had showed much less generosity to Geoffrey Arnett, who had married the Brentons' daughter, Caroline, the year before; she had been given a handsome dowry, but nothing approaching the sum he was prepared to spend to please Diana. But to anyone who might have known the secrets of his heart there was a simple explanation for his generosity to his titled daughter-in-law. The Arnetts were wealthy, but still in trade. The Carterets had class.

Charles Brenton had long wished to breach the walls of society but he despised upstarts like the American millionairess, Laura Corrigan, who lured titled guests to her parties with gold vanity-bags from Cartier and gold-tabbed braces. The Brentons might have new money, but it had the patina of discretion. Besides, he liked his new daughter-in-law. She had spirit – unlike his wife, and his daughter, too, more was the pity.

'What are you doing about furnishing the house?' he asked Howard, as the *entrée* was put before them. 'I should give the girl a free hand, if I were you. She'll know what to do with it.'

Across the table Charlotte's knuckles whitened on her knife and fork. She had not been allowed to choose even the wall-coverings in her own home, not once in thirty years.

Esther Gulliver woke in the darkness to find Anne shaking her with a rough hand. 'Wake up, Es. Something's happened.'

Esther heaved herself up on her pillow, trying to shake off sleep. There was fear in Anne's voice. Whatever was wrong it must be terrible.

'What is it?'

'How do I know?' Anne said angrily. 'I heard an almighty crash!' In the darkness Esther could sense that Anne was trembling. Light from the street lamp shone through a chink in the curtains, causing a ghostly glow to come from the dressing-table mirror.

'Shall I light the gas?' Esther said it reluctantly, unwilling to put a foot down to the cold linoleum and feel her way across darkness to the gas mantle by the door. There was a scrape of a match, and then the candle Anne kept by the bed flared into life.

'What are you doing, Annie?' The pet name of childhood slipped out, and for once Anne did not reprimand her.

'What does it look as though I'm doing? I'm going to find out what's happened.' She slipped from under the blankets and reached for the knitted shawl that lay on the velvet armchair. Esther watched her, a sinister figure in the flickering candlelight. Anne moved towards the door, and then halted and turned. 'Come on then, Es, get out of bed. You don't think I'm going down there on my own?'

Together they went onto the landing, Esther's fingers wound in the slack of her sister's nightdress, the brass candlestick held aloft in Anne's shaking hand.

'What if it's burglars?' Esther whispered.

But Anne did not answer, for the flickering light had already illumined what lay at the foot of the stairs.

'Is he dead?' Esther asked, halfway down, her legs threatening to give way underneath her.

'Dead drunk, more like,' Anne said scornfully, not knowing how near the truth her words lay. She moved down towards the inert figure, at first confidently and then more cautiously. At last she bent and put out a hand. She touched his shoulder, and then his hand, and only then did she recoil with a cry that made the hair stand up on the back of Esther's neck.

Sidney Gulliver, for once, was not in a drunken stupor. He was drunk, certainly, but he was also dead. A slight smile was on his parted lips, the lips from which a flow of blood had erupted and then ceased as the heart that was pumping it gave up beating.

'My God,' Anne said sitting down abruptly on the bottom stair.

Above her Esther started to cry, the wail of the frightened child she was. The sound stiffened Anne's nerves.

'Stop that!' she said fiercely. 'Don't you dare go to pieces on me now. I can't face this on my own.'

Esther sniffed and lifted the hem of her nightgown to wipe her eyes.

'That's better,' Anne said, in a more kindly tone. 'Now, go upstairs and put some clothes on. He's dead. Someone'll have to go next door for help.'

She held the candle aloft so that Esther might climb the stairs to the bedroom, her bare feet pink and pathetic in the flickering light. Anne followed more slowly, her mind racing furiously while she went through the mechanics of putting on her clothes.

4

It was late when Diana and Max returned to Scotland Gate from the Savoya. As they entered the darkened house he reached for her, his eyes hot and excited, his hands rough. She laughed and would have moved away to safety, but he took firm hold of her arm. 'Come on, Di – don't tease!'

There was a touch of anger in his voice and Diana bridled. That morning she had had an unpleasant intimation of the baby's presence. She had woken feeling nauseous, and had only been comforted by cinder tea, a concoction prepared by Nanny. Mumbling under her breath, the old woman had picked a red-hot cinder from the nursery fire and dropped it into a glass of warm water. After a moment the brew was ready to be poured down Diana's unresisting throat. If Nanny suspected Diana was pregnant, she made no mention of it. As soon as colour began to return to Diana's cheeks the old woman lost interest and tottered back to her own room. Loelia had asked no questions and Diana had offered no explanations. But all day she had been thinking, and now she faced the fact that her dalliance with Max must end.

'Let me go,' she said, but Max's grip tightened. Only the advent of Nanny on the landing, vague and incoherent but still in charge, saved them from an unpleasant scene. The next morning Diana asked the maid to pack, and used the telephone to send a telegram to Howard.

Loelia nodded with understanding when Diana told her

she simply must go home. 'Of course,' she said. 'You must be missing Howard.'

'It's not that,' Diana said, and then, 'well, of course, I do miss him terribly, but the fact is...' She paused and then came to a decision. 'I think I might possibly be pregnant. You know how sickly I was this morning? And – well, I just think I may be.' She would have liked to add, 'Don't tell Max – not yet,' but she didn't dare. Instead she said, 'Keep it a secret, darling, just for the moment.'

'How utterly marvellous!' Loelia said, and kissed her warmly. Neither of them mentioned Max's existence.

That afternoon Diana sped north. Knowing she was pregnant was beginning to affect her. She felt a little holy, and of much greater consequence. She sat in the train, magazines in lap, gazing out of the window. But she did not see the passing countryside. She was remembering the girl she had been and reflecting on the woman she must now become.

Howard was waiting for her on the platform, hat in hand, hair ruffled by the draught from the passing train. He was by far the tallest figure in the waiting crowd, and Diana felt a glow of satisfaction. He was not only handsome, he was dear and familiar and safe. She flung the carriage door open and threw herself into his arms, as the train juddered to a halt. 'I've missed you, Howard – and I'm going to have a baby! What do you think about that?'

Howard had been aghast at the change in her appearance wrought by Madame Iris, but when her words penetrated, pride and pleasure showed on his face. What did it matter that Diana was painted like a *demi-mondaine*? She was going to have his child!

'I'm so proud of you,' he said as he handed her into the car. 'And I've missed you so: more than I can say.'

'It's lovely to be home,' she said, squeezing his arm as he slid in beside her. 'And I'm going to be good, Howard: a model coalowner's wife. I shall visit that man's widow, and take junket to the poor, and positively exhaust myself with good deeds. Just you wait and see!'

Howard smiled as he negotiated the exit from the station yard, and shook his head as though in disbelief, but he was relieved at her mention of Mary Hardman. He had intended to visit her again himself, but he had shirked it. Now Diana would break the ice, and then he would follow. He glanced at his wife's flushed and lovely face, and thought of the coming baby. Truly, he was a fortunate man.

The Brentons were also shocked by their daughter-in-law's short hair and painted face. Sensing their disapproval, Diana launched into an account of the torture she had endured to achieve the desired effect – an effect that was in vogue among the grandees in Mayfair, she added and by the time she finished Charles was smiling. Charlotte was harder to reconcile. Howard saw her nostrils pinch at the sight of Diana's metamorphosis, but news of the pregnancy forestalled a protest. Charles called for Bollinger, and when they sat down to dinner that evening Diana's daring beige sheath dress caused hardly a quiver.

As the servants moved about, dispensing saddle of lamb and caper sauce, Diana regaled them with more tales of London, of Gertrude Lawrence at the Vaudeville, Chaplin's new film which had made her cry, and disturbing tit-bits about the Prince of Wales, who, according to Diana, was up to no good with his cousin, Dickie Mountbatten, and a score of well-bred but amoral young women.

Watching his vivacious daughter-in-law, Charles could barely conceal his satisfaction. She was a slight little thing, flat-chested like a boy – but Charlotte had appeared fecund enough and not lived up to that appearance. He glanced up to find his wife's eyes on him, their look unfathomable. He stared her out until at last her eyes dropped to her plate. 'Go on,' he said, turning to his daughter-in-law. 'Let's hear more of London.'

Diana was anxious to let her father-in-law see that his generosity about the new house was appreciated. She chattered through dessert, and afterwards sat down at the grand piano in the drawing-room and played Chopin for him. Howard sat watching her, smiling from time to time, and a small knot of content formed in Diana's chest. She had been right to come home. She would grow to love Howard in time; she half did already. In a little while they could escape to their room, the two of them alone. She beamed at Charles and rattled into a popular song, one she had heard ex-servicemen sing as they begged in the London gutters.

Though there's nothing in the larder, ain't we got fun?
Times are hard and getting harder, still we have fun.
There's nothing surer, the rich get rich and the poor get poorer.
In the meantime, in between times, ain't we got fun?

Charles frowned in mock-disapproval of her Cockney accent, but Diana could see he liked it. Charlotte's face was stony. Diana slipped into a chorus of 'Look for the Silver Lining', then announced she was ready for bed.

On their wedding night Howard had left her alone to undress. He stayed away for half an hour, timing it by his watch. Diana was ready in ten minutes and spent the next twenty in a fever of anticipation. She had not complained, because of an instinctive belief that a bride's ardour should not match, let alone outblaze, a groom's. But she had no intention of letting that happen again tonight.

One look at Howard's face when he reappeared from his dressing-room told her that what she had half-feared was true: now that she was pregnant, he was going to treat her as an object of veneration. And all she wanted was to be loved without restraint! She reached for his hand and placed it on her stomach, letting it rest lightly for a moment before she moved it to her breast. When that did not have the desired effect, she began to caress him, until at last he groaned and reached for her.

Afterwards, she fell asleep in his arms. Howard lay still, unwilling to move for fear of disturbing her. She had roundly dismissed his fears about her condition, but there were still limits. For a while it would be all right... but only for a while. He felt a wave of tenderness for the sleeping girl, and it was more than an hour before he freed his arm and turned on his side to sleep.

Diana was driven into Belgate the following day. Fox sat at the wheel of Charles Brenton's Daimler, disapproval in every line of his livened figure. In the *tonneau* there was a wicker basket full of nourishing food culled from the Brenton kitchen, and some items from the now-outmoded trousseau. Diana was feeling virtuous, and it was a pleasant experience. Her mother regularly took calves'-foot jelly to the poor and needy, but Diana had always shirked such things. Now, however, she was resolved to be a proper wife.

Last night Howard's ardour had finally almost matched her own and he had positively beamed at her over the breakfast table. She had not felt so sick; in fact she had enjoyed kidneys and bacon. Her good intentions increased with every yard of the journey. She must get to know this place and its people. Above all, she must be loyal to the Brenton name. It was wrong to joke about Charles Brenton's social pretensions and money-making zeal; there was no sin in making money work and using it to provide employment. The fact that her father considered the pursuit of money to be vulgar had not stopped him from marrying her into a mercantile family when the chance came. Snobbery was for the middle classes, always striving to look down on everyone else. Well, she was above such things. She sat in the Daimler, proud of her classlessness, smiling cheerfully at passers-by.

At the Shacks, Fox sprang out to open her door. 'Shall I fetch the basket, Mrs Howard?' As long as Charlotte was alive there could only be one Mrs Brenton.

'Yes, please, Fox,' she said and let him hand her from the car. He went ahead of her, hefting the basket as though it were feathers. A clump of pansies in a stone container caught her eye and lifted her spirits. It was nice to see people making the best of their surroundings.

As they waited for a response to Fox's rap on the door, Diana licked her lips. She felt great sympathy for the widow, but how to put it into words? When Mary Hardman appeared in the doorway, a pale, stern figure in black, Diana's composure deserted her. She brushed past her into the living-room, letting out a trill of nervous laughter. Inside, she held out her hand, thought better of it as being too formal, and withdrew it. Mary saw and misinterpreted the gesture. That Diana might be nervous or afraid never entered her mind. In her chagrin, she looked pointedly at Fox and then back to Diana, and Diana, understanding, told him to wait in the car.

It was easier when they were alone. Mary pulled out a chair and Diana sat down at the red plush table. It was warm in the room and she put up a hand to undo the sable collar of her coat. Mary felt a grudging admiration for the beautiful painted face, flawless beneath the sable hat.

'I would have come before,' Diana said. 'Perhaps my husband told you I had to go to London? I came back yesterday.' Her tone implied that she had come as soon as she could and expected credit for it, and Mary thought of what Frank had said the day before: *'They give us a pat on the head when we're good and expect their bloody feet kissed for it.'* That was about it.

Getting no answer, Diana blundered on. 'I've brought you some soup. And some clothes. They're quite new… part of my trousseau.' Her voice faltered as it dawned on her that some of her clothes might be less than useful to a woman in mourning. And then she remembered she had included her good grey wool, and her voice revived. 'Will they fit you?'

Mary's answer was flat. 'They'll alter for the bairns, likely. It was good of you to think of me. Thank you.'

Diana smiled, gratified by Mary's words and the pleasing quality of her voice. She wasn't difficult to talk to, not difficult at all.

'It's the least we could do. My husband and I are both very sad for you, and anxious to help. Was your husband a native of Belgate?'

Mary shook her head. 'He belonged Pelton Fell. I was born in Belgate, and he moved here when we wed.'

Diana nodded. 'I see, so you'll have family here. That must be a help. I'm a long way from home. My parents live in Berkshire.'

Mary was not listening. She was thinking of Stephen on the day they wed, a giant in unaccustomed blue serge, carrying her over the threshold of this room. *'Why did he die?'* John had asked her yesterday and she had not been able to answer.

She had looked forward to Diana Brenton's visit as a chance to get work and occupy her mind, but she had also dreaded the meeting. Diana had been to her only a dim figure in a grey coat and bright red hat, shrinking into the upholstery of her husband's car. Frank blamed Diana for Stephen's death, but some of his workmates, better informed, hinted that Charles Brenton alone had been behind the mad haste at the Scar. Mary, unable to hate them all, had decided to blame no one. And yet…

'So you see we really do need help,' Diana was saying. 'After the baby is born there'll be so much to do, and before that the house needs attention. There's a separate washhouse and a splendid new boiler, by all accounts. My husband tells me you were in service before you married. Do you like children?'

Mary turned to the fire and began to poke vigorously at the caked coal. It was more than she could bear, the monstrous unfairness of life. As if from other lips than her own she heard a voice: 'Yes. Yes, I like bairns. I must do, mustn't I, seeing as I have two of my own? Thank you, Mrs Howard. I'm sure I'll try and give satisfaction.'

They drank tea and made small talk, and as soon as she decently could Diana made her escape. When the car was gone Mary raised the lid of the basket and looked down on the finery. She picked up a dress of apricot voile, looked at it for a moment and then tossed it aside. But after a while she retrieved it and set about sorting out what could be made over for her children.

Esther's eyes were still swollen, and every now and again tears would come. Anne was dry-eyed, as she had been from the moment they had stooped over their father's body and realized he was dead. She had sat stonily through the inquest, hearing the coroner talk of her father's 'chronic addiction to alcohol, which had led to internal haemorrhaging and thus to his demise'. She had supported her weeping younger sister throughout the funeral service, and served tea and baked meats to the mourners afterwards.

'I can't pretend what I don't feel,' she said, when Esther reproached her for her composure. 'And you shouldn't cry for him, either. Save your tears for yourself, our Es. There's plenty to weep for there.' She had already inspected her father's accounts and seen the extent of the debt they faced.

Now they sat in the sitting-room, the curtains half-drawn over the window, and listened to their mother's brother prophesying doom.

'It's a mess, girls, and that's a fact. A dozen people demanding their due, and not a penny in the account. Still, I'm not here to criticize a dead man.' Her uncle's expression said he was there to accept martyrdom, and Esther's heart sank. He was going to take them both to his cold unwelcoming house in Stockton and begrudge them every bite that passed their lips.

But Esther was wrong. 'I shall do my duty by you. I know what's right for families.' Her uncle shook his head sadly. 'I'm afraid we can't stretch to take you in, so I've taken it upon myself to make arrangements. I spoke to the Brenton agent, and he says there'll be work in the house at the Scar for both of you. It's almost completed. By the time you've packed up here, there'll be places for you there...

Esther felt Anne quiver. Was it relief? She herself would go anywhere, as long as it wasn't Stockton.

But Anne was rising to her feet and her face was like a thundercloud.

'You needn't have bothered yourself for me, Uncle. I'll see to my own affairs. I've made my plans. Esther must do as she pleases, but I wasn't made to skivvy for a Brenton.' Before her uncle could speak, she was moving towards the door to the kitchen. 'I'll make some tea, I'm quite parched.'

Esther looked at her uncle's astonished face, and scuttled after her sister. 'What plans have you made?' she asked as they shut the door behind them. Suddenly the fears that had skittered around the back of her mind ever since her father's death came to the fore. '*What plans*?' she asked again, this time in desperation.

'How do I know?' Anne said, thumping the kettle onto the stove. 'But I'd sooner sweep the streets than do what he suggests.'

There came a sudden tap at the back door, and Esther, surprised, went to open it. Frank Maguire stood on the step, his cap clutched in one hand, a brown paper bag in another.

'I've brought some fresh eggs,' he said, lamely. 'I thought you might both need building up...

Esther turned to see what Anne's reaction might be; you never could tell with Anne.

'Thanks,' Anne said flatly. And then, 'You'd better come in. Wipe your feet.'

Frank came over the step, twisting his cap between his hands, lowering himself gingerly into a deal chair. Anne was clashing crockery and rattling caddies, but Esther watched as Frank gazed around the big kitchen, his eyes like saucers but trying not to look over-awed. He looked at the dresser crowded with willow-pattern plates; at neat tins labelled *Rice* and *Sago* and *Sugar*, at the gleam of the Aga, polished by Anne until it positively glowed. 'It's a nice kitchen,' Esther thought, a brief quiver of pride striking her.

He was looking at Anne now, a half-smile on his lips. 'She *is* lovely,' Esther thought, seeing the gleam of her sister's neatly parted hair, the tilt of her head, the snug fit of her cinnamon dress with its tucked bodice and puffed sleeves. Anne's hands darted hither and thither with cups and spoons, and once strayed to her neck to check that her enamel brooch was still in place.

She was scalding the tea when a furious knocking erupted at the front door. She went to the door at the entrance to the passage, and put her eye to the crack. Esther heard a man speaking, and then her uncle's reply, but she couldn't make out the words. Anne was leaning forward, straining to hear.

'Who is it?' Esther said, but Anne put up a hand for silence. There was more murmuring, and then came the sound of the parlour door opening and closing. Anne turned back to the kitchen, her face a mask of consternation.

'It's the bailiffs,' she said. 'They've come to clear us out. They're discussing it with Uncle now.'

'What does that mean – the bailiffs?' Esther said, afraid once more.

'The end,' Anne said. 'That's what it means.'

For a moment they were all silent, and then suddenly Frank was standing up. 'You'll have to move quick,' he said urgently. 'Take what you can before the bailiffs make their list. Small stuff: gold and silver if you've got it. Vases, anything fancy. I'll take them to Lansky, the Jew. He'll give you cash for them.'

Esther waited for Anne to wither Frank, but she was moving to the larder, reaching to the hook for the big straw bags they took when they went shopping for provisions. 'Here,' she said, thrusting one at Esther, 'you take upstairs, I'll do down – and don't let them catch you, Es.' She turned to Frank. 'You wait here and stop them if they come out.'

'How?' he said, but obeyed her just the same.

For a moment Esther's legs threatened to fail her, but then she remembered her mother's keeper chain, and the silver rattle with the mother-of-pearl handle that bore both Anne's teethmarks and her own. No bailiff was getting his hands on those! She sped up the stairs on tip-toe and set about salvaging anything of value that came to hand. As she rifled drawers and dressing-table tops her strength returned, and the bag grew comfortingly heavy.

Downstairs, as Frank kept guard, Anne scoured the back shop and living-room, and then hurried upstairs to help Esther. 'That's enough,' she said at last. 'They'll be coming to look for us any minute now.'

'All right?' Frank asked, as they tiptoed down to the hall.

'Yes,' Anne said. 'Now, let's get out of here.'

In Mary Hardman's small living-room they cleared the table and set out their booty: a clutch of china ornaments; the small pieces of jewellery that had belonged to their mother; a silver picture frame with their parents' wedding photograph inside; a small silver case; the silver rattle; a polished wooden box inlaid with mother-of-pearl...'It's not much,' Anne said.

'It's better than nothing,' Frank offered. He had a grin on his face and one hand inside his jacket. 'And', he said grandly, 'and – ' His hand came out of his jacket, clutching a fistful of cutlery. 'What about that?' he said.

'Can you do this?' Mary Hardman asked. 'I thought you couldn't cheat on the duns?'

'I didn't cheat anyone,' Anne said bitterly. 'We were the cheated ones, Esther and me. These were my mother's things, even the knives and forks.' She picked one up and flourished it. 'That's an S there, for Shipton, not a G for Gulliver. The debts were Gulliver debts. Let them take Gulliver things to settle them.'

The knot of misery that had been building in Esther's chest since her father's death was now threatening to choke her. 'What are we going to do?' she wailed.

Anne looked down at the table, moving the knives and forks into line with a forefinger. 'Survive, Esther. That's what we're going to do. Survive!'

'That's the ticket,' Frank said proudly, but Mary put a motherly arm round Esther's shoulder. 'Come on, chuck,' she said. 'You need a good cup of tea.'

As Howard and Diana drove towards the Scar it was impossible for either of them to forget Stephen Hardman's death. There was no wind today, and no crowd of gawping workmen, but the memory of the inert body could not be banished. 'I'm glad I went to see his wife,' Diana said as their house came into sight.

'Yes,' Howard said, and took his hand from the wheel to pat Diana's hand as it lay in her lap. They were silent then until the Suiza was halted at the broad steps of the front door, and Howard came round to help his wife alight.

'Will we be happy here?' Diana said apprehensively.

Howard smiled. 'Very happy,' he said firmly, and kept

hold of her hand as they pushed open the door and went into the spacious hall. Opposite them a wide staircase ran up to a landing where it divided, going right and left. On Diana's instruction the woodwork had been painted white, with here and there a touch of apple-green. It was still wet to the touch but it looked good. Charlotte had shuddered at the very mention of it, and Howard had been dubious, too. Now he saw that it was right for a house that was to be a symbol of all that was modern, and after the solid Edwardian opulence of his parents' home he found it a refreshing change.

When Diana had begged for a house he had wondered if she wanted to recreate the Elizabethan splendour of Barthorpe, her childhood home. But she had opted instead for a house that had New Age in every line. His father had come to see it and declared it a monstrosity, but he kept his opinion to himself whenever Diana was in earshot. It was what she wanted and that was all that mattered.

Standing at a window, they looked far out to the soft line of the Cleveland hills. 'I have such plans for this house,' Diana said. She had already commissioned spare, unpolished oak furniture from Ambrose Heal in London, and she meant to choose bold modern patterns for curtains and upholstery. A Durham carpet had been ordered, one colour to run throughout the whole house, and a few dozen boxes of glass and silver and porcelain from Barthorpe were waiting to be unpacked.

Diana turned from the window, her hands clasped beneath her chin. 'I love it, love it, love it, Howard. And I love you.' She moved forward and kissed him squarely on the mouth, catching his lip against his teeth. He drew his head back involuntarily, and instantly regretted it. The wary look returned to her eyes, and she turned away.

'I shall have to go back to London for a while to see to things there,' she said. 'You can't trust tradesmen, nowadays. You need to check what they're doing yourself.'

Knowing she was punishing him for his lack of response, Howard wondered whether he should reach out for her and kiss her soundly to make amends, but at that moment Cockcroft, the overseer, came into the hall below them, and the opportunity was lost.

'I do wish we were in our own home,' Diana said later. Already dressed for dinner, she was sitting on the ottoman at the foot of their bed while Howard coped with studs and cufflinks.

'Not much longer,' he said, smiling at her in the mirror. Tonight she wore a short evening-dress in two shades of violet, the skirt in what he thought to be chiffon, the bodice in lace cut in the fashionable flat-chested style. He pulled open the top drawer of his Wellington chest and took out a green shagreen case. 'This is for you,' he said. 'With my love.'

Diana's face lit up with anticipation. 'A present,' she said. 'How lovely!' The bangle was slim, made of gold and set with garnets and seed pearls, divided into quarters by rose-cut diamonds. 'Howard!' she said, her mouth forming an '0' of astonishment.

He took it from her and slipped it over her slim, telescoping hand. 'There,' he said. 'It suits you.'

But she was reaching for it and forcing it upwards until it clamped the flesh of her upper arm. 'That's better!' she said, and shook her head at him, so that her long, drop earrings swung in a crazy arc.

They went downstairs together, her hand resting lightly on his arm, he anxiously watching her feet in case she slipped and he had to catch her. The song she had brought back from London was ringing around his head. *In the morning, in the evening, ain't we got fun...* He was indeed a lucky man, to have such a wife, and soon to have a child.

In spite of the gift, with which she was genuinely pleased, Diana felt less euphoric. She was tired of Charlotte's perpetual disapproval, the raised brows when she lit an Abdullah, the audible tut-tutting when she asked Howard to pour her a drink. She did not love her own mother, but she tolerated her. She was not prepared to tolerate Charlotte. She must get away again, and stay away until their own house was ready.

For a little while she had enjoyed her power over her father-in-law, but now she was wearied by his constant enquiries as to the state of her health. His eyes running over her made her feel like a brood-mare, and it was no longer something about which she could joke. She knew Charles wanted a grandson, and perversely hoped the baby would be a girl – and a Carteret into the bargain.

Conversation at the dinner table was boring and predictable: Mussolini's Fascists taking over in Italy; how long Lloyd George could survive as premier; and, as always, the price of coal.

Charlotte hardly spoke but her hooded eyes flicked from one man to the other, taking in every word they uttered. They were on to unemployment now. In Jarrow 43 per cent of the workforce was idle; Hartlepool – which Diana had never heard of – had 60 per cent unemployed.

'Oh don't be so gloomy,' she said lightly, delighted to see that her intervention shocked Charlotte to the core of her quivering mauve bosom. 'Does anyone mind if I have a cigarette?' she went on, already fitting one into her holder.

She saw her father-in-law's mouth open, then close. His eyes flashed to his wife's face, and he frowned before turning back to Diana. 'Smoke if you must, but I hope you're going to eat dessert. Must keep up your strength, especially now. And get plenty of rest.'

'I haven't time to rest,' Diana said firmly, waving away the cream-filled, spun-sugar confection a maid was trying to place before her. 'I have so much to see to at the house.'

Charlotte cleared her throat. 'I've been thinking about

that,' she said. 'We can go into Sunderland next week and look at carpets. A good Turkey red is best. As for curtains...

'I've ordered a carpet,' Diana said airily. 'I sent for samples aeons ago. It's being woven specially, in Durham. And it's green: pale jade-green. It will look like a calm sea, everywhere you look. I can see it in my mind's eye quite ravishing!'

'Unpatterned?' Charlotte asked, and Diana waved her holder in assent.

Charlotte shuddered. 'Unpatterned...pale green. It will scarcely last the week.'

'Oh good,' Diana said, wickedly, winking at Charles. 'Then I can choose a lovely new one.' His eyes gleamed with amusement even as he shook a reproving head. 'He likes it when I tease her,' Diana thought, and she knew that he would like it even better if she tormented rather than teased. The thought made her uneasy, for reasons she couldn't quite understand.

'Actually,' she said, tipping the ash from her cigarette, 'actually, I'm off to London as soon as I can make arrangements. I've ordered everything, but they need to be chivvied. We must be settled in at the Scar in plenty of time for the Blessed Infant, and there will be so many things to arrange, even when the house is ready. Servants, for instance – and a nanny. I won't have a dragon like Nanny Carteret. I was glad when she died, and I'm not ashamed to say it.'

'I've spoken to Gallagher,' Charles said. 'He's engaging local girls to work as maids in the house. Other staff will come from Sunderland. We'll go as far as Newcastle, if we must.' He turned to Howard. 'Remember Gulliver, the draper? His girls need places. Their uncle came to see Gallagher, and I said we'd take them.'

He turned back to Diana. 'The father was a drunken ne'er-do-well, but the mother was good enough. They'll have skills and a genteel manner. You can decide what to do with them. As for a nanny, Nurse Booth will be there for as long as you need her.'

Diana raised her eyebrows. 'Nurse Booth?' Did she detect a degree of satisfaction in her mother-in-law's expression? If so, she must be on her guard.

'Nurse Booth was with me for Howard and Caroline,' Charlotte said. 'She's splendid, you couldn't do better. She goes only to the best families. She's strict, but you couldn't be in better hands.'

After his wife had endured two abortive labours, Charles had engaged the then youthful Nurse Booth. She had been the one to put his son into his arms, and he had never ceased to be grateful to her. He saw her as the talisman that would ensure the safety of his grandchild. In vain Diana pleaded. Charles would not defer.

'But will I like her?' Diana said, and saw from their amused glances that whether or not she liked the woman who would see her through the ordeal of birth seemed not to matter at all.

Esther had long since crept wearily to a bed ticketed with a bailiff's number. Frank and Anne sat on in the inventoried living-room, on either side of a dying fire.

'I'll bring you some coal tomorrow,' Frank said, bending to stir the feeble flames.

'There's no point,' Anne said. 'We'll have to be out of here before long.'

The terrible resignation in her voice moved Frank 'Cheer up,' he said. 'It mightn't be that bad.'

'Working for the Brentons?' Anne taunted. 'You've changed your tune.'

'No, I haven't. I don't want to see you skivvy to a Brenton any more than you do. But needs must – for the time being.'

'For the time being?' Anne was trying so hard to keep eagerness out of her voice that her nails were scoring the palms of her hands.

'Well…' Frank had gone a dull red and appeared to be short of breath. 'I'm a putter now. I'll be a hewer afore long, and making good money. Then we'll see.'

'See what?' Anne said, hoping she sounded disingenuous. Would the idiot never get to the point? A week ago she would have seen a Maguire as being far beneath her, but anything, even a Maguire, was better than a life of service. Once she was into a black dress and pinny, she would be there for life. But as a married woman... And she could make something of Frank Maguire. If she hadn't been sure of that she might have wavered.

'See what?' she insisted, watching him squirm.

'Well... you and me.'

Anne bent her head to hide her triumph. 'Don't be cruel,' she whispered. 'It isn't fair to tease me. Not now, when we've got so much trouble.'

That brought Frank down on his knees to her chair. 'I'm not teasing, Annie.' She winced at the distortion of her name, but there would be time to cure him of that. 'I've always had a soft spot for you, everyone knows it. I'll work hard... and there'll be a colliery house. We'll get it nice. In a couple of years... next year, even?'

She would have to take the plunge. A year in a basement kitchen with Frank as a follower – it would not do! She began to tremble and then to sag against him, her lips seeking out the fold of his neck and resting there, letting his arms come round her, letting her body fold to his until she felt him respond. This was not how she had meant her first experience of sex to be, but it was necessary. She let her legs fall apart ever so gently. Mustn't panic him, or let him think of her as anything but his victim. She moaned gently and then, as his lips sought hers and she felt him begin to quiver, she put a furtive hand to loosen the buttons of her dress.

Frank paused, and Anne saw his tongue pass over his lips; saw the question in his eyes.

She closed her own eyes, afraid of what he might see there, and kept them closed when she felt his hand tighten on her breast. She moaned again and moved slightly, so that her tilted pelvis came into closer contact with his. 'Annie?' Then his lips were on hers, wet but firm, and she felt a little flicker of pleasure at the sensation. He was moving his head, so that her lips parted and then she felt his tongue explore her mouth, tentatively, gently. She pretended to withdraw, as though afraid, and then gave way.

'I want you, Annie,' he said softly, pleadingly. 'I've always wanted you, even when you were a little stuck-up girl.' He was lifting her skirt, and she put out a staying hand but only for a moment. And then he hesitated: 'This isn't right, Annie. I really love you... I can wait.'

But Anne couldn't. Next week she would be driven over to scrub out Diana Brenton's new house. 'I want you, too, Frank,' she said, as childishly as she could manage. 'I need you to love me now!'

She heard his breath come out in a long sigh, and then together they laid aside the layers of her petticoats and pulled down the baggy lawn knickers she had taken from the shop an hour before, especially for the occasion, knowing her usual combinations would be the very death of seduction.

'Are you sure?' Frank asked one last time, but Anne could sense that for him it was already too late. When the pain came, a hot soreness followed by a brief agony, she clenched her teeth against it. He was moving and moaning, and Anne felt heat building up inside her. Then, as he slumped against her, she had the satisfying conviction that she would not be going into service at the Brentons, now or ever.

5

After Charles Brenton's refusal to give Trenchard a job, Howard had approached several firms with whom he did business, but they were all apologetic. For every vacancy, they had four or five applicants – good men, all of them, with excellent war records; some of them former employees. Howard was disappointed, but he resolved to keep on trying.

A week or two later he drove into Sunderland but Trenchard had left the address he'd given Howard and a search of the streets where they'd met was fruitless. In vain Howard told himself that Trenchard had moved on to better things. In his heart he knew the man had moved on rather than put him, Howard, in an embarrassing position.

So it was a relief to catch sight of Trenchard walking ahead of him, and about to cross Sunderland's main street, the day after Diana had left for London. Howard's call brought no response, and he broke into a run. Trenchard turned, eyes lack-lustre in a sallow face. 'Brenton?' He seemed confused, almost disorientated.

Howard stared at him. 'Are you ill, old chap?'

The eyes beneath the brim of the greening Homburg brightened. 'No, I'm perfectly all right, I promise you.'

Suddenly Howard realized Trenchard was on the point of exhaustion. It showed in his sunken cheeks and the taut line of his mouth. Ahead loomed the bulk of the Grand Hotel. It was one o'clock. He gripped Trenchard's arm and urged him towards the brass-edged portico, ignoring his feeble protests. A few minutes later they were seated in the dining-room.

Howard ordered soup and Châteaubriand steaks, and two whiskies to be brought at once.

'I've been looking for you,' he said. Then, seeing hope leap up in Trenchard's eyes, 'Nothing definite, I'm afraid. Not yet, but I'm still trying.'

Trenchard smiled. 'You were always the optimist. But you mustn't fret. I know it's difficult. No one is finding it easy at the moment.'

Around them the good burghers of Sunderland were eating their midday meal. The air was thick with Havana smoke; grease trickled down chins doubled by prosperity. Howard looked at the shabby figure opposite him and wondered how Fortune made her choice. The whisky had brought a little colour to Trenchard's face but he still looked ill. It was damnably unfair. Some men had stayed at home and prospered; others had gone to war. Trenchard's life had now lapsed into a kind of limbo, and there it seemed destined to remain unless his country had need of heroes once more.

They talked as they ate, slowly at first, and then more easily. Trenchard told of returning to his old job, the job they had promised to keep for him at the war's end. 'They were polite,' he said. 'I felt sorry for them... what could they do? Another man had my job now – he'd claimed a dicky back when we were mobilized. It may have been true. The firm offered me a fresh start at the bottom... I saw him grinning, and said, "No, thank you," – out of pride, I suppose. Besides, the place seemed to have grown smaller while I was away. I felt claustrophobic, and to start at the bottom... I was still confident then, you see. I thought it would be easy.'

Howard was remembering how they had sat in a dugout on the day the Armistice was signed. The world had gone mad with rejoicing but the front line was silent: impossible to forget, in a moment, four years of Hell.

'What on earth are we going to do with ourselves?' Howard had said.

'Work,' Trenchard had replied. 'Work.'

He was toying with his food and Howard had to bite back an exhortation to eat up. Instead he tried to move the conversation on to more general levels. 'What d'you think of the new Prime Minister? Will he make a go of it?' Bonar Law had held office for less than a week and Howard doubted whether he could stay there for long.

Trenchard shook his head. 'Not if he is Baldwin's choice. That fellow sold us into bondage over the War Debt. A child could have done better.'

It was true. The war debt, a massive thousand million pounds, was to be repaid to America on the most unfavourable terms. Baldwin had agreed to pay a rate of interest several times higher than that granted to other European countries. And now he had brought about the downfall of L. G., and manoeuvred his own man into the premiership.

'Do you remember what it was like when we got back from France?' Trenchard's face was more animated now as the food and drink found their mark.

Howard nodded, remembering the gaiety of the back-street clubs, the thrill of the baccarat tables, the sheer joy of being warm and dry and alive!

Trenchard was continuing. 'I went back there when my old job fell through – to London, I mean. There was such hope there, such excitement. I stood on the pavement as the King drove by with Woodrow Wilson. They were in an open carriage and the crowd were cheering like mad. The president was raising his topper right and left… I swear he looked right at me, as though he were acknowledging me, and I cheered like the rest. And then the Queen, straight as a ramrod, and the president's wife grinning away. The crowd were all talking about the League of Nations. "You see?" one old woman said to her husband, "I told you God was on our side." I wasn't sure whether she meant the Almighty or Woodrow Wilson.' He paused. 'It's a different tale now. The camaraderie is gone, and the money men want payment of their bills.'

He was silent for a moment and the hovering waiter seized his opportunity to clear away. Howard passed over his cigar case and Trenchard took one, lit up, and drew a lungful of smoke before he continued.

'After that it was downhill. There was no work in London – too many of us with the same idea. Everywhere there'd been talk of a boom, prices rocketing, money being spent like water... and then suddenly it was all over. Wherever I went, there was nothing. I'd become "officer class". I'd have done better if I'd come back as I went. It made people uneasy... and when I tried to hide it, they always knew.'

Howard nodded. It was true. They had gone through a metamorphosis in France, a change that had fitted them only for that moment in time.

They carried their brandies through to the lounge to drink with their coffee. 'Are you still with the brush company? What was its name?'

'Aztec. The Aztec Brush Co. No, they finally felt able to dispense with my services, and quite right, too. I was a bloody poor salesman.'

Howard chose his words carefully. 'There was a girl, wasn't there? You used to talk about her.' He saw Trenchard's face cloud and hurried on. 'And your mother's still alive, isn't she?'

Trenchard reached forward to shed ash from his cigar. 'Evelyn is married now. She waited for me...but I put an end to it when I saw how things were. Just as well. I have eighteen shillings a week now, as long as I am "genuinely seeking work". I go each day and try to look "genuine", but I'm not sure they're satisfied. And if they decide against me, it's the Board of Guardians and Outdoor Relief.'

He spoke flippantly but there was panic underneath the words, and Howard felt his own unease grow. This was not the Trenchard of Ypres or Hooge Wood. To cover his own emotion he spoke crisply. 'Look here: where are you staying? Write it down. I'll find something for you within a week or two, I promise you. According to my father, things are looking up,' Howard lied cheerfully. 'And he's usually right – about money, at least.'

Trenchard was writing on the back of one of the Aztec cards, before pushing it across the table. 'I live there. It's not much, Brenton, but it does have a view of the sea.'

Howard smiled and put it carefully into his wallet.

'And now,' Trenchard said, 'I want to hear about you. I'm weary of my own affairs.'

They talked about Diana and the child she was carrying, but Howard did not mention the house at the Scar. It made him feel guilty even to think of it in Trenchard's presence. His fingers itched to take out his wallet and press money on his friend, but he knew it would not do. A meal almost stuck in Trenchard's throat; a hand-out would choke him.

They left the hotel side by side and turned towards the river. The bridge was quiet at this hour except for the occasional tram trundling into town and small ships moving below in the waters of the Wear. The clamour of the shipyards at the river mouth was barely audible, and the stream of home-going workers was still two or three hours away. They halted midway across and stood looking down at the water.

'Sometimes,' Trenchard said slowly, 'sometimes I feel it all gone by me now. I'm twenty-nine years old, Brenton, but what's left to come? On good days I think, "Cheer up, old chap, there's bound to be something." But mostly I think, "England's done with me." Down the river a ship's siren punctuated his words and spared Howard the need to reply. They shook hands, there on the bridge, and went their separate ways.

'Two weeks... give me two weeks,' Howard called over his shoulder, and then turned towards his car. Someone, somewhere, must find an opening for Trenchard... and if the worst came to the worst he would have to beard his father again.

Two weeks later Fox drove to Belgate to deliver a brown-paper parcel to Esther Gulliver. The parcel contained a letter from Diana and a length of grey nun's veiling, enough for three uniform dresses. If Esther was unable make them herself she was to employ a seamstress and apply to Diana for payment, the letter said. The house would be ready in late November and Mrs Howard would be grateful if Esther would take up her duties on December 2nd. It was signed with a flourish, *Diana Brenton*, and the postscript crept almost to the end of the page. '*I do hope you are feeling better and will be happy in our employment. We looking forward to your joining our household.*'

A tight-lipped Anne cut out the dresses and helped the fitting, and now they were hanging out on the front of the wardrobe that would be carried away after tomorrow's auction, along with everything else in the house.

Today, though, Anne and Esther were concerned with dresses of a different colour. In less than an hour Anne Constance Gulliver was marrying Francis Joseph Maguire in St Benedict's Church with her sister Esther as her only attendant.

'Will it do?' Anne said, plucking at the blue dress they had tricked out with new collar and cuffs and tiny bunches of gathered lace for buttons. 'It looks lovely,' Esther said. 'And so do you.' She banished the last sliver of guilt at abandoning their mourning black. It was Anne's wedding day, after all, and must be celebrated. She looked down at her own pink dress, her favourite. There would not be much chance to wear it in future – and in fact it was getting a little too tight around her chest. But it was still pretty. The sound of rattling at the front door made Esther jump.

'That'll be Mary,' Anne said. 'Let her in.'

Frank had been forbidden to show his face on the wedding day, and their uncle had taken umbrage at Anne defying his edict that no member of his family could marry a collier. So it was Mary Hardman who came to help them with their bags, and with the locking up of the shop that had been the only home they had known.

'You'll be in your own place tonight,' she said to Anne, as they took a last tearful look around them. 'And Esther will be all right with me till she goes to the Scar.'

Anne braced her shoulders and pushed Esther ahead of her, over the step. 'No looking back, our Es,' she said. 'Don't ever let me catch you looking back.'

They lodged their bags at Mary Hardman's and then walked to the church. Curious eyes followed their progress but no one spoke until they were almost at the church door, when a sweep, covered in soot, stepped into their path.

'Good luck to you,' he said, tipping his tall hat to Anne. 'And may all your troubles be little ones.' He handed her a sheaf of garden chrysanths, slightly frosted in places, but flowers just the same. There was a smaller posy for Esther.

'Our Frank arranged that,' Mary said complacently. 'For luck! It'll cost him a pint, no doubt.'

'Well, we've had precious little luck till now,' Anne said, putting the flowers into the crook of her arm. 'So I suppose it's worth it.' There was an air of grim gaiety about her, but Esther felt like crying. This was not how she had imagined Anne's wedding. There should have been proper flowers and a veil, a carriage for Anne and pealing bells. Most of all, her father should have been there to give away the bride.

'Cheer up,' Anne said softly to her, as they stood in the church porch. 'I'll be all right with Frank, you'll see. And you won't be with the Brentons forever – not if you've got any sense.' The verger beckoned them and they moved slowly into the church on the arms of two of Frank's friends. There was the same queer smell Esther remembered from Stephen Hardman's funeral, and the priest looked down his nose at the Protestant bride, but Frank's face was full of joy, and he gave a special smile to Esther, as though to welcome her into his family.

Esther stood, as the Latin service went over her head, and wondered what was left to happen to her now, after the way life had turned upside-down in the past few weeks. At the end of the summer she had had a home and a place in her father's shop. Anne had been nothing but a girl like her, and both had had dreams of what the future might hold. They had had possessions, and even a degree of status in the village. Now they were orphaned.

Esther thought of the death certificate, the first official document she had ever seen, and the coroner's harsh words. '*The deceased was a habitual drinker. Death was caused by internal haemorrhaging due, in its turn, to cirrhosis of the liver.*' It was sad, said the coroner, to think that the deceased had paid so little attention to his responsibilities. Even Anne had flinched at that – she who had not had a good word to say for her father for months.

Esther closed her eyes and prayed that her father might find peace at last – and then Frank was kissing Anne, and Mary Hardman was weeping, and it was time to go back to Mary's for elderberry wine and a slice of spice in honour of the bride and groom.

Diana, too, was eating cake, a delicious moist sponge from the Dunane kitchen. The faint sound of a barrel-organ could be heard from the street and Loelia pulled the bell-rope beside the fire. 'Give something to the man outside,' she said to the answering maid. 'A shilling, I think. Cook will know.'

She went back to the tea-tray and a moment later the music ceased.

'The 0. M. says they're all Bolsheviks,' she said to Diana, 'but I think they're ex-officers. None of them can get jobs since the boom collapsed. I only hope Bonar Law will do something, but the 0. M. says he's weak.'

'It's awfully dismal,' Diana said, wishing that Loelia would drop her social conscience and talk about interesting things, as she had done before she took up with Henry Colville. He was never out of her conversation now. As if to confirm Diana's worst fears, Loelia produced a book which Henry had given her. It was called *England after the War* and appeared to provide depressing reading.

'It says here: "In the retreat from Mons and the first battle of Ypres perished the flower of the British aristocracy… In the useless slaughter of the Guards on the Somme or of the Rifle Brigade in Hooge Wood, half the great families of England, heirs of large estates and wealth, perished without a cry".'

'Like Derry,' Diana said, thinking of her brother.

'Yes,' Loelia said, solemnly. 'And Jocelyn Vane and Mark Arner, and heaps more. And it says in here,' She flourished the book, 'that the England they fought for has all gone to the profiteers.'

'And Lloyd George has put them all in the Lords,' Diana said glumly. 'Still,' she brightened, 'some good things came out of the war. We've much more freedom, you and I.'

'True,' Loelia said. 'And there's cocktails instead of that dreadfully boring Madeira. And jazz.'

'And lip-rouge,' Diana said, touching her own rouged lips with the tip of her tongue. They were giggling, now, and slopping their tea as they raised their teacups.

It was growing dark outside and a footman came in to

light the gas. 'I do envy you having electricity in your new house,' Loelia said. 'The 0. M. will get around to it in the end, but you know what he's like. He drives Max wild... but then Max is so easily riled.'

In spite of her good intentions Diana felt a little flicker of curiosity about Max. He had gone to Ireland with Henry, to visit the Colville family estates. Loelia was continuing: 'Max says if he meets a Sinn Feiner he'll strike him.'

'When do he and Henry come back?' Diana asked.

'Friday, I think. We're dining with the Cunningham-Reids on Saturday, so he's sure to be back by then. You're invited, too, of course.'

Diana pulled a face. 'What will I wear? Everything's tight.'

'You can borrow something of mine,' Loelia said. 'You're still thinner than me. It's horribly unfair.'

'No,' Diana said firmly. 'I trailed everywhere today to see to wretched hangings. Tomorrow I shall shop for myself and buy some wonderful, capacious clothes. Who's smart at the moment – is it still Madame Reboux?'

'Yes,' Loelia said doubtfully. 'But most people prefer Paris now... and lots of people are copying.' She raised her eyebrows in an expression of mock-terror. 'They say hems are going to go down again! I can't believe it, but people who know say they'll be down to the ankle next year. And the 0. M. doesn't understand about fashion changes. "Make do," he says. And at the same time he gives Max carte blanche. I could spit!' She plucked complacently at her faggotted bodice. 'Whatever you do about a maid, Diana, make sure you get someone who can sew. It's such a help. How many staff will you have?'

'Lots,' Diana said truthfully. 'I'm not sure how many, but lots. Remember the man who got killed in the wind? The blacksmith?' Loelia nodded. 'Well, Howard has promised his widow a place. And then one of the shopkeepers drank himself to death, and pa-in-law promised we'll take on the two daughters. I ask you: where will it end? It's a terrible place up there, all death and disaster –'

'– and you're a kind of soup kitchen for the widows and orphans,' Loelia said. 'How frightfully worthy of you. More cake?'

That afternoon Howard telephoned Edward Burton, a brewer in Sunderland, who had been at school with him. A gammy leg had kept Burton out of the war and Howard knew his conscience troubled him. Once Howard would have flinched from twisting the arm of a friend, but desperate situations required desperate remedies. The brewery employed a large staff; there might be a place for Trenchard.

Burton sounded eager to help. 'I'll try, Howard. Leave it with me.' Howard made a note to telephone again if he didn't hear but he felt reasonably confident that he would have good news for Trenchard before long.

He was moving away from his desk when the telephone shrilled in the next room. It was the line from the pit, and the tone of Gallagher's voice as he answered alarmed Howard. The agent was already struggling into his coat as Howard opened the connecting door. 'Roof fall,' he said tersely. 'The southeast face. No fatalities. One injured.'

Howard was behind him as they raced down the steps to the yard. Already men were grouped in twos and threes, muttering uneasily. Thank God the southeast district was almost worked out – no great concentration of men there. Still, even one man down was too many.

The wheel whirred as the cage came up towards the surface, and Howard braced himself for the sight of it. There was a sudden fierce hiss of steam from a bad joint in the pipes overhead, and he jumped. He glanced at Gallagher, and saw that his mouth was set in its usual implacable line. He had always detested the agent; loathed the clipped speech that sounded as though he bought his words by the pound and was determined to be sparing of them. Now he felt a grudging admiration for the man's composure.

Around them the volunteer rescue men waited, ready with face masks connected to heavy bags of oxygen that hung from their shoulders. All eyes were fixed on the vibrating rope as the cage at last appeared in the shaft and the safety gate lifted.

Inside it the men were crammed together, stinking of sweat and fear. It reminded Howard of his first days in France, he men fresh out from England crowding into the wagons.

The banksman threw forward the level, the cage dropped onto its bed, and the black-faced men poured out. The injured man was lying on the lower deck, and they carried him carefully out into the yard. He was young and, to Howard's relief, he was smiling. 'It's Watson,' someone said, 'Sammy Watson.'

A man appeared suddenly from nowhere, dressed not in the dark and serviceable clothes of a collier but in a serge suit with a jaunty yellow flower in the buttonhole. 'It's Frank Maguire!' a voice announced, astonished. 'And him on his wedding day, an' all.'

The newcomer crouched down and took the injured man's head in his arms. When he looked up at Howard his eyes were bright with fury. Howard, unable to meet that hostile gaze, looked instead at the injured man.

His trousers were torn and inside them the skin was peeled neatly back to show raw flesh, ingrained with coal dust around the jagged bone, which was white and shining where it protruded from the wound. Howard stooped down to him, too. 'We'll have you out of here in a moment, Watson. The doctor's on his way.'

The man's shirt was striped and had seen better days. Now it was patterned with blood. He grinned, lips moving back slowly from his teeth. His eyes were watery and bright and strangely transparent. 'There'll be Hell on when our lass sees the state of this shirt,' he said, and died.

Howard had seen death too many times not to recognize it now. After a moment, he rose grimly to his feet. 'How did it happen?' Watson's friends lifted his body to carry it away, and Gallagher fell in behind them, anxious to begin the routine that accompanied death in the pit. 'God,' Howard thought as they filed away. 'Why must there be so much pain?'

Frank Maguire heard Howard Brenton's question but at first he did not answer. He was remembering how the pit had rumbled yesterday, as though in anger. 'Let the bitch rumble,' he'd thought. And then there had been an ominous cracking as weight came down on the timber. Dust had filled the tunnel, bringing momentary darkness with it, and then, as the particles settled, Frank had seen a pile of dirt and stone where he had been working a moment before. He had thought it no more than the usual minor accident – yet now a man working that same face, a seam as hard as bell-metal, was dead.

He looked up at the coalowner. 'It was timber,' he said, the words grating between his teeth. 'Bloody timber props where there should've been steel. An' all to keep down the price of coal.'

Howard walked across the yard, looking reassuringly to right and left. 'The worst is over,' he said as he passed a group of watchful men. 'The rescue men are down, but it's just a formality now.' He felt anger mounting within him, elbowing aside the pain he had felt at first.

Gallagher was replacing the phone as Howard entered the office. 'I've told Mr Brenton,' he said. 'He's relieved it was no worse. We'll stop production for the day, except for an inspection – and with luck we can reopen the face tomorrow.'

Howard leaned forward, both hands on the desk, his face on a level with the agent's. His voice was soft and even. 'We agreed on steel props after the last inspection. Where were they?'

Gallagher gazed back stoically. 'We did agree on them, Mr Howard. Your father made note of the Divisional Inspector's report, and we laid in stocks. We're putting in steel props as we open up new faces. But you must understand we had large stocks of timber supports, which couldn't be written off. The southeast face is in decline. There was no point in putting good steel in there.'

Howard felt rage scorch his throat. He wanted to smash his fist into the face opposite, its skin pitted like an orange peel and beginning to ooze sweat. He had smelled sweat that day when the shell whistled overhead, and then the ground was spitting up at him and a thin, sharp pain was slicing his cheek. When he'd cleared the blood from his eyes he could see his corporal, head blown away, and the other bodies behind him. And Gallagher said there was no point. He sighed.

'Watson was the point,' he said quietly. And then, louder, 'Watson was the bloody point!'

Gallagher's eyes dropped. 'I'm sure we're all sorry, Mr Howard. But this is the coal-mining industry. We must expect –'

He got no further as Howard's hand fastened on his lapel. 'I want the men withdrawn from the southeast face and any other timbered working. I want them kept out until we've replaced wood with steel. And if I hear of one timber prop being used in future – just one – I shall break your neck.'

He let go and moved back from the desk, as he saw Gallagher's eyes flick towards the telephone. So that was his game!

'I'm going now to see my father and tell him my orders. If I find you have telephoned him in the meantime, I shall make it my business to see you are discharged.' Once more he leaned forward. 'I hope you believe I will have my way.'

He saw Gallagher's mouth twitch. Forced to choose between son and employee, Charles Brenton, Gallagher knew, would choose blood.

Howard went straight to his father's sumptuous office at the Dorothea, marshalling his arguments as he went. The Northern Division's Mines Inspector had stressed the need for more adequate supports in his recent report, but there was no legal obligation to use steel, only a moral one. That would not weigh with Charles Brenton – only money would count. And prestige! Howard chose his words carefully.

'This accident will cost us money, father, in compensation to the man's family and loss of production. Do the Brentons want to be listed as being behind the times? We're asking the Miners' Association to swallow wage-cuts. Where's the point in antagonizing them, just to save a few pounds' worth of timber?'

When he left the office, Howard had his father's word that his orders would be obeyed. It was the first time he had got the better of Gallagher and it would not be the last – on that Howard was determined.

The wedding party had been at its height in Mary Hardman's kitchen when word came of the roof-fall. Frank had squeezed Anne's hand by way of apology and made for the door, the yellow chrysanthemum she had plucked from her bouquet still in his buttonhole. At first she had been annoyed at his swift departure, and Mary had rushed to defend her brother.

'The men depend on him, Anne; he has to go. He's in the Union, one of the leaders. It's his place.'

Hitherto Anne had heard the miners' union spoken of only in derogatory terms, as troublemakers and anarchists to a man. But there was respect in Mary Hardman's voice, even reverence. Anne was unwilling to show interest, but she needed information.

'Leader?' she said. 'Hardly that, at his age.'

'It's true,' Mary said. 'They voted him in. He's their delegate to Durham: the big place.'

'I see,' Anne said. She looked at Esther. 'Come on then, Esther. Since it seems I've been deserted – not quite at the altar, but near enough. We might as well go round and see to the house.'

They walked through the village, once more the subject of curious eyes and whispered speculation, until Anne turned and addressed the spectators.

'He hasn't left me, ladies and gentlemen. He's off seeing to business: your business. I expect he'll be back by night-time.'

There was an uneasy titter as the two girls moved on.

They let themselves into No. 6 Ranelagh Row: one-up, one-down terraced houses named after a lordly friend of the coalowner. Inside there was no furniture except a broken chair and a selection of wooden crates that Frank had collected from here and there. These held Anne's few possessions, and an assortment of pans and dishes contributed by Mary Hardman's neighbours at the Shacks.

'How will you manage?' Esther ventured. Privately she wondered how Anne would bear it: proud Anne who had made no secret of her ambitions.

'I'll manage,' Anne said. She was unpacking bedding they had stolen from the shop, a sheet here and a blanket there from the numbered piles.

'Besides,' Anne went on, 'it won't be like this forever. Frank's a fool with money. He makes a good wage and squanders it – gives it to his family mostly. I'll soon put a stop to that. Now, take this corner. Stand away: that's it.'

They folded blankets and laid them in a corner by the fire that Frank had laid, and which they now touched with a match. They added flannelette sheets and pillows and topped the lot with a quilt their mother had embroidered for Esther's cot fifteen years before. 'There now,' Anne said. 'That's more like it.'

It was strange to think of Anne sleeping on the floor; stranger still to think of her sharing a bed with

Frank. And yet she didn't look scared – not in the least.

'We could've had a bed,' Anne said, 'a great wooden thing out of the Ark. And a table and chairs, and a scabby couch. But I'm not starting off like that. First...' She looked around. 'First, I want to bottom this place: scrub it and open the windows and send a great gust of fresh air through. It smells as though whoever was here before never washed. But I'll clean it, and paint it, and then I'll get what I want, bit by bit.'

'Of course you will,' Esther said, and hugged her sister until it felt as though their bones would break.

When Esther had gone back to Mary Hardman's, Anne sat down on the step, pulling a shawl around her, and waited for her husband to come home and take her to bed. She had a problem to solve before nightfall. To achieve an instant wedding she had had to tell Frank he had made her pregnant in that first coupling. She had wondered if he would question it, say it was all too soon – but he had said nothing, and his sister had seemed to assume they had been lovers for a while. Since then Anne had acted the distracted victim, and there had been no further sexual encounter. But now that they were married Frank would expect his rights, and as long as he believed she was pregnant he would not expect to have to take care. It would be up to her to make sure there was no slip-up.

She had taken the initial risk, that night by the fire, because it was both slight and necessary. And no one got pregnant the first time. But Anne had no intention of falling wrong – not now, with so much to be done; probably never, if she went on feeling as she did at present. In time she would have to feign a miscarriage, and bask in sympathy. For now, she would have to be clever.

When her new husband appeared at the end of the street she sucked in her cheeks and turned down her mouth, until she was a picture of ill-health. And she saw, with satisfaction, the look of solicitude on Frank Maguire's face.

6

When the day came at the beginning of December for Esther to go to the Scar, she felt both terror and relief. Her bones ached from sleeping in the short, narrow box bed set into the side of the chimney-breast. Catherine, the baby girl who usually occupied it, had been taken upstairs to share her mother's bed, in spite of Esther's protestations that she would happily sleep in a chair. Now Catherine could have her own bed again, and Esther would have not only a bed but a room of her own – for Belgate was agog with the news that live-in servants at the Scar had their own accommodation.

'You'll manage,' Mary told Esther when she wondered aloud how she would cope with her new duties. 'Just do as you're told, and remember I'll be there on Tuesdays and Fridays. I'll keep you right. We're family now.' Mary had already recounted her tales of service at the vicarage, but these had done little to cheer Esther. And Anne, when she came to say goodbye, was not a comfort.

'Mother must be turning in her grave today. When I think of all the things she told us about her family. Get out as soon as you can, Esther, whatever you have to do.' Her face darkened, and Esther couldn't help wondering if she was regretting her own chosen way of escape. But the next minute Anne's chin went up and a note of satisfaction came into her voice. 'Don't stand any funny business from the Brentons – or anyone that comes to stay. Remember that! They're buying your hands, Esther: nothing else.'

She put out a finger to touch her sister's cheek. 'I don't know. You're a baby in some ways. Fifteen years old! Still, you'll learn. And there's a place for you with Frank and me whenever you want it.'

'Remember to use the back door,' Mary said, and as Esther nodded she heard Anne's snort of disgust.

They had divided the things they had saved from the bailiff into three lots. The larger objects of no sentimental value had been taken straight to Lansky by Frank. Lansky had paid £4 18s for them which, according to Frank, was more than fair. The rest had been divided into two, with Anne getting a lion's share as elder sister. Esther had her own share safe in her Gladstone bag. Now Anne handed her £2 9s. 'Keep it by you, Esther, and try and save to get out. I won't have a decent night's sleep till I see you out of there.'

Anne stood at Mary Hardman's door, waving goodbye as though Esther were off to incarceration. Esther walked soberly, turning now and then to wave, but when she turned the Half Moon corner and was out of sight she swopped her bag to the other hand and began to trot briskly towards the hill.

The house at close quarters was massive and intimidating, when she reached it, but Cockcroft, the mine overseer, was there at the back door to greet her, a sheaf of written instructions in his hand. He riffled the pages until he found Esther Gulliver's name. 'It says "general duties" here, though what Mrs Howard means by that, God knows.' He looked quizzically at Esther. 'Anyone told you anything?'

'No,' Esther said, feeling more lost with every minute.

Cockcroft decided to take pity on her. 'Well, not to fret. She's got fancy ideas, Mrs Howard, but she won't eat you. Anyroad, they won't be up here for a while: we've still got the outfitters in. I'll take you to your quarters.' He consulted the list again. 'Yes, south side. That'll be nice for you. And Mr Howard will see you right.' He reached to chuck Esther under the chin. 'Cheer up. It won't be like school or your daddy's shop, but you'll get by. Eight staff, they're having – eight! Wait till word gets back to the old lady.' He chuckled. 'We're in for lively times.'

Esther's eyes grew rounder as she followed him through the house, where men with ladders and tool-bags seemed to swarm everywhere. She had never been in such a building, unless you counted Sunderland town hall, where once she had been for a concert recital.

Some of the servants were to live in the lodge, near to the gates, Cockcroft told her; but Esther had been given a room in the house, which might or might not be a privilege, depending on the way she looked at it. He led her up the stairs and along a maze of corridors, and then pushed open a door. 'There,' he said, 'this is yours. Get yourself sorted out, and then come down and make yourself useful.' Esther put her bag down on the linoleum and turned to say 'Thank you,' but Cockcroft was already gone, the door swinging shut behind him.

She looked around her. The walls were distempered a pale peach and a little frieze of green and dark peach ran underneath the picture rail. The linoleum was beige with a pattern of green, and the curtains were green with bands of peach and brown near to the hem and a ruffled pelmet above. In one of her darker moments Anne had told Esther she would doubtless be consigned to a gloomy attic. If this was it, it would do!

Esther crossed to the dormer window and leaned against the glass. To the left she was sure she could see the sea – or perhaps it was sky? Ahead, in the distance, she could see the gentle line of the Cleveland hills. Beyond them lay the outside world, dangerous but exciting. If she had to run away from this place she might go there one day, and make her fortune.

Esther turned back into the room, the prospect of needing to run seeming as remote as heaven itself. For the first time since her father's death – even before that, if she was honest – she felt a sense of happy anticipation. This room was her own place, her eyrie: far from the anxieties of the shop, or the grime of the pit, or the squalor of the Shacks in spite of Mary Hardman's kindness.

Esther's eye was caught by an apple-green switch beside the door. Surely not electric light! She had heard it was coming to the Scar, but surely not for servants? She moved to the door and clicked. The bulb that hung from the ceiling had escaped her notice, inside its peach shade with green thonging, but now it sprang to life. She clicked again, and it went out. Click, and on. Click, click, click – until Esther feared it might explode.

She went back to the window for one more look, and then changed quickly into one of her grey dresses and went in search of work.

In her new home Anne Maguire was looking around her, seeing the bare boards, the peeling walls, the chipped hearth... imagining the house at the Scar. All green paint, they said, like garden railings – and costing the earth. She sank to her knees and began to brush up the hearth. In all her life Diana Brenton would never have lacked for anything. By all accounts, she had come from a big house, and now they were building her a better one – while she, Anne, was coming down in the world. The shop hadn't been much, but this…!

She sat back on her haunches and looked up at the mantelshelf. The small beaten brass candlesticks she had brought from home stood at either end, and in the centre, where she would have a handsome oak clock one day, stood the crucifix Frank had brought with him. All he *had* brought, come to that. 'Every good Catholic home has a crucifix and a Sacred Heart,' he had said and Anne had wondered when she should break it to him that this was not going to be a Catholic home. Common people were Catholics; the Gullivers – and more important, the Shiptons – were Church of England. She had not argued over the wedding, but now that she had marriage-lines she would have her own way.

Anne levered herself to her feet as a wave of heartburn struck her. She went to the kitchen and took her mother's fob watch from the cupboard. She could remember it pinned to her mother's breast when she was a child, its gilded face an attraction for her small hands. Now it was her only means of knowing what time of day it was. And five good clocks sold off by the bailiffs for little more than a shilling apiece!

It was half-past eight. Soon Frank would be in from the pit. She began to assemble the makings of a meal, taking them from the built-in cupboard beside the stone sink, greasing the pan before she laid in thick slices of streaky bacon and black pudding. Frank had the appetite of an ox! Still, he tipped up his money, which was more than some men did. She added an extra knob of dripping to get the pan nice for the fried bread, and stood dreaming daydreams until it was time to welcome her husband home.

When he came stooping through the door Anne could see he was pleased about something. 'How would you like a brass bed?' he said. 'With a brand-new flock mattress.'

Anne put the plate before him, wincing at its heat. 'Where from?' she asked suspiciously, afraid to let Frank see how much it would mean to her to have one good bit of furniture, a symbol of better times to come.

The bed was for sale in a house in a respectable street where the colliery overmen lived, and the price was £5.

'We can't afford it,' Anne said, wanting it desperately but knowing it would take everything they had, and then more.

'We don't have to afford it,' Frank said smugly. 'It's a present from our Mary.'

'Oh yes,' Anne said ironically. 'Your Mary's just dripping with money. Besides, she gave us the tea-set for a present – it's the one decent thing we did get.'

Frank tapped his nose and looked sly. 'Our Mary has a bob or two put by: money young Brenton gave her when Stephen was killed.'

'How much?' Anne said.

'Don't ask me that because I don't know. But it wasn't fourpence. Anyroad, she's seen this bed and she's mad keen on getting it. She says she can't sleep in her own bed for thinking of us on the floor.' He filled his mouth again, shoving the food into his cheek so he could keep on talking. 'I'll see our Mary all right, you needn't worry. She'll get her money back, one way or another.'

'Well,' Anne said grudgingly, 'I suppose it'll be better than nothing.' And then, afraid she had been too matter-of-fact: 'I can't give birth on the floor, can I?'

Frank chewed for a moment and then the smile spread slowly from ear to ear. He would have stood up and embraced her, but Anne turned away, her conscience suddenly pricking at the thought of how she was deceiving him.

Diana and Howard arrived at the Scar in the early after noon, anxious to see what progress had been made. 'It's beginning to look like a home,' Howard said, surveying the specially commissioned, pale-green Durham carpet, source of such annoyance to his mother, that ran as far as the eye could see. They went from room to room, seeing evidence of the workmen still, but looking now at whole rooms put to rights. The furniture from Heals was unusual, after the mahogany splendour of his boyhood home. Privately, Howard thought it more suitable to a cottage, but it was what Diana wanted and he had paid the enormous bill without flinching. They came back into the hall and were just about to ascend the stairs when they saw the Gulliver child coming down the staircase, dressed in regulation grey. Her fair hair was looped back from her face into a thick plait that was wound into a bun which looked too heavy for her slender neck. 'And who are you?' Diana asked.

'I'm Esther Gulliver, Mi... Mrs...' Esther floundered over what to call her new employer.

Howard stepped in to rescue her. 'I'm Howard Brenton and this is my wife. You call her Mrs Howard, or madam.'

Esther flushed and finished '– madam.'

Howard was reflecting that if he had realized how impossibly young the girl was he would have made other arrangements, but Diana was noticing the neat cut of the grey dress, the delicacy and cleanliness of the girl's hands, and her open expression.

'Do you sew, Esther? Good. Then you shall be my personal maid. No, don't look so scared. I'll teach you all you need to know. Now, let's see upstairs, and then perhaps you can find someone to make us some tea.' She indicated that Esther should follow them up the stairs. They went from room to room, Diana's satisfaction deepening as she saw how her wishes were being faithfully carried out. She even inspected Esther's room and hoped it was satisfactory, before they went back to the staircase.

'She's beautiful,' Esther thought, observing Diana discreetly. Never mind that people said she was selfish and proud: she looked like a picture-postcard in her smart beige suit with its side drape and dipping hem, her dark hair cut short and curling over her cheeks. As if she sensed Esther's curiosity, Diana halted, one hand on the light oak newelpost, the other resting gently on the small mound of her belly. This house was her own creation and it pleased her mightily.

'See, Esther,' she said proudly. 'This is *my* house, and it's right, isn't it? Just right.' It was true. Carteret taste allied to Brenton money had created a masterpiece. It was light and modern and airy; a pleasant place in which to live. And, most important of all for Diana, it was a comfortable distance away from her husband's parents.

While Esther scuttled away in search of tea, Howard took Diana into the room that was to be their own private sitting-room, smaller than the huge reception rooms and looking down towards fields. They stood, hand in hand at the window, looking out, until they heard Esther at the door, struggling with a huge silver tray. Howard hurried to take it from her.

'I can manage, sir… Mr…

'Sir, will do,' he said comfortingly. 'Now give it to me. Isn't there a man about the place yet? This is too much for you.' He saw Esther bridle, as though slighted at the suggestion, and his lips twitched. When he had first looked at her, on the stairs, he had thought her a queer little thing. Now he could see she was in the ugly monkey years of adolescence, the good-looking woman she would be struggling to break through the childish shell. She would never be a beauty, Howard thought, but there was character there.

He set the tray down on the floor beside Diana and told Esther she could go. 'We hope you'll be happy here,' he said to her.

'We mean this to be a happy house,' Diana added. 'Not just for us, but for everyone.'

When Esther had gone Diana set about pouring tea, suffused with a comfortable liberal glow. It was nice to have patronage to bestow, and she would be the very best of employers.

'The house is going to be divine,' she told Howard as she handed him his tea. 'I will never want to leave Durham again. Well, hardly ever.' And then, as he smiled his disbelief, 'Oh, darling, you know what I mean!'

*

The brass bed had been carried through the streets, piece by piece, and set up in the bedroom. The flock mattress looked almost new and smelled faintly of camphor. 'It's nice,' Anne said grudgingly, and Frank, who was learning about his wife, knew she was very pleased.

They made it up with sheets and blankets, and aired it with Mary Hardman's stone hot-water bottle, and it was ten o'clock before Frank blew out the lamp and climbed into bed beside Anne. She had turned on her side, and he fitted himself against her. 'We're going to be all right here, Annie.'

'I suppose so.' Her words were brusque, but Frank felt her relax a little within his arms, in the darkness.

'How does it feel to be a Maguire?' His lips were against her neck now, nudging aside the weight of her hair.

'Much the same as it felt to be a Gulliver: uphill work.' Anne was silent for a moment and then she posed a question. 'Why are there so many Irish in Belgate?'

'Strikes. The old owners brought strike-breakers over from their Irish estates and used them to starve the miners back to work. Time and again, they did it. They say the cobbles used to run with blood, some of the battles they had. It's different now; we're all strong for the union.' Frank's hand moved to her belly. 'This little lad'll grow up in a better world, I promise you that.' His hand was questing now, moving to stroke her thighs and slip between them.

Anne sighed and turned to face him.

'Is it all right?' he asked cautiously, even as she felt him harden against her.

'Of course it's all right,' she said, and laid her cheek against his. *As long as I'm quick enough when the time comes,* she thought, getting ready to twist away as soon as she sensed his climax.

'I love you, Anne Maguire. And I'll make you proud of me, see if I don't.' Frank had raised himself above her, and she saw his head outlined against the grey square of the window. It was a good head and she put up a hand to caress it.

'Be sure you do, Frank Maguire. I shall have something to say if you don't.'

The brass bed began to sing as he moved inside her, and for a while at least Anne gave herself up to the tune.

When it was over she slept; but she awoke to an awful nausea that was like no other sickly feeling she had ever experienced – vile even when she lay still, unbearable if she sat up. She crept down to the kitchen and tried to vomit, but nothing came. The waves of nausea continued until, in the cold grey light of morning, Anne had to face the fact that the lie she had told Frank had in fact, unknown to her, been the simple truth.

At the Scar Esther finished her bedtime wash-down and made her way back to her room. Only three of them were sleeping in as yet, and it was a good feeling to shut her door and slide home the bolt. She put out the light and then drew back the curtains, hoping she would wake before day break. Somehow she would have to get an alarm clock. She thought of her £2 9s and resolved to try and save for the clock, so as to keep her capital intact.

She knelt down and folded her hands, praying first for Anne and Frank, then for Mary Hardman, and lastly for Mr Howard and Mrs Howard. His face had been so kind when he took the tray that she had wanted to wrap her arms around his waist and cling to him. A nice carry-on that would've caused. Esther grinned in the darkness, resolving to watch her tongue when she went to Anne's. She would have to think up a grumble or two to keep Anne happy. It would never do to tell her everything was rosy.

When she climbed into bed, she thought ahead to the time when Mrs Howard came to live at the Scar and she took her place as a personal maid. If she stuck in and learned all the tricks, she could go to London and do very well. Esther closed her eyes on a vision of herself attending to someone famous, like Mary Pickford or that nice little Bowes-Lyon lady who was to marry the Duke of York. The bed was soft and warm, and smelled of scented soap. Anne had been scathing about life in service, but so far it had been all right. Better than all right. Somewhere far off in the house a clock chimed. Esther began to count the strokes but was asleep before the last one sounded.

7

Christmas was only ten days away when Diana and Howard moved to the house at the Scar, but Diana meant to make the most of it. She borrowed her father-in-law's Daimler, enlisted Fox to carry her parcels, and raided the Sunderland shops.

She began at the dark and redolent grocers patronized by Charlotte Brenton. There was a wonderful smell of fresh ground coffee in the air, and she sniffed appreciatively while Fox went to acquaint the proprietor with her identity. He came scuttling down from his glass-fronted eyrie above the shop, twitching at his jacket and tumbling over his greetings.

Diana saw a gleam of amusement in Fox's eye but the next moment his face was impassive again. She had never really looked at Fox until then, seeing only the gaitered uniform and the peaked cap. Now she saw that he was young, no more than twenty-four or twenty-five and handsome. She turned back to the proprietor and gave him a dazzling smile. 'I've come to buy Christmas, Mr Heslop. I do hope you can help.'

Not only could Mr Heslop help, his army of aproned assistants could help as well. They piled up boxes of glacé fruits and Chinese figs, sugared almonds and crystallized ginger in fat, blue-and-white jars, peaches in brandy and dark cherries in liqueur, white sugar mice and pink sugar pigs, and boxes of crackers that glittered promise of untold delights.

From the grocers Fox and Diana crossed the street to a gentlemen's outfitters where she bought a splendid cherry-wood cane for Howard. It had a silver mount, and she ordered it to be monogrammed H.C.B. and delivered as soon as possible. Then she sent Fox back to the car and went into the department store that dominated the main street, wishing all the time that she was in Bond Street or Regent Street or Piccadilly. Still, Christmas was Christmas wherever you were, and this first Christmas as mistress of her own home must be a memorable one. Any lingering longings for London vanished when she caught sight of herself in a wall-mirror. There was a decided thickening about her whole figure now, a blurring of shape. No, she must hide in Durham until she was her old self again, and then there would be no holding her.

The prospect of Christmas had also spurred Anne Maguire to action. The house in Ranelagh Row had been cleaned to her satisfaction, although she had often had to pause in her work when the terrible nausea overcame her. Then she would sit and weep over her pregnant state. Trust her to fall wrong *the first time*! She had never had a day's luck in her whole life. Her sister-in-law, Mary Hardman, had offered to help Anne during her sickness, but when she came she brought her children with her and they whined or cried for attention the whole time, until Anne declared she could manage better on her own and shooed them out of the house. If that was motherhood, she told herself, it would indeed be purgatory – a word that she had noticed spattered the conversation of Frank and his Catholic family.

She thought of all the old wives' tales she had heard in the shop about what could happen if husbands were greedy in the first months of pregnancy. She wouldn't care if something did go wrong with this baby. She felt remote from it: unbonded. At nights she encouraged Frank to such excesses as he was capable of, but it was useless. The baby had taken hold and would not be dislodged.

Once the house was clean, Anne took out the things she had retrieved from the break-up of her home. She had kept the best for herself, stifling her prickings of conscience about robbing her sister by telling herself that she would put a roof over Esther's head when the inevitable happened and she was driven from the Brenton house.

More and more she saw Diana Brenton as her oppressor. The tale of her insensitive visit to Mary Hardman had percolated around the village and there had been bitter mutterings. Anne held herself aloof from village gossip; she might've come down in the world but she was still a cut above colliery folk. All the same, it galled her to think that Diana Brenton was nineteen, the same age as she was herself. Not for her the struggle to scrape a home together or prepare for a baby. But in a strange way, Anne's resentment fuelled her determination.

When she had sorted out the items of value among her possessions, she selected a china shepherd and shepherdess, wrapped them carefully and carried them to Lansky's shop.

She had never been at close quarters to the Jewish pawnbroker, content to eye him furtively when they passed in the street, noting the proud carriage of the bearded head and the excellent quality of his clothing, but disliking him as a stranger. Now she confronted him and held out the items for sale.

He offered her fifteen shillings for the china. She thought that a good offer, but she wasn't going to give in at once.

'No,' she said, drawing them towards her. 'They're worth more.'

Lansky shook his head. 'I made you a fair price – fair for us both. Take it.'

Anne saw that he was not to be moved, and although it irked her she had to concede defeat. 'I've got more at home,' she said, as he counted out the money.

He nodded. 'You've had your troubles, I know that. Bring what you have to me. Your father – I knew him for many, many years. I won't cheat his child.' There was a note in his voice that convinced Anne that he would be straight with her. All the same… he was a dirty Yid, making money out of other people's misfortunes.

That day and the next she went back and forth to Lansky's, and when she was done she had £13 7s 6d to add to the money she had shared with Esther. There had been 30s in the till, when her father died, but her uncle had impounded that for the creditors. She had been slow there, but never mind; she was learning.

In the weeks Anne had been married to Frank she had managed to save £4 from his weekly wage. It all seemed a small fortune, but when Anne had counted her money she sat and cried for the old days – the days before her mother died and her father took to drink and the shop ran down and she and Esther were reduced to living like animals. When she had cried herself out, she dried her eyes, put on her one good dress and set out to walk into Sunderland where she would get better value for money.

The goods she bought came to Belgate that night on a horse-drawn cart: a red and brown carpet square, worn but clean: a pine table and three bentwood chairs; two chests, one for upstairs, one for down; and best of all, two upholstered armchairs in faded velour. Anne had longed for the comfort of the chairs at her old home, and had cursed herself for not going to the auction, where everything had been sold for a song.

The velour came up with soft soap and a scrubbing brush; table, chairs and chests were also scrubbed. By the time they took to the brass bed, Anne and Frank felt like a proper married pair.

'You're a little wonder,' Frank said, squeezing her gently. She knew what would happen next but she didn't particularly mind. 'Say if I hurt you,' he said as he straddled her. She sighed and closed her eyes, thinking of all the years ahead when she must go through this same procedure. All the same, she must make the best of it: a man who was not kept happy at home would not thrive. Her father had been an example of that. So she must pleasure Frank, and cosset him, and make sure he lifted her up and out of Belgate one day – and if lying on her back with her legs open was the way to do it, that was what she must do. She even threw in a moan or two of pleasure.

When it was over and he had kissed her and turned away, she patted his rump. It had not been too bad, she thought; and now she was free to lie and work out how long it would take her to furnish her house to a standard that befitted her upbringing and background. She thought of the little valuables she had given to Esther – who, after all, was a child and too young to appreciate them, and was living in the lap of luxury into the bargain. It wasn't really fair that Esther should have so much when she, the elder sister, was having to struggle. As Anne's eyelids drooped, she resolved to ask Esther if she wouldn't be better off giving her share to Anne for safe keeping.

Howard had received one hopeful message from Edward Burton, but no definite suggestion by the time they met up at the gentlemen's club. Occasionally they dined at one another's homes, but their most frequent meeting-place was the club and Howard was always pleased to see his friend's slender figure and kindly face beneath the stiff, centre-parted hair.

'Howard,' Edward Burton said, his face lighting up. 'I haven't forgotten your friend, Trenchard, but we have nothing at the moment, I'm afraid. There are openings for manual workers, but nothing for such a man as you've described. However, Ferry, the builder in Durham, handles our outside work; it's lucrative for him and he's anxious to please us. I'll ask him to keep an eye open.'

Howard felt relief wash over him. Perhaps he wouldn't have to face his father after all. He seized Burton's hand and shook it gratefully.

As soon as he was back in his office he wrote a note to Trenchard: *A prospect in view. Will let you know as soon as something is settled.* Then he summoned Gallagher. 'I want this sent by express. It's important.' He thought of Trenchard's face when at last he could tell him there was a job for him. It would be a good moment for them both.

All in all, Howard felt a happy man. It was a pleasure to go home at night to Diana. He was brimming with satisfaction at the way the new house was taking shape, and the preparations for Christmas and the birth of his child.

Diana seemed happy. She liked to keep Esther at her side, arranging and rearranging the house, giggling together over the Christmas preparations, hiding gifts from prying eyes, and competing to see who could tissue-wrap gifts in the most artistic fashion. She was wonderfully indiscreet, referring to her mother-in-law as 'the Armadillo' and Charles Brenton as 'the Lord High Executioner'. This meant she could carry on secret and wicked conversations with Esther when others were present, even Howard. Esther was Diana's devoted slave, watching her with eyes like saucers and admiring her every mannerism.

Diana was constantly changing her mind, condemning brand-new furnishings and ordering others as though they cost nothing but fresh air. Eventually Esther felt bold enough to ask if she might retrieve some of the cast-off curtains and bed-linen; but when she took them excitedly to Anne they met with a decidedly cool response. Anne pronounced them 'tarty'. 'I'll use them,' she said, 'because I'm forced to use what I can get. But she's got no style, for all her money. As for him, we all know what stock he's from!' She threw the things on one side until Esther had gone, and then she spent a happy hour trying them here and there until she found their right niche.

On Christmas morning Diana presented her gifts. In addition to the handsome cane, she had bought Howard a copy of Hugh Walpole's new novel, *The Cathedral*. They were thoughtful gifts and pleased him, but his greatest pleasure lay in watching his wife's face as she handed out her presents to the staff.

For Esther she had bought a leather handbag and matching kid gloves. Conflicting emotions struggled for possession of Esther's face at the sight of them: gratitude, and pleasure, and horror at what they must have cost. Howard glowed. His mother had always bought her servants serviceable nightwear. He was glad his wife had more imagination, for each of the servants received a present suited to their needs or aspirations. When the giving was done with, Howard set up his camera, and master and mistress were photographed with each of their servants. 'Right,' said cook when it was done, and the staff hurried away.

After the Christmas meal was served and cleared away the servants were free to go for the rest of the day. It was the first time Howard and Diana had had the new house entirely to themselves and they made the most of it, moving from room to room like children. 'I love it, darling,' Diana said when at last they stood together in the hall.

She was wearing a red velvet gown in honour of Christmas. There was white Brussels lace at neck and wrist and her small face glowed under the black bob. Howard had never seen her look lovelier. 'I'm glad you're happy with the house, Diana. And thank you for making it a home.' He did not argue when she took him by the hand and drew him upstairs to bed.

*

In March, Nurse Booth arrived at the Scar.

She lived for her work. She had no life of her own, no home except the houses of the people she served. Her hair was hidden by a blue veil; a silver-buckled belt spanned the waist of her tailored blue dress; a nursing badge was pinned to her sterile bosom. She moved in before a birth and stayed until the baby was well established. There was always a waiting-list for her services, for there was a certain social cachet in employing her. Nurse Booth knew her power, and she enjoyed using it.

From the moment of her arrival she watched Diana closely. She drove the kitchen staff mad with her demands for bland food, and she banned tobacco and alcohol from the house. Diana and Esther became partners in outwitting her, and Diana was warm in her gratitude for Esther's support. 'When this is over I'm going to *live*, Esther! I shall go to London, and you will come with me. I'll have such fun. Howard will have his precious baby and the Dragon Nurse will smother them both. Oh, I can hardly wait.' But even the thought of London did not ease her gloom as Nurse Booth's dictatorial regime took hold.

Diana appealed to Howard for support, but he had been brought up to revere the nun-like figure, who had paid quarterly visits to monitor his progress and given him a Book of Common Prayer when he was confirmed. He was not prepared to evict her from his home. When the baby was safely delivered, he said, Diana would be grateful and all would be well.

Nor was Charles willing to give way. Nurse Booth was the essential to the safety of his grandchild's birth. In vain Diana pleaded. Charles would defer to her on most things but on the question of Nurse Booth she could not move him. The Dragon Nurse had come to stay.

Diana meant every word she said about going to London after the birth. She was willing enough to hide in Durham while she was pregnant and ungainly, but as soon as it was over she wanted to see Loelia again.

And there was another and more compelling reason for the trip: she knew that husbands expected to be admitted to their wives' favours a month after the birth. Before then she must be prepared. She had hinted as much to Dr Cunningham and had received no satisfaction except a muttered assurance that she could rely on her husband's self-control. Diana did not want an abstinent husband, and she meant to get the best possible advice on birth-control from the best possible source: Harley Street. According to Loelia it could be done. She would have other children; it was her duty… but she would dictate the timing. And the next baby would be born in civilization, as far away as possible from the cold and unfeeling hands of the Dragon Nurse. As the weeks went by she thought nostalgically of Nanny Dunane with her cinder tea and dripping nose. She was dirty and untidy and definitely odd, but she was human and that was an endearing trait.

At Nurse Booth's suggestion Howard had moved into another bedroom. Diana missed him, but for Howard it was a relief. He felt there was something almost sacrilegious in making love to a heavily pregnant woman, and yet Diana seemed determined that he should. His insistence that he wanted above all her comfort and safety seemed to pique her more.

Diana missed Esther on her afternoons off. She was bored when she had no company, and tired of Howard and his parents expecting her to be full of a sense of her own good fortune.

I look like a pumpkin, she wrote to Loelia. '*A hideous, swollen toad. Any bigger and I will float away like some terrible hot-air balloon, and end up God knows where. Pray for it all to be over soon, darling Lee, and then what fun we will have!* She signed it *With love* and, as an afterthought, sent her regards to Max. It was the thought of Loelia and Max and Scotland Gate that sustained her through the weary months of her pregnancy.

As her pregnancy proceeded, Anne Maguire could not have conceived of Diana Brenton's desperation; of her sense of imprisonment in the fourteen-roomed house because she knew no one outside it except one or two boring middle-aged people with whom she had nothing in common. As week succeeded uncomfortable week, Anne could scarcely see anything but her own desperate need to improve her lot, now that the coming baby was tormenting her with its kicking. She spent her waking hours looking for ways and means.

On her last trip to Lansky's she had noticed a sewing machine. For days she brooded about whether or not the machine could be made to pay. She could use it to prepare the layette for the baby, a job that could not be postponed much longer. But that could be done by hand, and by itself didn't justify the spending of money on a machine. But if she could sew for others… then the machine might be a boon.

She broached the subject with Mary, half-hoping her sister-in-law might offer to buy the machine for her. But Mary did not seem disposed to part with more of her precious compensation, and Anne was not yet close enough to ask outright. 'I don't know about paying customers,' Mary said, pursing her lips. 'But alterations, maybe – and for weddings. You Gulliver girls were always smart. People said you had style. If they were going to come to anyone, they'd come to you.'

Anne should have been pleased at the compliment but it had been couched in the past tense: 'You girls *were* smart.' When Mary had gone, Anne looked in the mirror and was shocked by what she saw. She was bloated by her pregnancy, and yet her face looked gaunt. There was a ridge to her nose that had not been there before and purple shadows around her eyes. She resolved to smarten herself up, and went to see Lansky.

The machine was £2. 'But to you, thirty shillings,' Lansky said.

Anne hesitated, her heart sinking at the thought of parting with money. Lansky tugged at his beard, thinking.

'I have it,' he said. 'You take the machine, and if you change your mind I take it back – for the same price.'

Anne carried it home by the handle on the lid, mimicking Lansky's accent as she struggled. He thought he was buying her approval with his favours but in fact she only despised him more. Anyone could dole out favours if they had money behind them!

Her anger was only mollified when her first customer turned up, secured by Mary Hardman; she paid Anne two shillings for altering a winter coat.

By the time Esther came to visit again, there was money in a jar, fruit of the new machine. Esther heard Anne's version of its purchase, but she could see through her sister's dislike of the old Jew. He was being kind to them because of their father, and if Anne wasn't grateful for it, Esther was.

Anne was sewing a baby's dress, cut from one of her own lawn petticoats. 'It's lovely,' Esther said, looking at the faggoting on the bodice and the drawn-threadwork at the hem.

'It'll do,' Anne said, sniffing. 'I don't suppose her ladyship's sewing, is she? Might prick her fancy blue-blooded fingers.'

Esther thought of the boxes and parcels that had been delivered to the Scar: a dozen of this and a dozen of that, silk and lace, lambswool and lawn, some of it embroidered by nuns, all of it the best that money could buy. She looked at her sister's hostile face and improvised rapidly. 'She's knitting... every spare moment. She's not very good, but she's trying.'

Diana's one attempt at knitting, prompted by the Dragon Nurse, had ended in tears and the wool and needles being hurled to the hearth, but Esther didn't want to show her employer in that unfavourable light.

'Oh, well,' Anne said, cheering up a little. 'We can't all be handy.'

They talked of the christening, then, and the pressure the priest was putting on Frank to get Anne to church. 'He'll get me to church when I'm ready and not before,' Anne said. 'And that'll likely be feet first.' She looked down at her sewing machine. 'I hear there's a party at the Scar tonight?'

'Mr Howard's parents,' Esther said. 'And some people called Pratt.' Diana had refused to open her eyes that morning, when Esther carried in her breakfast. 'It's Black Thursday, Esther,' she had said. 'Doom, doom. Still, I've ordered everything the Armadillo detests, so it isn't all bad.' She had sat up in bed, then, and allowed Esther to place her tray on her knees and put the napkin across her chest.

'They'll be having the fat of the land, no doubt,' Anne said now. 'Mary's up at the Scar, working till all hours, and we've landed with her children. Still, as long as her ladyship's happy…'

Privately Esther wished Anne would leave Diana out of her conversation. Aloud, she said, 'Let's not talk about them, Anne. There's heaps more interesting things than that.' She produced an old copy of *Vogue* and for the next hour they poured over the advertisements for French hats and corsets from Paris and 'original gowns' at inflated prices.

'Seventy-five guineas for that!' Anne said, tapping an illustration. 'I could make that for less than seventy-five shillings if I had the pattern.' She looked up. 'Can I keep this?'

'Of course,' Esther said, vowing to bring a magazine regularly from the piles that littered Diana's rooms.

On the way home she worried about how weary Anne had looked, quite unlike Diana who was positively glowing with health. The sooner both babies were here, the better, for neither mother-to-be was happy with her lot. Esther looked at the spring landscape, seeing green shoots here and there, faint budding on the trees and a general shrugging aside of winter. 'I love the spring,' she thought. And was suddenly glad to be alive, and young, and, most of all, not carrying a child.

8

Howard had not forgotten about Michael Trenchard but he was reluctant to see him again unless he could be the bearer of definite good news. He saw Burton several times but there was no new development. And then, in June, he suddenly heard from his friend.

There was a job in Durham, unless Trenchard failed miserably at interview. The pay would be £3 a week, with annual increments. Best of all, a rent-free house went with the job. Howard decided to take Trenchard the good news without delay.

He was mounting the stairs to his office when Gallagher appeared above him. 'You're wanted at home, Mr Howard. They've been on the telephone more than once. I think her ladyship's time has come.'

Howard was running to his car when Gallagher called after him. 'Shall I inform Mr Brenton?'

Howard shook his head, remembering Diana's injunction: '*Don't let them come near me till it's over, Howard. Promise me that.*' He turned on the bottom step and looked up. 'No, thank you, Gallagher; no need to worry them too soon. I'll tell them when it's over, that's the best way. But get word to Dr Lauder and Dr Goodfellow in Sunderland. They're both standing by for the birth.'

Diana's labour had begun during the morning, a sudden pain that brought her up sharply as she crossed the hall. Her one thought was to keep it from the Dragon Nurse as long as possible. She might look like a nun, but to Diana she was an icy-fingered fiend. She mounted the stairs to her room, calling for Esther as she went. Esther took one look at Diana and fled in search of Mary, who was washing clothes in the laundry down below.

By the time Mary arrived Diana's waters had broken, reducing her to tears. Mary had been through two labours and her voice was soothing. 'No need to fret, Mrs Howard: it's only natural.' She fetched towels from the dressing-room to stem the flow, but the appearance of dark meconium on the white cotton frightened them both.

'I'll get the nurse,' Esther said and Mary nodded. Diana, biting her lip, agreed. 'All right – but help me get undressed first. Her hands are so cold.'

Within an hour the temperature of Nurse Booth's hands was inconsequential. Diana was racked by pain that left her breathless without appearing to advance the labour. She screamed with rage, not only at the pain but at the indignity of it all. The nurse's cold fingers probing her vagina were an assault, one to which she must submit, but not without reviling Howard and the coming baby and anyone else who might bear the least responsibility for her plight.

Nurse Booth stood at the foot of the bed, disapproval in every line, while Esther held hands with Diana. Afterwards the bruises made by Diana's slender fingers would show black for a week, but at the time Esther was too absorbed to notice.

Dr Lauder arrived first and applied his trumpet to the mountain of Diana's belly. He warmed it first with his breath, but Diana was cursing too loudly to notice. She cried for Loelia, for her mother, and for Nanny Dunane who always knew what to do for the best. She never called for her husband, as Esther could not help but notice.

Howard arrived at eleven o'clock but before he was allowed into the room Nurse Booth attempted to cover

Diana with the bedclothes, raising them discreetly to her patient's neck. It was too much! Diana balled her fist and struck out. 'It's all *his* fault!' she screamed, incoherent with fear and rage. 'Never mind covering me, let him see what he's done!' Nurse Booth's cuffs had been removed and her sleeves rolled up in preparation for labour. She was not prepared for a fight. The two women wrestled with the bedclothes until Diana fell back exhausted, and Esther could move forward to smooth the bed.

When Howard appeared, Diana turned away her head. 'Be a good girl, Diana,' he said at last. 'It won't be much longer now.' It was less than adequate and he knew it.

He went downstairs to pace his study and Diana was free to scream again.

Anne was busy at her machine when the first pain came. She shifted in her seat but carried on sewing. She had just eaten a lump of turnip: served her right for greed. The second pain came, low in her belly and demanding. The third brought her from the bentwood chair to her knees on the carpet square, calling for Jesus. It couldn't be the baby; she was scarcely eight months pregnant.

When the next pain came, and even she could recognize it as a contraction, she waited for it to subside, feeling oddly philosophical. She had never wanted a child. Conception had been a risk that she had taken as a means to an end. If the baby died it would be sad, especially for Frank; but at least it would give her a chance to get turned round. When she could get her breath she crawled to the door and called to a passer-by to fetch Mary, newly returned from the Scar.

When Frank came in from his shift he found Anne installed in the brass bed with Mary in attendance. 'Get a doctor,' Mary said, and then, lowering her voice, 'and be quick about it, Frank.'

Frank ran to the house where Dr Lauder took messages and held his surgery in the front room, but the woman who lived there was adamant. 'He's been called to the Scar, Frank. You'll not get him away from there.'

He turned back to the street, a man demented, to see the pawnbroker, Lansky, regarding him from the opposite sidewalk.

'You have trouble?' There was nothing the Jew could do to help, Frank thought, but it was a relief to gabble out his dilemma.

'I've got to get help. It's my wife's first, and it's coming too soon.'

The massive head under the broad-brimmed black hat bobbed agreement. 'There's a doctor in Brandon – a good man though he's in poor health. I'll take the pony-cart to fetch him.' The next moment the Jew was off in a flurry of black tailcoat, leaving Frank to call down Catholic blessings on his head, before setting off for home to see how his wife was faring.

He told Anne that help was on the way, and then went down to sit beside the fire and gnaw his knuckles. He was more afraid than he had ever been before – more afraid of losing his wife than he was afraid of the pit. The birth of a child was to be an occasion for him, his mark upon the world. And it was not going according to plan.

Lansky whipped up the horse on the ride to Brandon, something he had never done before. He had a son of his own, his most precious possession since the death of his wife. Besides, he was tired of death and disaster in Belgate, and it suddenly seemed vital that this particular child should be born alive. But was Patrick Quinnell the man to bring it about? He was thirty-two, but the war had taken its toll of him. He was an alcoholic, now, and a creature of moods. With Lansky's help he had opened a surgery in Brandon a year ago, and ministering to the dust-ridden lungs of his patients had restored a little of his self-esteem. But the women of Brandon all preferred to go elsewhere. How would Quinnell cope with a difficult premature labour, when his hand trembled, there were shadows beneath his eyes and his hair had suddenly whitened at the temples?

'I need a favour,' Lansky said to him haltingly, standing on Quinnell's doorstep. 'There's a woman in labour in Belgate and no doctor to help her; the child, a first-born, is coming before its time. Will you help?'

Patrick Quinnell reached for his coat, not even grabbing a drink before he took up his bag. If this was a premature birth and a *primigravida* into the bargain, he would need as steady a hand as possible and he was not too far gone in drink to know it.

By the time they reached the narrow house with its sparse furnishings, Anne was lying in a pool of sweat, mucus cascading from her nose, her palms torn where her nails had scrabbled for relief of pain. Mary Hardman was at her side.

Quinnell felt, gently, expertly. The head was already in the birth canal but the foetal sounds were distressed. He patted the mother's hand. 'Not long now,' he said. The small, fair-haired woman on the other side of the bed regarded him steadily. She was weighing him up, and she did not attempt to disguise it. She looked at his hands, his mouth, and then deep into his eyes. At last she smiled and Quinnell knew he had passed inspection.

'I'm Mary Hardman, doctor. I know what's to be done.'

'Good,' he said. 'I'll need your help.' They set to work while below, in the living-room, Lansky, still wearing his hat, did his best to soothe the terrified father-to-be.

*

Diana's baby was born at seven o'clock, a fine boy with a mat of black hair and the longest fingernails Nurse Booth had seen on a new-born infant. The two doctors jostled for the chance to deliver it, but Diana didn't care. She had been quieter during the last stage of labour and now she lay still as Esther and the Dragon Nurse cleaned and prettied her for her husband. 'I'll never go through that again,' she said once but Nurse Booth smiled tolerantly.

'I've heard that before, Mrs Howard. You'll change your mind.'

Howard had been prepared for a wave of emotion when he saw his son, but the reality outstripped his expectations. He looked at the tiny face, puckered with all the cares of the world, and then met his wife's eyes. 'Thank you,' he said.

Before he left the bedside they had named the baby. Diana knew Charles Brenton wanted his grandson to bear his name, but some core of loyalty demanded she give her own father equal right. That made a third name a necessity. He would be Charles for the Brentons and Neville for the Carterets and Rupert for himself.

As Howard crossed the landing Esther came towards him, carrying clean linen. She looked drawn and weary, and somehow more mature than her fifteen years. 'Come downstairs when you can be spared, Esther. I want you to drink a toast to my son.'

She nodded and went past him into Diana's room.

Anne felt easier when the doctor was there. He had the voice of a boy but the face of an old man. As the waves of pain came and went she was conscious of him and Mary, two profiles above her, their eyes often locked together. Sometimes she thought she heard herself scream; at other times she seemed to be gabbling. The uppermost thought in her mind was guilt. She had ill-wished this baby, if the truth were known. She had conceived it for her own ends, and then wanted rid of it. Now it was threatening to be the finish of her, and somehow that seemed only fair.

When she tried to tell this to the doctor, he hushed her and wiped her brow with a wet towel. 'Hold on,' he said. 'Hold on.' Mary had carried the crucifix up from down below, and as time went on it seemed to grow until it was larger than the mantel-shelf itself. Anne found she was focusing upon it, willing it to come to her aid. 'Let me live,' she prayed. And then, for no reason that she could understand, her plea changed until she was begging that the baby should live. When she heard the first sickly cry it seemed as though her prayers had been answered.

'It's a boy,' Mary said, smiling. 'You've got a son, Anne.'

'Thank God,' Anne said, and she meant it with all her heart.

Patrick Quinnell spent an anxious hour with the baby before he was prepared to say it had a chance of survival. Mary brought him hot, sweet tea in a mug, and he managed to stem his craving for a drink. He had brought a life into the world; something he had never done in Brandon where the women preferred Dr Gibb for their confinements. He had saved one life, perhaps even two. It was a small return for the lives he had lost in Flanders.

The father was standing at the foot of the stairs when Quinnell went down, his face contorted with anxiety. 'It's a boy,' Quinnell said. 'Small and he'll need watching... but I think he'll live.'

The father put up a scarred hand to wipe his eyes. 'Is Anne all right?' he said.

'Yes.' Quinnell's voice was definite. 'She's exhausted, but she'll be fine, with rest.'

Now the father seized his hand in a crushing grip and pumped it up and down. 'About money…' he said. 'I've got –'

But the doctor put up a hand. 'I'm not allowed to take anything,' he lied. 'Besides, it was a pleasure to bring a child into the world.'

He saw that Lansky was weeping a little with emotion. 'Thank you, my friend,' the Jew said, but Quinnell shook his head.

'Thank you,' he said. 'The gratitude is mine.'

Frank was allowed to see the baby and kiss Anne's cold, damp brow, then Mary shooed him from the room. 'Go out, our Frank. Go and tell someone. Tell Esther. She has a right to know.'

Frank let himself out joyfully into summer night air, and half ran through the village, up towards the Scar. Halfway up the hill, he went behind a bush to relieve himself, chuckling as the urine spattered the ground. He had a son! A little thing, but it was life and proof of the life in him. He wiped his face on his sleeve, and tidied his blond hair as he went through the gate that had killed his brother-inlaw, and knocked, suddenly nervous, on the kitchen door.

A young girl in a blue dress and white apron answered, and he asked for Esther Gulliver. A moment later she was there, a strange, remote figure in her grey dress. 'There's nothing wrong with our Anne, is there?' she asked. Her voice was rising, and Frank hastened to give her the news.

The next moment he heard a man's voice behind her. 'Who's out there? Tell him to come in.'

Esther made as if to close the door, but Howard Brenton appeared and pushed it wider. He looked jubilant, his spotted silk tie awry and a lock of dark hair falling into his eyes. Behind him the servants stood, glasses in hand, and Frank was quick to notice. Something was up! 'This is my sister's husband, sir,' Esther said awkwardly. 'He's come to tell me she's had her baby safe and sound, too. A boy.'

In spite of his good intentions Howard had been out of his depth in the kitchen, dispensing Bollinger to a group who would probably have preferred cider. The tweeny's eyes had rolled as bubbles got up her nose, cook had looked disapproving, and the whole thing had been a strain. The advent of another man, and a new father into the bargain, was a godsend. He drew Frank into the kitchen.

'A son! This is a great day for us both, Mr...?'

'Maguire,' Frank said, 'Francis Maguire' – and then, reproachfully, 'I'm a putter in Belgate. I work for you, Mr Howard.' Howard nodded, but Frank was far from sure that he had been recognized and it irked him.

'Indeed you do, Mr Maguire. I remember you now.' Howard held out a brimming glass, and then refilled his own. 'To your son, Maguire. And to my son. May their lives be long and peaceful.'

'Aye, sir, I'll drink to that.'

Above the rim of his glass Frank watched Howard Brenton, fascinated to see him like this, in close-up and off his guard. The white scar was there under his eye, and he was thin for a man his height. It was true what they said: he wasn't half the man his father was, the old sod. But this one would still come in for it all.

And what did he know of the pit, with its scabby whinstone roof and walls bleeding water? He only owned it! It was the men who worked it who knew it like they knew their womenfolk. Frank thought of Stephen dead on the hill, and Sammy Watson's life tossed away to make Brenton profits. One day they would take over the Brentons' concerns, and then they would see where they stood. Frank had always believed he was cut out for something better than squatting on his honkers. One day, God willing, he would get his chance. He swallowed his first Champagne and smiled defiantly into his master's face.

Howard had no idea of Frank's low opinion of him. He was pleased that their paths had crossed like this, and felt they were drawn close by the mysterious bonds of fatherhood. He caught Esther's anxious eye and smiled. 'It's been a good day,' he said, raising his glass. 'I'll remember it all my life.'

'What weight was the baby?' the cook asked Frank, wrinkling her nose at the Champagne bubbles; and the conversation became a little easier, as Howard refilled glasses, even that of the giggling parlour-maid, who had suddenly flushed a deep red and taken off her cap. It attracted cook's attention and she gave the girl a glare.

'Oops,' the girl said and backed into the pantry. Howard saw, and kept his face straight.

'Come,' he said to Frank. 'We've toasted our sons. Now let us drink to our wives.'

9

Diana was quick to recover from the trauma of childbirth. After three days she announced that the two-week lying-in period decreed by Nurse Booth was ridiculous. 'Women in Africa', she said firmly, 'give birth behind bushes and then go back to the fields.'

Nurse Booth was ready with her answer. 'Savages are built like that, Mrs Howard. My task is to look after gentlewomen.' The accompanying sniff suggested that this time she might have made a mistake. 'Two weeks is the usual time my patients need to recover their strength. Lie still, and we'll see what doctor says when he arrives.'

But Diana was determined. 'I've been cooped up here for months,' she said, shaking off the nurse's restraining fingers. 'I'm perfectly well, and if you try to keep me in bed I shall see to it that you're discharged.' The nurse's wintry smile did not flicker. She stood back as Diana stepped to the floor. Four days in bed had left her weak; her head swam and she swayed. 'There you are!' the Dragon Nurse said smugly, and made to put her patient back to bed. Her smugness was the incentive Diana needed. She straightened up, thrust the nurse aside, and made her way to a chair.

She was sitting there when Howard came in to see his son. As usual his eyes flickered first to the crib and then to her; it was the same when Charles paid his visits, or Charlotte arrived to clutch her grandson to her bosom. The baby was the cynosure of all eyes; his mother the sloughed-off skin.

To be sure, they were lavish in their praise and with their gifts. Howard had given her an aquamarine pendant and matching bracelet; Charlotte an exquisite cameo in a heavy gold setting. Charles had told her she was a clever girl and had given her 100 preferential shares in the Brenton parent company. It was, he said with a rare chuckle, the most appropriate gift he could think of. Diana had thanked him prettily enough but she would have been more gracious if she had known they represented a holding of £25,000.

In front of visitors, or in the presence of the Dragon Nurse, Diana's attitude to the baby was casual. Secretly, or when Esther was there, she allowed her fondness to show. Writing to her parents, she told them their new grandson was a splendid little fellow with the Carteret chin, and that before the summer's end she would bring him to Barthorpe for inspection.

She thought of little else but getting away from Durham. She longed to see Loelia again, and there was that other compelling reason why she must go soon. Diana had no intention of sleeping with Howard until she had had advice on birth control. In time she would steel herself to go through the terrible process of childbirth again, but not yet. Her body was still sore, but it was the bruising of her spirit that hurt most. She would never forget being at Nurse Booth's mercy, or too thick and ungainly to have chic. Clever women did not spend nine months of every year pregnant; neither would she.

But before Diana could go to London, the baby must be weaned. She could not whisk the Brenton heir to London at such a tender age – and, besides, she had a curious reluctance to appear at Scotland Gate encumbered by motherhood. For a few days she wanted to be a girl again. She wanted to dance, and flirt, and exchange confidences with Loelia. She had given them their precious baby; surely she was entitled to a little fun?

Nurse Booth kept the baby swaddled in a blanket, delivering him to Diana at feeding times. Diana dreaded the moment when she must offer her swollen breasts, blue-veined and leaking milk. Only the fact that they were engorged persuaded her to suckle the baby. She feared that small intense face, the greedy mouth keeping a perfect 0 even when it lost the nipple, although the possession of nipples at long last was a source of satisfaction.

At last she told Dr Cunningham that the baby would be better for artificial feeding, and the doctor, sensing tantrums ahead, agreed to prescribe something to take away her milk. Nurse Booth's scandalized face gave Diana a moment of triumph, which was quickly forgotten when she had to endure the pain of her unrelieved breasts.

It is pure and unadulterated purgatory, she wrote to Loelia, *but I mustn't give in. I have so much to tell you, and I will simply shrivel if I stay here much longer. You can't imagine what it's like – but more of that anon. I should be with you within a week or ten days.*

If she had had a choice, Diana might have waited a little longer; there would have been no question of Howard forcing his attentions upon her against her will. But it was already June. London would empty abruptly during July. To be seen in London in August was out of the question for anyone of consequence, and certainly for the Dunanes. The Carteret town house had been shut up to save expense, ever since Diana's wedding. If she waited much longer the blinds would be drawn at Scotland Gate, dust-covers spread over the furniture and only a token footman left on guard. Loelia would be gone to Goodwood or Cowes and then off to the grouse-moors. If she wanted to stay with Loelia she must go now or leave it until the autumn – and she could hardly avoid Howard's bed until then.

When she announced her intention of going to London, Howard was aghast. He appealed to his mother, and Charlotte arrived to remind Diana of her duty to the Brenton heir, and to the brothers and sisters who must follow. This last firmed Diana's resolve as nothing else could have done.

Esther was subjected to a fine display of temperament when Diana discovered she could no longer get into her clothes. Esther unpicked and eased frantically, until at last Diana could cut a presentable figure for the journey. The bags were packed, the Suiza brought round to the door, and a kiss planted on the baby's head.

'Take care of Rupert,' she told Esther. 'I do love him, but I *must* get away for a little while. He won't miss me with you and the Dragon hovering over him, and if I stay here I shall die! Then where will he be?'

Esther carried the baby down to say goodbye, acknowledging to herself that Diana Brenton was too wild a spirit to be kept anywhere for long, and that the sooner they all came to accept it the better it would be.

As the days passed Howard missed Diana. Several times he telephoned her at the Dunane house, hoping to find her bored and ready to come home. He was disappointed. It was a long time since he had heard her so animated, so like the girl he had married. Loelia was still in London, he was told, together with her brother and some of his friends, and they were making sure Diana had a good time.

He told Diana to convey his gratitude to Loelia, and said she must stay in London as long as she wished. He found it hard to understand how Diana could leave the baby when it was so small, but everyone had different attitudes to love and responsibility, and he had no doubt she would come home soon.

In the mean time Howard was cementing his own relationship with Rupert. Each evening, when Nurse Booth was changing for dinner, Esther would bring the baby to him. He liked to think the blue, hardly focused eyes lit up at the sight of him, the mouth curved in a smile. If it was simply wind, Esther was too kind to tell him so, and their half hour together fortified him for dinner *à deux* with the Dragon Nurse. She made him feel like a child again, a small grubby boy at the nursery table, until he found she had a weakness for vintage port. Thereafter he plied her with it, and spent his own time in longing for Diana to come home.

It was at dinner one night that he suddenly remembered Michael Trenchard. The promised job was to start the following week and he had not yet arranged the interview. How could he have forgotten? His feeling of self-disgust threatened to overwhelm him, until he telephoned Edward Burton and found that the job was still open.

The following afternoon he drove into Sunderland, crossing the bridge to the north side of the town and turning towards the sea. He soon found Trenchard's lodging: a small, terraced dwelling with lace curtains at the windows and heavy drapes, almost drawn, to block out the light. He knocked and stood back. Out of the corner of his eye he saw the curtains twitch. A moment later the door was opened by a small, thin-faced woman, her sparse hair pulled back from a centre parting.

'Mr Trenchard?' Howard enquired.

'Are you a relative?' the woman asked. It was a strange question and for a moment Howard was lost for an answer.

'No,' he said at last, 'I'm a friend.'

The woman stood back from the door. 'You'd best come in.'

Howard stepped into a narrow hall, panelled in sage green. The woman shut the outer door and ushered him into the front parlour. It was dim and smelled of disuse, and Howard hovered uncertainly in the doorway until she gestured to an overstuffed chair.

'Is Mr Trenchard out?' he said, lowering himself gingerly to a seat.

The woman sank her teeth into her lower lip. For a moment she sucked, ruminating, and then she spoke. 'He's dead. He took his own life. I did what I could, but it was too late. The doctor says he must've been determined.'

There was a glass vase behind her, suspended in a gilt frame. A few stalks of mimosa stood in it, the fragile yellow balls seeming to hang in the air. Howard would never see or smell mimosa again without remembering that moment.

'Dead?' he said stupidly.

She nodded, folding her hands across her narrow waist.

'Laudanum…they proved it at the Infirmary, but the bottle was beside the bed as plain as I'm standing here.' Suddenly her eyes narrowed. 'Would you be Mr Brenton?'

'Yes. Did he ask for me?'

The woman shook her head. 'No. He never spoke to anyone. Just said goodnight same as usual and went upstairs, like he always did. I was expecting him down the next day to pay his rent. When he didn't come down, my man went up and found him. He was gone, but we still got the doctor out, and he got the police. We've never had anything like that before and never will again, I hope. But he left some letters, and one of them was to Mr Brenton. The police took them away. I expect you'll get yours eventually, but there's a procedure for that sort of thing.'

A terrible weariness had overtaken Howard. He wanted to rise from the chair but it was beyond him. Motes of dust were swimming in the sun that filtered through the curtains. It was too late. If only he had come in time.

As if she read his thoughts she spoke, 'It happened three days ago.'

With an effort Howard heaved himself to his feet. 'How much did he owe you? You must let me make it good. He was a friend of mine, you see.'

The woman's tone when she replied was shocked. 'There was nothing owing, Mr Brenton. Mr Trenchard was a good tenant. He left the week's rent beside the bed, and the money for his milk and papers. They took it away, but we'll get it eventually.' Suddenly she was struck by an afterthought. 'Of course I won't be able to let the room for a while. A thing like that gets around. I dare say I'll be out of pocket that way.'

Howard took out his wallet. 'Will this cover it?'

She demurred but he pressed notes into her hand. 'Well, if you're sure. It's very good of you.' She folded the money and tucked it into the pocket of her cardigan.

'He was a friend of mine,' Howard repeated. 'We went through the war together. Has anyone contacted his mother? I'm sorry, I don't know your name, Mrs…?'

'Ward. Mrs Ward. We sent word to his mother straight away. The police arranged it. But she can't be responsible for anything, they say. The Guardians will pay for his burial, after the inquest.'

Howard asked if he could see Trenchard's room, and she led the way up the narrow stairs with their thin red carpet. The room was clean and bare, the bed stripped to the mattress. A brown cardboard suitcase stood at the foot. 'His things are in there,' Mrs Ward said. 'I don't know what's to become of them, I'm sure. He packed it himself before… well, before he lay down. Everything neat and tidy.'

Howard looked around. There was nothing of Trenchard here. No sense of occupation. He crossed to the window and looked out over a crowd of chimneys. What had Trenchard said? '*I have a view of the sea.*' It was there between the roofs, a tiny triangle of blue.

Howard turned back into the room. 'I'll be seeing to everything,' he said. 'I'll need his mother's address.' They lifted the case onto the bed and opened it. The few things it contained were neatly folded – shirts, ties, a shabby suit. There was a small volume of poetry, bound in suede leather: *The Shropshire Lad*. They had read it together in France and the cover was trench-stained still.

His mother's address was on an old letter, and Howard copied it down. As they went downstairs he asked where he would find Trenchard's body, and Mrs Ward told him it was in the mortuary at the town's Infirmary. 'But you'll have to see the coroner's officer first. That's the procedure.'

'I'll let you know about the funeral,' Howard said as he left.

Mrs Ward nodded. 'I wish you would. We'll want to pay our respects. He was a gentleman... but he should have spoken up sooner. There was no need for him to go so far.'

As he drove back across the bridge, Howard felt a steady rage building inside him. 'I feel England has done with me,' Trenchard had said. They had all done with him, especially Howard himself. He could have helped much sooner, if he'd forced his father's hand – but it hadn't seemed imperative. And then, when a real opportunity had offered, he had forgotten to tell him. Trenchard had made no demands. He had borne it as long as he could, and then he had died quietly, leaving his dues beside his bed. Howard changed gear, averting his eyes from the place where they had stood together on the bridge. Had it really been only a few months ago?

An hour later he stood in the hospital mortuary, looking at Trenchard's dead face. It was pinched and waxen, the lips drawn back from the teeth, and there was a terrible neatness about the body under the winding sheet. Howard's nostrils twitched at the overpowering smell of Lysol. It reminded him of the day he had stood by Stephen Hardman's bier. A terrible weight of responsibility seemed to be settling on him lately, and he was not sure he was up to it. He had learned that Trenchard's letter would not be available until after the inquest; he could see the coroner's officer next day for details. He lifted his hand in a last salute and turned away.

Sitting in the Grand Hotel, drinking brandy, he tried not to laugh aloud at the irony. He and Trenchard had come through the war in France together, unscathed, and now it had ended like this! His guilt was so overwhelming that he wanted to vent his anger on someone – but who? Around him sat solid, middle-class citizens, drinking aperitifs and waiting to dine. Once the head waiter approached him. 'Are you dining, sir?' Howard shook his head. 'Not tonight.' He doubted whether he would ever eat again. If he had faced up to his father and demanded that a place be made for Trenchard, the man would be alive today. If he had not been carried away by excitement at the birth of his son…!

At eight o'clock Howard phoned the house: he would be late; no one was to wait up; he would not need a meal.

For the first few days after his birth, Anne Maguire had been almost afraid to handle her son. They had agreed to call him Joseph, after Frank's father. Frank had suggested they add Stanley, her own father's name, but she had scorned the suggestion. 'Plain Joseph,' she said. 'I like it.'

The baby was tiny, the skin of his limbs loose and empty, his head monstrously large for the tiny torso. But he had a scream on him like the colliery whistle, and when he caught one of Anne's fingers, his grip was determined. Most of all he was greedy, voracious for her breast, and Anne liked his fierceness about getting what he wanted.

When Dr Lauder arrived and would have shaken a doleful head, Anne cut him short. 'He'll thrive,' she said.

The doctor grudgingly admitted she had been lucky. 'I'd have come if I could but I had to assist Dr Goodfellow at the Scar.'

'Why?' Anne asked bluntly. 'What was wrong?'

'Well, nothing,' the doctor said. 'It was a normal delivery – a fine boy. But one likes to be sure.'

'Of course,' Anne said, smiling to hide the murder in her heart. 'You can't take risks with the Brentons.'

So Diana Brenton had been attended by every doctor within earshot, while she, Anne Maguire, had been left to the tender mercies of a drunk – for Frank had painted in Patrick Quinnell's shaking hand in lurid detail. Anne chalked up another debt to be repaid in full to the Brentons one day, and gave the doctor her last half-crown for his pains.

When Esther came down from the Scar bearing a hand-knitted matinée-coat that she had laboured over for weeks, and congratulations and a satin-bound blanket from Diana, Anne's rage was not assuaged.

'What's this for?' she asked, tossing the blanket aside.

'Mrs Howard is pleased for you,' Esther protested. 'I told her about you being pregnant, too. She used to ask…

She refrained from saying Diana used to ask how the other poor victim was, for fear Anne might not see the joke. 'Have you been out yet?' she asked, to change the subject.

'Of course not,' Anne said, opening her dress and putting the baby to the breast. 'I haven't the strength. Besides, I haven't been churched yet. Where could I go?'

Esther was not exactly sure what churching meant, but she'd heard Diana's views on the church's need to purify a woman after childbirth. 'They've already been crucified,' Diana had said. 'How much purer can they get?'

'Mrs Howard says churching's a lot of nonsense,' Esther ventured, expecting Anne's scorn for everything Catholic to surface. Instead her sister's eyes dropped.

'She would think that,' she said, and Esther could have sworn that for once Anne was beat for words.

In fact, Anne was at a loss as to how to explain to her sister that the prospect of being a good Catholic no longer seemed the terrible fate she had thought it to be. The crucifix had been a comfort to her in the agony of labour. She had fixed her mind on it, and it had helped. She had even prayed, and God had heard her and sent a doctor. Not much of a one – but a doctor, just the same. Her son had been blessed by the priest, and even since he had thrived. A lot of it, Anne felt, was still mumbo-jumbo, but somewhere in all the tarradiddle there was something to cling to. Since she had realized that, she had felt better.

'There'll be a christening,' Anne said, lifting her head to face her sister. 'But you can't be godmother, Es. I'm sorry, but with you not being Catholic…'

'It doesn't matter,' Esther said, trying hard to sound sincere. She had been sure she would be godmother to her only sister's child. They had even discussed it once. Now, apparently, Anne had changed her mind.

'I'm asking Mary,' Anne continued. 'She's been good to me, and she is Frank's sister.' She bent her head again, her conscience pricking her. 'You'll still be important, Esther but they have their rules, the Catholics. I don't want to cause a stir.' She paused. 'As a matter of fact, I'm converting. Well, it seems to make sense.'

Esther couldn't resist a small gasp of astonishment, and Anne bridled. 'I don't know what that's for; I could do many a worse thing – like drinking with the gentry. Yes, you may well look sick: I've heard it all from Frank. And you no more than a child, still. They'll draw you in to their flighty ways, Esther. You know what they do with domestics: look at the King when he stopped with the Londonderrys. Never out of bed. There's more royal bastards around there than dogs have fleas.'

Esther stood up. 'I'm going if you're going to talk like that, Anne. Mrs Howard was downright nice about you when she heard – and they've been kind to me, both of them. Besides, if your Frank didn't tell you there was Champagne for the whole house, he should've done.'

She left with another dire warning ringing in her ears and an uncomfortable pricking of the nose that meant tears before long.

*

It was ten o'clock when Howard left the Grand Hotel. He was drunk and he knew it. His wounded leg rarely bothered him, but tonight he stumbled again and again. It seemed to take hours to start the car and manoeuvre it on to the road, but at last he managed it.

When he left the town behind and was out on the open road, he let out a harsh sob. The gas lamps of Sunderland were receding, and suddenly the pale night sky of summer was luminous with stars. Trenchard would never see a night sky again, and it wasn't fair. It wasn't fair! In his mind's eye Howard saw Hooge Wood, the hastily dug graves and the chaplain, wrapped in a waterproof against the rain. *And there shall be no night there*, he had read aloud from a shabby Bible.

As the car mounted the Scar the engine laboured because he had not changed gear for the climb. It seemed not to matter. He wanted to see his son: that was all that counted. If Diana had been there he could have turned to her for comfort, but she was miles away. Even if she had been there, Howard was not sure he could have made her understand. He had never been able to explain about important things, not even when he saw frustration in her eyes at his lack of words.

He closed the car door gently and mounted the steps to the front door. From inside the house he could hear the telephone ringing. He tried to hurry but his feet were awkward, his fingers thumbs. His key refused to enter the lock, and it took several attempts to set the door open. A single electric light burned in the hall, throwing light on to the shrilling telephone. But as Howard hurried towards it, the impatient bell ceased. Whoever it was, he had come too late. He left the light on and turned towards the stairs, remembering half-way up that he had forgotten to lock the front door. But he was in no mood to turn back.

A night-light was burning in a bowl beside the cot. The baby lay peacefully on his side, nose tip-tilted above the pouting mouth. From the next room came the steady rumble of the Dragon Nurse's snoring. Howard touched the small cheek. It was warm. There was a rattle in his throat, and he moved backwards, feeling for the low nursing chair. He should not be in his son's room fuddled with drink, and he felt ashamed. He buried his face in his hands and let out a long moan.

'Are you all right, sir?' The Gulliver child stood in the doorway, a shawl clutched over her nightgown and her hair about her shoulders. 'I heard the telephone ring but I was too late to answer it.'

Howard sank on to the chair. 'Yes, I'm all right, Esther. Thank you. I've had some bad news... that's the reason I'm late.'

Esther moved forward. 'It's not the mistress?'

Howard shook his head. 'No, nothing like that. An old friend of mine, someone I knew in the war, died three days ago. I found out this afternoon, and there were things I had to do.'

Esther went to the fireplace, where the fire was always lit, on Diana's instructions. It had been banked up to last till morning, but a dull glow showed through the bars. She unlatched the big brass fireguard.

'Come to the fire, sir. I'll get you some tea by and by.'

Howard moved to a fireside chair and watched her coax a blaze from the coals. 'Thank you. It's nice to see a flame.' They were speaking in whispers, fearing to wake the baby. Their eyes met, and he saw pity in the way Esther looked at him. How could he tell this child that his own lack of care had probably caused a man's death?

'You shouldn't be up at this time, Esther. You need your sleep. I'm sorry for making a fool of myself. To you, of all people – you've had more than your share of grief. I shouldn't burden you.'

Her young eyes were fixed on his face and in the firelight he could see she was half-smiling in sympathy. It was too much. Howard felt tears welling, and it made him afraid. The amount he had drunk was running away with him and there was nothing he could do about it. His head drooped.

After a moment's hesitation, Esther put out a hand and patted his arm. 'It's all right, sir,' she said. 'It's all right.'

Howard put up a hand and caught her hand, squeezing it because he couldn't manage to speak.

They stayed there, his hand on hers, not moving or speaking, while the fire flared up in the grate. Neither of them had heard Charles Brenton's Daimler draw up to the front door, or the feet on the parquet of the hall, running lightly up the carpeted stairs. They were still in that tableau of unconscious intimacy when the light snapped on, and Diana stood in the doorway, a flustered Dragon Nurse behind her.

No one spoke. Then Diana turned away. Howard stood up instantly, and left Esther without a word, hurrying after his wife. Esther stood, transfixed, as Nurse Booth rushed for the cot, and then she slowly made her way back upstairs. She could hear Howard's voice, in explanation, as she passed the master-bedroom, but she knew he was wasting his time. They had done nothing wrong, but she had seen something more than indignation in Diana's eyes. There had been a kind of relief, too… as though something that had been difficult was now resolved. As for the Dragon Nurse, there had been more than suspicion in her face – there had been the certainty of sin, and satisfaction that the servant who had usurped her place in her mistress's esteem would no longer be a threat.

Diana did not doubt Howard's explanation of the scene in the nursery. Esther was a child, and Howard was too upright ever to betray her. But as he had sat with Esther, Diana had seen more open emotion in his face than she, his wife, had ever roused in him. She was not jealous, or even angry – she was hurt. But pride prevented her from saying so.

There was in Diana a great capacity for sin, and an even greater desire to be good. She had left London on a tidal wave of remorse, jumping into the train at King's Cross without wiring ahead. She had been missing Howard and longing to feel her baby in her arms once more. Besides, Max was making no secret of his desire for her now, and Loelia was starting to look distinctly anxious.

'She doesn't trust me,' Max had teased one night, while Loelia's lips tightened across the table in the Savoya. He sounded smug and gloating, and Diana felt an unexpected stir of distaste. She looked around her. The men were all like Max: complacent, aware that, since the war, eligible men were in short supply and must therefore be cultivated. 'They're spoiled,' Diana had thought. 'Almost a whole generation was wiped out, and the survivors can take their pick.'

Suddenly she had remembered Howard. He, too, was a survivor of the carnage of the trenches; more, he was a hero. Max, however attractive, was merely a boy. At that moment she had felt his hand upon her thigh. She had drawn on her cigarette and then smiled at Loelia. 'By the way, darling, I must go home tomorrow. It's a frightful bore, but absolutely essential.'

All the way home in the train Diana had imagined Howard's face: the surprise and pleasure she would see there. They had not shared a bed since the Dragon Nurse had separated them; even Howard would be eager for love after such abstinence. The Dutch cap and rather messy cream she had obtained in Harley Street were safe in her bag: 'Put it in every night when you brush your teeth,' the doctor had advised, and Diana meant to obey.

She had telephoned the Scar from the station at Durham, but the operator had got no reply. There was nothing to do but ring Charles Brenton and ask for Fox to come at once. In her haste to see Rupert, she had thought nothing of the unlocked door, the lighted hall. While Fox carried in her bags, she had run ahead up the stairs to the nursery. And then she had seen Howard with Esther, in the dim, fire-lit room, both of them apparently lost to the world. She had come home to be a good and dutiful wife; now she must play out the charade of a wronged one.

'Get out,' she said angrily to Howard, now, and locked her bedroom door against him.

At six she roused Nurse Booth, and told her to pack. 'I'm taking Rupert to Barthorpe,' she announced to the astounded and toothless face on the pillow. 'And you must come along to take care of him.' As Nurse Booth packed, elated at the prospect of visiting a stately home, Diana telephoned her father-in-law to beg once again for Fox and the Daimler.

If Charles disbelieved her story of Sir Neville Carteret's sudden illness, he was too wise to say so. Fox was dispatched to take mother, child and nurse to the station, and by noon they were on their way.

10

Esther had taken refuge in her room, but she did not sleep. Suddenly the house at the Scar, which had been her haven, was no longer welcoming. It did not even feel safe. She had not fully understood the scene in the nursery, but she could not dismiss how important it had been. She had seen and heard Anne's rages, but Diana's silent fury had been far more frightening. It had left Esther with only one desire: escape.

It never occurred to Esther that Diana, too, would choose to fly. At daybreak she dried her eyes, folded her grey uniform dresses neatly and left them on the bed, then began the walk into Belgate. Her bag bumped against her legs as she made her way towards Anne's house. It was cramped and overcrowded, but it was the only refuge she had now, and Anne would not turn her away.

She offered no explanation of her arrival. 'I've left,' was all she said.

Anne's eyes were bright with curiosity. 'You'd better come in,' she answered.

The baby was lying in a drawer, placed across the arms of a chair. It was a pretty baby, Esther thought, the small head a ball of blond fuzz, the mouth still guzzling in sleep. It reminded her of the other baby, back at the Scar. She had loved Rupert Brenton from the moment he slithered, blood-streaked, into the world, shocking her with the ferocity of his coming. Now she would never see him again, unless at a distance. She realized Anne was speaking to her and turned to face her sister.

'What's happened, Es? You might as well come out with it.'

Esther put down her bag. 'I decided to leave. No special reason. I just got fed up.'

Anne's look of derision was instant. 'I see: you just got fed up. Last week you had the best job in the world. Today you can't stand it. A likely story! Still, no matter – I think I know what went on. He tried it, didn't he? I told you he would.'

The sheer unfairness of Anne's assumption stung Esther to tears. 'No, he didn't. He was lovely. It wasn't him, it was her. She didn't want me there.'

It was only half-truth but Anne seized on it. 'The bitch! The la-di-da faggot! Well, you sit down there. Here: I'll blaze up the fire. Poor bairn. Well, you shan't go back, no matter how much they beg and plead…'

When Frank came home from the pit the house was filled with Anne's sense of injustice, and her satisfaction at having had her worst fears about Diana Brenton confirmed. Frank patted Esther on the shoulder and joked about two women being better for a man than one, but his eyes spoke volumes. 'See,' they said, 'this is what comes of drinking Champagne with your master.'

Howard could scarcely comprehend the events of the past twenty-four hours. Yesterday he had driven into Sunderland, a happily married man bearing good tidings to a friend. Now his wife had left him, he had caused trouble for a child (for that was what Esther was), and he was preparing to attend an inquest upon his friend's death.

In the early morning he had gone in search of Esther, anxious to make amends; but he was not surprised to find her gone. She had done nothing except comfort him in his distress, but there could be no future now for her at the Scar. Once or twice, as he'd reasoned with Diana, it seemed she believed him, but in the end she stuck to her original accusation: he had been too familiar with one servant and humiliated her in front of another. Now she was gone, God knew where, taking Rupert with her. She had muttered something about Barthorpe, but in her present state… As Howard drove into Sunderland he wondered where it was all going to end.

The coroner's officer sympathized with him in the loss of a friend. The man had served with the Durham Light Infantry in France, and knew what links were forged between comrades in war. He motioned Howard to a seat. 'The inquest won't take long, sir. They never do, these open-and-shut cases. I'll arrange for you to have your letter afterwards. They won't need it after today.'

Mr Ward gave evidence of identification, since Captain Trenchard's mother, his only living relative, was unable to travel from her home in York. The hospital pathologist said death had occurred from inhibition of the respiratory function due, in his opinion, to an overdose of alcoholic tincture of opium, commonly known as laudanum.

A few moments later it was over. 'Suicide while the balance of the mind was disturbed…the only possible verdict in the light of letters left behind by the deceased.' There were, the coroner said, a great many men who found themselves unable to adjust to peacetime living. It was sad, but it was part of the aftermath of war. Here he glanced in Howard's direction, his pince-nez glinting like stones. He had been informed by his officer that friends of Captain Trenchard's had made themselves responsible for the arrangements. There would, therefore, be no charge upon the townspeople of Sunderland. This was laudable in the extreme.

A moment later coroner and spectators had gone about their business. 'If you'll just follow me, sir?' the constable said and led the way.

Howard stood at a high desk to sign a release for the letter. 'Sorry it had to be opened, sir, but we needed sight of it. It made everything plain. I've sealed it up again.' Howard put the letter into his wallet, unable to read it yet. He hesitated, wondering whether or not he should offer some sort of tip. The officer shook his head. 'No need, sir, I assure you. Glad to be of assistance.'

When he got back to his office Howard telephoned Edward Burton to tell him that the post he had so carefully arranged would not be taken up, then he went in to see his father. There would have to be some explanation of Diana's sudden departure, but he had no intention of telling the truth.

The interview with his father was easier than he had imagined. It was as though Charles Brenton knew something was wrong but refused to acknowledge it might be significant. His smile implied that all women were difficult, and beautiful women were more difficult than others. He shook his massive head at news of Trenchard's death. 'What a waste,' he said. 'Suicide's never a solution.' There was regret in his tone but no remorse; no suggestion that he, Charles Brenton, might have affected the outcome. The next moment he was discussing the failure of a ventilation shaft at the Dorothea, and Howard let himself be carried into the painless world of work. Tomorrow he would go and look for Esther Gulliver: she had wages due to her, and he wanted to make sure she was safe. After that, he would think what was best for his marriage.

That night Esther slept in a chair, tucked under an old coat. Frank had come back from the Half Moon in an expansive mood, following Anne around, seizing her by the waist whenever she stood still. 'How's our lass, then?' he asked jovially each time, and each time she pushed him away. 'Get off, Frank. We've got company.' Esther was glad when at last they made their way up to bed, carrying the baby, and she could go to sleep.

It seemed she had hardly closed her eyes when Frank was up and about, pulling on his pit clothes over his longjohns and blazing up the fire. He brushed aside her embarrassment. 'Lie still, Esther, I've got nowt to hide. Dinnat fret. There'll be tea by and by.'

She huddled in the chair, sipping the tea he gave her, while he wolfed bread and dripping, and filled his bait tin with more. He offered her another mug of tea and then emptied the pot into his can. 'Our Anne'll be down when she's fed the bairn,' he said, and then he was over the step, whistling as though he were off to the seaside.

As Esther poured water into a bowl for washing she looked around the squalid kitchen. It was clean and tidy, but the walls were crumbling, the floor uneven and cracked with terrifying nooks and crannies in the corners that might hold all sorts of unimaginable horrors. How could Anne bear it? And yet she seemed happy enough… and willing to take in her sister when she was in need of shelter. All the same, Esther thought, she would have to get out of there as soon as she could, and this time there would be no offer of sanctuary at the Scar. She would have to make her own arrangements.

When Anne came downstairs, the sated baby on her shoulder, Esther set bread and tea and a boiled egg in front of her. 'Eat that. I'll buy more when I can get to the shop.'

Anne looked scandalized. 'I was keeping that egg for Frank.'

Esther nodded. 'I've told you, I'll buy more.' She had three pounds and seven shillings in her purse, saved from her wages at the Scar. It had felt like a fortune when she was in work. Now it seemed little enough, but she could still afford a tray of eggs.

When the breakfast was cleared away she offered to help with bread-making, and was up to her elbows in dough when a knock came at the door. Anne's brows lifted. No one ever knocked in Belgate. She went to the door and opened it, and Esther heard a man's voice.

'Is Esther here?'

Anne stood back, her face wooden. 'You'd best come in.' Once Howard was over the step, she folded her arms across her chest and tucked her chin into her neck as though preparing for conflict.

Esther was dusting off her arms and rubbing her hands on her borrowed pinny, terrified that Howard Brenton would speak in front of Anne. But if he and she went outside to talk, every tongue in the street would wag. Inspiration struck as Howard stood awkwardly, clearing his throat. She took a handful of silver from her purse and pressed it into her sister's hand. 'Please, Anne: I'll be all right. Get those eggs I promised you, and whatever else is needed. Mr Brenton won't be long. Please, just for a moment!'

Anne's eyes blazed with the desire to stay, but the silver won. She left the baby in its drawer and went, casting a look at Howard as she left that threatened death for the least bit of hanky-panky. He would have smiled if he had not felt so wretched.

'Is this the new baby?' he said, to ease the tension, as they turned back into the room. 'He's a fine boy.' They sat down at the table. 'I hoped I'd find you here.'

Esther's face was impassive. She could manage as long as he didn't go on about it; all that she felt now was a terrible embarrassment and a great desire to forget. Last night she had wondered if Mrs Howard might swoop down on her in the Daimler and carry her back. Now, suddenly, she knew that would not happen, and that she would not go even if it did. Her time with the Brentons was over. Now all that mattered was that she made it easy on Mr Howard. She drew herself up and folded her still-floury hands at her waist.

'I'm sorry about last night,' Howard said hesitantly. 'I behaved very badly. I'm afraid I'd had… I mean, I was upset

– I told you about my friend. I went to his inquest today. They said it was suicide.' Esther noticed the way Howard said 'suicide', as though he didn't agree with the verdict.

When Howard spoke again his tone was formal. 'It's all been an unfortunate misunderstanding, and I blame myself. What will you do?'

'I'll manage, sir,' Esther said, blinking as tears threatened.

Howard looked at her. She was still little more than a child but there was a dignity about her that moved him. He wanted to reach out and pat her arm, but he had done damage enough already.

'You're due wages,' he said instead, and took out his wallet. He would brook no argument. Esther was due to wages in lieu of notice, and she must take them.

'That's too much,' Esther said when she saw the white Treasury notes, but Howard would not be gainsaid. So she thanked him, and saw him over the threshold just as her sister returned from the shop.

Anne was unburdening herself of her purchases: eggs and bacon; a pound of rice and another of sugar, both in blue paper bags; potatoes and carrots; and a tin of bully beef. She tumbled rice into a dish and left it to soak. There was a quart of milk in a can in the sink, and a nice rice pudding would be a treat.

Once it was underway she turned to her sister. 'There's no change. You did say to spend it all, didn't you?'

Esther nodded, counting the money well lost. Anne swung the kettle on to the fire and turned back. 'Well?' There was no mistaking her meaning.

'Well what?' Esther said feebly.

'What did he want?' Anne insisted. 'I'm not daft, Esther. You didn't light out of there without a reason. You said it was her, but if it was why did he come? When Frank told me about you drinking with him I knew what'd happen. I hope you didn't let him get away with anything. You're the one who'll lose, you realize that?' She did not say, 'How far has it gone?' but the question hung in the air.

Esther went back to the dough, kneading and pulling as though possessed. 'You're wrong,' she said at last. 'I told you last night: I wasn't up to the work. Mrs Howard had her own ideas – fancy ways. I gave it up, that's all. And he came down because I had wages to come.'

Anne looked disappointed and then brightened at the thought of the money. 'How much? Not what you'd a right to, I bet. That's how they make their money, greeding it off people like us.'

The dough was ready to rise. Esther covered it with a cloth and carried it to the hearth, collecting a batch of proved dough in return. 'He's not like that. He had no need to give me £15, but he did.'

The moment the words were out she knew she'd made a mistake. Anne had reached for the kettle, now she set it back on the coals.

'What £15?' There was suspicion and hostility in her voice. 'What £15, I said? On top of your wages?' The suggestion was plain: whatever the money had been given for, it could not be anything good. Esther went on kneading the dough, without reply. She was acknowledging a dreadful truth: that the days of the old intimacy with her sister were gone. She could no longer be completely open with Anne, or rely on her for comfort, except in the short-term.

Their ways had diverged. But while Anne had Frank and her baby, she had no one. From now on she was completely on her own. Esther felt tears prick her eyes and concentrated on shaping the loaves, white and smooth and plump, before they faced the ordeal of the oven, while Anne went on and on about the wages of sin.

*

Michael Trenchard's funeral took place the following day. The coffin was lifted from the hearse and the organist, sensing the approach of the cortège, began to play. Howard and the Wards formed up behind; not much of a following for a dead hero. They were well into the church before Howard saw the two men. Edward Burton he recognized at once, but the other took a moment – until he saw the uniform covered by the fawn waterproof. It was the coroner's officer. For the first time he felt tears threaten and hastily reached for the hymnal.

Afterwards, by the graveside, he shook the constable by the hand. 'I don't usually come, sir, but this one was a bit special.' 'Thank you,' he said. Howard tightened his grip on the man's hand.

Edward and he walked together to their cars.

'Come and lunch with me at the club when you can,' Edward said.

'I will,' Howard answered. He wanted to thank Edward for his efforts on Trenchard's behalf, but he was afraid of sounding maudlin. And how would he explain his own laxity?

The brewer's eyes were shrewd. 'I know, old chap,' he said. 'I know.'

But kind though Edward might be, he could not know all of it, Howard thought, as he climbed into his car. Last night, alone at the Scar with a cold supper laid out for him, he had at last read Trenchard's letter: *Some good things came out of that mess, Brenton. Friendship was one of them... and pride and hope and good intentions. Perhaps I am not man enough to wait until it all works through. Perhaps, as I suspect, the good that arose then has dwindled away...*

Trenchard had seen death as a way out, not only for himself but for his mother. *I have been a poor reed, she will do better without me.* Howard was on the bridge now, the tram-lines shaking the car as they caught the wheels. What sort of country cared better for a widow if her son was first sacrificed? And what sort of friendship had he offered Trenchard? As he reached the main street Howard could hardly see the way ahead for tears.

While Howard was attending Trenchard's funeral, Patrick Quinnell came again to Belgate, sitting in Lansky's trap.

'I've come to see the baby, if I may,' he said as Anne opened the door to his knock. He saw her bridle, and smiled to placate her. 'Not a professional visit. I haven't delivered a child for a long time, so your son is quite special to me.'

Not even Anne could resist such a plea – and the fact that the doctor didn't expect to be paid made a difference.

'Come in,' she said, glaring at Lansky to show the invitation did not extend to him.

'You could have let the Jew in,' Frank said later, when Anne told him of the visit. 'We'd have done badly without the old man that day, there being no doctor an' all. He went all the way to Brandon and never took a penny for it.'

'He's made plenty out of us,' Anne said. 'And besides, your Mary was here, making sheep's eyes at the doctor.' She let fall the accusation lightly, just to make Frank shut up about Lansky. Now, as his brow darkened, she saw it was a mistake. 'I'm only joking,' she said uneasily. 'Mary was here and she seemed pleased to see the doctor, that's all. And don't go all hoity-toity about your precious sister, I've got enough trouble with me own.'

'Where is Es?' Frank asked but received only a roll of Anne's eyes in return. Esther was, the glance implied, off on some pursuit of her own and heaven help them all with the consequences.

In fact, Esther was taking flowers to her father and mother's grave. The stone said only: 'Maude Gulliver, beloved wife' – there had been no money for an inscription to their father. But there were fresh flowers in a tin vase: yellow daisies and purple stocks. They had not come from Anne, that was certain. So who had put them there? The question perplexed Esther as she arranged her own marguerites in the jam-jar she had brought for the purpose and, kneeling, asked direction as to what she should do next.

11

Diana had been home at Barthorpe for only four days and already she was bored. At the merest hint that all was not well with her marriage, her parents had retreated into their shells, pausing to coo dutifully over the baby and compliment Nurse Booth on his condition. The Dragon Nurse took one look at Barthorpe's vaulted hall and recognized it as her spiritual home. Henceforth she would be more tolerant of Diana's wildness, putting it down to a rare intensity of breeding.

Diana loved Barthorpe's mellow walls and the clumps of Turkey oaks and Spanish chestnuts that surrounded them, but there was nothing to do. She had looked forward to seeing her dog, Mephisto, whom she would have brought to Durham long ago if Nurse Booth had not vetoed it. But Mephisto's eyes were rheumy, the liver-and-white coat dull. The spaniel had grown old, and it made Diana sad. She made endless rounds of the stables, offering sugar on a flat palm, thumb tucked out of the way, as her father had taught her when she was five. She visited the home farm and the glasshouses, but even they soon palled, and there was only a limited welcome in the nursery, where Nurse Booth resigned supreme.

There is nothing for me to do here, Lee, she wrote. *It is as though I have grown out of my old home. And yet I must let the parents see their first grandchild. It's the least I can do.* She made no mention of the real reason she had left the house at the Scar. Loelia might wonder, but she would come nowhere near the truth. Thinking of what had happened that night, Diana felt guilty. Had Howard actually been to blame? Or had she run away because it suited her to do so?

She began to look forward to meals as a kind of punctuation to the day, but her father's obsession with cooking smells was worse than ever. The green baize door from kitchen to dining-room had to be hidden behind a tall six-leaved leather screen, and a maid stood behind it, fanning the air with a serving-cloth. Still, Sir Neville swore that odours entered the room and destroyed his appetite. It was all so trivial.

The long country days seemed to stretch ahead interminably, and she was full of regret. She had been too quick to make judgements, and much too quick to walk out. Howard had faults, but they were minor ones: sins of omission. The capacity for love was in him, Diana was sure of that. If only she had stayed in Durham. Instead she was stuck here, with Mama vaguer than ever and the Dragon Nurse behaving like a feudal serf. 'Bloody woman's soft in the head,' Neville Carteret said after Nurse Booth had used his title seven times in as many minutes.

On the tenth day, the Dragon Nurse went down with colic, and lay, sans teeth and dignity, moaning in her bed. Diana showed little compassion. 'This is what comes of too much rich food, Nurse,' she said wickedly. 'We have only ourselves to blame, haven't we?' She shook an admonitory finger, and the nurse's eyes rolled in the only retaliation she could manage. Diana returned to her own room, smothering a giggle, wishing Esther was there to see her discomfort their old enemy.

She now felt extremely uneasy about the way she had left the Scar without a word to Esther. The child had hardly been to blame; what must she be thinking? She contemplated writing a note to Esther. Not an apology – that would never do – but a simple note, expressing certain wishes about the house or her clothes, a note couched in friendly terms, to set Esther's mind at rest. She wavered, but in the end she decided to leave making amends until all this horridness was over and she could return to Durham.

Esther knew she must leave the Shacks as soon as possible. Frank had made her welcome enough, and Anne was positively feasting on her sister's need for refuge. But Esther knew it was not good for any of them for her to stay. Anne could not let the idea of Brenton villainy rest – and then there was the money. If Anne carried out her threat to fix up the box bed by the chimney-breast, and if Esther stayed, all would be well until the money ran out. There was no work for her in Belgate. How would she and Anne get on once Esther had no way of paying for her keep?

On the day following Joseph's christening she went to Lansky's pawnshop. The door opened with a clang and she closed it carefully behind her. The shop was dark and apparently empty, apart from the clutter of pledges, boots and Sunday suits.

The next moment Lansky was there, appearing from the back shop. It was the first time Esther had seen him without his coat and hat, and he looked strange to her. A small embroidered cap covered the crown of his head; his white shirt had the dull gleam of silk; and there was a curious knotted fringe at his waist. He laid down the book he was carrying and smiled. 'I never thought to see you here.'

Suddenly Esther wondered why she had come. She hardly knew this man; he might tell her to go away. She licked her lips, and gathered her courage. 'I've come for advice, Mr Lansky… if it's all right with you?'

Teeth flashed in the grey beard as Lansky laughed. 'Advice? The first customer of the afternoon, and it's advice she's after!' He waved a hand around. 'A fine piece of china, a little silver... with these I can't tempt you?' And then, seeing her confusion: 'But I shouldn't tease you. Not when you pay me such a compliment.' He lifted up the flap of the mahogany counter and drew her through. 'Advice I keep in the back. It's too precious to put on display.'

Esther had always averted her eyes from Lansky, fearing the bearded face beneath the side-brimmed hat. Jews were a rarity in the collieries, and Lansky was still regarded as a foreigner after twenty years. Now she looked up at him and saw there was nothing to fear. He was less old than she had thought, and his voice, with its faint accent, was firm. Besides, her father had always spoken well of him.

They drank tea out of fine bowls, thin green tea that soured her palate at first and then refreshed it. The bowl had no handle and she had to turn it round in her hand to escape the heat. The back shop was warm and dark and lined with books: books on shelves and in packing-cases, spilling from every surface, all of them well-thumbed.

With a conjuror's ease Lansky extracted Esther's story. She had £20 18s in cash and some bric-à-brac, but she had no home and no work, and was looking for both. 'It didn't work out at the Scar,' she said and hoped it was enough. In case he asked questions she hurried on: 'I want to get a job in Sunderland, and you're the only person I know who lives there. Can you tell me where I can go to find a place?'

Lansky smiled. 'You're young and strong. Not in the hand or the wrist – these are penny skills. You have a core, a strength inside. Now that does not come so cheap. We Jews have a word for it; we have a word for everything. It is *chen*: something in a person that cannot be described but is good. I saw it in you from the start, Esther Gulliver, when you were a little girl holding your father's hand.'

Once more he smiled. 'Your namesake is revered by my race. That Esther was a Jewish queen, who risked her life to intercede for her people, and saved them from slaughter.

She had *chen*. There is much about you that reminds me of that Esther.'

Esther was not quite sure what he was talking about, but she smiled just the same. Lansky drained his tea and put down the bowl. 'Now you want this old fool to stop philosophizing and give you what you came for. How are you to manage? It is a *she'alah*. But twenty pounds and eighteen shillings... empires have been built on less.'

He gave her the address of his shop in Sunderland. 'Come to me there tomorrow, and we will see what can be done. Can you walk as far as Sunderland?'

Esther nodded, suddenly elated. 'Of course I can,' she said gratefully, and got up to go.

Howard's arrival at Barthorpe a day or two later, in the Suiza, was the answer to Diana's prayer. Only the night before she had asked God to work it out, and he had. She was filled with the pleasure that the first sight of Howard always gave her: he was so absolutely right for a husband. She blessed her mother for having insisted that, as a married woman, she should occupy a double room instead of her old bedroom. Once bedtime came, she and Howard would work everything out.

Howard, too, was anxious to make up. They had been foolish, and it must stop now. He had never seen Diana look more beautiful, and he was sure he could detect a note of warmth in her muted welcome. Dinner seemed to drag interminably, and the time spent in the library with Sir Neville and his precious vintage port was an agonizing waste of time. In another home the butler would have attended to such things, but Neville Carteret insisted that no one knew how to handle port as well as he did. So Howard sat while his father-in-law took the cobwebby bottle fresh from the cellar and set it between his knees.

The cork must not be drawn for fear of disturbing the sediment. Instead, the neck of the bottle must be snapped off cleanly with the cork in place. The special tongs were heating in the fire, cold water was to hand. The red-hot tongs were applied, a cold cloth replaced them, there was a crack and then the port was trickling through a silver strainer into the decanter. Now it must be left to take the temperature of the room and all this while, precious time he could have spent with Diana was trickling away. Would she want him so soon after their quarrel? Had enough time elapsed since Rupert's birth? Howard's head swam with a combination of vintage port and desire and anticipation and fear.

Diana had already made her escape from the drawing-room, pleading the need to see to her baby. Rupert was sound asleep, lulled by the snoring of the Dragon Nurse on the other side of the wall. Diana sped to her room and began to undress. She chose a nightgown of white crêpe de Chine, exquisitely smocked in shades of pink by Belgian nuns who themselves wore coarse linen habits and wooden shoes. It showed her new and much prized nipples to advantage, and clung to her thighs.

She sat down at the dressing-table and looked at herself in the mirror. She had not made love for months and months. Now, the Dutch cap safely in place, she could do it without fear. And without guilt! She was beautifully and safely married to Howard. When he had said he was sorry she would be so good to him, so loving. She seized her hairbrush and began to groom her hair. With each stroke she imagined how completely she would love him.

But it was almost two hours before Howard appeared, and by then Diana had worn herself out. A heaviness had settled upon her chest, the taste of anti-climax was on her tongue. She watched through the mirror as he began the process of taking out studs and cuff-links, winding and correcting his watch, removing the contents of his pockets and laying it on the walnut Wellington chest. The ritual had always irritated her, spinning out the foothills when she was eager to ascend the peak. She looked at his face, still and closed, bereft of the eagerness she had wanted to see there. Suddenly she no longer wanted to make love with Howard. She wanted to bring him down!

'Has she gone?' she said at last, sitting upright in the wide bed.

'Who?' Howard asked, surprised by the question.

'You know who!' Diana said accusingly. 'The Gulliver girl.'

Howard shook out his shirt and lowered it into the linen basket. 'If you're speaking of Esther, she's gone to her sister's, I believe.' He frowned, wondering why he had uttered the small lie. He knew Esther had gone to her sister's; why had he not said so?

Diana saw the frown and it stiffened her resolve. 'You mustn't think our sharing this room means I have changed my mind, Howard. Mama arranged it, and I chose not to argue.'

Howard inclined his head. 'Of course.'

Diana glared at him.

'You could try saying you're sorry. I'm not saying it would make a difference, but you could try.' It was the point of no return and each of them knew it. Howard sought desperately for the right words; Diana held her breath in the hope he might find them.

'I'm sorry you misconstrued the situation,' he said at last. 'Other than that, I have nothing for which I need to apologize.'

'Are you sure?'

'Quite sure.' By now his tone was clipped.

'I should never have married you, Howard. I made a terrible mistake!' Diana was climbing from the bed as she spoke, shrugging into a wrap, turning to face him. There was only a yard or two between them and suddenly she felt an urge to cross the divide and press her face against his chest. His arms might come round her then and it would all be all right. But his face was implacable, his eyes as impenetrable as ever. 'We're strangers,' she thought and turned away.

They spent the night at opposite extremes of the mattress, moving their legs gingerly for fear of a stray touch being mistaken for an olive branch.

In the grey light of dawn Howard abandoned sleep and went downstairs. Over a bleak breakfast table they made plans: Rupert's christening would take place in London, and for the time being the two of them would continue to present a united front. In private, they would go their separate ways.

'I will keep up appearances for my son's sake,' Diana said grandly, 'but I would be grateful if you would not pester me.' It was an unfortunate choice of words and she regretted them as they left her lips, but by then it was too late.

'There is no fear of that,' Howard said. 'I have no desire to do any such thing.' His voice was icy, and it stung.

'Good,' Diana said, and did not give way to tears until she was safe in her room again.

The following day Esther packed her bag and took her leave of Anne. 'You'll rue this,' Anne warned. 'Off to a strange town, with no one but a Jew-boy to rely on. It's crazy, our Es, when you could stay here.' But Esther kissed the baby and made for the door.

'Don't come back here licking your fingers when they're burned,' Anne added, but by then Esther was out on the path and turning north towards the smoky blur of Sunderland.

She had never been to Sunderland except in the company of her father or Anne, and as she walked the five miles her heart began to sink. It was a big town and she knew no one there. Lansky lived there and had his shop just off the main street, but she couldn't rely on him to do more than point her in the direction of work. The rest would be up to her. Her bag grew heavier as her spirits drooped, and by the time she reached the shop she was weary and aching, and not far from tears.

Lansky greeted her like an old friend. Esther saw the gleam of silver behind mesh-fronted cabinets and a row of telescopes on the counter – none of the clutter of the Belgate shop. But they were not to talk there.

'You're being very kind,' she said, as Lansky put on his hat and placed the *Closed* sign on the shop door.

He locked the door before he answered. 'It is my pleasure to help you, Esther Gulliver, and you will help me, too, before long.'

An hour later Esther had taken a room in a house in a quiet street in Hendon, the lower part of Sunderland, belonging to someone Lansky knew. The boom of the docks could be heard in the background, but there were trees in the street and birds to sing in them. It would cost her three shillings a week until such time as she found work. Then she could move to the lower floor and rent a larger room with an off-shot kitchen, for six shillings and sixpence. In the meantime, she had the use of a kitchen and bathroom on the lower floor, and a key to her own door. On the Jewish Sabbath she would earn two shillings for lighting Lansky's fire and doing those jobs an orthodox Jew could not do for himself on that day. Most important, Lansky would give her a letter of reference to show to possible employers – and he already had one such person lined up. Before he left Esther in her room she tried to thank him, but he put his finger to his lips and shook his head. 'What's a little help for a friend?'

When he had gone Esther sat on the edge of the bed and looked around. After a moment she reached into her bag and took out the photograph of herself with Howard and Diana taken on Christmas day. It annoyed her to admit it to herself, but once it was set upon the mantelshelf she felt as though she was at home.

She spent an hour or so placing her things around the room, and moving the furniture to her liking. There was a fawn hair carpet on the floor, a floral-patterned toilet set, and the gas jet had a pink shade. The furniture was oak: a wardrobe, a table and two chairs. The room was clean and dry and quiet, and she liked it.

When she had finished Esther put on her best coat, took the handbag Diana had given her, and made for the corner shop, drawn by the smell of baking bread. She bought a cottage loaf wrapped in tissue-paper, and then set out to walk to Lansky's house in Tunstall Road, following the directions he had given her. His housekeeper would be there to hand her the precious letter, and to show her what work must be done on the Sabbath. She grinned at the thought: Esther Gulliver cleaning up for a Jew. What would her mother have made of that? Or Anne – Anne who now blamed every Jew for personally assisting at the Crucifixion? A few months ago Esther would never have believed any of it possible.

Suddenly and gloriously there was a park ahead, with iron railings and a green hill topped by a statue. She found a seat in the sun and broke the top off the loaf. It was just right, crusty on the outside and creamy within. When she had eaten her fill she tore up the rest of the loaf and threw it to the wheeling seabirds. It was the first time she had seen a gull at close quarters, and it reminded her how near she was to the sea.

Down below she could see tram-cars rattling along the main street, with busy little motor bikes threading between them, and motor cars, and horse-drawn vehicles. Beyond, the rooftops seemed to go on for ever.

A woman was on her knees in front of Lansky's house, stoning the steps to a proper whiteness. She dried her hands on her apron at Esther's approach. 'Esther?' Her voice was strange and guttural, but she was smiling. 'I was expecting you. I am Rachael Schiffmann – *Miss* Rachael Schiffmann.' She stressed her single state as though she was not ashamed of it.

She waddled up the steps, and Esther saw that her left foot was encased in a brown surgical boot and turned in at an angle. But she was nimble for a fat woman. As they went through the door she put up a hand to touch a small box on the jamb. Esther looked at it curiously, but it seemed to have no useful purpose.

Inside the woman handed over the letter of reference, and a slip of paper. 'You must go there and ask about a job; it is arranged for six o'clock. There you will be all right.' Rachael was nodding vigorously to emphasize her words, and Esther found herself nodding in unison.

She looked at the paper: *Philip Broderick,* it said. *17 Valebrooke. 6 p.m.*

'Who is he?' Esther asked, unable to contain her curiosity.

'He is a friend of Mr Lansky,' Rachael said. 'A good man, a scholar – but afflicted.' She glanced at her own misshapen foot and sighed. 'Yes, afflicted. Still, you will do good work for him, and he will be kind. You'll see. It is meant to be, this – the right one for the right place. Now.' She rubbed her hands together to indicate the need to make progress. 'Now, I show you all you need to know.'

They went from room to room on the ground floor while Rachael explained the layout of the house, and the duties of the Sabbath.

It was the most magnificent house Esther had ever seen, with heavy curtains that looked like silk, and gleaming carved furniture. Everywhere there were huge glassfronted cabinets stretching to the ceiling and filled with books, most of which had tooled leather covers and titles in gold.

'There is no need for you to care for all this,' Rachael

said. 'All week I see to everything, but on Shabbos I do no work. I, too, am a Jew. It is forbidden to work on the Sabbath. So you will see to the fire…'She looked around. 'And the cat. It is a good beast, no trouble. And anything,' she waved a hand, 'that occurs.' It all sounded a little vague to Esther but Rachael seemed satisfied. 'Now we have tea!'

They sat in the stone-flagged kitchen for tea and honey cake. Esther thought it rather dry but Rachael pressed it upon her guest. 'Eat, eat,' she said, pushing the plate forward with a big red hand.

Suddenly there was a clatter of footsteps and a boy burst into the kitchen, a small skull-cap perched on his untidy black hair. 'Esther, this is Samuel Lansky,' Rachael said, gazing indulgently at the newcomer.

The boy advanced, holding out his hand. 'So you're the new Shabbos *goyah*?'

Esther's brow wrinkled in incomprehension and the boy laughed. 'You'll come to us on the Sabbath day,' he said. He had eyes like shiny black buttons, and when he smiled, Esther could see his resemblance to Lansky.

'Pleased to meet you,' she said, shaking him by the hand.

The boy, who was about twelve, turned on Rachael, seizing her by the waist. 'Come on then, Schiffy. Where are *de kich'lers*?'

Rachael shook her head vehemently. 'No, no: honey cake if you must, but cookies: no!'

He squeezed her tighter, revelling in her screams of protest. 'Come on: one or two cookies for your boy. You know you love me, Rachael Schiffmann. Now I'm asking you to prove it!'

She slapped at him feebly. It was obviously a familiar ritual. 'Such *plaplen*!' She reached for a blue jar and took two small cakes from its depth. 'Now out of my kitchen, *boytshik'l* – before I take my hand to you.'

A burst of conversation followed, in a totally strange language. It seemed to amuse them both, but left Esther bemused. Then the boy backed away, munching. 'I always win, Rachael. Why do you make a fight of it?' He blew her a kiss and turned to Esther. 'Shalom, Esther. See you on Shabbos.'

When he was gone Rachael smiled. 'Such a good boy: a *mentsh* like his father.' Suddenly Rachael shook her head. 'A *mentsh* – a good man. I forget you have no Yiddish.'

Her words startled Esther. 'Dirty Yids,' Frank used to say and she had thought it a term of abuse. Yet here was Rachael using it herself. She had only understood half of what had been said between the boy and the old woman: she would have to learn.

Rachael looked at the big clock. 'Nearly time,' she said. 'You mustn't be late on the first day.'

At five minutes to six Esther was standing outside the address Rachael had given her: a large red-brick house. She tucked her hair under her hat, nervously, and straightened her coat. The new handbag dangled awkwardly from her wrist; today was the first time she had carried it, and it felt strange. She tucked it under her arm, and marched resolutely up to the door.

At first she thought it was a child who answered her knock, but as her eyes became accustomed to the gloom inside the hall Esther saw that it was a man. Thin and pale and unnaturally stooped, but an adult all the same, dressed in the dark coat and striped trousers of a businessman. A sudden lump filled her throat, but she swallowed her fear, and spoke out.

'I'm Esther Gulliver, sir. Mr Lansky sent me.'

'Come in, please. You're very prompt.' His voice was surprisingly deep and pleasant, Esther thought, as she followed him down the hall into a small back room. Like Lansky's house, the room was full of books neatly stacked behind glass fronts. The curtains were heavy brocade velvet, and everywhere was dusty, the motes swimming in sunlight that came between the half-drawn curtains.

'Do sit down,' Philip Broderick said courteously, and Esther sank on to a hard, over-stuffed chair.

Seated, Philip Broderick looked even smaller, his head too big for his shrunken body, his eyes gleaming behind wire spectacles. He reminded Esther of the humpty-backed man who came to Belgate twice a year to grind knives, but his expression was pleasant. She tried to guess his age, but it wasn't easy. Were the lines on his face lines of age or lines of pain?

'Mr Lansky tells me you are accustomed to domestic work. Do you enjoy it?'

The question took Esther by surprise. 'I suppose I must.'

He was laughing a little, mouth open to reveal good teeth, and Esther was discomfited. 'I'm sorry, Miss Gulliver. I didn't mean to be impolite, but you sounded so astonished.' It was true. No one had ever bothered to enquire whether or not she liked housework – not even Howard Brenton, and he had meant well enough.

Esther smiled. 'It's all I've done – all I know. I used to help my mother, and then my sister, and then I went into service. I don't dislike it, if that's what you mean.'

The grey eyes behind the wire spectacles were kind. 'But you'd rather pick flowers?'

She knew what he meant. 'I expect I'd like that.'

Philip waved his hand at the bookcases. 'These are my flowers, and I pick them when I can. But during the day, alas, I must work for my bread and butter. I have an office in town, a ship-broking company. Very dull.'

Esther was entering into the game now. 'It's a hard world, sir,' she said, and heaved a sigh, and saw a smile twitch at his lips. She felt a little intoxicated by the conversation, and by sitting here on an upright chair clutching her handbag for all the world as though she were thirty.

Philip Broderick had grinned at her remark. Now he put his fingertips together and touched them briefly to his lips as though considering. 'I need someone to care for my house, dust my books, cook for me. Simple food. I have had a succession of ladies since my mother died, but they never stay. I think they are a little afraid of me. You don't seem at all afraid. However, you are very young. How old are you?'

'Sixteen, sir,' Esther said, and tried not to look guilty. Her sixteenth birthday was still a few weeks away.

'How would you feel about being in this house alone during the day, keeping it clean and preparing my evening meal? I'm back by six. And I don't require help on Saturday or Sunday.'

Esther had already decided to take whatever he offered. It was a job, and if Lansky approved of Philip Broderick he was bound to be all right. 'I'd like to give it a try, sir… and we can see if we suit.'

He offered her what seemed like riches – fifteen shillings a week – to cook and clean and buy his groceries, five days a week. She could keep her job at Lansky's, whom he spoke of as one of his closest friends. When he took her on a tour of the house, she saw that he only came up to her shoulder, and yet his hands and feet were normal, even large, the legs long. It was the chest that was folded in upon itself.

From the hush of the carpeted hall they came into a passage floored with dark green linoleum. The windows had lower panels of red glass which added to the gloom, but the place was clean. A huge black Eagle range dominated the kitchen, with a saucepan bubbling on top: some sort of stew, to judge from the smell. Poor man, Esther thought, coming home to make his own meal. She would soon change that.

'Emmanuel Lansky tells me you lost your parents,' Broderick said as they returned to the hall. 'I know how that feels. Don't be afraid of the work here. If there's anything you need to know, or don't understand, I will explain it. And you must tell me what you need to make the work...' He paused and smiled again. '...as near to picking flowers as we can manage.'

He walked her to the front door. 'Goodnight, Miss Gulliver.'

Esther had the key to the front door and a sovereign for groceries in her pocket.

'My name's Esther, sir, if you'd prefer.'

He stood at the door until she reached the gate. 'Goodnight then, Esther. Until next Monday.'

That night Esther wrote to Anne to give her new address and to say she now had a good job in a respectable household. She left out any mention of Lansky, knowing what Anne would make of it, but then her conscience pricked her. *PS*, she wrote. *The old Jew has been very kind.*

12

Diana went early to London to arrange the christening, in the church where she and Howard were married, leaving Nurse Booth to bring Rupert a little later. They did not have much time before the end of the season. She was to stay at Scotland Gate until the Carteret house was ready to receive her parents and their guests.

It was bliss to be reunited with Loelia, and she had hardly cast off her hat and gloves before Max was there, as attentive as ever, with the ubiquitous Henry Colville in tow.

'Diana,' he said, bending to kiss her hand. 'You look lovelier than ever.' His lips on her hand were like butterflies and she was relieved when he let it go.

They had tea, delicious Dunane nursery tea, in Loelia's sitting-room, and then rolled back the carpet to dance to the gramophone. 'This is the rage,' Max said, putting on the first record. 'There isn't an errand-boy in London who isn't whistling it.' He put his thumbs into imaginary braces and began to caper about, singing: 'Yes! We have no bananas. We have no bananas today.'

'It doesn't make sense,' Diana protested, but Max shook his red head. 'None of the best things make sense, Diana darling. Don't be such an old stick-in-the-mud.'

That night, Max took Diana to the Riviera, with Loelia and Henry into. But when the evening was almost over Diana and Max slipped away to his car. 'I'll show you the eighth wonder of the world,' Max whispered as they drove. It was the new neon lighting on the tower of the Coliseum Theatre – the first neon lighting in London. It gave a sunset glow to the sky.

They sat in the Napier for five minutes while Diana drank in the wonder of it, oblivious to the West End traffic hooting all around them. 'I love, love, love London. I never want to leave it again,' she said. Max's answer was to leap from the car and fill her arms with Parma violets from a street-seller's basket.

'You mustn't leave,' he said, as she lifted the flowers to her face. 'I couldn't live without you.'

After that, Max took her out every night: 'Making up for lost time,' he called it. He was so attentive that nothing seemed to matter to Diana except the warmth in his sparkling eyes – a warmth that was for her alone – and the touch of his hand on her arm, urging her on to new excesses of pleasure every evening. 'I'm happy,' she told her mirror as she shed her evening finery in the early hours of the morning. 'I'm happy. This is how life should be.'

She managed to ignore Loelia's pained expression, and to dismiss her own occasional doubts by snuggling up in her room to read Max's copy of the newly published *Ulysses* by James Joyce, in a discreet brown wrapping. It was badly printed on coarse paper, and had been bought in Paris.Reading it, Diana blushed to think that Max knew she had read it, and then went back to read the worst bits again.

When Rupert eventually arrived, and was carried into Scotland Gate, he was seized on by Nanny Dunane, much to the chagrin of the Dragon Nurse. 'There now, Master Brenton,' Nanny crooned, nuzzling him with her moist nose.

'So unhygienic,' Nurse Booth told Diana, pursing her lips and puffing out her grey-clad bosom. 'I refuse to be responsible for the consequences.'

It was a relief when the servants came down from Barthorpe to open the Carterets' London house, and the two nurses could be separated. But Diana knew which of the two old women was her favourite. It was not Nurse Booth

Rachael had explained to Esther something of the Kiddush on Friday evenings, the lighting of the Sabbath candles, the singing and the feel of the family safe within the home, but nothing had prepared Esther for the splendour of silver and glass and white lace as the Sabbath began, and for the feast laid out – and enough to spare. And apart from the celebration itself there was all the pleasure of preparation. Esther hurried through her duties at Valebrooke to get round to Lansky's before darkness fell and the Sabbath began.

That first week Rachael showed her how to make *challah*, a golden egg bread, usually shaped into a plait but sometimes more eccentric shapes if Rachael was in the mood to please Sammy. Then she would put in raisins and other dried fruit, and always she would nip off a small piece of the unbaked dough and cast it into the fire as a symbolic offering, muttering a prayer as she did so.

Rachael baked all day on Friday: *lokshen kugl*, a pudding of noodles; *gefilte* fish and herbs; roast chicken; great pans of soup. It was all strange and wonderful to Esther, seeing the beautifully set table, each piece blessed by Rachael, who sometimes sang weird, wordless songs as she worked. Philip had excused Esther serving his meal on Fridays so that she could be at Lansky's in time to carry out her duties, and she was grateful to him.

Emmanuel Lansky came in for the lighting of the candles and the making of the Kiddush, the prayer, over the wine. A beautiful candelabra, a *menorah*, stood on the table, and Emmanuel told Esther that this ceremony was the kindling of the Sabbath light. She was invited to share the strange, exotic food; and Sammy mocked her round eyes and open mouth until she blushed redder than the fire she tended.

Singing and praying seemed to go on for most of the Sabbath, as Esther came and went. There was, in fact, little for her to do. The summer was made for the Sabbath, Rachael had said, and it was true. In winter she would have the gaslight to attend to and more coal to bring in, but at this time of year it was still daylight when she let herself out of the house next day, as the Sabbath drew to a close and the Lanskys settled to their final prayers.

The park was grey and deserted, but she always went into it just the same, climbing to the top of the hill to see the lights springing up in the town. It was a big town. Esther could almost hear it breathing, feel it throb. It was the first time she had been part of such a place. She would stand there, looking down, thinking of all that had happened in the last year and all that was to come. 'I'm independent,' she told herself proudly, and actually felt her stature increase. Her sixteenth birthday came and went, but she told no one. Anne sent a card with a loving message and a warning to behave herself in brackets, and Esther treated herself to a new blouse in a lovely mauve paisley cotton.

On Sundays she usually carried her midday meal into the park. Around her children played, much as the children of Belgate played – but here the air was clean, the grass was green under their feet. She watched them splashing at the drinking-fountain and wondered if they knew about the men toiling in the pit, the children playing on the tip. She decided it was unlikely. At Sunday School they would learn to love the children of the Niger and the Yangtse, but no one would mention the children of Belgate.

Esther's principal pleasure on Sundays, however, was thinking ahead to the moment when she would let herself into the silent Valebrooke house again and set about cleaning and polishing to make it a pleasant place for Philip Broderick to live in.

When he returned on Monday night his house was always polished to a nicety; the fire lit, in spite of summer, because it was welcoming; two grilled lamb cutlets in a hotwater dish to keep warm. The first day she had served up peas, and mashed potatoes, and parsnips in butter, and had topped it off with a pink blancmange. 'There now, eat up,' she had wanted to say, as if to a child, but she had held her tongue. Philip Broderick was a man, and a man who paid wages, and she had better remember it.

He had greeted her shyly and then gone upstairs to wash and change from his sober office suit to a velvet jacket with braided lapels. When he returned he sat down at the table, laying his evening paper beside his plate. She realized he was waiting for her to withdraw.

'What about the dishes, sir? And will you be wanting tea?'

He had a nice smile. She watched it start at the side of his mouth and spread. 'This is treat enough, I think, Esther. Time for you to go home, before it gets dark. I can see to everything else myself.'

She had left him in the big chair in the empty dining-room in the quiet house. It was a queer set-up, and no mistake – but he was a gentleman. That morning she had dusted a shelf of books on keeping house. Tomorrow she would cook him something special.

It had taken her a week to plumb Mrs Beeton, and two days to read *Every Woman's Book of Household Management*. Each day her cooking improved. She was just in time: very soon he asked her to prepare a meal for three. 'My brother and his wife will be coming to supper. Don't worry about it. Whatever you cook will be splendid, I'm sure.'

Esther was about to panic until pride came to her rescue. She served three courses: a clear broth, roast pork with apple; and a plum tart with custard. She made sure the table was well-dressed, buying three penn'orth of roses from an allotment she passed on her way to work, and arranging them prettily in a vase. The young Mrs Broderick's look was frosty, and her husband ignored Esther, but they said the meal was 'very nice', and the expression on Philip's face gave Esther all the thanks she needed.

Before she left that evening she lit the plopping gas-jet in the kitchen and washed up the good china – a lovely pattern that Philip called 'Indian Tree'. She wasn't having him skivvy tonight, not in front of that pair, even if it meant her crossing the park in almost complete darkness.

A week later, as she was laying out his meal, she heard voices in the hall. Philip came into the kitchen, his face flushed. 'You have a visitor, Esther. I've shown her into the drawing-room. Run along.'

Frank had brought Anne into Sunderland in a borrowed trap, having union business, and she had seized the chance to find out what Esther was up to. She didn't put it in those words but her meaning was plain: 'I had a job to get the baby minded, but I thought I ought to come.'

'You never said he was a cripple when you mentioned the job,' Anne said, when greetings were over. Her eyes were round as ha'pennies.

'He's not a cripple,' Esther said defensively. 'He's small, and he's not strong, but he's no cripple.' Why, oh why, had she even mentioned Philip in her letter?

Anne nudged Esther with her elbow. 'Any rate, there's no chance of you being led astray with that one, is there? Just as well.' For the first time, Esther noticed how Anne's speech had coarsened since they left the shop. She had grown used to Philip's courteous way of speaking, and to Lansky's measured tones, and Anne's lack of refinement came as a shock.

'Still,' Anne continued, holding out her arms. 'Come and givvus a kiss. It's not your fault if you're skivvying. And I didn't forget your birthday.' She produced a blue silk scarf, not new but one of her own which Esther had always admired. 'It's the best I can do for the time being, but you're welcome.'

Esther kissed her warmly again, and enthused over the gift. 'How's Joseph?' she asked. 'And Frank?' Father and son were both well, and Anne dismissed them in a word or two so that she could get down to really important things.

'How much does he pay you? Does he treat you well? What's your room like? I'm dying to see it.' Esther reassured her on all counts, halving the amount she earned, and seeing that Anne was still suitably impressed. She promised to visit Belgate and lend a hand as soon as she could, and finally saw Anne over the doorstep with relief. 'By the way, how did you find out where this place was?' she asked. 'Frank asked Lansky,' Anne said, turning as she shut the gate. 'Trust a Yid to know everything.'

'It was my sister,' Esther said apologetically when she returned to the dining-room, where Philip had served his own meal. 'And please God she didn't hurt your feelings,' she added under her breath. As she passed the hall table she saw his paper lying there, forgotten. She was about to carry it through to him when she saw a headline halfway down the page. The first son of Mr Howard Brenton and his wife, formerly Miss Diana Carteret, was to be christened in London with the Hon. Loelia Dunane as godmother and Mr Edward Burton and Captain Greville Carteret, a cousin of Mrs Brenton, as godfathers.

Charles Brenton was pleased when his son told him they were all to stay at the Carterets' London house for the christening. It must mean that whatever had been wrong between Howard and his wife had been settled. Diana was an acquisition, a step upward – but any hint of scandal, any suggestion that Howard had not come up to her expectations, would ruin everything. Charles had viewed her flight from the Scar with unease, but if they were all to meet up in London the difficulty must have resolved itself. He was tolerant of Charlotte on the journey to London, and affability itself to Diana's parents.

He drank in every detail of the Carteret house: the delicate De Wint and Harrington watercolours that graced the walls, the Georgian table-silver, and the worn but glorious *famille verte* service. In his own home he had solid Victorian oils and heavy King's Pattern silver. Diana was above gloating, but as she watched her father-in-law's eyes narrow in thought she felt a sense of pride that her own family did things so well.

In the afternoons the men chatted or dozed in the library while the women took part in the tea ceremony. Lady Carteret would ring for the parlourmaid to wheel in a trolley, dripping with Brussels lace and bearing a silver spirit kettle, a walnut caddy of the right Darjeeling blend, thin bread and butter, tiny sandwiches and gingerbread. The kettle was lit by the maid, and a tapering silver douser left for Eleanor to put out the flame. Six minutes to boil, three minutes to brew, a silver strainer over each cup, and Eleanor's face rapt, as though at a shrine.

Charlotte Brenton sat through it all, handsome and impassive, going to any length to avoid using the first person singular, that dreadful egotistical word 'I' that should never pass a lady's lips. 'One feels a certain reluctance to come up to London,' she said one afternoon. 'But one makes an exception for the christening of one's first grandchild.' Diana was longing to say, 'How frightfully good of one,' but her mother's pained expression stilled the words on her lips. Instead, she asked Charlotte for news of Howard's sister, Caroline, marooned in Devon in the final stages of her first pregnancy.

'She's well,' Charlotte conceded. 'Weary, of course, but it will soon be over. And Geoffrey is so good.' Privately, Diana thought Geoffrey the world's greatest bore and was relieved that neither he nor his wife had made the journey to London.

Aloud, she said: 'I wish they could have been here. We must see them later in the year, and compare offspring.'

It was on the eve of the christening that Charles dropped his bombshell: he wanted Diana to look for a house the Brentons could all use when they came to London in future. Diana squealed with delight, and rushed to kiss his cheek. Her own house in London! So this was how he was going to outdo her father: outspend him!

Howard was equally surprised, but he had a different explanation for his father's generosity. Charles, he saw, was trying to mend the cracks in his son's marriage with the only cement he understood: money. If Diana had tired of the Scar they would build her a gilded city cage – anything to keep her.

Diana was disconcerted to find that Howard had asked Max to stand proxy for Edward Burton at the christening. Max entered into the ceremony with gusto, but Diana was uneasy. In vain she told herself that nothing had happened between them. At confirmation classes she had learned that a sin of the mind was no different from a sin of the flesh, and she had sinned with Max in her mind more than once. As she fussed over Rupert's robe, she knew her cheeks were flushed, and she hoped no one would notice. All through the ceremony she was conscious of Max's presence close beside her, and once, when their eyes met, she saw his were amused.

Loelia was resplendent in lilac wool crêpe, a delicious dress from the Mesdemoiselles Lehman in Wigmore Street. Skirts had suddenly dropped again and Loelia's skirt was almost to her ankles. When Diana admired it Loelia told her to visit Wigmore Street without delay: 'Soon simply everyone will hear of them, and their prices will rise.' The dress was cut high at the neck and fell behind in a cowl, and it made even the dumpy Loelia look chic. Diana looked down at her own grey crêpe de Chine, which had seemed perfectly satisfactory a moment before, but now looked dowdy and too short, and she resolved to visit Wigmore Street without delay. She knew she was the better-looking, but Loelia had an awful habit of outstripping her. It was living in London that made the difference.

Rupert slept serenely in the Honiton lace robe that had graced a dozen Carteret christenings, waking in time to receive his godparents' gifts of silver and gold. A large bubble formed on the perfect lips and exploded when he smiled.

'Thank you,' Howard said when he and Diana found themselves alone. 'Thank you for making things go so well today, and for giving me my son.' Diana wavered. It would be so nice to move towards him, to forget all the silliness. And then Charlotte sailed into the room, and the moment passed. Howard smiled at his mother, but inwardly he rued the missed opportunity. The gulf between him and Diana was widening, and he felt less and less able to bridge it. All he could do was behave like a gentleman – and he had a feeling that this inadequate response was not what Diana wanted. She was going to Dalesworth with Loelia for August. When would he see her again?

The next afternoon he went north with his parents, leaving Diana to house hunt. As the train rattled out of King's Cross, Howard brooded on Edward Burton's hint, dropped before Howard left for the christening celebration, that he should join the Conservative Party. Was that where he belonged?

Certainly it was no time to sit on the sidelines. The industries on which Britain's prosperity had been based for a hundred years were now out of touch with world demand. Their owners had dreamed of, and prepared for, a long-term boom after the Armistice, but a Europe in postwar chaos could not afford to buy. *The Times* had stated that British shipbuilders had the capacity to supply the whole of the world's demand, but what hope was there that Britain would succeed in dominating the market, let alone gobbling up all of it? And if the shipyards failed, the steel and engineering industries would suffer, which would in turn reduce the demand for coal. He looked across at his father. Surely Charles, the shrewd businessman, could see the writing on the wall?

But Charles was not thinking of the economic situation as the train sped north. He was giving thanks that he had spent his last night under Sir Neville Carteret's roof. Henceforth there would be a Brenton house when he came to London, and money enough to keep it open all the year round. Let Carteret suck on that! He looked up to find his wife's eyes on him, flat and yellow like amber beads. No point expecting Charlotte to trek to London too often; it would be up to Diana to run the London house. She was a temperamental little thing, and Howard was making a poor show of holding her, but he, Charles, would always be on hand. He reached for a cigar and began to roll it backwards and forwards between his fingers.

Two days later the Carterets also went back to the country, leaving Diana to despatch Rupert to Durham and close up the house. When she came back from Dalesworth she would move in with Loelia at Scotland Gate until she found the right property for the Brentons.

At the station she kissed Rupert fondly and handed him into his first-class compartment. 'Take good care of him, nurse. I'll be coming to Durham soon.' Max, who had driven them to the station, then took Diana's hand and tucked it under his arm.

'There, little mother. Duty done. Now I'm going to cheer you up.'

*

As soon as Anne Maguire's legs would carry her again she went back to her sewing-machine. There was not a lot of work to be had in Belgate. Most women sewed for themselves or did without. She got the odd job of making-over, cutting down adult clothes for children, or letting out or taking in a deceased's wardrobe for the lucky heir.

But Anne also made use of all Diana Brenton's cast-offs, carried to Belgate by Esther when she worked at the Scar. The material made her mouth water: silk and velvet and finest suede. The stitching was fine, the trimmings luxurious, the ease with which Diana had discarded them almost unbelievable. It grieved her to be beholden to the Brentons, but she was not in a position to indulge her pride. If she wanted a nice home and the wherewithal to finance her plans for the future, she must make use of whatever came to hand.

So Diana's curtains and cast-off clothes were unpicked and pressed and cut and sewn into all sorts of new garments and furnishings, to be sold to the women of Belgate for the most that Anne could wring from them.

Now, though, she had even greater reason to stitch until her fingers ached. Her periods had resumed after the birth, but then stopped again. Anne had thought it was just an after-effect of the birth, until the familiar nausea returned. In vain she prayed, and wept, and retreated to the privvy every five minutes to check; she had a terrible feeling that she had fallen with a child again. Frank was an enthusiastic lover, and Anne had a presentiment that she was too fertile for her own good.

She was sitting at the sewing-machine one day when the horror of it all swept over her. They could hardly manage with one child; two would be the end of all her hopes. She put her head down upon the trunk of the machine and wept.

That was how Mary Hardman found her when she came to bring a ham-shank that had been boiled with split peas along with one for her own family. 'You're tired, Anne,' she said, setting Catherine on the settee and putting the covered dish on the table. 'Put that bloody sewing aside, and get a moment's rest.' From his crib in the corner the baby Joseph let out a whimper, as though to add weight to his aunt's argument.

Anne raised a white face in which her dark-ringed eyes looked sunken. 'Rest? There'll be no rest for me in nine months' time.'

Mary Hardman sighed. 'It's that way, is it? Our Frank must've lost his senses.' Her five-year-old son was plucking at her skirt, and she slapped his hand lightly to make him desist. 'How far gone are you?' she asked.

Anne shook her head. 'A few weeks. I don't know exactly. It can't be more.

'No,' Mary said slowly. 'No, I suppose it can't.' She bit her lip for a moment. 'You're sure?'

Anne nodded and Mary made a decision. 'I'll ask Cissie White if she'll fix you up. Not a word to anyone, mind.'

Anne's eyes widened. She knew Cissie White: the woman who laid out the dead and came for confinements if you had no one else. She smelled of gin and unwashed clothes, and had more than a hint of the witch about her. 'What about the priest?' she asked. 'I thought we weren't supposed –'

'What the eye doesn't see, the heart doesn't grieve over,' Mary said firmly. 'Besides we're only talking about a draught. Mebbe you're that way, mebbe you're not; you can't be sure – not dead sure. She'll give you some herbs…' She left it there and Anne straightened up.

'I'm probably not,' she said. 'Still, it can't do any harm.'

'They say the Brenton baby's been christened,' Mary said. 'Up in London, with the world and his wife there.'

Anne put up a hand to wipe her eyes but her mouth bristled in fury. 'And while I'm going through this, Mary, all this trouble – *she's* in London for a fancy christening. *She* won't be worrying about another mouth. Come one, come all for the Brentons – they can afford it. What've I ever done to deserve all this? It isn't me wanted pampering and spoiling till a good man like yours went west! Oh God, I can't bear the unfairness of it. I'll drink poison if I have to, but I'm not going to go down. For God's sake, don't let Frank know. I've got to keep it from him.'

'He'll hear nothing from me,' Mary said. 'Now cheer yourself up while I tell you about Robinson's lass – she's run off with the carter from Houghton, and her man's up in arms.'

Anne had kept her fears to herself, not out of tenderness for Frank's feelings but because she could not bear to acknowledge them to be true. Now she knew she must keep it from him because of his fear of the priest.

That night in bed he held her in his arms and kissed her fondly. She had been strangely subdued while they ate Mary's ham and pease-pudding, with fresh baked bread and taties and turnips fried up with lumps of white ham fat. 'All right?' Frank said, his lips against her hair. He would have kissed her then and moved onto her to love her, but Anne turned on her side.

'Go to sleep, Frank,' she said, and, anxious to please her, he did.

Max Dunane often reflected that for a man who loved women there could be no better time to be alive than now. There was a new mood of freedom abroad. It was fashionable to have affairs, daring to talk about them, and quite permissible to mention sex, formerly the great taboo. There was no longer a need to look for fun in the brothels of Soho or keep a mistress in a quiet London terrace; the girls and young married women of his own class were undergoing a liberation. A blemished reputation no longer meant social ostracism; a love affair no longer produced an unwelcome baby. Women might drink a lot, and smoke too much, and their passion for driving fast was to be deplored, but they were the most tremendous fun.

Max had had a summer dalliance with the elegant Elinor Fairfax, but now that Diana Brenton had made a reappearance his affair with Elinor had palled. He could not make up his mind whether Diana was genuinely naive, or whether she was a tease, and he meant to find out.

One night, soon after her return to London, he took her dining and dancing at the Embassy, and the Prince of Wales was there. Max admired the Prince of Wales for his fashion flair. Last year he had launched the Fair Isle sweater, a brilliant innovation. Tonight his fair hair gleamed, and his evening wear was immaculate.

Max saw the royal eyes flick past Diana and then return to her, and it filled him with pride.

'You don't have to be back for any special time, old girl, do you?' he asked as they circled the floor. Diana felt a quiver that might have been excitement or apprehension. Time for decisions now. She licked her lips and widened her eyes, playing for time. She was living alone in the Carteret house, except for a handful of servants, and she had told them not to wait up. Should she tell Max this? Or should she beg for discretion, and go home to safety? For a moment she weighed the implications, but the decision had really been made before she left the house, in the moment when she had slipped her contraceptive device into her bag. She smiled up at Max, and then laid her hand quite deliberately against his neck.

'No, darling, I'm quite my own mistress – for tonight, at least. But I mustn't be too late and upset the servants.' She was warning him that they must be discreet, that she must be home before morning, and Max understood. The key to Henry's flat in Conduit Street was safe in his waistcoat pocket; he could feel it, hard and unyielding, against his ribs, a constant reminder of joys to come. They sat on in the crowded, noisy nightclub, each unwilling to show too much eagerness, longing for the other to make the first move. Diana felt her own fervour peak, and then wane. Perhaps she should go home after all?

And then Max leaned close to whisper. 'Let's go somewhere quiet for a nightcap, old girl. I've got the key to Henry's place. We'll have it to ourselves.'

Max felt an almost unbearable excitement as they reached Conduit Street. He had waited a long time to possess Diana, and had never quite been sure that she would do it in the end. Besides, there was the added thrill of knowing that Diana was someone else's wife; she was not a paid courtesan, or a woman of blemished reputation. Such women bored him now – they were second-hand goods. But Diana… he had good reason to believe that she had had no other man except for her husband. He, then, would be her first lover, and he meant to make it memorable for them both.

He mixed her a cocktail and took her wrap, and then, discreetly, showed her the bedroom – 'In case you need… anything.' He left her there and poured himself a stiff measure of Henry's brandy.

In the bedroom Diana sat down on the bed and wondered whether or not there was time to change her mind. Did she love Max? Did he love her? If he did, it somehow would make it all right. She got up once or twice, and moved to stare into the dressing-table mirror. Her own face stared back at her, flushed and shadowed, eyes unbelievably large and hectic, drowning out all other features. In the end she went back and sat down on the bed. That was where Max found her when he entered the room, satin slippers neatly together, red-tipped fingers folded in her lap like the well-bred young lady she was.

The coverlet of Henry's bed was a Moorish blanket, dark and exotic. Max stood in front of the bed and held out his hands, until she rose and came into his arms so that he could begin to slip off her straps and ease the red satin dress from her body, to expose the tiny confection of silk and Brussels lace that was the latest thing in underwear, the teddy.

He could feel his own body hardening against her as he struggled to free himself of his clothes. 'You are a sport, Diana,' he said and, too late, realized it was not the right thing to say.

She frowned and drew back a little. 'Put the light off,' she said. But when Max hastened to obey, she seemed suddenly afraid. In the end he lit the bedside lamp, shedding his trousers and underpants as he did so, and then they were together on the bed and he was gently stroking her limbs, her hair, her face… holding himself back in order to excite her the more. And all the while he murmured to her, something she had always longed for Howard to do.

That night, in Henry's small bedroom, hung with mementoes of his Oxford days, Max and Diana became lovers. Afterwards Diana could always summon up a picture of Max's rapt face, the red hair curling like a cherub's and spangled with sweat. And behind him, on the wall, a crossed pair of rowing sculls.

After a long period of caressing her until Diana thought she would die for need of him, Max made love to her as though laying siege to a city, attacking from every angle. Their skins grew sweaty so that they stuck together and had to be torn apart with every change of position. It was the passion Diana had only imagined until now. All the while, Max went on uttering encouragement and appreciation in equal measure. 'Oh yes, yes, yes... darling, darling, darling. That's it. Oh, yes. Good, good, good.'

Diana had enjoyed making love with Howard, but she had never been able to believe he shared her pleasure.

Once, touching him, she had asked, 'Does that please you?' There was silence for a moment and then he had said, 'Yes.' Thereafter neither of them mentioned it again, making love in silence. Or rather she had made love to him. That was it: all the loving had come from her! The thought of how Howard had cheated her made Diana angry, and anger gave way to desire. When Max was ready to desist she was just ready to begin.

'Do you like this?' she asked. 'And this?'

'You *are* a clever girl,' Max said and then fell to loving her again.

Afterwards, when they sat propped up on pillows, Max told her again how good it had been, and how good she had been. At last he put out a finger and traced her mouth. 'I love you,' he said.

Howard had never said those words unless Diana prompted him, and then he would repeat it parrot-fashion, as though to appease a child.

'Was it good for you, too?' Max asked, as he lit two Abdullahs and put one between her lips. Diana drew on the cigarette before she replied.

'Yes.'

'The best ever?'

She was suddenly seized with loyalty to Howard. How could she betray her husband by telling the truth: that never, ever, had he roused her as Max had just done? To avoid answering she leaned to nuzzle her lover's neck and, to her relief, he let it go.

When it was still dark they left the flat and drove back to the Dunane house, dark and silent in the dawn. Max took her hand as they stood on the step and raised it to his lips. 'Soon,' he said, and followed her quietly into the hall.

13

Diana quelled any qualms about the way her life was going by throwing herself into the search for a London house. After all, it was her father-in-law's wish, and her duty to obey. When she telephoned to make sure Rupert was well she didn't mention returning to Durham herself and Howard could not bring himself to raise the matter.

He knew he should have broached the subject. He had not been a coward in war; increasingly he was competent in business. Why could he not deal more forcefully with the emotional side of his life? But he stayed silent on the subject of the chasm that was growing between them.

When Diana telephoned from time to time to report on her house-hunting, they were polite to one another, even friendly. She was solicitous in her enquiries about Rupert, about her parents-in-law, about Howard himself and the running of the house. Such behaviour assuaged her guilt over her adultery, at least for a moment or two. Howard, in his turn, was polite about the house search, about the Dunanes, about anything that allowed him not to address the subject of when his wife was coming home.

By the end of September Diana had found a house in Mount Street at what Howard considered to be an astronomical price. His father winced at the sum, and then agreed to pay it. 'You must go and see it,' Charles growled. 'It can't all be left to a woman.'

So Howard telephoned Diana that evening and announced

his intention of coming to London to inspect her choice. His call came less than an hour after her return from an energetic afternoon of love with Max. She tried to persuade him to delay his visit – 'Just until I'm sure we've got it, then we can really make plans.'

But Howard had made up his mind. 'I'm coming,' he said. 'Expect me the day after tomorrow.'

Loelia's fears for Diana and her brother Max had grown daily as she watched the chemistry between them through a haze of smoke and music at parties and in clubs. She had welcomed Diana to Scotland Gate in the belief that motherhood, if not wifehood, would be an effective bar to anything improper. She saw she had been wrong; and now, when Diana told her that Howard was coming to inspect the Mount Street house, and asked if he could possibly stay in a separate bedroom as she, Diana, had a cold, it did not deceive Loelia for a second. It merely confirmed her worst suspicions.

Dinner on the night of Howard's arrival was a painful experience for them all. Max had pleaded a previous engagement and persuaded Henry to take his place. The men talked about the madness that was afflicting the German mark and the new race for sports cars that had been introduced at Le Mans earlier in the year; Diana went into raptures over Rudolph Valentino's performance in *Blood and Sand*; but tension hung in the air above the *entrecôte* and the *crème brûlée*. Howard tried repeatedly to meet his wife's eye, but she kept the shingled head downbent except for sideways glances at Henry or Loelia.

Diana had not abandoned her marriage. In the schoolgirl recesses of her mind she sometimes pictured a touching reconciliation, a moment when she would renounce both her lover and her evil ways, and be clasped in her husband's forgiving arms.

Looking at him across the dinner-table whenever he was engaged in conversation with the others, she decided that he had always been handsome, but that now there was a new air of resolution about him that made him even more attractive. But she did not now want him in her bed. Some odd Puritan streak forbade it. Later she would show him how she had learned to love, but not now; it would not do.

Howard had raised no objection when his bags were taken to a separate room. He had allowed his clothes to be unpacked and hung up, and had smiled his thanks to the maid who turned down his bed. But he knew where he was sleeping tonight, and it was not alone. On the train from Durham he had decided that he owed it to Rupert to end this nonsense without delay.

He mounted the stairs with Diana and turned away from her on the landing without speaking. In the room allocated to him he paced the floor for a few moments, breathing deeply, trying to convince himself that what he intended to do was wise. At last he began his routine, undressing, laying his things neatly or consigning them to the linen basket, washing, cleaning his teeth and combing and brushing his hair. When at last he was ready he let himself out on to the landing, closing his door quietly behind him, and made his way to his wife's room. He opened the door without knocking and found it in darkness except for the light from the landing. So she had not expected him to come!

In fact, Diana had known he would come since they had parted on the stairs. He had not said goodnight, simply released her arm and turned away. She had contemplated locking her door, but she could not risk a scene on the Dunane landing and, sensing a change in Howard, could not be sure he would not make one. She was listening for his step on the landing as she lay in the darkened room, eyes resolutely closed.

Now, as he closed the door behind him and crossed the room, she feigned sleep. She heard him slip out of his dressing-gown and then turn down the sheet on the other side of the bed. She felt it move as he climbed in, punched the pillows, and lay down. They lay for a while, side by side, each listening to the other's breathing; then Howard put out a hand and laid it on the flat of Diana's belly. She flinched at his touch, and then sat up in the bed.

'I can't, Howard,' she said, her voice small.

He took away his hand and turned towards her. 'I love you, Diana,' he said firmly. 'I don't know how we got into this mess, but I know that I love you.' As he said the words, for the first time of his own accord, he wondered if they were strictly true. But he did regret the mess they now found themselves in. 'I want us to be happy again,' he said. 'I need you. Rupert needs you – needs us to be together.'

But Diana was thinking of Max, who was never solemn or censorious. As Howard reached for her her nerve broke. 'I can't, Howard. Don't ask me – not now. It wouldn't be right.' Her meaning was plain.

After a moment Howard swung from the bed, gathered up his robe, and left Diana to lie, heart pounding, staring into the dark.

At the beginning of December there was another death in the pit, and again the dead man was a friend of Frank Maguire. They had gone down in the same cage on their first descent into the pit, and had drawn lots together on cavilling day for a good place to work. They had even bought twin pocket watches from Lansky with their winnings on the Cesarewitch, though Frank's had long since gone back to the pawnshop. Now there had been a rock slide, the buzzer had blown, and the crakeman had gone round to lay the pit idle for a day. On Gala day there would be a black drape on the banner. Otherwise the man would be forgotten, except by his family.

'There's no consoling Frank,' Anne told Mary. 'Well, you know your own brother: he's got feelings. "I cannat get over it",' he keeps saying. "I cannat get over it".' Anne was noticeably pregnant now, and resigned to it; Cissie White's draught had failed to work.

They sat by her kitchen range peeling apples for sweet mincemeat. There was a good smell of Christmas in the air and for once Anne felt almost content.

'What's going on up at the Scar?' she asked, as they cored and chopped.

'Nothing much,' Mary said. Howard Brenton was unfailingly kind to her, and she was not disposed to tell Anne of what she believed to be his misery.

'Come on!' Anne said derisively. 'Him stuck up here with a bairn, and her on the loose down London. It stands to reason something's wrong.'

'Well, I only wash for him,' Mary said. 'I don't read his mind. He looks all right to me.' She tried to change the subject. 'Is your Esther coming for Christmas?'

Anne was scooping the browning peel into a bowl to go in the hen's mash. Frank had an allotment now, with three good layers in a cree, and root vegetables in rows. 'Yes,' she said. 'If she can tear herself away from the Yids and the cripples, I expect she'll honour us with her presence. Still, she's the only family I've got so I shouldn't grumble.' She winced suddenly and put a hand to her belly. 'My God, this one's a kicker. He's started early, and no mistake.'

'It's a girl,' Mary said. 'I can tell by the way you're carrying.'

'No,' Anne said. 'Girls are trouble. It's a bonny little lad, and we're going to call him Stephen, after your Stephen.'

'That's nice,' Mary said, trying to smile. It would be nice, she told herself later as she made her way back to the Shacks, Catherine toddling beside her. But in her heart she knew it would not be nice at all to have a baby in the world that bore her man's name but was no part of him. She consoled herself with the thought that if ever she had seen anyone ripe with a girl-child it was her sister-in-law: the baby would be a girl, and a right little trouble-maker into the bargain, if its behaviour up to now was anything to go by.

Mary made tea and sat at the table to drink it, watching the clock for John's return from school, smiling occasionally at Catherine as she played contentedly on the mat. She was a good bairn: like her father. Mary waited for the pain to strike at the thought of Stephen, but this time there was only regret. She was coming to terms with her loss. She liked her job at the house at the Scar, where the cook encouraged her to do more varied duties once the washing was out of the way. Howard was benevolent, and Diana the best kind of employer: an absent one. Mary had a bob or two in her purse, and food in the cupboard. She was going to manage, after all.

Life at Scotland Gate came to a standstill one day when Nanny Dunane collapsed. She had finally withdrawn from the last remnants of reality, sitting propped upright in her chair, clawed hands gripping the arms.

'I'm here, Nanny.' Max was a little boy again, frightened for the peace of the nursery if Nanny was not there. 'You must eat, Nanny darling, there's a good girl. Eat up for Max.' Roles were reversed and it was an incongruous sight: a twenty-two-year-old man, dressed in the height of fashion, down on his knees, with a dish of pap in one hand, a spoon in the other.

'How long will it go on?' Loelia asked the specialist. She was pale and composed except for a nervous wrenching at her lawn handkerchief.

'Not much longer. She's immobile, refusing to move, and that will affect her chest. After that it will be quick.'

Max continued the spoon-feeding until Loelia led the specialist away, then he put aside the dish. 'We've got to get her walking, Diana. You heard what he said. If she doesn't move about she'll die.' They supported the old woman between them, head dangling, skinny legs drawn up in protest. For five minutes they walked up and down, sometimes lowering her so that her feet dragged on the carpet. She did not speak, but her head shook from side to side. 'Please, Nanny, please. Do it for me,' Max pleaded.

'It's no good,' Loelia said from the doorway. 'She's made up her mind.'

As Diana left the room she reflected that Nanny Dunane, who had held them all in thrall, now weighed no more than a child.

A week later the old woman was dead. 'I don't know her name,' Loelia wailed. 'I need it for *The Times*. She was always just Nanny, darling Nanny Dunane, but she must have a name of her own.' In the end the announcement went in under the Dunane name. There was no other way.

The Dunanes stood together at the funeral, the Old Medieval for once subdued, Loelia and her mother dry-eyed and expressionless, Max letting tears flow unheeded down his cheeks. It was left to Diana to shepherd them into the cars and give orders for the return journey. 'Janet McLeish. That was it. I had forgotten she had such a pretty name,' Lady Dunane said suddenly from the back of the Delaunay-Belleville, and there was wonder in her tone.

As soon as the funeral was over Diana threw herself into the refurbishment of the Mount Street house. A craze for all things Oriental was growing, inspired by the British Empire Exhibition to be opened at Wembley the following spring. One department store had an Indian pavilion, and other shops were beginning to stock the silks and splendoursdours of the East. Diana considered these things briefly, and then discarded them. She knew what was right for a town house.

She had made a success of the Durham home but at Mount Street she surpassed herself. Acres of grey carpet; white walls with lilac panels; ceilings in pale clover; reeded I:screens to divide some of the rooms; furniture of ebonized wood, thin-limbed and upholstered in grey silk or velvet. She found a cabinet-maker who had studied at Nancy with the great Émile Gallé. He listened while Diana outlined her plans, and then went away to transfer them to paper.

The first bills so alarmed Charles that he made a special trip to London to see for himself. He came away mollified. He would have to pay through the nose, but the Brenton house would be the talk of London.

In the house at the Scar Diana had achieved a feeling of light and space. Here, as winter drew on, in the confined setting of a town house, she achieved elegance. The austerity of Diana's design, so different to the art nouveau that had been the vogue, caused a sensation. People 'dropped in' to criticize and left to sing her praises.

'You're becoming frightfully well-known,' Loelia told her. 'I think you're very clever. I bask in all the praise, and say I gave you your best ideas.' For a moment she had forgotten her disapproval of the affair with Max, and Diana sensed it.

'I do love you, Lee,' she said, flinging her arms about her friend. 'When you marry Henry I shall design you a palace.'

Loelia disentangled herself. 'You'd better make a start then, Di.'

She was blushing and Diana stepped back to look at her more closely.

'What is it?' she said excitedly.

'I didn't mean to tell anyone,' Loelia said. 'Not yet but…' She beamed. 'I can't keep it secret any longer. Henry proposed last night.'

Esther was increasingly happy in her work with Philip Broderick. Her cooking had improved enormously and now she enjoyed surprising him, liked to see him flush with pleasure or smile his quick, crooked smile. He had given her employment, and she was grateful, but it was more than that. He treated her as though she had brains, showing her items from the paper and explaining them if she didn't understand.

He left the daily paper for her each morning, laid out neatly on his breakfast-table. It was strange to see pictures of the bogey-men Frank ranted against, and find out they were ordinary men, without horns. Bonar Law had lied, but Stanley Baldwin was left, and Winston Churchill. With Philip's help she was coming to see that politics were not as simple as Frank and Anne made out.

Soon there would be an election, although Mr Baldwin had only held office for six months. 'He'll go to the country,' Philip told her one day, as she set his meal, 'but he's a great fool to do it with Asquith and Ramsay MacDonald both poised for the kill. Your brother-in-law may get his Labour government, Esther, but it won't have a majority. It will have to combine with one of the other parties, and that won't mean good government.'

In her head Esther knew Philip was right. All the same, someone would have to do something about the sad-faced men on the street corners in Sunderland.

'I can't see the point of any government,' she said diffidently. 'Not if it lets good men go to waste. I see them every day on my way here, standing around with nothing to do.' She wondered if she had said too much, but Philip's face lit up.

'Sit down,' he said as she put out the tureen. 'Let me explain about unemployment...'

One day he lent her a novel by Sir Arthur Conan Doyle.

His mother's name was on the fly-leaf: *Catherine Maude Broderick. 1890.*

'The year I was born,' Philip told her. So he was thirty-three. Esther had never been able to work out his age. She read *The Sign of Four* with relish, and swapped it for another. She had always enjoyed reading, but since her father's death she had never had access to books. 'Borrow what you like,' Philip said, and she carried his books to and from Hendon wrapped in a clean tea-cloth.

She had never known a time of greater contentment. She kept the house nice, no doubt about that, polishing the mahogany till it shone, attacking the grates with Zebra polish and spit, putting flowers in vases, and scrubbing the floors on her hands and knees. Young Mrs Broderick paid surprise visits to run a white-gloved finger along the dado, but she was wasting her time. Her husband, like Philip, worked in the family ship-broking business, but his wife was the one with backbone – and sharp eyes! When she was around Esther never looked at Philip for fear her affection for him should show on her face. If young Mrs Broderick thought Esther was getting above herself, she would be out.

It pleased Esther to keep Philip's house warm and welcoming for him on winter days. As she walked to and from her work she planned what she would give her employer for Christmas. A present and a half, that's what it would be. She could afford it now – in spite of the loss of the week-end florin from Lansky, for she could no longer take money from a friend.

Over the last few months she had learned much about the Jewish faith, and with understanding had come respect. Rachael had explained the *mezuzah*, the tiny ornamental box fixed to every doorway. Inside was a copy of the Sh'ma, the profession of faith, and the name of the Almighty was shown through a tiny peephole. The very pious would kiss it as they passed; most contented themselves with a touch.

Esther loved to see the gesture, as she loved to see Sammy Lansky shawled for prayer. From what Esther could make out, Jewish women were free from ritual, but men must wear a four-cornered fringed shawl called a *tallis*. Very pious men, like Emmanuel Lansky, wore the shawl as an undershirt all day, and each morning men put on *tefillin*, little black leather boxes tied on to their foreheads and left arms. These were another version of the *mezuzah* as far as Esther could see, and even Sammy treated them with respect.

'I'll still come, Mr Lansky,' she told him. 'If it's all right with you. I like coming, so I'll carry on. But I won't take money.' When he held up his hands to argue Esther was ready. 'Sh,' she said, in perfect mimicry of his own tones. 'What's a little help for a friend?'

He had smiled, then, and acknowledged defeat. 'You're growing up, Esther,' he said. 'A woman with a mind of her own, no less.'

She intended to buy gifts for the Lanskys at Christmas, and Rachael, too. It was not their festival, but they would understand that it was hers, and had certain customs just like their own did.

The election took place on 6 December, and its outcome filled Max with fury. 'That fool, Baldwin,' he said, as the results were coming in. 'He had a comfortable majority and he throws it away. For what? Because he wants a mandate from the people for his tariff changes. He's there to lead, not beg the electorate's permission. If he loses – and he damn well might – Asquith and the Liberals will be in there, urging free trade. Or Lloyd George: don't think we've heard the last of him. He won't play second fiddle for ever.'

Tory seats tumbled. Winston Churchill was defeated in West Leicester, and when the final tally was taken the Tories were 100 seats short of an overall majority. 'They won't survive,' Max said. 'Then the King will ask Ramsay MacDonald, that damned Bolshie, to form a government. My God, what's the world coming to?'

He could talk of little else as he took Diana to King's Cross to catch the train for Durham. Howard's letter asking her to come home for Christmas had read like a command, and there was something in Loelia's expression that told Diana it might be wiser to go.

'What will I do?' Max moaned. 'Henry is wrapped up in Lee these days and you're deserting me. It isn't fair!'

Diana consoled him. 'I know, darling,' she said. 'It's too boring. Howard only wants me there to hand out largesse to the Brenton serfs. There's no one so keen on *noblesse oblige* as a son of the middle-class.' It was a beastly thing to say, and she did not need Max's moue of distaste to tell her so.

It was also untrue. Diana knew Howard wanted them to be together as a family. She herself was longing to see Rupert again, and make friends with Howard. It was only beastly sex that stood between them. If only everything were not in such a muddle! She remembered last Christmas, alone with Howard at the Scar. It had been fun, but now they had a houseful of servants and the forbidding figure of the Dragon Nurse would be everywhere. Instead of leaving to take charge of a new confinement, she had opted to stay on with Rupert, and Howard, bereft of his wife, had agreed.

When Max handed Diana into her compartment, with chocolates and flowers, she kissed him urgently. 'I'll miss you,' she said. He stood, bareheaded, to wave her away as she blew him kisses with gloved fingertips.

It was Fox who met her at the station, bearing Howard's apology. On arrival at the house she half-ran from the car, anxious to see her son, and found him being changed by Nurse Booth. Diana's conscience smote her as she watched the bony hands circling Rupert's plump legs. How could she have abandoned her son to those icy fingers for all the months she had stayed away? As soon as the London house was ready she would take him there and care for him herself, for at least part of the day. In the meantime, she would start with bathtime. She girded herself in an apron and set to with a will as Howard returned, full of contrition.

Watching her with Rupert, Howard felt hope stir. Perhaps it would all work out, after all? But the Dragon Nurse was a constant presence, and Diana resented it, especially now that there was no wide-eyed Esther at her beck and call. She took refuge in her room on the pretence of wrapping gifts, leaving Howard hurt at her renewed neglect of their son.

Diana knew that Howard's gift to her would be a sable coat. Charlotte had let it slip, her tone suggesting that sack-cloth and ashes might have been more suitable. Diana was unrepentant: whatever was wrong with her marriage, it was no business of her mother-in-law.

She had brought her gifts from London, something for everyone – even the Dragon Nurse. She had chosen Howard's gifts with care: a black-silk, silver-mounted umbrella from Briggs, and an expensive wireless set. Max was intoxicated with 2LO, broadcasting now from the roof of Marconi House in the Strand, and Diana had been infected with his enthusiasm. There was a second transmitter in Manchester, and Howard should soon be able to pick up a signal, even in the wilds of Durham.

Two days before Christmas Diana's preparations were complete, and she felt excited and happy at the prospect of Christmas morning. That night she and Howard dined alone. Since she had come back to the house at Scar they had mounted the stairs together each night and parted on the landing like polite acquaintances. She preferred not to think what the servants made of it. It was probably the talk of the neighbourhood. Tonight, though, she felt things might be different.

If Howard came to her room – if he came… well, perhaps…! She spent a long time on her appearance and went down to dinner simmering with anticipation. He was her husband, after all, and he had been very patient.

They enjoyed the meal, and afterwards she played the piano for him, the new Gertie Lawrence numbers, and the old songs from the war which he always enjoyed. Watching her, Howard wished that this intimacy could last and deepen.

It was midnight before they went upstairs to the nursery, drawn there by Rupert's soft whimpering. They found the room in total darkness, the fire out, and no nightlight by the cot. Diana switched on the light and ran to pick the baby from his blankets. 'There now, my darling. Mama's here.' As the whimpering subsided she put the baby into Howard's arms, and went in search of Nurse Booth.

When she returned, Howard had never seen her so angry. 'She ordered this, Howard – that fiend, Booth! No fire, no light. Apparently it's good for Rupert; it will make him a man.'

Howard's closer acquaintance with Nurse Booth had destroyed his boyhood illusions, and he did not argue when Diana went on to tell him the Dragon Nurse must go. In the flurry of anger and activity needed to light the fire and the lamp, their rekindled ardour cooled. When their son was settled again, Howard and Diana said goodnight and went their separate ways.

'But I've cancelled my other engagements to be with you,' Nurse Booth wailed the next morning. Diana had cooled down overnight, but she was ready with her argument.

'You're much too experienced to be tied to a toddler, Nurse, and Rupert will not be a baby much longer. It's my duty to let you go, so that you can help others as you've helped me.'

The words were little comfort, but the cheque for a year's salary was balm. Within the hour Nurse Booth had convinced herself of the nobility of her employer's character in letting her go where there was a greater need. It was just what you would expect of a Carteret.

'I must have some help with Rupert, Howard,' Diana said firmly, when the Dragon Nurse was gone. The following day three Belgate girls, all elder daughters of large families, presented themselves for inspection. Diana chose a plump, fair-haired girl called Susan Baharie, and appointed her nursery-maid at four shillings a week. Susan's mouth was gentle, her fingernails clean, and her references said she was very good with children. 'There now,' Diana said, triumphantly. 'That's everything sorted out for the better.'

Philip was to spend Christmas Day with his brother's family. He and Esther exchanged their presents on Christmas Eve, although she had already received Philip's most important gift.

The week before she had decided to have her hair bobbed. When she had gone to Philip Broderick's for the first interview she had wound her long fair hair into a bun and secured it with pins, and since then it had stayed that way. However, it was always coming down and straggling, especially when she was over the wash-tub or the sink. It would have to go. A woman's crowning glory it might be, but Esther had had enough of it.

It would cost a shilling to have it bobbed the first time, and sixpence each time it was trimmed, which seemed outrageous to Esther – although perhaps with time she could learn to do it herself? A Marcel wave was all the rage, but she would die before she parted with £1 lOs.

Telling Philip of her intention, Esther foolishly confided that she could not afford a Marcel wave.

'Are you sure you want to cut off your hair?' he asked her, looking grave.

'Yes,' she said defiantly, and he smiled.

'Then a Marcel wave – is that what you called it? – shall be my gift to you for Christmas.'

Esther had sat in the brown-and-white salon and shivered, half in excitement and half in apprehension. And then they had showed her the finished effect, and she had known it was good. She had bought Philip a fringed silk scarf and embroidered his initials in a corner in satin stitch, and she had bought him a book, too, on the recommendation of the bookshop owner. It was poetry written by a man called Yeats, and the cover was green suede.

When Esther gave them to Philip on Christmas Eve, she thought for a moment that he was going to cry. Instead he reached into a drawer and produced a flat box. 'But I've had my present,' she said, fingering her hair.

'Take it,' he said. 'I bought it for you.'

It was a little silver watch attached to a pin in the shape of a bow. She looked down at him, her eyes shining, and then she pinned it on her lapel. Only afterwards did she realize that it was a long time since she had remembered that Philip was a cripple, and not like other men.

She walked to Belgate on Christmas morning, her feet ringing on the frozen track. The cemetery was already open, and she had brought a holly wreath for her parents' grave. After she placed it, she closed her eyes, remembering. They seemed a lifetime ago, those days at the shop. Esther stood on until cold struck through the soles of her shoes, and then she hurried to Anne's, to be drawn over the step by Frank. He kissed her on the cheek and wished her a fervent 'Merry Christmas', before Anne summoned her to join in the flurry of peeling and coring and basting and stirring.

Anne shook her head mournfully at her sister. 'I think you've spoiled yourself, our Es, cutting off your bonny hair.'

Esther smiled cheerfully. 'I may look a clip, Anne, but it feels a lot lighter.' She could see the sweat beading Anne's brow in the heat of the kitchen, and damping the great weight of hair on her neck, and she felt sympathy for the heavy figure.

'You go and sit down, Anne, and leave everything to me. Mary'll be here directly. We can manage between us.'

Anne subsided gratefully into a chair and Esther set about making Christmas.

Diana and Howard exchanged gifts in Diana's room. He was thrilled with the wireless set. He had already experimented with a crystal set, using earphones and a roof-top aerial, but Diana's gift was the latest six-valve set, with a loudspeaker that reared up like a gramophone horn. He fiddled with it like a child with a new toy, and was rewarded with the distant crackle of a human voice.

The world's changing, Howard thought. But was it changing fast enough? There were sullen faces on the streets; dockers, railwaymen, cotton-workers had all been forced to accept lower wages, although prices had soared in the boom. And nearly two million men were out of work altogether, expected to exist on a pittance. It was all very well for the rich to exult over crackling, disembodied voices. What would the people do, with little or nothing to divert them from their misery? He turned the various dials and tried to look not only pleased but carefree.

'Thank you,' he said to Diana. 'It's a wonderful gift.' She had put the sable coat over her wrapper and was stroking it lovingly. She smiled at him in appreciation. He had long since realized that Max Dunane was Diana's lover, but pride forbade his making an issue of it. He had no great opinion of Max's staying-power: sooner or later Diana would come to her senses, and perhaps her return to London would speed the process? Besides, seeing her here at the Scar, more beautiful than ever, Howard doubted his own self-control – and he would not risk another rebuff. It would be easier when she was gone; and he knew she would go sooner or later.

But for now it was Christmas and the house glowed with the magic of that season. At Diana's request, holly had been brought in from the grounds, and it decked every ledge and balustrade in the place. A tree in the hall was ablaze with lights, and gifts for everyone were piled beneath it. When the Brentons arrived on Christmas Day, Diana stood under the mistletoe and kissed her parents-inlaw warmly.

'Welcome,' she said and led them to where dry sherry was waiting in the long drawing-room.

'I hope you won't be leaving us again,' Charles Brenton said to Diana as they ate their Christmas dinner. But he did not labour the point, and Howard was relieved.

They dined well, and the claret went down with favour. By the time the men carried the port to the library and left the women alone, Charles was in a mellow mood. The real business of the evening could begin.

Howard had been preparing his plans ever since they acquired the London house. It was bad enough to live in splendour above the pit, but to have a fashionable second home while his workforce lived in squalor was more than he could bear. Something must be done about the Shacks, and surely Christmas was a time of goodwill.

As they settled in their deep leather chairs, Charles looked around him. 'She has a way with a place, that wife of yours. The London house is splendid. The place does her credit!' His self-satisfaction was almost tangible.

'Speaking of houses, father...'

Charles heard Howard out in silence as he spoke of the Shacks, the shared privies, the night-soil men removing the filth, above all the lack of a proper water supply. 'We'll have to do something about that slum sooner or later, father. Why not now?'

Charles sat for a moment and Howard felt hope flare. 'I appreciate your concern, my boy. More than that, I respect you for it. But you must try and appreciate the breadth of the problem. The mining industry is in a state of flux – it has been since 1913 – and all the government can do is pour in subsidies and set up another damned commission. Home demand has dropped, and we'll never get the export markets back. The net value of a ton of coal is down to only 15s 11d, as you know. None of us envisaged this. I was more farsighted than most, and I diversified, but some of the other owners are in a bad way. We must stick together, Howard, make no mistake about that. I could spend money on Belgate, but where would that put me with the other owners? Not in their good books! And what about the men? We've had to ask them to take less money in return for more work. I can hear what they'll say if I put money into improvement schemes! "Where's the need for cutbacks?" – that's what they'll say, and they'll have a case.'

Privately Howard doubted that any Belgate man would quibble about the demise of the privy and the open drain, but he did not wish to antagonize his father.

'Nothing is the same now,' Charles mused, through a haze of cigar smoke. 'I expected changes after the Armistice – I was resigned to that – but the whole country seems to be in decline. Old families falling by the wayside and a new aristocracy springing up… all the riff-raff of Europe, and beyond. Even the damned Yankees!'

One by one, he grumbled, the English castles were falling to rich foreign upstarts. Not even noble houses like Barthorpe were safe! Howard couldn't repress a smile at the way his father now classed himself among the aristocracy.

For the next fifteen minutes, before they rejoined the ladies, they discussed with enjoyment the worthlessness of all foreigners, and of Americans in particular.

14

Loelia was to marry Henry on Thursday 24 April in St Margaret's, Westminster, dressed by Worth in white guipure lace, with a retinue of six in eau-de-Nil silk chiffon. After that the happy couple would enjoy a motoring honeymoon in the black and white Rolls-Royce that Henry had recently acquired. Latimer, Henry's chauffeur, would accompany them, as would Loelia's maid, and the journey would take them to Paris and then via the Route des Alpes to Cannes, Genoa, Florence, Venice, Lake Como and Lausanne.

'Exhausting,' Loelia said.

'Heaven,' Diana replied.

She had returned to London in February, but now she had finished the Mount Street house she was increasingly bored with life. She cheered up when Max held a costume party to celebrate his birthday. *Come as your secret self*, the invitation read. Max came as Nero; Loelia was Cleopatra; Diana, in white, was the Madonna. 'I always thought you a virginal creature,' Max teased, but Loelia's eyes narrowed. Diana looked at her friend, so soon to be lost to her in marriage, and resolved to live up to her costume and be good for one night at least. She danced with every man in the room, gave Max a wide berth, and was rewarded with a goodnight kiss from the Queen of the Nile.

It had been a circumspect party, compared with most of the affairs Diana attended with Max. Quite often these took place in sleazy back-street clubs, where they were first scrutinized by a bruiser in evening dress who would ask if they were members. 'Of course,' Max would say grandly and sign the book as William Smith or Robert Brown. As far as Diana could see, the book was filled with Smiths, and Browns, and the odd Jones.

Once inside, there was the regulation moaning of a saxophone, drink in oceans, gambling, and abandoned dancing on the tiny centre floor. It both shocked and fascinated Diana, until such time as she gave herself up to drink. After that, nothing seemed to matter. She would sit with Max, wondering if she were dreaming, as a half-naked *danseuse* took the floor to writhe and twirl erotically until some couples, overcome, took refuge in the curtained booths that lined the walls. Often there would be hysterical laughter; sometimes it was tears; sometimes a man would seize a girl by the waist and hoist her over his shoulder as though she were booty.

Now that Henry had become engaged and respectable, and his flat was out of bounds, Max had hired a dinky little maisonette in Canton Mews, where he and Diana would usually wind up.

Diana did not abandon herself completely, as other women did – even titled women. Anthea Stubbs-Gore, who had been at school with her, had became a platinum blonde and was obsessed with a man called Oscar de Marr, who was reputed to peddle dope. 'That swine,' she told Diana one night, her voice slurred. 'I wish I wasn't so sozzled, Diana. I wish I didn't want him. He's got such a lovely body, though; he can give me thrills. I must have thrills, Diana... Oh God, how bored I am!' De Marr had come then, and pulled her away, and Diana had asked Max to take her home.

Max, too, was more and more careless of convention, seeming to enjoy flaunting their affair. If Diana urged caution, he would become angry. She suspected he was also flirting with drugs, but when she taxed him with it he laughed. 'Of course I'm not, goose. But what if I were? Everyone's doing it now.'

It was true! 'Orgy' was the fashionable word in the new nightclubs, jazzy music a noisy requiem for the old standards. Diana had seen young men and women lying blotto in the gutters of Jermyn Street as dawn broke, and had almost landed there herself once or twice. She didn't like it, but these people were her sort. So she joined in the wild car-chases and the treasure-hunts and the eternal seeking for thrills. If she deserted her friends, what would be left to her? She closed her eyes to the worst excesses, and tried to stifle her irritation with her lover.

Max was preoccupied with style, with the cut of his jacket, the width of his trousers, the fitness of the body beneath. As he alternately preened or peered anxiously in the full-length mirror, Diana remembered Howard's reticence about nudity. She had thought his behaviour prudish; now she thought it might have something to recommend it. But she made a determined effort to close her eyes to Max's egocentricity. It was necessary for her to feel that what she felt for him was love. It was the only way she could retain her self-respect.

The death of his friend in the pit still rankled with Frank. He blamed the agent, Gallagher, for it, and every time he saw Gallagher's arrogant face about the yard his resentment stirred again. One day in April Frank saw his chance. The men paid a penny a shift for the lamps they took underground with them, but the lamps were seldom in good working order. As Frank queued at the lamp cabin he saw one duff lamp after another handed out. It was not only dangerous, it was robbery. If the men paid, they should get a proper return.

At that moment Gallagher was passing by with the overman. Frank stepped forward. He saw the overman's eyes widen, but it was Gallagher he spoke to. 'See these lamps?' The overman would have stopped him but he brushed him aside. 'I'm talking to the engineer, not the oilrag.'

'What do you want, Maguire?' Gallagher asked. A thin white line had appeared, running from his nose to the sides of his mouth.

'I want what I'm owed,' Frank said. 'What we're all owed. We pay for a lamp, a penny a shift – that's more than a pound a year. And these lamps have been used since Adam was a boy. At a penny a day, we've paid for them a dozen times, and still you don't replace them! And men go down the hole with duff lamps...'

Gallagher would have turned away, but Frank, suddenly remembering the horror of the time his lamp had gone out when he was a trapper boy, seized Gallagher by the lapel of his suit. 'Don't turn away from me, you sod!' As he spoke he saw the smile of satisfaction grow on the overman's mouth, and knew he had blundered. Ten minutes later he was walking away from the pit, no longer a Brenton miner.

Anne took the news tight-lipped. Frank thought it was courage; in fact it was anger. If she had given way she would have screamed until her lungs burst: with rage at the Brentons for their power; at Frank for his stupidity; at life for its sheer bloodiness; and most of all at the prospect of having no food to feed her children.

By the next day she had recovered her nerve and had seen a possible solution. Frank would never go down a pit again: a miner who set his lip up to the agent was blacklisted everywhere, from Land's End to John o' Groats. And if there was no job as a collier, there would be no preferment in the union. Besides, the union had proved itself a sorry thing, unable to defend Frank and demand his reinstatement.

If he could not be a collier, then, Frank must be something else. He had no other skills, but Anne did. She could sew; there was money there. She could also run a shop; that would be their salvation.

While Frank went out to grub for coal on the pit-heap – coal he might sell – Anne wrapped Joseph in a shawl and went to the Shacks. She found Mary at the poss-tub, suds flying everywhere, the room draped with washing in various stages of drying.

'That money,' Anne said, without preamble. 'The £200 you got from Brenton when Stephen died. We need it, Mary. Frank'll never go down the pit again; you know that. But if you lend us the money we can open a shop. I should never have let me father's shop go.' Anne did not mention that she had had no choice; this was not a moment for reservations.

'I can't part with what I've got left,' Mary said. 'It's nowhere near £200 now, but I need to keep it by. You know I'd do anything for Frank... but I can't do that.'

Anne was not deterred. 'Please, Mary, please! Think how you'd feel, if your Stephen was still alive and I had money to get him out of the pit. I'd give it to you like a shot.' It was a lie and they both knew it. Anne played a final stroke: 'Think how you'll feel if Frank comes to any harm – when you could've saved him. He'll get into trouble if he's got nothing to do; you know that. We could make a shop pay, Mary. I've always fancied a shop. You'd get your money back in no time.'

Mary was sitting by the fire, her younger child in her arms. She looked down at the sleeping face. Perhaps she should help them out? As it was, the £200 had been nothing but a bloody nuisance!

Anne sensed that Mary was weakening, and there was suppressed excitement in her voice. 'Think it over, and come round later on. Frank'll be back for his dinner. Come round then.'

Mary appeared in Anne's doorway just after Frank had arrived back, dirty, from the Blast where he had gone for coal, instead of the tip.

'Hallo, our Frank. I'm glad you're back,' Mary said.

Frank shrugged out of his jacket and sat down at the table. He never washed until he had eaten, and it was one of the things Anne had against him; but today she held her tongue.

As Frank ate, Anne outlined her plans. They would all be tycoons within the year – if Mary obliged. Frank heard her out, chomping grimly on his food.

'Well, go on,' Anne said at last. 'Tell Mary it'd work.'

Frank laid down his knife and fork. Sweat had run through the grime on his face, causing comic white rivulets on either side of his nose and mouth.

'It well might work,' he said slowly, 'if we did it. Which we'll not. I'm no shopkeeper: a penn'orth of this and a penn'orth of that! I'm a pitman – a collier. Like it or lump it, my girl, that's my road, an' you better all take notice of it.'

Mary felt respect stir within her. Frank meant what he said. Anne, too, recognized finality in her husband's voice. She resented his autocracy, but respected him for it just the same. She folded her hand on her swollen belly and held her peace.

Frank ate his rice with gusto. That'd teach them to make plans for him. He made his own plans. He hadn't sweated thirteen years in the hole to leave it now. One day he would own that mine in the name of the people. When things picked up and coal was needed, the miners would strike – and this time there would be no going back. And when the miners ruled the pit, there would be room in plenty for a man like him. Until that day dawned, they would have to get by one way or another. He could always get coal from the Blast, and there were vegetables in his plot, and chickens, too. He would rustle a sheep before he would see his bairns go hungry; many a one had done it before him. All the same, he would miss the pit – and his mates and the union most of all.

Mary saw the determination in her brother, and knew he would die if he was separated from the hole. He hated and feared it, but he needed it just the same. There was only one way out of the mess, and it was up to her.

Philip was caught in a sudden rainstorm in the middle of April, and in spite of Esther's ministrations the resultant chill went to his chest. 'Don't tell Eleanor,' he begged Esther. He looked like a child lying in the bed, eyes bright with fever, his dark hair tumbling on to his forehead.

'We'll see,' Esther said, smoothing his sheet and plumping his pillows.

She was nearly seventeen now, and conscious of her grown-up state. If Philip's condition worsened she would have to let his brother and sister-in-law know. In the meantime she would respect his wishes. Eleanor, with her tight mouth and permanent expression of disdain, was not exactly a tonic.

Esther stayed with Philip that night, sleeping in the cold spare room, waking instantly if he coughed or even stirred in his sleep. *How much I like him*, she thought, on one of her trips to his bedside. In the lamplight his face was almost handsome, not contorted with pain as it sometimes was when he was awake. His mouth moved as though in a smile, and Esther tiptoed away, hoping that if he was dreaming it was only of pleasant things.

The next day the fever had broken and the doctor pronounced Philip on the mend. Lansky called, and the two men drank the tea Esther carried in and talked about Fascism, which seemed to be their favourite topic of conversation now. A man called Adolf Hitler had been sent to prison in Munich, but Lansky did not think the sentence was heavy enough. Philip was worried about Mussolini, who was fighting an election in Italy and would, according to Philip, soon hold the Italians in the palm of his hand.

'That's enough now,' Esther said firmly when Philip

began to tire. Lansky's teeth gleamed in his beard and he lifted his hands from his knees in a gesture of resignation.

'*Dino d'malkuto dino*,' he said, and Philip laughed.

'What did he say?' Esther asked curiously when Lansky had gone.

'He said you must be obeyed,' Philip answered, eyes twinkling.

'Well, I'm sure...' Esther said, not knowing quite what to say. But Philip suddenly caught hold of her arm.

'Oh, Esther,' he said, 'when the time comes that you must leave me, whatever will I do?' And then, as if he regretted his words he reached for the book that lay on his bedside table. 'I came across this this morning, when you were downstairs. In the eighteenth century, when tulip mania was at its height, there was a sultan in Istanbul who filled the gardens of his *seraglio* – the place where he kept the women he loved – with tulips, in every colour of the rainbow. And at night, in case the women missed the splendour of the day, he put tortoises among the tulips, each with a lighted candle strapped to its shell, so that the light would illuminate the tulips and give pleasure to his consorts.'

'That's lovely!' Esther said.

Philip nodded. 'To have such imagination... I envy him. He hid trinkets there, too, and the women would search for them among the flowers by candlelight – or moonlight, if there was a moon.'

He told her more of the harem, of beautiful women wearing the *yashmak*, tempting the sultan with exotic sweetmeats while fountains played like music in the back-ground. And Esther drank it in, wide-eyed, and took the book home to read in her lodgings far into the night.

A week later Philip was well enough to go back to his office. The following day, when Esther let herself into the gloomy house, she found the kitchen table filled with tulips, surrounding, in the centre, a single candle burning in a jar.

*

Mary Hardman had made up her mind to speak to Howard Brenton about Frank's dismissal from the pit. She waited in the back kitchen, where she laundered the clothes, until she heard his car sweep over the gravel to the front door, and then she tidied her hair in the cracked kitchen mirror, laid her apron over the back of a chair, and made her way upstairs.

If Mary had met the housekeeper she would have been cross-questioned, and she was ready to stand her ground, but no one interrupted her. When she knocked on the door of the morning-room where Howard usually sat, she heard him call, 'Come in.' He looked surprised to see Mary, but not displeased.

'What can I do for you, Mrs Hardman? It's not your children, I hope?'

'No, sir.' Mary had meant to lead up to it gently, but the words came tumbling out. 'It's not my bairns; it's my brother, Frank Maguire. He's one of your workers, Mr Howard. A good worker. He's a hewer now… well, he was. The thing is, he's fallen foul of Mr Gallagher, and he's been dismissed. And you know as well as me that he won't get work at any other pit, and he's got a bairn, and another one –'

Howard held up a hand. 'Wait. Tell me: why was he dismissed?'

Mary decided not to mention that it had been for gross misconduct: laying hands on the agent.

'It was over the lamps,' she said. 'Frank says if the men pay to use them, they should get good lamps, but mostly they're scabby and –'Again Howard interrupted.

'But they don't pay, Mrs Hardman. Lamps are provided by the company: they're tools of the trade.'

'They *do* pay, Mr Howard: a penny a shift. It's in the conditions. Every man signs for it when you set him on.'

Howard frowned and looked at Mary for a moment.

'Your brother worked at Belgate, not the Dorothea?'

'Yes,' Mary said. 'Since he was thirteen.'

'I'll speak to Mr Gallagher,' Howard said. 'I'm going to London tomorrow, but before I go I'll make it my business to find out what has happened. I think there's been some misunderstanding, but if your brother has been unfairly treated you can rest assured that I'll put matters right.'

Howard summoned Gallagher to him the next morning. 'Maguire,' he said. 'Frank Maguire. You sacked him. Why?'

'Because he assaulted me,' Gallagher said hotly. 'He seized my lapels in his usual belligerent fashion. I hope you're not suggesting I should have let that go?'

'Why did he do it?' Howard asked.

Gallagher shrugged. 'Some petty grievance. Men like Maguire don't need excuses to misbehave.'

'It was over a lamp,' Howard said. 'That much I know. Now tell me why he was aggrieved – and don't make me have to drag it out of you, word by word.'

'He was grumbling over the state of the lamps,' Gallagher said. 'You know the wear and tear of the pit. He seemed to think we should provide brand-new lamps for each trip down.'

'But we do *provide* the lamps?' Howard asked. 'The men don't pay to use them?'

He saw Gallagher's eyes flicker. 'Of course we provide them,' he said, buttoning his jacket. Howard had seen that gesture before. It meant unease.

'Do they pay for the use of the lamps? Yes or no?'

'They pay a nominal sum, a penny a shift. It's a token, that's all. The revenue from –'

'Be quiet,' Howard said. 'By what right do you charge them for something so essential?'

Gallagher left off toying with his jacket and squared his shoulders. 'By authority of the conditions of service drawn up by your father, sir.' He turned on his heel and went into his office next door, returning with a paper which he handed to Howard. Howard looked down at it and read it to the end before he replied.

Conditions of Service between the Brenton Collieries Ltd and Workpersons employed by them, it said at the head. The first clause demanded eleven days' work in each fortnight; the second demanded and promised fourteen days' notice except in cases of misconduct; but that right was taken away by clause 3 if a collier was ill or injured. The fourth and fifth clauses made a collier responsible for loss of, or damage to, tools; but it was the sixth clause that concerned lamps. Every collier would be supplied with a lamp, and for this he would pay one penny per shift – by Order of Brenton Collieries Ltd.

Howard looked up at Gallagher. 'Who drew up this – this *thing*?'

'I did, with Mr Brenton's full approval. It has been in force for long enough without trouble, and but for that hothead Maguire –'

Howard tore the paper into strips and then again. 'Destroy the rest of these.' He looked down at his desk, struggling to maintain his composure. 'I will draw up new and equitable terms of service.' It seemed to him that Gallagher's lip lifted, and Howard looked down, afraid now of what he might do if he let himself go.

'I want Maguire reinstated,' he said, when at last he could look up. 'Fine him, or punish him for laying hands on you how you will: as long as it's fair. But I want him back in the pit today. And the levy for lamps is to be dropped as of now. I will speak to my father today, and tell him what I've done. And when I come back from London I will inspect the stock of the lamp cabin. I hope I will find it in good order. That's all.'

*

Howard went down to Exeter from Durham. He had not yet seen his sister Caroline's baby daughter, and it troubled him. He was not close to his sister, but blood was blood.

Caroline was as quiet and passive as ever, her husband full of the Tories and the wicked Labour threat. Was Geoffrey really his kith and kin? Did he, Howard, belong in a party whose members believed in a Divine inequality? He kissed his sister, pronounced his niece adorable, and then drove on to Mount Street to see his wife for the first time in eleven weeks.

He found Diana more beautiful than ever, her hair in soft waves now, from a side parting, a jumper in pale georgette under her tailored suit, her skirt discreetly covering her knees. As she reached to kiss Howard on the cheek, he smelled expensive perfume and something more: a whiff of alcohol.

'You look well,' he said carefully. In fact he thought Diana looked tired. There were lines of strain about her mouth, and shadows beneath her eyes.

'I'm very well,' she said firmly as if daring anyone to contradict her. Rupert had been installed at the house in London for a month, with Susan in attendance. Now Howard went upstairs to be reunited with his son. 'He remembers me,' he said joyfully when Rupert smiled, and saw a look of remorse on his wife's face as he held his son against his cheek.

'Of course he remembers you,' Diana said. 'He's a big boy, now, and very smart for his age.'

That night they went to see a Noël Coward revue, just the two of them because everyone at Scotland Gate was caught up in a fever of wedding-eve excitement. It was two days to Loelia's wedding to Henry, and the following evening Howard must join the groom-to-be and his friends in one last evening of freedom.

'You don't mind, do you?' Diana asked. 'They invited you, and I didn't like to say no.' Howard knew that Max would be there, and that Diana was afraid he might object. She knew he had realized she and Max were lovers. Half of her wanted him to knock Max down; the other half could not have borne a scene.

'Of course not,' Howard said. 'I expect they could do with an old married man there to curb their excesses.'

Diana was oddly hurt by his calm acceptance of her adultery: he must care for her not at all, she thought, if he could be so controlled. Inwardly Howard seethed, but pride would not let him show it.

On the way home from the theatre they talked about the British Empire Exhibition, due to be opened at Wembley the following day by the King.

'It might be fun to go,' Diana said. 'And we have invitations.' So the next morning they joined the crowds in the stadium to hear the King perform the opening ceremony, which was being broadcast on the wireless to the six million people who now owned receivers.

The exhibition had cost almost £10 million, and although the Empire itself might be in a ferment of tension the organizers had clung to their Kiplingesque illusions. An imitation Taj Mahal out-glittered the real one; there were Burmese dancing girls and Ashanti war drums; even the Prince of Wales himself, cast in best-quality Canadian butter.

Howard smiled at the full-scale coalmine, complete with 'real coal', but Diana was fascinated by Pears' Palace of Beauty where the ten loveliest women of all time were on display – from Helen of Troy to Miss 1924 (as portrayed by Miss Mimi Jordan). Pears soap was on offer at $4^1/_2$d and 7d a tablet, unscented (scented, from one shilling); and the models portraying the ten lovelies looked as though they had used nothing but Pears soap all their lives.

There was a huge funfair too, although Howard and Diana shirked it, and dance-halls where popular music was played, and the new Exhibition song, 'Wembling at Wembley with you'. But in spite of the laughter and the loud music and the vulgarity and the cheerful faces everywhere, and the sheer commercialism of the whole vast extravaganza, it was the scale of the Empire, from the mystic East to the frozen north, that caught the imagination.

As the massed bands of the Brigade of Guards played 'Heart of Oak', and the songs of the war, Howard felt his patriotism, which he had long thought dead, stir once more. There was something noble about a commonwealth of nations. Perhaps he should do as Edward Burton suggested, after all, and join the Conservative Party officially.

'We must visit the exhibition again,' Diana said, impulsively, taking Howard's arm. 'Don't rush back to Durham too soon. There are so many things I want to show you.'

That night she accompanied him to Scotland Gate, and watched him greet Max with dignity and no apparent resentment. *I admire him*, Diana thought. *And I think I could love him; perhaps I already do*.

She kept Loelia company that evening until ten o'clock. They sat on Loelia's bed to choose Diana's new writing paper. It was a weighty problem. Scented paper was damning; mauve not at all good; deckle edges seedy; and if the address was framed in inverted commas the writer was not to be cultivated. They settled on a thick speckled paper in greenish-grey, with the Mount Street address diestamped in charcoal. 'It will do,' Diana said, flopping back onto the pillows. 'I suppose it will do.'

She was driven home to the Brenton house in the Dunanes' car. Loelia came on to the doorstep to kiss her. 'See you in church,' Diana said, but Loelia gripped her by the arms and spoke seriously.

'Is it all right being married, Di?'

'Of course,' Diana said cheerfully, but Loelia shook her head.

'No, seriously, Di – while I still have time: have you ever had regrets?'

What could Diana say except, 'No, not ever'? But Loelia needed more. 'I'm not the best person to ask, Lee,' Diana said uncomfortably. 'I don't think I was meant to be a wife. But it's all right – nothing to be afraid of.' Had Loelia and Henry made love yet? Diana looked into her friend's face and concluded that they had not. 'Truly,' she said, embracing her lovingly. 'Love with the man of your choice is heaven, you'll see. No regrets.'

She stepped into the limousine and waved to Loelia, trying to remember which of the many regrets that she had had in the last two years could be directly attributed to her marriage.

When Diana was ready for bed she left a light on in Howard's room and set the connecting door ajar. When he came home he was sure to come into her room, just to say goodnight. Did she want him to stay? She wondered, while the far-off tones of Big Ben marked the hours. She rather thought she did. Howard came in just after three and she lay tense, waiting to see him silhouetted in the doorway. She heard him put his cuff-links and change on his dressing chest; go to his bathroom; return to his room and wind his bedside clock. The next minute the lamp went out, and she heard his bed creak. For a little while she wondered if she should go to him; then she turned on her side, and tried to think instead of tomorrow, and how Loelia would look as she walked down the aisle.

Gallagher had summoned Frank and told him he had reconsidered: Frank would lose a week's wages, and be on night-shift for three months. No mention was made of Howard's intervention, and as Mary had not told her brother of her appeal Frank thought that Gallagher had simply changed his mind.

'See,' he told Anne, 'I'm too good a worker to lose.' Anne filled his snap-tin, trying not to cry with relief as she did so.

When he left the house she sank to her knees in front of the Crucifix. In desperation, the day before, she had asked the slumped figure of Christ to feed her children. As usual, her plea had been answered within a day. As Frank went back to crawl on all fours through a low seam, Anne, too, prostrated herself: first, to give thanks, and then to ask for Divine retribution on the coal-owners and all their kind.

The following morning Loelia Dunane became Loelia Colville, in a church filled with arum lilies, imported from France like the gowns of the fashionable ladies who thronged the pews.

Loelia looked splendid in her white guipure lace with a tulip skirt and a veil of Honiton lace. The bridesmaids, in eau-de-Nil chiffon, wore head-dresses of crystal and sea-green organza to match their satin slippers. Henry's beam of joy threatened to split his face, and Diana wept with emotion, until Howard had to lend her his handkerchief. It reminded her of her own wedding and the clear view she had then had of the future. Nothing had turned out as she had hoped. She glanced up at Howard, who was gazing resolutely towards the altar. *I don't know him*, Diana thought. *I know him no better now than I did on the day we married.*

The O.M. smelled strongly of camphor, and Loelia swore afterwards that when asked if he was giving her to Henry in marriage, he had replied '*Rather*,' in tones of utter joy.

It was a jolly wedding, awash with Champagne and lobster, ending in a grand evening reception at Scotland Gate after the bride and groom had left for Dover.

As the music lulled them in the dance, Diana and Howard moved closer together. Diana was waiting for him to ask her to come back to Durham with him, but all he said was that the band was better than most. In the end, mad to stimulate a reaction of any sort, Diana began to make eye-signals to Max to rescue her from her husband's clutches.

He moved through the dancers to claim her. 'Do you mind?' he asked Howard – and Howard, never taking his eyes from his wife's face, said, 'No. I don't mind at all.' It was true. Suddenly he felt only a profound distaste for the woman who was his wife, pouting now as though abhorring his words.

It was, Diana thought afterwards, the most final thing she had ever heard Howard say. He did not want her. If Max did, he was welcome to her. That night, when they mounted the stairs at Mount Street, she held out her hand.

'Goodnight, Howard. I expect you'll be gone before I wake up. Do telephone and let me know you've arrived home safely. And give my regards to your mama and papa. I hope I'll see them at Mount Street soon.'

He bent to kiss her cheek, the kiss of a distant relative. 'Sleep well,' he said. 'Take care of Rupert... and yourself, of course.'

A moment later their doors closed and neither of them gave the connecting door even a second glance.

While Howard and Diana went their separate ways, Anne Maguire was trying to ignore the pains that were gripping her. 'It'll be colic,' Mary Hardman said. 'You've got three weeks to go yet.' But it was not colic. She mounted the stairs with Mary and gave premature birth once more, this time quietly and with the minimum of noise.

Frank sat by the fire in the downstairs room while his wife laboured in the bedroom above. His son and Mary's children played on the floor with one of Anne's precious fairings, taken down from the mantelpiece to keep them quiet. He wondered if he should explain to them what was going on but decided against it. Explaining such things was women's work.

When Mary came down to tell him he had a daughter, small but sturdy, Frank was relieved. It was over, and soon Anne could take back the reins of the family. He kissed her clumsily when he went upstairs, and patted her hands, clammy with effort. It was, he pronounced, a fine bairn. 'No need to fetch the doctor till tomorrow,' Mary said. 'They're both doing well.'

Ten minutes later Frank was on his way to the Half Moon to celebrate the birth, leaving Anne in Mary's charge. He had a week's pay in his pocket, for in the flurry Anne had forgotten to relieve him of it. It had been a short week, and his pay was thin. He separated the two sovereigns and put them in the pocket of his waistcoat. The seven shillings that remained were his to do with as he pleased. He was a hewer now, an aristocrat of the pit, and entitled to his spends.

As he received the congratulations of his friends, Frank's satisfaction grew. He could father bairns, no doubt about that: two in a twelve-month and both healthy. He grinned at the sly digs. 'God help your lass,' they said, winking. 'She's got a handful with you.' It was true. Many a man stood head and shoulders above Frank in the pit, but none were so well-endowed. He flexed his shoulders beneath the rough grey-flannel shirt and called for more ale all round. It wasn't every night a man had a child, and there was nothing to go home for with Anne lying-in and the house full of women. 'Set up the drinks again,' he said. 'It isn't a birthing every day.'

When at last Frank reeled home, he saw the Brenton Daimler driving towards the Scar. It went by him in a rush so that the gobbet of phlegm he spat at it missed the car by a mile. 'Never mind,' he told himself, as he hitched up his trousers and made for home. 'The pits will be ours one day – and then we'll see who has the motor-car.'

BOOK TWO

1929

15

Esther turned in through the cemetery gates, shifting the pinks she carried to her other arm. It was a few weeks since her last visit, so she expected to see the grave overgrown. It was June, and along the road to Belgate the grass had been lush and green, spangled with purple vetch and yarrow and red campion.

She cleared the weeds, slotted the pinks into the jar, and stood for a moment, remembering; then she set off for Anne's house. It was Durham Big Meeting, and she had promised to look after Anne's children, all four of them,while Anne accompanied Frank on his march in with theBelgate banner.

'It's the only day out I get, Esther. I'll go if I drop,' Annehad said last week. So Esther would look after Joseph, Estelle, Philomena, and the baby Gerard, until Anne and Frank arrived back, full of booze and comradeship and political fervour. Anne was red-hot for socialism now, and, as Mary Hardman had said more than once, more Catholic than the Pope.

She was trying to get ready when Esther arrived, shoving the luckless Joseph into a corner. 'Get over there, out of my way,' she said. 'And as for you…' She took the back of her hand across Estelle's ear. The child winced, but betrayed no other emotion, and Esther's heart sank. Estelle was a handful and no mistake. 'Move over, Philomena,'Anne said to the three-year-old, and 'Sit still, pet,' to the baby, Gerard.

Anne's children descended in the pecking order as they grew older. Gerard, being the baby, would be king of the heap until a newer and more helpless infant succeeded him – and then he would have to watch out.

'Are you sure you want to go, Anne?' Esther said, looking anxiously at her sister's flushed face. 'Why not stop home with me?'

Anne shook her head. 'I'm going. I'm getting a lift in a trap, but I'm coming back after the speeches. That's the important part.'

Frank handed Anne into the trap when they were ready, and went to his place at the head of the column. Keir Hardie's picture was emblazoned on the banner, with small portraits of Lenin and Ramsay Mac as supporters. *All for One* it said, and a length of black crêpe festooned the right-hand support in memory of two men dead in the pit that year. Frank, looking at it, was saddened, but Anne was angered by it rather than dismayed. Each death in the pit was a casualty of the class war, to be avenged when the time was ripe.

She folded her hands in her lap now, and looked to left and right as they went. She was Frank Maguire's wife, after all, and he was someone in the union. People regarded her with respect, which was no more than her due. As the trap jolted uncomfortably on the road, she reminded herself that she could not have let Frank loose on his own on Gala day. Better men than him had strayed, and the streets of Durham would be full of hussies today. Still, he was a good man – never complaining and working till he dropped.

Marching ahead of her, Frank felt his spirits rise as the miles passed and the column came in sight of the tower of Durham cathedral. He was walking into the city to the music of silver and brass, to add his banner to the field.

From the first time he had gone to the Big Meeting, astride his father's shoulder, it had been the high spot of his year. But this year, 1929, he was looking forward to it more than ever. He was a union man now, with a task to perform. No longer was this simply a day out: a chance to booze and guzzle and make love along the river bank. Now it was a platform, a chance for the miner to hear leading politicians and, more important, to let them know the feeling of the coalfield.

Today Durham belonged to the miner, and other, lesser, citizens had better step aside. Never mind that the miners' Sunday best had been redeemed from the pawnshops, and would go back there in the morn; for a few hours cares would recede. He could get as drunk as a fiddler's bitch today, and no one would say him nay, not even Anne. He helped to plant the swaying banner, lifted Anne down from the trap, and they went in search of ale and hot mutton pies from the basket-women clustering like flies along the narrow streets.

In Belgate Esther sat quietly in the deserted kitchen. Outside, the children played, Estelle's voice loudest of all. She was five years old and already the boss. Suddenly, there was a crack, and then a cry. When Esther went to the door she saw Joseph struggling to hold back his tears. His knee was bleeding and a paling of the fence was snapped away.

'You'll get murdered, our Joseph! Me mam's told you about climbing,' Estelle said. Her blue eyes were bright with satisfaction, her mouth pursed above the determined chin and the blue-and-white gingham pinafore.

Philomena was only three but already she had the pale, smooth face of a martyred saint. 'Naughty,' she said sanctimoniously.

'That's enough, you two,' Esther said, scooping Joseph up in her arms. 'If you can't say something kind, say nothing.' She carried Joseph into the kitchen and set him down on the table. He was stoic as she washed the knee, his eyes already brightening at the prospect of a reward for bravery.

Esther sorted through the cupboard: arnica, camphorated oil, eucalyptus, and three jars of homemade raspberry vinegar ready for winter coughs, but nothing to disinfect a wound. 'There's some knitbone outside,' Joseph said helpfully. 'Me mam always puts knitbone on when I fall down.' Just then Esther found iodine, and he squeezed his eyes shut and his hands together to take away the sting.

When the knee was cleaned, Esther took a white paper poke of ju-jubes from her bag. 'Share them out, and you can have one extra for being a big lad.' Joseph's face was as open as Philomena's was closed. He would get hurt as he grew, but Esther preferred him to the girls. God forbid she should ever show her partiality, but it was there just the same.

She looked around the cluttered kitchen, contrasting it with the order and comfort of her own home. She had a flat in a nice street now: it cost 12s 6d a week, but it had a patch of garden and a window looking out into a spreading sycamore. It was her pride and joy. Once Anne had been a meticulous housekeeper, but her standards had dropped with the years and the increased size of her family. There was dust on the mantelshelf with its mountain of Catholic bric-à-brac, crosses and statuettes and prayer-cards of every conceivable shape and size. 'Still,' Esther thought, seeing the well-used sewing machine, 'at least she makes ends meet.'

The alcove at the side of the range had been clumsily shelved, and was stacked with books, all of a political nature, and well-thumbed newspapers. Anne was as militant as Frank these days, and even keener on revolution.

Now that the voting age for women had been lowered to twenty-one, Esther was more interested to know about the political scene than she had been. She had studied the candidates standing in Sunderland in last month's general election, and had voted Liberal; but Anne had actively campaigned for the Labour candidate, and had cried tears of rage and frustration when the result was a stalemate.

Esther looked from the bookshelves to the kitchen range. It was a week or two since that had seen black lead, and the clippy mat gave off a cloud of dust when she stirred it with the toe of her shoe. The rest of the floor was stained and dirty, and littered with crumbs. She thought of her own Axminster: she had run her new carpet-sweeper over it before she left, but only to bring up the pile. She was seized with a sudden sense of her own good fortune to be earning twenty-eight shillings and sixpence a week, and of her sister's burden; it lasted until she had put on the kettle for hot water, found a bucket and brush and a ticking apron, and rolled up her sleeves.

The room was sparkling and the children washed and ready for bed when Anne came back, descending clumsily from the trap. 'Eeh, I'm whacked,' she said, subsiding into a chair. 'It's been a grand day, but I'm exhausted.' Her hair was dishevelled and there were bright spots of colour in her cheeks. As Esther poured her a cup of tea, she wondered how long it would be before Frank returned. He was probably laid out in a Durham gutter by now.

As if she read Esther's thoughts, Anne sighed. 'By, there's been some drink got through today, and no mistake. I wouldn't like Frank's head the morn, but there's no telling him.'

The children had been waiting quietly for their treats, but patience was wearing thin. Joseph gave a small, hinting cough. A smile flickered on Anne's face. 'That's a bad cough you've got, our Joseph,' she said. 'Ask Aunt Esther to give you some raspberry vinegar.'

The child's expectant smile did not waver. He knew the game. Estelle was made of sterner stuff. 'I want sweeties,' she said, advancing on her mother.

Anne pushed her away. 'I want never gets, miss,' she said tartly, but she gave her a thin wooden box of Turkish delight just the same, and dished out three more to the others. In a moment they were covered in sticky white icing-sugar.

'That's nice,' Anne said, when the children were settled and the women could sit to their tea. Her face lit up suddenly. 'By, they had a right carry-on before the speeches. You know Pease?'

Esther nodded. She knew Pease, the coal-owner Frank hated even more than old man Brenton. A few years ago the price of coal had plummeted, but the men had been in no mood to sympathize with the owners when they demanded more work for less pay. Pease had put match to tinder: 'I cannot see why they object so much to working an extra half-hour when they have nothing particular to do with their time.'

'Well,' Anne said, slurping her tea in her haste to tell her story, 'this man came along, all dressed up in his spats, and one of the lads says, "There's Pease!" and someone else says, "Let's duck the bugger!" Frank says they never laid a finger on him, but the man was that frightened he went backwards, head over tip into the river.'

Esther's eyes widened. 'Then what happened?'

Anne chuckled. 'Someone with a boat pulled him out. But the thing is, it wasn't Pease after all!' Tears of mirth were springing up in her eyes at the recollection. 'And someone says, "Never mind, the bugger needed a wash anyway".'

Esther grinned. 'It's a pity it wasn't Pease.' She leaned back in her chair. 'I'm worn out, Anne. I don't know how you manage day after day.' In truth the children had not tired her, but she wanted an excuse to get back to Philip, and she couldn't tell the truth to Anne.

'You've tidied up,' Anne said, looking round. Esther had not expected gratitude, and there was none forthcoming. 'I hope I can find everything!' She looked at the children. 'Time to get washed for bed,' she said, and proceeded to drag a flannel wrung out in soapy water across sticky mouths.

Esther watched while Anne dosed them with Gregory powder on the grounds that they looked pasty, and then smacked them for crying at its foul taste. Before she left, she took Joseph between her knees and smoothed the fair hair from his eyes. 'Next time I come I'll bring you a slate, our Joseph. And some chalks, all ready for school.'

Estelle was nothing if not her mother's daughter. 'And don't forget me, Aunt Es – I'm a good girl, too!'

Esther gave Joseph and Estelle a shilling each, and left two others on the mantelpiece for Philomena and the baby. 'Not such a baby now,' she said, looking down at the lively face.

'He's a handful,' Anne said darkly.

Esther shook her head. Already the baby was slipping from grace: Anne was broody again.

Outside in the street children were kicking a pig's bladder, blown up and tied at the ends – no gaily coloured balls for Belgate children. The boys wore cast-off caps on their heads; the girls tottered in their mothers' high-heeled shoes... anything to hasten the process of growing up. *And for what?* wondered Esther. The boys would be pit-fodder, and the girls would cook and wash and put a black cat briefly into the oven for luck on cavilling day. Thank God she was out of it.

The revellers were returning in twos and threes, some of them with children astride their shoulders. One man, alone, had paper streamers around his neck, and the belt of his trousers was gone so that he had to hold them up by hand. He was addressing a street lamp, practising excuses ready for homecoming. 'I never meant it, pet,' he said, pleading. 'Don't get yer rag out now, while I tell you what happened.' He held out his hands in supplication and his trousers fell about his ankles. He scooped them up and began again. 'I've had a canny drink, I'm not denying it, but it's only once a year.' When Esther passed him his trousers were round his ankles once more, his long white galluses bagging around his knees, the explanations flowing from his lips.

Esther wiped away tears of laughter, and schooled her face for fear of hurting his feelings, but she needn't have bothered. He was oblivious of passers-by, lost in his own private world of explanation.

Esther looked at the house up on the Scar as she passed. She had been happy there, and watching Lady Diana had been fascinating; but if all the stories she heard were true, it was not a happy house now, with its mistress away in London and its master living alone like a monk. She remembered Howard Brenton the night his son was born, pouring Champagne for everyone like a man lit up. It was a funny world, and no mistake. He was a good man, and deserved better than a lonely life. Esther quickened her pace, anxious to get back to Philip. She knew she was indispensable to him now, and it was a good feeling.

Today was a Saturday and he would not be expecting her. She pictured herself, slipping quietly into the house, blazing up the range, lighting the gas-jets, sending the cooking smells along the hall to signal her presence.

His study door would open then. 'Esther?' he would say in that shy voice of his. 'Esther? Is that you? You shouldn't have come.' But he would be pleased. He was always pleased to see her, showing it in a thousand acts of kindness, even if he was sparing with words.

She had covered four of the five miles to Sunderland now, and her thoughts turned to her only worry: the problem of Sammy Lansky. She loved and respected Emmanuel Lansky, and she hesitated to cross him, but she could not agree with his attitude to his son. Sammy was now eighteen, and a man – in spite of Rachael's efforts to keep him a baby. Like every pious Jew, Emmanuel's ambition was for his son to become a scholar, an expert on the Talmud. Sammy had other ideas.

'Twenty years, Esther, twenty *years* it takes even to begin to understand. I should live so long! Me in a yeshiva? Fat chance! I'm a trader, I want to buy and sell. My father does it, so why not me?' Each year Sammy went to Paris, to see his maternal grandparents. 'One day I won't come back, Esther,' he had told her, darkly. 'I'll stay there, and make my way.'

Esther had carried this conversation to Rachael. 'Why won't Mr Lansky let the boy have his head, Rachael? Sammy is a man now. He needs his chance.'

The old woman's eyes had filled with tears. 'Don't blame Emmanuel, Esther. He loved his Cecelie so much. When she died and the baby lived, I fell on my knees to pray he would take to the boy and not reject him. For seven days and nights he mourned, and then he asked to see the baby. Such love he has for this *boyt'shikl, oy vey* – such love. For him, only the best: a rabbi no less. He loves him, more than I hoped.' There was a note almost of fear in Rachael's voice.

Last week Sammy had begged again for a stake to build a business of his own, but his father had refused him, and Sammy was becoming sullen and defiant. Yesterday Esther had seen him in the street without his yarmulke on his curls. Worse than that, he had been down on his knees throwing dice with a group of young men – and she had recognized the look on his face. She had seen gambling fever before in Belgate. He was trying to win his stake – and if he didn't win, who knew what he might do? Esther had mentioned her fear to Philip, but he was Lansky's friend and unwilling to interfere. Now, as she walked between the flowered hedgerows, she made up her mind. She had saved £87: she would lend it to Sammy, and if it went, it went!

Last week Philip had given her a sovereign in a tiny kid-skin purse. She was smiling at the recollection as she let herself into the Valebrooke house and hurried through the hall. She knew the fire in the range was out before she opened the kitchen door: the room was chilly, the stone floor striking through the soles of her shoes. She had counted on Philip banking it up if he went out, but the fire had not been touched for hours and hours.

She unpinned her hat and struggled out of her coat; something perhaps could still be saved if she hurried. But for some reason she felt uneasy. She was hanging up her coat in the cupboard under the stairs when something made her cock her head and listen. It was then that she heard the harsh breathing from above. Philip's misshapen chest often affected his lungs. Esther had heard him fight for breath before, but never like this.

A moment later she was in the bedroom, smoothing Philip's sheets and raising his pillows. 'There now,' she said, matter of factly, 'you'll be all right now. I'm here.'

Loelia was lying back on her pillows, eyes bright with exertion, her red hair curling about her plump face. 'Have you seen him?'

Diana deposited *Vogue* and *Good Housekeeping* on the foot of the bed, and bent to kiss her friend's cheek. 'I've seen him and he's scrumptious. It made me feel quite maternal, but I beat the feeling down. How was it? Awful?'

'Beastly,' Loelia said with feeling. 'But worth it, I suppose. He is *sweet*, isn't he?'

'Very sweet,' Diana said. 'And you are a clever girl! I've brought you some of that divine Chanel scent to raise your morale.'

'Good. I could do with a treat,' Loelia said. 'I am *so* depressed, Di.' She looked down at her satin-upholstered chest. 'When I get out of this bed they will drop right down to my knees! I won't be able to get clothes, and I'll be hiding in my room like an ape.'

Diana was flipping through one of the magazines. 'No, you won't. You'll have to have one of the new brassières. They're called Kestos, and they lift you up.' She gestured with her hands to demonstrate uplift. 'Everyone's wearing them. Here you are!' She held out the magazine triumphantly. 'Crêpe de Chine, flesh-pink or ivory, and extra for black.' She looked quizzically at Loelia's ample chest. 'They do Outsize, too, at 23s 11d.'

'Beast,' Loelia said but she was devouring the advertisement just the same. '*Gives the breasts the small, firm, rounded contours which are the essence of youth and charm*. I like the sound of that. Perhaps I'll try one.' She struggled up in the bed. 'We've chosen a name: Anthony Gerald Hugh Colville. I can see the AGHC on his trunk when he goes to Marlborough.'

'Is Henry pleased to have a second son?' Diana asked. She had taken the brocade armchair and was helping herself to grapes.

'Delirious,' Loelia said complacently. 'It's cheered him up, because he was terribly depressed about his American shares – even General Motors. And Henry says when General Motors goes down, nothing's safe.' She peered at Diana's grey crêpe dress. It had a knee-length skirt with chevrons down the side, and a low, loose waist. She wore a bunch of Parma violets at the asymmetric neckline, and her cloche hat was a matching shade of deep violet. Her shoes and stockings were mauve, like her buttoned suede shoes and pochette handbag. 'You look divine,' Loelia said enviously.

'Do you like it?' Diana turned to view herself in the mirror. 'It's a new man – Norman Hartnell. He's in Bruton Street, beavering away. You should try him whenever you're on your feet. I'll go with you, if you like?'

'I thought you were going back to Durham?' Loelia asked. Her face had clouded and Diana felt a spasm of annoyance. She and Max had been lovers for more than five years. They did everything together, and the rest of society seemed to accept it. Howard, too. Only Loelia refused to acknowledge that Diana's life did not revolve around the wilds of the Durham coalfield.

'I was,' she said. 'But Max wants me with him at Ascot, so Durham will have to wait.'

Loelia sighed and plucked at her coverlet. 'Durham will wait, I suppose, but what about Howard?'

Diana popped a grape into her mouth, and chewed it with delicacy. They had been through all this before.

'Howard has what he wants,' she said at last. 'Rupert has been up there now for three weeks, and I have no doubt Howard is revelling in it. They'll be perfectly content, Lee. And I'm happy to leave them to it.' She tried to change the subject. 'There's a photo of Janet Gaynor in the paper today. She's won this new Academy Award. I can't say I've ever liked her, but Max simply swoons over her.' Why had she mentioned Max? She tried again. 'I've bought a skull-cap. I know I said I'd never wear one, but it's gold tissue, and too divine. And...' She lifted her mauve legs and regarded them complacently. 'I've decided I will never wear beige stockings again – never, as long as I live.'

She had said the right thing this time. Loelia's face lit up, and a lively discussion on the rage for coloured hosiery ensued.

The movement on the American Stock Exchange was filling the financial pages of Howard's newspapers. No one had an explanation, but Howard was not particularly worried by it; the Brenton fortune was solidly British-based. More worrying was the state of the coal trade. Already Welsh miners had walked from the Rhondda Valley to London, carrying their pit lamps into Trafalgar Square, and holding aloft banners depicting the Communist hammer and sickle.

Their leader, A. J. Cook, had predicted that the government would be compelled to take over the mining industry, and there were times when Howard wished with all his heart that someone would take the responsibility for the Brenton pits from his shoulders.

Putting aside such problems, he read Diana's latest letter. He knew better than to expect that it would contain anything but trivia. As the years had passed, he and Diana had grown less able to discuss anything that really mattered.

Lee's baby is a small but lively boy, fortunately with the Colville nose, who hardly ever cries, and seems to have none of the Dunane temper. Poor Lee hates her nurse. How I sympathize, remembering the Dragon. I hope Durham is well and producing oodles of coal. Isn't the news depressing? London is full of Americans who look as though they are ready to jump out of fifth-floor windows.

I know I promised to come north this week but I can't possibly leave Lee at the moment. You know how she depends on me. Tell Rupert I will be with him soon. We must find him the right governess; my brother had a tutor who was much too amiable, and that led to his flunking everything. However, when I'm there I'll see to it all myself.

Much love,

Diana.

PS: Regards, as ever, to your ma and pa, and kisses galore for the boy.

Howard folded the letter and slipped it into the drawer of his desk. There was a tap at the door and then Rupert, in striped flannel dressing-gown, was advancing to say goodnight, his nursemaid Susan in attendance. The boy was six now, tall for his age, with a mass of fine dark curls on his head and his mother's eyes. He allowed Howard to lift him on to his knee and looked up into his father's face. 'Susan's going to read me a story, papa.'

Howard smiled. 'That's good. Do you think she'd let me listen, too?' The child's eyes flicked to the nurse and back again. He pursed his lips, delighting in teasing his father, then nodded.

'Yes. You can come.'

Howard set his son down and went to the tall, glass-fronted bookshelves that lined the room. He took down a slim dark-blue volume: Rudyard Kipling's *Jungle Book*.

'I'll read to you tonight. I'll read this book, about the Indian jungle, and a boy who lives there with the animals.' They walked up the stairs together, talking of lions and tigers.

'I might go to the jungle one day,' Rupert said. 'I want to fly an aeroplane when I grow up,' and made engine-noises with his small, determined mouth. 'Then I can go anywhere.'

When at last Rupert tired of hearing of Mowgli and Bagheera and Shere Khan the tiger, he slept, but Howard sat on watching his son. The sight filled him with such emotion that he felt his nostrils flare and his eyes prick. How could Diana stay away from her child for such long periods? He was grateful for the opportunity it gave him to grow closer to the boy, but he knew it was not fair on the child that he should be divided between his parents in this way. *What a mess*, he thought for the hundredth time, then he kissed Rupert's brow and tiptoed from the room, leaving the light burning on the side table in accordance with Diana's wish.

His spirit lifted a little as he descended the stairs. For once he was about to indulge himself, and it was a pleasant feeling. He rang the bell and enquired whether or not Mary Hardman was still downstairs. The Brentons' housekeeper had been in Chester for a month, attending to her ailing mother, and this morning she had written to say she would not be returning to the Scar. Howard had engaged Miss Darnton when it had become obvious that Diana had no interest whatsoever in running the home. The woman had come with excellent references, and had done a splendid job. Throughout, she had encouraged Mary, teaching her other aspects of household management than the laundry, raising her wages, and creating for her a new blue uniform dress that set off Mary's fair hair, now neatly bobbed, and her trim figure.

When Miss Darnton had rushed away to care for her mother, Mary had taken on most of her duties and supervised the running of the home. Now she presented herself at Howard's study door, an anxious expression on her face. Howard smiled.

'Come in, Mrs Hardman. I wanted to thank you for all the extra work you've undertaken with Miss Darnton away. She's not coming back to us, I'm afraid. Her mother will be ill for a very long time, perhaps indefinitely. So you see I shall have to find a replacement.' He gestured to a chair. 'Sit down. I want to ask you if you'll take the position.'

Mary's face lit up, and then fell again. 'I'd like it, Mr Howard. I could do with the extra money, and I enjoy the work. But Miss Darnton lived in, and I couldn't leave my children. Anne, my sister-in-law, takes them now when I'm working, but she has a handful of her own. It couldn't be a daily thing; not forever. And not for the longer hours I'd need to put in if I was doing the job properly.'

'I've thought of that,' Howard said. 'You know how I've wanted you out of the Shacks ever since... well, for a long time? I mean to pull those houses down, and one day I will.'

Mary had smiled at his use of the colloquial name for Rosemary Row; now she sat forward, intent on his words.

'I can't expect you to live in, as Miss Darnton did. You need a home for your children, and room for them to play. We built stables when we built this house, but we've never used them. My wife doesn't ride now, and although we have Rupert's pony to consider it doesn't need a big block. My idea is to convert the space above the stabling to an apartment for you and your children. I'm told there's space enough for three separate rooms, with a kitchen, and a bathroom. A staircase comes down the outside of the building, and there's a gate into the paddock behind, to the woods and the hillside… so there's plenty of room for children to play. And they'd be playmates for Rupert, if they'd put up with a six-year-old.'

'Catherine is only eight,' Mary said abstractedly. Howard could see he had taken her by surprise, but there was something that looked like a gleam of excitement in her eyes.

'So you'll take it?' Howard asked.

Mary shook her head. 'I can scarcely believe it, sir. I'm just not sure I can manage the work in the way…'

He saw her hesitate, and understood.

'My wife will be delighted, I promise you.' Privately Howard wondered whether Diana would care at all. He wondered even more what Mary Hardman must make of his marriage. 'My mother remarked the other day on how well you've coped recently, and my mother's standards are high.' Their eyes met, and simultaneously they grinned: Charlotte's almost daily visits to the Scar were ostensibly to see her grandson; in reality they were tours of inspection designed to make sure that her son's establishment ran as smoothly as her own.

'Well, then…' Mary said slowly. 'If that's the case, I expect it'll be all right.' She thought, incredulously, of bringing Catherine and John to a new home, to the clean air of the Scar. And she thought, too, with gathering pleasure, of the status her posh new job would carry. Let Anne bite on that!

*

Philip was breathing more easily now. The doctor held his wrist once more, studying his gold half-hunter as he did so. He smiled at his patient. 'You'll live, Philip, but you must rest for a while. Take your medicine, eat, and rest: that's all. In a while you can go off somewhere for some bracing sea air, but first, bed and more bed.' He turned to Philip's sister-in-law, who stood at the foot of the bed, hands folded, face a picture of solicitude.

When Esther had discovered Philip he had begged her not to tell anyone, but he had been so ill that she had taken fright, and disobeyed him. Now, banished to the landing, she was regretting her impulse.

'I shall engage a trained nurse for a least a week,' Mrs Broderick said when the doctor had been seen to his car and she and Esther were alone in the hall. 'But I can't do that before morning. I have to go back to my children. It's unfortunate that Cedric is away, but it can't be helped. Can you stay here for one night?'

Esther was careful not to appear too anxious. She frowned, all the while in fever to get the woman over the step and run up to minister to Philip's every need. 'I suppose I can,' she said at last, and kept a grudging expression in place until the ogress had pinned on her hat and departed in a hail of instruction and stricture.

'Now,' Esther said, as she hurried to Philip's bedside, 'what would you like best in the world?'

His hands were white and blue-veined where they rested on the coverlet above the ugly arch of his chest. His fingers were long and slenderly jointed, and tipped with oval nails. Esther loved his, hands, watching them sometimes when they played chess so that she almost missed her moves. He laced them together now in supplication.

'I would like a little brandy and soda, and a lot of Dickens. *Bleak House*, I think. As many chapters as you can manage before you have to go. I don't want you walking to Hendon when it's too late.'

Esther was already turning to go and fulfil his wishes, but she spoke as she reached the door. 'I'm not going home tonight. I'm staying here with you.' 'She saw his look of alarm and lifted a finger. 'No, don't fret: Mrs Broderick asked me. And I was careful to hum and hah, and then say I'd stay if I must. You know she doesn't like to think I'm getting above myself. But I'd've stayed whether or not she let me. I'll be here as long as you need me – until you throw me out and get in someone who can make a galantine.' They both smiled, remembering her unsuccessful culinary efforts. Then she was running downstairs to find the book and the brandy, not knowing that he had turned his face to the pillow, uncertain whether he was crying for joy or fear of what lay ahead.

16

Howard went to Mount Street for the Colville christening, taking Rupert and Susan with him. Diana was waiting at King's Cross, waving frantically as they made their way through the barrier, swooping on Rupert with cries of delight and welcome home. She gave Susan the evening off, and entered into bathtime with gusto.

When Rupert was safely asleep she went to change for dinner, carrying on a conversation with Howard through the open door between their rooms as they dressed. He told her of Charles's gout and Charlotte's sponsorship of a new welfare clinic for the children of the coalfield, and Diana promised to help with it herself when she came north again.

'And Caroline and Geoffrey want to come up to London,' Howard went on, as he put in his studs.

'And stay here?' Something in Diana's tone alerted him.

'I suppose so. It is all right, isn't it?'

'How long do they mean to stay?'

'I don't know… a week or two, probably. They'd hardly come all the way up from Exeter for less.'

Diana made no reply, and Howard wondered whether he should remind her that Mount Street was a Brenton house and not her personal possession; but before he could speak she appeared in the doorway, dressed in a gown of ochre georgette, with a dipping, flaring skirt and a spray of orange flowers at the shoulder. He would have told her she looked splendid, but the tense expression on her face forbade it.

'It will be all right, won't it?' he asked again, trying not to let a note of annoyance creep into his voice. But the telephone shrilled suddenly in the hall, and Diana turned on her heel and fled.

Howard finished dressing and went out on to the landing. He had not intended to listen, but it was hard to resist trying to make out her whispered words.

'Of course I do, you know that. Of course not! How could you dream that I would?'

Howard knew who was on the other end of the phone, and he knew exactly what they were talking about. He turned back into his own room and closed the door, acknowledging that he had now waited too long to intervene, and despising himself for being the cuckold he was. At first he had been shocked and hurt: unbelievably hurt. He had contemplated ending his marriage. Then he had thought of Rupert; when Diana was with her son, she loved him, and the boy loved her. Perhaps half a mother was better than none? There were his parents to consider – and Diana's parents, too. Howard had thought of the harm scandal could do, and hesitated. It was fatal. Before he knew it season had followed season, year had followed year. He had given up hoping Diana would tire of Max – but one day, perhaps, Max's attention might stray. It was little enough to hope for, but it was all Howard had. In the early days he had longed to thrash Max, but he knew Diana: opposition made her defiant. As it was, they had the outward appearance of a marriage, and better that than a messy divorce.

They dined at opposite ends of the long table, keeping the conversation going, all the while occupied with their private thoughts. Howard was wondering how much longer he could live with a wife who was betraying him. Diana was wondering how she could possibly entertain her stuffy sister-in-law and her equally boring husband without their realizing that Max and she were lovers.

'Tell me more about your mother's clinic?' she said as they ate their fish course.

'It's not her clinic,' Howard said. 'A rather splendid chap started it, a Doctor Dix. He was struggling on on his own in a church hall, and then mother and one or two others – Miss Pratt and Mrs Darnley, you know the crew – decided to help. I think it thrills them to roll up their sleeves once a week, but the end result is a good one. They have cod-liver oil to give out, and the children are weighed regularly. It has to be beneficial in the end.'

'What does your father think about it?' Diana asked, eyes twinkling.

'Oh, he predicts doom as usual: cod-liver oil today, revolution tomorrow. You know how he is. I think it's a damned good idea.'

They talked of America, then, and Herbert Hoover's new presidency; and then of Edward Burton's suggestion that Howard should enter politics.

'It would mean your living down here,' Diana pointed out, smiling. 'I don't think you'd survive for long away from Durham.' She sighed. 'I envy you your roots, Howard. I don't feel I belong anywhere. I love Barthorpe, but in a strange, detached way. And London, where I'm happiest, is not a place for belonging.' She shook her head. 'I think you'd make a good MP. But if you intend to stand as a Conservative, and you want to be elected, you'd better hurry. Henry says this country will be red in ten years' time. Look at Wedgwood Benn.' Captain Wedgwood Benn, a Liberal MP for twenty-one years, had been elected for Labour in a by-election in Aberdeen. Some had cried defection, others conversion.

'He won't stick to it,' Howard said. 'He'll be back in the Liberal fold before long, you'll see.'

When they had eaten their lamb cutlets and melon sorbet, they went through to the drawing-room. There were flowers on a side-table, and the room was heavy with the scent of mimosa, reminding Howard of Trenchard. 'We must go to *Show Boat* while you're here,' Diana said. 'It's wonderful. I saw it…' She hesitated suddenly, and then put up her chin. 'I went with Max and Loelia.' She sat down at the piano and began to sing:

'Why do I love you, why do you love me,
Why should there be two happy as we…

It was the wrong song and they both knew it. She changed to playing 'Old Man River', which Howard had heard before, but it was too late. They were both relieved when they could mount the stairs and go their separate ways to bed. As she undressed, Diana pondered apprehensively about how she and Max would manage if Howard got into the House, and had to spend months of the year in London. But she couldn't deny him his chance, not if it was what he really wanted.

After that night when she had been allowed to care for him herself, Esther had to bear the frustration of handing over Philip's welfare to a trained nurse. But at the end of two weeks he was well enough to dispense with the nurse, and their lives returned to normal. She cooked him nourishing meals, and made him wear a muffler if he went as far as the door. He submitted to her, saying teasingly that now that she had a vote, he dared not disobey. They played chess each morning and evening, and in the afternoon he lay on the *chaise-longue* while she read to him, choosing the books carefully, marking her place with a suede bookmark when at last his lashes lay on his cheeks and he slept. Then she would gently disentangle his spectacles and put them on the table, raise the comforter to cover his hands and arms and tip-toe from the room. When he woke she would be there with the brass-railed tea-tray and homemade biscuits in a blue and white barrel.

At the end of July, Philip's doctor pronounced him fit to travel, and his sister-in-law arranged to rent a cottage for him at Whitby.

'I'd better go, Esther,' he had said ruefully, when the plans had been settled. 'We must keep the peace. But you will come to visit me, won't you? Otherwise I couldn't bear it.'

Now she sat upright in the carriage of the train that was carrying her to Whitby. She had never been in a train before, and it scared her. But she was eager to see Philip after three weeks apart, with nothing except postcards of Whitby to cheer her.

Time without Philip to care for had dragged unbearably. The first week Esther had spring-cleaned Valebrook. Thereafter she had haunted the Lansky house, where she was always welcome. Sammy was off on his annual visit to his French grandparents, and she missed him, too. She had sighed, and moped, and not even chess with the old Jew could cheer her. At last Lansky's patience snapped.

'He *lives*, this employer of yours. That is cause for thanksgiving!'

Esther had touched Lansky's arm to show contrition, and had turned into the nearest church on her way home to give thanks for Philip's recovery.

When he had sent her a ticket and instructions for the journey, she had thrown herself into an orgy of baking so that she would not arrive empty-handed. The results were in a basket beside her on the seat.

The train rattled along the coastline, and Esther sat upright at a window-seat, clutching her precious leather handbag, her straw hat pulled well down over her newly waved hair. As they passed Hartlepool she caught sight of her reflection in the window, smart in her new grey suit and the grey crêpe de Chine blouse that had cost her £2 4s. She thought she looked her best, but would Philip agree? His face, as he handed her from the train, gave the answer.

He laughed as she unpacked the basket: mutton pie, plum cake, beef mould... 'Am I being fattened for Christmas?' he teased.

In spite of Esther's protestations at the cost, they ate their midday meal in a hotel. She knew they looked an odd pair, but it seemed not to matter. Then they wandered through the streets, oblivious of curious eyes, buying toys for the Maguire children, and for Rachael a glass jar of humbugs with *Welcome to Whitby* in gilt letters. It was cold near the sea, but they walked a little way along the sand, collecting tiny pieces of coloured glass worn smooth by the action of the sea. 'Boody', Esther called it, a name she had known from childhood. Philip complained that it was not a proper word. 'It's a word if I say so,' she retorted.

Above them on the hill the ruins of the great abbey of Whitby stood out in gaunt silhouette. 'They called it "The Lantern of the North",' Philip said. 'It was built by the King of Northumbria to celebrate his defeat of Penda, the heathen King of Mercia. Two centuries later the Danes destroyed it, but the people of Whitby built it up again. And then Henry VIII ruined it during the Dissolution of the Monasteries.'

'Why did he only half-destroy it?' Esther asked,interestedly, hoping Philip would continue the history lesson.

'It was left as a landmark to sailors. This was a famous whaling-port once upon a time. It has quite a history, this town. It's where Bram Stoker conceived the idea of Dracula. On a hot day, when the wind blows from the North Sea, mists blow in – frets they call them, or the haar – that's when Dracula walks!'

Esther pulled a face of mock-horror, and Philip smiled. 'Don't worry, the haar always goes with the turn of the tide. I'll protect you until then.'

He looked much better for his convalescence by the sea. There was a tinge of colour in the pale cheeks, and he laughed a lot, teasing her about her new outfit, and how pleased she must have been to be rid of him for three weeks.

I want this day to last forever, Esther thought, even as the sun began its descent into the west.

'We still have time,' Philip said. 'Don't talk of leaving yet.' He took her hand once to help her over the sand, and Esther knew he was reluctant to let it go. If it had been left to her she would have let him keep it, but a sudden shyness overcame them both and their hands fell to their sides.

They sat on a rock to catch the last watery rays of afternoon sun, and sang sea-shanties to a deserted shore. 'Oh Shenandoah, I took a notion...' As dusk fell, Esther saw that he was becoming sad, and she wanted to leave him cheerful. It was twenty past seven, and the last train went at eight o'clock. 'There's time for a cup of tea at your cottage,' she said. 'Just a quick cup, before I go.'

They settled before the fire and drew the chintz curtains to shut out the gathering dusk. Willow-patterned china filled the dresser, and brass gleamed on the walls. In her mind's eye Esther saw the train approaching the station. She knew she should go, but the power to get out of the chair had left her. She waited, terrified that he would notice the time and urge her to go. She went on sitting there, in the firelight, as the train came and went, and they could both breathe easy again because it no longer had the power to separate them. They started to chatter, then, of anything and everything – like children in their pleasure at being together. Neither of them mentioned the fact that the train had gone, and that with its going a fateful decision had been made.

When they had talked themselves to a standstill, the tension in the room grew deeper. At last Esther dropped to her knees to mend the fire. She knew that any move would have to come from her, and she was ready to make it. She put the tongs and hearthbrush neatly back in place, and then turned to him, as he sat on the wicker armchair, holding out her arms.

'Esther,' Philip said, not meeting her eyes. 'I am not used to this.'

She felt such love for him that she feared her heart might burst with it. She put up a hand to lift off his spectacles, seeing in his naked face the boy he had been. He was lovely to her, the sight and the feel and the smell of him. She drew him from the chair and down, until they lay together on the soft hearth-rug, the fire's glow flickering on the ceiling, making the room a cave of delights. *This is what I have always wanted*, Esther thought, amazed. *This is what life really means.*

Philip's head was in the hollow of her neck, his hair soft and fine and smelling of soap. She traced his features with her fingertips, feeling the bones beneath the skin. Once she had held a fledgling in her hands and felt the bones telescoping under her fingers: now she remembered. She kept her touch gentle. 'There now,' she said. 'There now,' and went on holding him until she felt his fingertips in return trace her eyes, her cheeks, her mouth.

'We must think,' Philip said at last. 'We mustn't be foolish.' There was desperation in his voice, but Esther felt only strength and certainty. For the first time in her life she knew exactly what she wanted.

'I'm tired out with thinking,' she said and put her lips to his cheek. He kissed her, then, his mouth at first like a child's, and then firm and gentle like a man's. She sat up in the firelight and unbuttoned her blouse, slipping it from her, seeing the fire reflected in his dark eyes, lying down again to unbutton his shirt until they touched, skin to skin.

'I have no knowledge of how things should be done,' he said against her hair. 'Except in books.'

'Oh,' she said, pretending to be shocked, 'I never knew you read books like that.'

Philip did not respond, and she realized it was not a time for teasing. 'Listen, my love,' she said, suddenly hearing his heart labouring in his chest, 'I know no more than you, but we can learn.' She took off the rest of her clothes, then, feeling proud of what she was doing, relishing the courage she gave to him so that he, too, was soon naked beside her. He was pale and slight, except for his misshapen chest, and when he lay above her he was hardly the weight of a child.

As firelight danced on the ceiling, Esther thought of the tulips in the Sultan's gardens, and the thousand other delights she had discovered since she knew him, and she understood then that this was the greatest discovery of all. There was pain for them both, and he would have drawn away, but Esther held him fast. 'I love you, Philip.' And then they were moving together, suddenly finding a rhythm, and at the end she cried out, 'God Almighty!' at the wonder of what they had just achieved.

The Brenton miners had been on short time for two years now, and the men were becoming restive. They had met in the Welfare Hall and elected three men to carry their discontent to the owner. Stephen Gilbert was chosen because he stood head and shoulders above the rest; Martin Botcherby, because he was chairman of the lodge; and Frank Maguire because he had, so they said, a tongue like a windy-pick. 'There's only one thing Frankie likes better than talking,' one wag said. 'And that's lying in bed at home makkin' bairns.'

Their appeals to Charles Brenton fell on deaf ears. He pointed out that the Durham coalfield was not making a profit. If a quarter of a million or more other miners were without work at all, should they not consider themselves lucky to be on short time? If they didn't feel like that, would they be willing to surrender their unsatisfactory jobs to people who would be more appreciative? It was a threat and they all knew it. Only Frank spoke out.

'The Brenton pits *are* making money, Mr Brenton – even the Dorothea, and that's from clapped-out seams.'

Charles fixed Frank with what should have been a withering stare, but Frank gave him eye for eye.

'Well,' Charles said at last. 'As long as there's excess capacity and the resultant cut-throat competition in this industry, I'm afraid we'll do well to keep you on, short time or no. Good-day, gentlemen.'

'I'm sorry about that, sir,' Gallagher said when the door had closed on the deputation. 'Maguire is too free with his tongue. I got rid of him a while ago but...' He paused carefully, to choose his words. 'Mr Howard is always so concerned for the men, and Maguire's wife was with child – an almost permanent condition in their case, I believe. I took him back, even though he'd actually laid hands on me.'

Gallagher had hoped to rouse Charles to anger, but all he got was a grunt. 'Keep an eye on him,' Charles said. 'That sort of man always repeats his folly. We'll have rid of him sooner or later.'

He lit a cigar and blew smoke in a steady stream across his desk. 'They have only themselves to blame, Gallagher. Until the General Strike we kept our share of world trade. But returning to the Gold Standard priced us out of some markets, and then a seven-month lock-out... what else do the fools expect? However, enough of them. Mrs Brenton and I are going up to London next week. You wanted me to see that boy of yours?'

Gallagher was nodding and performing washing motions with his hands, an action that always irritated Charles. He decided to cut short the eulogy of his son and heir that Gallagher was sure to give.

'Do we have something for him? Of course we do. Get him in and let's see how he shapes up. Perhaps Mr Howard could do with some help.'

Charles chuckled to himself as he went down to the new Daimler that Fox had inveigled him into buying. The Gallagher boy had the face of a ferret; let him keep watch on Howard and channel everything back to his father, and thence to Charles himself. No harm in knowing what was going on; no harm at all. He remembered Maguire and his insolence; so, he had Howard to thank for that, had he? Well, the sooner some of his son's quixotic impulses were restrained, the better, and setting on young Gallagher might be the way to do it.

On the way home from the colliery office, Frank was remembering the look in Charles Brenton's eye when he had challenged him. There would be a price to pay for that small moment of triumph. All the same, it had been worth it. He felt his stomach rumble with hunger: he had not eaten since his snap – cold bacon and bread, washed down with water – and that had been nine hours ago. He wondered what Anne might be cooking: a nice ham shank, maybe, or a sheep's head with barley and leeks and lumps of tatie. Frank felt saliva flood his mouth, and then he remembered that Anne had said something about going to church. She was there more often than the priest nowadays, with the children in tow. They said there was no one more fervent than them that came to it late, and Anne was the living, breathing, proof of that.

Frank felt in his pocket and found a threepenny bit – the price of a drink, and no harm done because Anne would not be home to dish up for another half-hour or more.

As Frank turned into the Half Moon, Anne was offering up a prayer that he might forsake drink and save his money and get them all out of their two-bedroomed hovel and into a three-bedroomed house. God knew they needed it!

She lit a candle and placed it at the feet of St Teresa of Avila, then she offered another prayer – this time that Esther might break free of the Jew and the cripple, two no-hopers by anybody's standards, who would surely drag Esther down before they were done with her. She added a note to the effect that if her parents were still in limbo, for their failure to provide for their daughters, it might be time to consider their release; but that if, in God's opinion, they had not yet suffered enough, she, Anne, was quite happy for them to stay there meanwhile.

She looked to right and left to see if she dare break wind, and decided against it. Instead she rose to her feet and set off home to boil up the sheep's-head broth. The following day she heard that they had been given a three-bedroomed house – but in the Shacks!

Diana wore beige for Loelia's son's christening in September; a suit in fine wool crêpe, with a tailored white silk blouse, a row of pearls, and white gloves with embroidered gauntlets. Her hat, from Madame Simone, came down low over her eyes, so that she had to tilt back her head in an almost coquettish way in order to see. She was ready on time, holding Rupert, in his ice-blue tailored coat, by the hand as they waited in the hall for Howard to bring her car round from the mews. She had declined Max's offer to pick them up: Loelia was restive enough without their arriving with Max *en famille*.

She drew Rupert onto the steps and stood, tapping her foot, until the car appeared. A sudden spasm of indigestion seized her, a wave of nausea that came and went, and then returned again. Diana looked in her bag to see if she had a stray peppermint, but there was nothing there but violet cachous. Howard drew up at the door, and stepped out to help her into the car.

Loelia was already in the porch when they arrived, a smear of baby-sick on the shoulder of her Vionnet dress. 'Stand still,' Diana said, and licked her hanky to take out the mark.

When it was done Loelia looked up at her. 'Diana, you are my dear and oldest friend, and I could not live without you. If only you weren't such a fool.' Their eyes met and held, and then Henry was ushering them down between the pews, and the organ was playing, and Anthony Gerald Hugh was being accepted into the family of the church.

Max was godfather to Loelia's first-born, so this time he stood in the front pew without a part to play. He looked incredibly stylish this morning, his hair gleaming above his choir-boy face. Diana felt a wave of love for him. Her Brenton shares were doing well, and the money in her account simply seemed to multiply. Tomorrow she would buy him a present, something especially nice for just being Max. She looked up to find Howard's eyes on her, smiled at him, and went back to singing, 'All things bright and beautiful', feeling just a little ashamed.

Diana was enthusing about the purple-headed mountains when nausea overtook her once more. She was glad when the hymn ended and she could resume her seat. 'All right?' Howard murmured, and she nodded without speaking. She had had *fruits de mer* at dinner last night; perhaps she had food poisoning?

But even as she thought it, the coloured window behind the altar began to shimmer, and terror overtook her as she tried to count back to her last period. She couldn't, mustn't be pregnant – and yet the only time she had ever felt like this was seven years ago, when she had known without doubt that she was carrying a child.

17

The three days she spent with Philip in Whitby were the happiest Esther had ever known. The Whitby fishermen, in their blue ganseys, paid no attention to the lovers, or, if they noticed the unusual pair, they were too polite to remark on it. Esther paddled in the cold North Sea while Philip sat on a rock and urged her on. They browsed the shops, buying gifts for one another; she a warm jersey knitted in one of the traditional Whitby patterns for him, he a Dresden china shepherd and shepherdess for her.

In the evenings, as the sun went down, they held hands and watched it disappear, and at night they made love: gently, tentatively, sometimes one of them weeping and the other comforting, sometimes laughing together at their own limitations.

On their last night together before Esther returned to Sunderland Philip was unusually quiet.

'What will we do?' he said at last.

'What do you mean?' Esther knew what he meant, but was afraid to put it into words.

'When we go back – what will we do then?' She didn't speak and he continued, 'I don't think this is wise?'

Esther raised herself on to her elbow and put a finger to his lips.

'Hush. I won't have you talk like that about us.' She lifted her shoulders in an imitation of their friend, Lansky. 'Wise? So what's wise?'

Philip smiled, but he was not to be diverted. 'You're twenty-three, Esther. Still a child. I'm thirty-nine, and I'm a cripple. You have come to know me, and I honestly think you don't care… that I'm not as other men, I mean. But the world cares, Esther. The world jeers and taunts, or pities, me. I'm not sure which is worst.'

She was about to speak, but this time it was he who stayed her words with a gesture. 'I won't have you hurt by it, Esther. I know you, I know your courage and your determination. If I asked you to be my wife you'd say "yes" without a moment's hesitation. Well, I won't ask you – although I can't think of anything of which I'd be prouder than having you for a wife. But I know what they'd say: they'd say you married a cripple for his money. "She took the dwarf into her bed for greed" – that's what they'd say about you, and it would break my heart.'

Esther would have argued, but as Philip spoke she could hear Anne's voice, echoing his very words.

'But we can be together, Philip,' she said quietly, after a moment. 'They can't spoil that. We'll keep it secret – we won't even tell Lansky, if you say not. It'll be all right…

'Will it?' Philip sounded rueful. 'We've had three days out of time, Esther: three days during which I've behaved more foolishly than I could ever have dreamed of behaving. If I've harmed you, I'll never forgive myself. You know what they say about bastards; well, what would they say of a bastard with a cripple for a father? If we go on…'

And here he smiled at her, his eyes lighting with laughter until he remembered the peril of their situation. 'If we go on one day, there might be a child.'

Esther knew that she must reassure him if they were not to lose all they'd gained.

'We will go on, Philip – but there'll be no child, I promise you that. I'll go and do something about it as soon as I get home.'

They loved one another, then; incompletely because now they were both afraid of what might come about. But in the end, pleasured, they curled together in the high brass bed, and in a little while Esther thought Philip slept.

She lay awake, thinking how she loved him. It had begun out of pity, and gratitude for the job he had given and the respect he showed her. And then somehow love had cast out pity and gratitude, and any other emotion she might have felt. She turned gently so as not to wake him and kissed his naked shoulder where it showed above the blanket. She could see the twisted vertebrae of his spine sticking out awkwardly where there should have been a concavity, and put her mouth to the skin above the bones. In the darkness she heard him say, 'I love you, Esther.'

The following day he saw her on to the train. 'I'll be home soon. I can't wait to come home.'

Secretly Esther was glad of a few days to herself. She had heard of a Dr Dix who held a welfare clinic for children: some people said he helped women who wanted no more babies. But would he help her? She bought a thin brass wedding-ring from Woolworth's, and presented herself at the doctor's surgery.

The waiting-room was dark and full of harassed women with crying children clinging to their skirts. They talked together with an amazing frankness that made Esther's heart beat faster and brought a blush of agitation to her cheeks and throat. Would there ever be a time when she would be prepared to sit and discuss the most intimate details of her life?

She looked up to see the receptionist's eyes on her from her eyrie behind the blue and green bottles with their Latin labels. Long before the bell rang to signal her turn, Esther lost her nerve and half-ran from the room, a ripple of laughter following her into the street.

The baby had been presented for inspection, kissed and cooed over, and carried back to the nursery. Now Loelia swung her plump legs on to the *chaise-longue* and gave forth on the subject of fashion. 'Skirts are definitely getting longer, Di, and those dreadful uneven hems are back. First it was up and up, till they were almost out of sight. Now "they" – whoever "they" are – say down again. Up, down; zig-zag; those dreadful *robes de style* that made us look like teapots; handkerchief prints, so transparent that all your underpinnings showed – why don't we rebel? The waist is going back to its proper place, and that won't flatter me so soon after baby.'

'I know, darling,' Diana sympathized, feeling a bead of sweat on her upper lip. She couldn't face the thought of losing her figure again ... and what would people say?

Everyone in London admired her and Max for their daring, for their style. But a baby would ruin all that. People would know it couldn't be Howard's child. She remembered Althea Smith-Whyte, who had been ostracized for the very same thing; frozen out of absolutely every social occasion. Life would be insupportable… unless Howard would divorce her, and she and Max could marry in time. People could be very tolerant if you managed to scrape within the rules.

Diana, feeling a flood of relief at the idea, turned her attention back to Loelia, who was onto the subject of hair.

'We've had Eton crops, waves, medieval pageboy cuts, spit curls, shingles ... all in the space of five years or less! Now Enrico says I must let my hair *grow* if I don't want to be left behind. Well, I've a good mind to take a stand, Di.' She giggled and reached for another *marron glacé*. 'I think I'll have my head shaved. That will show them all.' She wiped the corners of her mouth with a pink fingertip, and changed the subject, her tone becoming a little acid. 'How's my dear brother? I never see him now he has a place of his own.'

Max had acquired a house in Grosvenor Street, and he and Diana had played with it for months, turning it into the most stylish house in London with its black-and-white decor, and striped wool curtains and upholstery. But the furbishing of the house had not been the end of it: there had been staff to engage, and knotty problems like choosing between *Punch* and the *Sphere* and *Country Life* to have delivered along with *The Times* and the *Morning Post*. In the end, Max had ordered them all and thrown in *The Illustrated London News* for good measure.

His footman wore a dark-green tail-coat with crested buttons and black dress trousers. His maids were to wear yellow by day and dark blue after tea. Max seemed to have a passion for designing and commissioning uniforms, although his own dress was becoming more casual by the hour, showing the new informality that was sweeping fashionable circles. He was immensely proud of his bird's-eye tweed knickerbockers, which had cost an astronomical price.

'Max has been terribly busy lately,' Diana said, as casually as she could. 'You know how fanatical he can be. He wants Grosvenor Street to be just right.'

'He's not taking anything, Di, is he?' Loelia asked suddenly. 'You know what I mean: silly things.'

'Half of London is drugging, darling,' Diana said. 'As for Max, he's tried it, I suppose; probably still does. But if you mean, "Is he overdoing it?" the answer is no. Anyway, I'm seeing him today: we're going to choose some pictures for the new house.' She tried not to think of the party they had attended last week, when excess had been the order of the day. 'You are a sport, Di,' Max had said; and she had tried to feel pleased but only felt uncomfortable.

'He's not buying, is he?' Loelia said. 'The Old Medieval has pictures laid down like claret. Tell him to poach some of those.'

Diana shook her head. 'He wants modern pictures. Terribly stark things to go with the decor. Besides, if he chooses well – if he lets *me* choose for him – they'll appreciate like mad.'

'That would be nice,' Loelia said, popping another chestnut into her mouth. 'The O.M. grumbles all the time, and threatens to cut Max off if he doesn't marry and do the decent thing. They threw Bunty Gascoigne at him at Christmas, but it didn't work. And now he has such a marvellous valet, I suppose marriage is further from his mind than ever. He's almost twenty-nine, Di. He ought to settle down.'

The mention of Bunty Gascoigne irritated Diana. The girl was knock-kneed, and fat, and whinnied when she laughed. 'Perhaps he doesn't want to marry?' Was Loelia trying to upset her? She felt a twinge of heartburn and put a hand to her throat.

'Men never want to settle down,' Loelia said firmly. 'But when they meet a suitable girl, they do.' There was a definite emphasis on the 'suitable'. 'After all, Diana, you and I did it. We took on responsibility, we have children. It comes to us all in the end. And remember how boring it was just rattling around, not belonging.' A note of complacency had crept into her voice. 'I *like* being married – and you should, too. Howard is an angel: you're very lucky! And Max must be brave, and do the right thing, too. Do tell him, old thing. He listens to you.'

I can't bear this, Diana thought and leaped at a chance to change the subject. 'I've brought you the most shocking book. It's called *The Well of Loneliness*, and it's been banned. This came from Paris.' Loelia's eyes had widened. 'It's about –.' Diana looked in mock-guilt from side to side. 'It's about love between *women*.' Loelia's face fell. 'No, goose,' Diana said. 'Not love like I love you. But IT – you know, S-E-X.'

Loelia brightened. 'Oh, good, I'm all for a naughty thrill.'

By the time Diana came out on to the pavement in front of Henry and Loelia's Belgravia home, she had made up her mind. She could not be sure she was pregnant, but she was almost sure. The sooner she told Max the better.

In the cool, grey-walled Kensington art gallery they walked around, occasionally stepping back to view a picture from a distance, speculating what would look well in the hall, discussing what would need lighting from above or below.

Diana waited until they reached the far end of the gallery, and then she put a gloved hand on Max's arm. 'I have something to tell you, Max.' She felt his arm tense, as though he were already anticipating bad news. 'I'm going to have a baby.' She put her head on one side in what she hoped was an appealing fashion, and made a little moue of apology.

Max's response took her breath away.

'Is it mine?'

Diana felt the room shake, and then steady. 'Of course it's yours. Whose else would it be?'

'You have a husband.'

Diana shut her eyes, resisting the impulse to strike him. 'You know I don't sleep with Howard. I haven't for years. What do you take me for?'

Max was moving away, pretending to study his catalogue, speaking quietly as though to stem her wrath. 'I think you are my dearest, closest friend, Diana – and more fun than any other woman in London.'

'He is putting me away,' Diana thought, and hurried to catch hold of his sleeve, lowering her voice in case she was overheard.

'I'm going to have a child, Max: *your* child! What are you going to do about it?'

She saw his face whiten, and his eyes close momentarily with shock. When he spoke he sounded suddenly older.

'My dear Diana, what do you expect me to do? Take you from Howard and hustle you into a registry office? We're not free agents, either of us. You're dependent on Howard; I'm accountable to the O.M. – for every penny. I couldn't marry you, even if I would.'

'*If* you would...!' Max turned to face a Diana, whose face had gone paper-white except for red spots of colour on each cheek-bone.

'Grow up, Diana. We both know what I have to do. I have to make the right marriage, just as you had to when you took Howard Brenton. I need a rich bride, preferably not in trade – although I may have to give a little there. And preferably a virgin. You know the rules: you're one of us. You can't opt out now. It's too late.'

The accommodation Howard had provided above the stables for Mary and her children came completely furnished. Everything was of good quality, and although Howard had left it to his mother to do the choosing he had made sure she chose well, even returning one set of curtains because he thought them too dark. Secretly, Mary wished she had been allowed to choose for herself, but if she had she'd have felt bound to pick the cheapest, so she had probably done better as things were.

All she took to the Scar herself were personal things, and objects of sentimental value: Howard had arranged for a handcart to help her. John and Catherine were enthusiastic about a move to be near ponies and motor-cars and the great rambling outbuildings of the house at the Scar. John was tall for his eleven years, broad and dark-haired like his father; but Catherine, at eight, was a Maguire, with golden hair that tumbled constantly from the single plait Mary braided every morning.

Mary was not given to displaying emotion, not even to her children, but she was excited about the adventure that lay ahead. It was what Stephen had always wanted for them – a chance to get away from the pit. 'If he knows,' she thought, 'let him be glad for it, too.'

When she had packed the few things she wanted to take

to the Scar, she told Anne she could have her pick of the rest, except for the stone sink of pansies which was going to the Scar on the barrow. Anne's eyes lit up: 'Everything?' Her tone was incredulous, her eyes flicking right and left, and again and again to Mary's fine, proggy mats.

'Everything,' Mary said.

When the time came for her to leave, she closed the door for the last time, and stood for a moment on the step. Miners in twos and threes were making their way home, black-rimmed eyes in curdy faces, shoulders hunched in weariness. Mary looked at them for a moment; then she summoned her children, picked up her bags and walked resolutely away.

As she led her children up the quarter-mile towards the Scar summit, and the house came into view, she remembered the day of Stephen's death. She had run up this hill, then, her heart hammering against her ribs, her eyes fixed on the long green roof. She paused now at the entrance and leaned her forehead against the cool wrought-iron of the gate Stephen had made. How strange life was; too much for ordinary mortals to comprehend. He had died on this hill, and now it was giving her children a new life. She took her daughter's hand and walked on towards the house.

Her new home above the stables was light and airy, with a shingled roof and a view from the hilltop to the fields outside of Belgate. Mary went from room to room, admiring her new furniture and kitchen gadgets, discovering that she could see the pit from none of the windows. At the last one she opened the casement and leaned out, resisting the impulse to shout her pleasure aloud. In the end John said it for her: 'It's wonderful,' he said. 'It's really wonderful!'

There were two bedrooms, and Mary decided to give one to each of her children. 'See,' she said to each of them, 'this is your own room, and I'll be sleeping out here in this room, so I'll always be there if you need me.' She made herself a bed up in the living room, draping it with a shawl by day. When she had set her own possessions on the mantel and shelves, she positioned her wedding photograph where she could gaze on it last thing and first thing, and then knelt down in front of the Holy Virgin to give thanks for all her blessings.

She was roused from her devotions by whoops of glee as the children discovered the light switches, and she had to run to restrain them in case they fused the lot with over-use!

Mary soon felt at home in the flat, delighting in its cleanliness and space. John was taken up with the cars in the garage, but Catherine missed the closeness of the Shacks, the noise and bustle of the pit, the constant presence of other children… until the day she looked from the window and saw Rupert Brenton. Thereafter she followed him at a distance, watching as he rode his pony, or bowled a hoop along the cobbled yard at the back of the house.

The six-year-old Rupert saw her watching and, to Howard's amusement, began to perform for his audience. 'Mayn't they play together?' he asked Mary Hardman, one day when he saw her trying to draw Catherine away from Rupert for fear of annoying her master. 'The boy is lonely up here. Some companionship will do him good.'

Mary agreed readily enough, but over the next few weeks, as the pair became inseparable, she reflected uneasily that oil and water never mixed. If Rupert had fixed on John for a playmate, he would have met his match, but Catherine was too pliant. Rupert, though younger, was the master in the playground as he would one day be in the pit, and it was good for neither child.

Though Mary was uneasy, Howard was relieved. It would do his son good to have childish company. Rupert's tutor was an elderly, retired schoolmaster; Susan was no longer the young girl who had come to them; she was a young woman now, less inclined to gambol with her charge. Whenever he could, Howard drove Rupert into Sunderland to meet the children of acquaintances, but it was not enough. Howard listened to the sound of the children playing in the grounds, and it eased his cares.

He had many things to worry about: the ever-present problem of the low price of coal; the need to find places for the men who trekked to Belgate every day from other pits in the area, hoping for work. Last winter had been bitter, and some families had had to exist through it on a few shillings a week from parish relief. Howard had asked Gallagher how the men they took on fared, and had been told that most of them had trouble with their hands. After a period of idleness a day's hacking with a pick caused terrible bruising. 'It passes,' Gallagher had said; but Howard gave orders that men taken on after six months out of work should be set duties other than hewing, until their hands hardened again. He meant it as a kindly gesture. The men saw it as an attempt to consign them to menial and less well-paid jobs.

He was worried, too, about his parents. They had never been affectionate towards one another, but when he tried to remember his childhood Howard seemed to recall a degree of respect between them. Now his mother displayed a cold indifference to his father, who in turn lost no opportunity to humiliate his wife. Howard had tried, and failed, to ease the tension between them. They had nothing in common except their children; in a sensible society they would now have reached an amicable agreement to live apart. But even as he arrived at that conclusion, Howard realized that that was almost the solution he and Diana had settled for, and it had not brought happiness – to him, at least. He cared for his mother, although there had never been between them the open affection he saw between Rupert and Diana, in spite of their many separations. It grieved him to see Charlotte so ill-treated, and it made him think a great deal about his own marriage.

Had his motives in marrying Diana been any nobler than Charles's? He had fooled himself into believing he loved her, when in fact he never had. She had captivated him, amused him, pleased him; but only on the day of Rupert's birth had he felt the deepest stirring of emotion. Surely, in a real love-match, such strong emotion should be present for most of the time?

After her retreat from Doctor Dix's surgery Esther spent an hour in the park, panicking about what she should do. She knew Philip's determination; if she could not reassure him that there would now be no threat of a baby, he would put her away from him. The thought of losing the intimacy they had so recently achieved was unbearable to Esther. For the first time in her life she loved someone wholeheartedly, and it seemed that everything in the world had taken on a rosier aspect.

Lansky, seeing her euphoria, commented that if Whitby air had done so much for her in a day it would have done wonders for Philip in three weeks. If he realized she had stayed in Whitby for three days, he didn't remark on it, but Esther knew it would be impossible to fool him once Philip returned. She could only hope Lansky would understand. In the meantime she must sort out her own particular problem.

In the end she walked into Belgate to pick Anne's brains. Even if she had been prepared to confide in her sister, she would have received no help; Anne, a Catholic now to her fingertips, believed any form of birth control to be a sin. But Anne, who spent half her day gossiping, must nevertheless know about it. If Esther could inveigle her into conversation, she might get the information she needed.

She found Anne hunched over her sewing machine, patching curtains for a neighbour. 'I need the money,' Anne said, and kept on with her work. Esther brewed tea, and then casually she told Anne the tale of a fictional maid-servant in

Sunderland who had undergone a botched abortion. 'Blood everywhere,' Esther said, letting her imagination loose.

'Serves her right!' Anne pulled the material from the machine, and bit through the threads with her teeth. 'If you do what you shouldn't, you have to accept the consequences. God didn't give love for pleasure.'

'People do *do* such things, though,' Esther said. 'I've heard of all sorts of tricks.' She tried to sound disapproving, and hoped to God Anne wouldn't ask her to cite examples.

'Oh, yes,' Anne said, 'there's all sorts of tricks.' Her eyes narrowed as she inspected her handiwork, and a look of satisfaction crossed her face. 'That's that nearly done.'

Don't stop now, Esther thought – but Anne appeared to have lost the thread of their conversation. Aloud Esther said, 'What d'you mean by tricks?' She was glad Anne was still peering at the stitching: if her sister had looked up at her, and raised her eyebrows at the question, she would have melted away on the spot.

'Well,' Anne said, 'some soak newspaper in vinegar and well, you know... push it up. Many a one's been taken to the Infirmary with that. It turns to septicaemia in the end, and serve them right. And some wait till after, and wash it out with salt water. There's all sorts, if you'll stoop to it. But that's prostitution – or little better. You can see them going in and out of that dirty little shop down High Street, near the docks, wickedness in their faces. There's a price to pay for everything in this life, Esther – everything worth having. Don't you forget it.' A gleam came into her eyes, as it occurred to her that she had never before had a conversation like this with Esther.

'It makes you think,' Esther said hurriedly, trying to sound as disapproving as possible. 'I mean – some folk get away with it.'

She saw Anne's face light up and knew *she* had got away with it. For the next ten minutes Anne dissected the moral future of Belgate, and then, worn out, moved on to the scandalous price of hens' eggs at is 6d a dozen. Even rabbits, *vermin*, were a shilling a piece, and potatoes were sixpence a stone. The Public Assistance man had been round and forced Annie Caswell to sell her dresser before she could get relief.

'It's been a hard year,' Anne said. 'Still, I'm better off than you, I suppose. How you stick slaving over that lot I do not know.' She stood up, flexing her shoulders to ease her tired muscles, and Esther saw there was a tear in her sleeve. The old Anne would have died to be in such a state. Esther, hugging her own happiness to her, tried to look downtrodden. If it made Anne happy to look down on her single, employed state, it was a little enough thing to oblige.

'You can stop for your tea if you like,' Anne said. 'I've boiled a nice shank, and there's taties.' Esther had smelled the ham shank as soon as she entered the house – smelled, and remembered Anne's words in the shop a lifetime ago: *'When I have a home of my own, I'll never have a ham shank across the step.'*

Esther turned down Anne's offer of tea, and walked home contentedly in the late-afternoon light, secure in the knowledge that all she had to do was find the dirty little shop in the High Street.

She called in at Lansky's as she went, and found father and son at loggerheads again. As usual, their conversation was peppered with Yiddish and French, for the boy was recently back from visiting his mother's family.

Now, though, he stood defiant, yarmulke pushed to the back of his curly hair. He had been caught gambling in a public street, and the horror of it was etched on Emmanuel Lansky's face. 'So I gamble a little?' Sammy was saying. 'So where's the harm? It's the only way I have to make myself a stake.'

'*Shlemiel!*' Lansky said. 'The only thing you'll make there are enemies. You mix with *ganovs* and *shlubbers*, and you talk of a stake.' He turned to Esther. 'The boy's *meshuge!*'

Sammy's eyes blazed at being called a fool. 'If I'm *meshuge*, you made me!'

Esther drew in her breath. 'Stop it,' she said. 'You two have done this almost from the very day I came into this house, and I do believe you're capable of keeping it up for the next twenty years. Then what? Will you say Kaddish for your father when he's gone and beg his forgiveness? And will *you* die knowing you left your son unhappy?'

Neither of them looked abashed but at least they were listening to her. Esther turned to Lansky. 'You want Sammy to be a learned man. Well, I don't know much about that, but I know he's learning nothing at the moment but how to do things behind his father's back. And he doesn't even do that very well! As for you, Sammy Lansky, you say you want to be a responsible trader, a businessman, and you play in the gutter with *drek*.' Her use of the Yiddish word for rubbish surprised even her. 'Yes, I may be a goy, but I can use my ears. I learn. Which is more than can be said for everybody.'

'So what would you do?' Lansky said. 'Give him money to throw away?'

'See,' Sammy said, triumphantly, 'that's the trust my father has in me. He thinks I'm a *shmuck*.'

'Stop it,' Esther said again. 'I'll tell you what you should both do. Give him his stake, Mr Lansky, a small one. And give him three months. If he makes good with it in that time, then help him. If he doesn't, make him go your way.' She turned to Sammy. 'And you: stop your fooling about with the rag, tag and bobtail of Sunderland, and do your trading. If it doesn't work, then become the man that your father wants – and do it cheerfully.'

They both thought for a moment, and then Sammy spoke: 'I'd agree to that.' They held their breath for Emmanuel's decision.

'How much of a stake?' he said at last.

'A hundred pounds,' Sammy said.

'Fifty,' Lansky said firmly.

'Right,' Esther said. 'Now, who puts on the tea kettle?'

The following day she also gave Sammy £50, more than half of her savings. 'I meant to do it sooner,' she said. 'But Mr Philip got ill, and it slipped my mind. Don't tell your father – and don't forget your promise to him. If it doesn't work out, if you lose your stake, then you'll buckle down to study, and stop grumbling.'

'It'll work,' Sammy said, with confidence. He waved the white notes Esther had handed him. 'I'll give you this back ten times over.'

'Only ten?' Esther said. '*Oy vey*!'

18

The Colvilles were off to Cornwall, for a late holiday, and Loelia was pre-occupied with packing for every eventuality. Diana sat in the cluttered bedroom and tried not to show the acute misery she was feeling. She had always been able to confide in Loelia in times of crisis, but not even she could be expected to do anything but disapprove of the situation Diana confronted now.

As if she were reading her friend's mind, Loelia sat down on the dressing-stool and heaved a sigh. 'I feel quite strange, not at all as I usually feel at this time of year. Henry says the most peculiar things are happening in America and that we will feel the after-effects. I don't know; according to Max, things are booming over there.' She turned to the mirror and studied an imaginary blemish on her upper lip. 'He's thinking of going to New York soon, but I expect you know that.' She turned back. 'In a way, a chapter in our lives is coming to a close, darling – don't you feel it? We have to grow up: you and I, and Max, and everyone. We're fearfully lucky, all of us, and I think we should appreciate our position – and all its privileges and responsibilities.'

She knows about the baby, Diana thought. *Or at least she suspects*. Aloud she said, 'You're being tiresomely serious, Lee. Let's not talk about gloomy things. I'm much more interested in your packing.' She paused, remembering the dreadful humiliation of the moment when Max had turned her down. If Loelia knew, or half-suspected, then other people would also know, or guess. She couldn't bear that.

'I'm off to Durham soon but first I'm having some divine outfits made in the new colours: almond and cedar and rose-beige. All bias-cut, with seven-eighth coats to match.' They talked of hat widths and heel heights, and the importance of remembering to put on cotton gloves after one's hands were creamed at night: all the minute but essential details that made it seem as if the world were not rocking on its axis, after all.

By the time Loelia's hats had been pinned to pads inside bonnet-boxes for the journey, Diana had made up her mind. She would go back to Durham and sleep with Howard. That was the only way to give her child a proper start.

'I shall be glad to get out of town,' Loelia said as Diana took her leave. 'Nowhere is fun any more. The really nice places are full of jockeys celebrating wins, or brash young Americans showing off their disgusting money. If their businesses all collapse, as Henry predicts, at least we'll be spared that. And when we come back, we'll all have changed and behave terribly well, won't we?' This time there was definite anxiety in her voice, and Diana bent to kiss her friend's chubby cheek.

'Of course we will, Lee, if it makes you happy.'

Diana walked out into Chester Square, tears welling up in her eyes. What would she do without Max? He was a sinner, but he was so full of life. After she had had this baby, could things ever be the same again? Could she make a bearable life with Howard? Or would she constantly yearn for Max; for the excitement, the danger, the exhilaration of being at his side?

As she walked towards the corner where she might pick up a cruising cab, Diana pulled herself together. She had to devise a strategy for getting Howard into her bed, that was the first thing. And if she couldn't manage that, none of the rest would matter at all.

*

Howard had not thought it possible to dislike anyone more than he disliked Gallagher, the Brenton agent, but in the weeks that Stanley, his son, had been installed in an office adjacent to his own, Howard had almost come to see the agent in a rosy light. He was alighting from his car in the colliery yard when he heard an altercation in young Gallagher's office. A woman's voice was mingled with the precise tones young Gallagher adopted, and from the sound of it the woman was weeping.

Howard pushed open the door. A woman was indeed there and weeping, holding her black shawl under her chin with one hand, dabbing her eyes with its crocheted edge with the other.

'What's going on?' Howard asked.

The young man flushed, but met Howard's eye. 'It's nothing to worry about, Mr Howard. I can handle it.'

Howard tried not to let dislike of Stanley overtake him. 'This lady seems to be worried – what's upset her?'

The woman broke in then, letting her shawl fall back from her head. 'He's given my lads over to the pollis, Mr Brenton. For one-and-a-tanner's worth of coal.'

Stanley Gallagher defended himself.

'They'd demolished a fence, Mr Howard, to get to the coal. And they gave verbal abuse to the guards who caught them. I had no option but to call in the constabulary.'

'*I had no option...*' The phrase irritated Howard, but there were conventions to be observed.

'I wonder if you would wait in the next room, Mrs…?'

'Renshaw, Mr Brenton. My dad worked for you in the Dorothea. I married a Murton man, who was took with the dust. My lads've been laid off since last year, and we had no fire. I know they shouldn't't've done what they did, but it was only one-and-a-tanner's worth, the makkin's of a fire.

If they're up at court, they have a chance not to get back when Ryhope takes men on again. You know what it's like once you get a name.'

Howard nodded. 'Wait next door and I'll see what I can do.'

When she had gone out, Howard closed the door and turned back to Stanley Gallagher. 'You called in the constabulary for eighteen-pence worth of coal?'

'And the broken fence, Mr Howard. I had no option –'

'Don't say that,' Howard said sharply. 'You had the option of consulting those who own the coal and the fence.'

'I was told not to run to you with minor matters,' Gallagher said sullenly.

'I'm sure you were,' Howard said, 'and I think I know who told you that. Ignore it. I want to know if a mouse runs across the stock-room floor, Mr Gallagher. Do I make myself clear? As for these wretched boys, the charges are to be dropped.'

'I'm not sure that's possible, sir.'

'Make it possible,' Howard said smoothly. Young Gallagher's eyes met his and for a moment defiance gleamed, and then the boy's eyelids dropped before Howard's steady stare. 'Right?' Howard said, and then again, receiving no answer, '*Right?*'

The boy nodded, and Howard let the boy go before he turned on his heel and left.

Howard went to speak to the woman. 'I'm seeing to this business, Mrs Renshaw. I'm sure we'll sort it out in the end.' Her shoulders slumped in relief and he saw that she was weary. 'Did you walk over from Murton?' She nodded. Howard went back to Gallagher's office. 'Do you know how to drive?'

The young man brightened. 'Yes, Mr Howard.'

'Good,' Howard said. 'My car's at the door. Drive Mrs Renshaw to her village – and treat her with some respect while you're at it.'

He went back to his office in a rather complacent mood, hoping young Gallagher would get the message. He would if he had any sense. His father had arrogance bred into him over years, but the boy was green. He might turn into a reasonable prospect, given the proper training.

Howard's satisfaction was to be short-lived. Before young Gallagher had returned from his enforced errand of mercy, his father came to tell Howard that Belgate was at a standstill. 'A dispute over piece-work, Mr Howard. And the ringleader's your friend Maguire.'

'Maguire again,' Howard thought, and went wearily out to deal with the dispute.

By the time of Philip's homecoming the Dresden ornaments were in place on the mantelpiece in the morning-room, the cosiest room in the house. 'They're to remind us of Whitby,' Esther said. 'Where our happiness began.'

But Philip shook his head. 'Happiness began for me when I opened my door to a strange young woman who had the effrontery to apply for a housekeeper's job while scarcely out of her pinafores.'

Later on, when they were sitting by the fire, Esther said quietly, 'There's nothing to worry about. Everything's been seen to.' Philip's brow furrowed, and she saw doubt in his mind, so she got to her feet and fetched the red-backed book that had been the fruit of her visit to the rubber shop down by the docks in Sunderland, where she had thrown herself on the mercy of the shopkeeper and confessed her ignorance.

It was called *Wise Parenthood*, and it was written by a woman doctor, Marie Carmichael Stopes. It was subtitled *The Treatise on Birth Control for Married People*, but the little old man behind the counter had seemed not to care whether or not Esther was married. All he cared about was extracting £1 for the book, in spite of the 3s 6d marked inside the cover.

Esther had carried it home and pored over it, feeling despair as she turned the pages without finding any practical help. But when she reached page 37, everything began to come clear. The doctor recommended the wearing of a special cap to cover the entrance of the womb, but Esther doubted her own ability to fit it, and she could not face another visit to Dr Dix. She had settled instead on cocoa butter and quinine suppositories, which ought to cost 2s 6d a box, according to the book, but which were also priced at £1 when she went back to the High Street shop. She bought douching equipment, too, for the book recommended douching with two parts of water to one of vinegar as an extra precaution, if you were worried. As she was leaving with her purchases and a sheaf of leaflets, another customer went furtively past her – and Esther realized just why the shopkeeper could profiteer so blatantly. No customer would dare to expose him.

Philip and Esther sat by their fire that first evening, and made plans. Esther would keep on her flat in Hendon for appearance's sake and to all intents and purposes would go home each evening. In reality she would live in Valebrooke, keeping her possessions discreetly out of sight.

'We won't fool Mr Lansky,' she said, and Philip nodded. 'Lansky will understand.'

Lansky both understood and approved. Nothing was said, but when he and Philip sat down to their chess ofter dinner, Lansky pulled a third chair to the fire. 'Time for you to understand the real mysteries of the game, Esther. Then you can give my friend the beating I can never quite manage.' It was a recognition of the changed situation, and as Esther's eyes met Philip's, Esther saw her own satisfaction mirrored there, If Lansky approved, what other permission did they need?

At nights they lay together in the big double bed that had been Philip's mother's, talking, holding hands, above all making plans. 'There are so many things I want to show you, Esther. Life will not be long enough.' A shiver went through Esther, at these words. She couldn't bear to lose him now. But his breathing was steady and there was warmth in his limbs when they entwined with hers, so she put her fears aside. Sometimes they put out the lamp and turned to lie side by side, her arm around him as though she would protect him against all the dark invaders of the night. Sometimes he slipped his arm beneath her head and drew her in against him, seeking her lips, cupping her breast in his hand, whispering against her hair, until she felt desire well up in her and reached for him like an impatient child.

They were learning together, moving from lesson to lesson slowly, because there was so much to be enjoyed. She carried out her birth-control practices faithfully, and when, sometimes, Philip was fearful, she reassured him with words – and once with the tangible proof – that precautions had been taken.

There must not be a child. Philip's words '*a bastard with a cripple for a father*' never left the forefront of Esther's mind. She would have delighted in a child of his, but on each of her visits to Belgate Anne offered her cruel examples of how little the world would understand.

'I think you need a medal, our Esther. Stuck in that black hole with a freak-show. What does he look like without a coat? A clip, I bet! He's like a monkey: all arms and legs. A spider, more like, I say. I hope you're getting well-paid.'

Anne had long since renounced the careful speech of their upbringing. She was coarser now than Frank, seeming to glory in the roughness of her own tongue. Esther, on the other hand, was slipping into Philip's ways. She noticed he never said 'didn't used to', he said 'used not to', and it sounded right. He never said 'pardon me' or 'pleased to meet you'. Often he forsook words and simply inclined his head in a gesture that said all that was necessary. 'By, you're gettin fancy, our Es,' Anne commented one day. 'Has the Jew-boy sent you to elocution?'

A month after his return from Whitby, Philip celebrated his birthday. Esther had sought out Lansky and demanded a birthday idea to surpass all others. He found her the ideal gift: ivory scrimshaw, carved by some long-gone sailor with an intricate pattern of lovers in a setting of trees and ferns. It was so exquisite that it seemed to glow as Esther held it in her hands. It cost five guineas, but she counted the money well spent. On his birthday Philip surprised her, too, with a gift: a green leather writing-case with her initials embossed in gold.

'What's this for?' she said.

'It's our anniversary,' he replied. 'A month together – the best month of my life.'

That night Emmanuel Lansky came to share their evening meal, with an unusually serious Sammy in tow. Esther was pleased to see them, but Philip led them away to his study and closed the door, while she got on with preparing the meal. When Sammy came to find her in the kitchen, she couldn't resist a whispered, 'What's going on?'

Sammy rolled his eyes and whistled softly. 'Secrets, Esther. I'd tell you if I could, but they'd cut my throat.'

The evening meal passed in a haze of companionable laughter and much teasing of Sammy about his business plans. Esther had never mentioned the loan she had made him, so it was Lansky alone who bemoaned the fact that he would never see his £50 again.

'Just wait,' Sammy said. 'When I'm riding by in my Rolls, you'll all be sorry you scoffed.'

When the Lanskys had gone home, Philip told Esther he had made a will, witnessed by the Lanskys, in which he left her everything he possessed. Esther cried, then, her tears splashing down onto her breast. They were not tears of gratitude, but tears of terror that the happiness she had now might one day be taken away from her.

*

Diana paid a flying visit to Barthorpe to get up courage for what she had to do. In the walled gardens there were peaches, and nectarines; figs and melons were ripening in the hothouses, but she found her mother vaguer than ever and her father incensed about the latest vagaries of the Prince of Wales. 'The biggest bloody rake in Europe,' he said. 'Utter bloody bounder.' The next day she kissed her parents, and apprehensively took the train north.

Diana had known and approved of Howard's decision to make Mary Hardman his housekeeper, but she was a little taken aback to see Howard on the station platform, holding Rupert by his left hand and a fair-haired girl, a little older, with his right.

'This is Catherine Hardman,' Howard said, after greeting Diana with a polite kiss. 'She's Mary's daughter.' Rupert had flung himself at his mother, and was clinging to her, but now he gestured towards Catherine.

'My friend,' he said in a proprietorial tone, and smiled as Diana shook Catherine's hand.

'They play so well together,' Howard said apologetically. 'And Rupert has been so alone at the Scar.'

Was this her opportunity? Diana wondered, as she took her place beside Howard in the car while on the back seat the children squabbled amiably. Enticing Howard to her bed after a lapse of years had seemed an almost impossible task, but if she could suggest that it was an act of noble self-sacrifice, in order that Rupert could have a companion of his own sort…? She relaxed into her seat and tried not to see the squalor of the pit villages they drove through on their way from Durham to the Scar.

At dinner they talked briefly of Loelia and her family, and of the Marchioness of Londonderry, who had been nicknamed Circe as a child, and had had a snake tattooed on one of her ankles. She gave brilliant musical evenings and intimate supper parties, and had recently admitted both Loelia and Diana to her charmed circle.

Diana widened her eyes. 'It's his Lordship who is really interesting!' she said. She was trying to flirt with Howard, to bring about a return to the mood of those first heady days when they had bolted dinner in order to go to bed. But as she toyed with her lemon mousse, she wondered if memory was deceiving her. Had she and Howard ever been enthusiastic lovers? And if they had, why ever had she let it go?

They carried their Armagnac into the library where the coffee tray was waiting. 'What do you think of the new government?' Howard asked. It was three months since Ramsay MacDonald had announced his cabinet, the first to contain a woman.

'I try not to think of it,' Diana said 'but Henry Colville says Ramsay MacDonald is behaving well so far. And papa has no grumbles; he's so busy fulminating against the Prince of Wales that he has no venom left – not even for socialists.'

'MacDonald is too dependent on Liberal goodwill to be radical,' Howard answered, thoughtfully. 'Most of the senior cabinet posts have gone to the right-wing of his party. And I'm glad he's going to do something about unemployment; there are men in Durham who haven't worked for a twelvemonth. They're living on air, Diana – fresh air.' He thought of the black-shawled woman of the afternoon, at her wits' end. 'Thank God we've managed to keep most of our men in work.'

'He's appointed that dreadful man Thomas to shorten the dole queues,' Diana said. 'The union man.' She uttered the word 'union' as though it were blasphemous.

'I don't think he'll go too far.' Howard was smiling at her, and Diana tried to look abashed and naïve and infinitely, infinitely desirable. 'I hope he doesn't,' she said, touching her tongue to her upper lip and fluttering her eyelashes. 'Now that they're restoring diplomatic relations with Russia, and calling for disarmament, we may all be murdered in our beds by Bolsheviks if we're not careful.'

'Don't worry,' Howard said. 'Tories and Labour have one thing in common: they hate the Liberals. And Lloyd George is their *bête noire*. "Keep the Welshman out": that's their slogan. So we'll have good middle-of-the-road government – until they all fall out again. Then we'll have another election.'

By the time the two of them were ready to go upstairs, much of their old rapport had been restored. Diana rested her hand on Howard's arm as they mounted the stairs. 'Come and say goodnight when you're ready for bed,' she said. 'I've something I want to speak to you about.'

She waited by her window, her long, white silky nightgown, with its bias cut, trailing the floor. It was lavish with Brussels lace and showed just the right amount of *décolletage*. She had tumbled her hair on her forehead to suggest abandon, and now sat at her dressing-table, anointing herself with perfume, and planning her moves. She would be serious and straightforward: Howard would appreciate that. No apologies, no silly seduction – just an acknowledgement that they were husband and wife; that they had one child and should have more; and that she was willing to play her part. Then, if Howard moved towards her, or even smiled, she would move towards him and bury her face in his chest to save further embarrassment. Diana felt quite calm about what she was going to do until Howard's knock came at her door and then she started to tremble.

He had on a dark silk dressing-gown, and she thought he looked tired and anxious. 'Come and sit here,' she said and went to the ottoman at the foot of the bed.

'I've been thinking, Howard.'

She paused and moistened her lips. 'About Rupert when I saw him today with Mrs Hardman's child. Well, one child is not a good idea.'

She felt suddenly impelled to stand up and move to the dressing-table, where she could watch the effect her words were having on Howard indirectly, through the glass. 'I know that you and I… that we…'Suddenly she looked at her own reflection, strained and dark-shadowed because she was about to commit a sin. She picked up a silver-topped perfume bottle and squeezed it, trying to collect her thoughts. She knew what she had to do: she had planned it, and it was simple.

'I'm going to have a baby, Howard,' she said. 'And needless to say, it isn't yours.'

Anne and Frank were in bed, too, propped up on pillows, while Frank explained to Anne the cause of that day's strike at the pit. For a while he had suspected that a deputy was taking bribes to give out rich stretches of the face; that men who didn't or couldn't pay were set on at the unproductive parts of the seam, so that their piecework earnings were sparse. Today Frank had obtained proof of his suspicions.

'So I fettled him, Annie. I slammed him up against a tub, and I fettled him. Then the under-manager suspended me and the lads came out. We're stopping out. I know it'll be hard...'

'Hush,' Anne said. 'We'll manage. I'll eat neeps before I'll give in to that one.'

'Who?' Frank asked.

'Brenton.'

Frank was taken aback at the venom in her tone.

'It's not his fault, Annie. I don't suppose he'd like it any better than I do, if he knew – not bribery. Or corruption, more like. Yes, that's what it is.'

'He bloody well should know.' Frank could tell Anne was whipping herself into a fury, and he took the only way out. He began to unbutton her nightgown and feel for her breast. If he didn't divert her, she might ask why he hadn't told Brenton the facts, and he didn't fancy explaining to Anne that you didn't betray fellow-workers, not even when they were corrupt. Sex was the panacea for all woes. He stroked and petted until he felt Anne's nipples harden, and the slight involuntary movement of her legs that signalled she was ready to receive him.

As he levered himself above her Frank smiled into the darkness, remembering the first time he had taken her, on the floor in the back shop. One brief encounter, and she had fallen. Nine months later he had sat downstairs, listening to her crying and straining above, marvelling at what he had done. In the whole of his life that far he had seldom if ever been able to dictate its course, and yet, in one small burst of passion, he had brought about the noisy affair upstairs. He had still not got over the wonder of it.

Now he set himself to pleasure Anne, liking to hear her moan in ecstasy and to feel her fingers making urgent circles upon his back. There was a brief moment when he wondered if it was wise to risk another mouth to feed, with a strike upon them – and then he was too far gone to care, and there was nothing to be done but match his own abandon to his wife's and hope that the good Lord Jesus Christ would sort it for them in the end.

19

In the lonely years when he and Diana had lived more or less separate lives, Howard had thought deeply about his marriage, and had reached the conclusion that he had done Diana a great wrong in marrying her. He had not been in love with her, he had been in love with the idea of establishing a home and family. If he had been more forthcoming in the beginning, making an effort to match her sensuality, might it all have been different?

So though the news that she was carrying Max's child, and that Max had abandoned her, at first outraged Howard, he saw, when his temper cooled, that it offered him a perfect way to atone for his own past mistakes. He would stand by his wife, and take her child as his own. Diana would find sanctuary; he would find absolution; and Rupert would have a companion.

Howard had crashed from Diana's bedroom in a fury at her words, but when he calmed down he went back, to find her lying on the bed, eyes swollen with weeping.

'Sit up,' he had said firmly, 'and dry your eyes. We need to talk.'

Diana sat up slowly, and he was suddenly filled with pity for her plight. He smiled. 'Cheer up,' he said. 'Things could be worse.' That made her smile, too. He went downstairs, then, and returned with two brandies.

'We'll sort this out,' he said. 'I don't know how, but I know we will… for Rupert's sake, if for no other reason.'

Within a week of that decision, and Diana's grateful acceptance of it, news came of Max's engagement to an American heiress, Laura Millward. When Diana cried about her betrayal to Loelia, she found her friend uncharacteristically hard and unsympathetic. 'He must have known her before, Lee – when he was still making love to me,' Diana wept.

'Face facts, Diana,' Loelia said harshly, stung to frankness by Diana's abandonment of self-control. 'What do you expect Max to do? Valesworth was built by my family five centuries ago. Now the roof needs repairing, the corridors are ice-chambers, the conservatory is in ruins, and we have a quarter – a *quarter* – of the staff we had before the War. And those that are left are doddering. I doubt whether Laura Millward's blood is as blue as yours or mine, but she is from the Fifth-Avenue set, old America, not the dreadful *nouveau-riche* Park-Avenue crowd. She's not pretentious or vulgar, and she has two things Max needs: an unsullied history, and oodles and barrels of money. He may never love her, but she will restore his name, give him children and – dear God, I do hope – keep him out of trouble.'

'I could have done those things,' Diana said but even as she spoke she knew it wasn't true. If she divorced Howard she would be virtually penniless; and together she and Max were more likely to seek out trouble than avoid it. The only thing she could have done – was, in fact, doing – was give him a child: and that was a secret she could never divulge, not even to Loelia, her closest friend. But she could give thanks for being married to Howard. He was the one rock in a disintegrating landscape.

Max and Laura Millward were married in New York on 10 October, 1929, and sailed on the *Berengaria* to Europe. There was a brilliant, if delayed, luncheon reception at Scotland Gate for those members of the Dunane circle who had not journeyed to America for the wedding.

'I don't know if I can face it,' Diana said on the morning of 24 October.

'You can,' Howard said. 'It's important, not least for Rupert's sake.' He did not add, 'and for the sake of the child you're carrying,' but they both knew that if they were to carry off the deception they could not shirk this occasion. Howard must not only be seen with his wife, he must be seen to be both proud and happy when her condition became known. Diana took him at his word, put on her new Chanel suit and hat, and enough *maquillage* to hide the dark circles under her eyes.

There may have been side-long glances as they entered and were introduced to the bride and members of her family, but by noon Howard's relationship with his wife was of minuscule importance to the assembled guests, for at about eleven-thirty that morning the bottom dropped out of the US stock market. Wall Street had crashed, and the news, which had begun to break at breakfast-time, was flashed around the world.

One by one the American guests at the luncheon fell silent, as news came in that New York's leading bankers had held an emergency meeting. 'How can they have been so blind?' Howard said quietly. 'It was bound to come. In ten years, dealings have more than quadrupled. There was bound to be a day of reckoning.'

Diana hardly heard him. She was looking at Max, the freckles standing out on the bridge of his nose as his face paled at the prospect of being tied for life to an heiress who might inherit nothing but a pile of worthless paper.

In the years she had come and gone from the Lansky house, Esther had begun to understand something of the Jewish way of life, but she also knew it meant different things to different people. For Emmanuel it meant scholarship and charity; for Sammy it meant a series of constraints and responsibilities; for Rachael it meant food and service. According to Rachael, each celebration should be 'half and half': half for God and half for people. 'Always Jews have to struggle,' she told Esther. 'Sometimes they starve. So when God is good and food is there, you enjoy!'

Before each special day, Rachael's kitchen became a factory for the production of naches or pleasures: *lekach,* the honey cake, peppery chickpeas, *gefilte* fish with *kichl* or crackers, *shashlik* with rice, blintzes and cheesecake, chicken, stuffed cabbage-leaves, strudel, and hard-boiled eggs, and *lokshen kug*l, almond cakes, bitter-sweet *charoset* for the Passover, and for the Purim festival triangular *hamantashen* with poppy-seed filling which was a favourite of Queen Esther, according to Rachael – all of these good things had their place, on the separate occasions. There were also a host of rules to add complication. Meat and milk must never appear together in any form; Rachael had separate crockery and pans for each, and she and Emmanuel would take great trouble over meat or poultry to make sure it was kosher.

Rachael negotiated her way through the rules with a look of serenity which never slipped, not even when Sammy raided the oven before things were well done. Sammy fretted eternally against the strictures of the *halachah,* or religious law. At five he had begun to read the Bible; at ten he was given the oral laws and traditions to study; at thirteen he was 'bound to the commandments' at his Bar Mitzvah. Now, at nineteen, he wanted to be free.

This year he had even resented the total fasting of Yom Kippur, the Day of Atonement, which brings to an end the ten days of reflection after the Jewish New Year. He had not, in fact, eaten or drunk on that day, but he had grumbled; and Esther saw the pain on his father's face. As soon as Yom Kippur was over Sammy threw himself into his dealing, trying to demonstrate to his father that he was serious about the small amount of buying and selling he was doing. Seeing how hard the boy was working, Esther looked to Lansky for his approval. All she got was a rueful smile, and when she queried it he took down his Bible and opened it at Exodus, Chapter 13. Esther read where his finger pointed: *Consecrate to me every first-born...*

'He is my first, my only son, Esther. I want him for a scholar, a rabbi. But this one... he seems to believe in nothing.'

'Give him a chance,' Philip said, when Lansky spoke of his fears for Sammy. 'Remember Tennyson: "There lives more faith in honest doubt, believe me, than in half the creeds..."'

The day that Wall Street tumbled, Esther was scrubbing the pine table in Philip's kitchen when Sammy's knock came at the door. Usually he came in search of comfort, or a consoling currant bun. Today he had a mission. 'See, Esther – there is our fortune!'

Esther peered from the yard door and saw a handcart piled with wooden cases. Sammy hefted one down and staggered with it into the kitchen. It contained cans of New Zealand condensed milk, their labels ornamented with a grinning cow that looked more like a gargoyle than a beast of pasture. The brand name was Evox, printed in a deep maroon.

'Look at that,' Sammy said. 'No wonder it didn't sell.'

'Didn't sell?' Esther asked, weakly.

'The Co-op couldn't shift it,' Sammy said proudly. 'I can. But first we have to change all the labels.' The side of the crate said: *48 tins*. Esther thought of the piled handcart.

'How many?' she said.

'A hundred cases – the rest are still at the auction house.' He waved a sheaf of new labels. 'Four thousand eight hundred tins for £50. You strip, I'll re-cover.' The new labels were butter-yellow and white, with the brand-name 'Choice' embossed in leaf-green.

'An improvement?' Sammy asked.

Esther gave a grudging nod, wiped down the pine table, and began stripping off the old labels.

Sammy had bought the unsaleable stock at just over a penny a tin. He sold them in the market over the next few weeks for 31/2d a tin. The profit was almost £90, when the cost of the labels was deducted. Sammy had practically doubled his outlay in one transaction. 'It won't always be so easy,' he said cheerfully. 'But it won't take me long to make you rich, Esther.'

The strike at Belgate pit lasted for six weeks and two days. Anne and the other wives had banded together to set up a soup kitchen, in the chapel, serving a hotpot of vegetables and bones and bread begged from nearby Sunderland, where men were still in work. No child went hungry, and pride at their achievement filled the empty bellies of their parents.

A miner's house without a fire could not be called a home. The men gathered wood from the surrounding countryside, and collected cinders from the ash heap where the weekly netty-emptying was flung. Shallow veins of coal near the disused shaft at Belgate were gouged from the earth, the colliery spoil heap was sifted and plundered, and somehow every Belgate chimney kept its plume of smoke.

Children went to school in boots and shoes mended with strips cut from motor-tyres and their inner tubes; a sheep was rustled from a night-time field and shared around. Belgate survived the battle but it lost the war. In the end Frank's suspension was lifted, but the corrupt official kept his place; and the men had to go back and work their guts out for money to pay their debts.

Esther helped Anne with both food and money. Mary Hardman helped, too, but honesty prevented her from taking Howard Brenton's left-over food to the men who were striking against him. She left the groaning Brenton kitchen, to carry what little she could from her own larder to the village below, but Anne was never satisfied. The strike was in full swing when she realized she was pregnant again. She sat staring into the fire, rocking her last baby in her arms, and then shrugged philosophically. It was God's will, and must be accepted. She kept the secret to herself until Frank was back at work and strong enough to bear it.

When at last Anne told him, Frank hung his head, appalled at the thought of another mouth to feed. At last he put out a clumsy hand in consolation, and then, gathering up his eldest son, he walked up and out of the village, to a place just below the house on the Scar, where he could look down on Belgate and the autumnal countryside surrounding it. As Joseph ran about, finding blackberries beside a rocky outcrop, and rousing a startled bird from its lair, Frank scanned the landscape.

He saw the rubble-walled squalor of the Shacks; the narrow, crowded streets of colliery houses; the fever hospital, where three people had died of smallpox less than two years before; the solid bulk of the Half Moon and the welfare hall; the aged miners' homes; the main street with its lock-up shops; the towering, brooding presence of the pit – and beyond it all, the spacious green surrounds of the colliery manager's house.

In some of the colliery houses there lived a father, mother and seven children, their ages ranging between two and twenty. The colliery manager and his wife had two children, of eight and ten, and five bedrooms. 'It isn't fair,' Frank said aloud. 'It isn't bloody fair!'

But when Joseph stopped, and looked round at the sound, Frank shook his head as though to dismiss his own words.

He whistled at a bird that was singing its heart out above them in the sky, and they set off together down the hill. His day would come sooner or later. First they must get piped water: each time he looked at his bairns, Frank thought of the way diphtheria could lay waste a village. A proper water-supply would mean the end of open sewers and nightsoil men. Peter Lee, the miners' leader, had promised them a reservoir that would mean the end of stand-pipes. First he must go for the clean water, then for the taking of the pits for the people. By the time the bairn in Annie's belly was ready for school, he might have achieved both these ambitions. All he had to do was work for the union with might and main, and put his faith in God – that way, anything might be accomplished.

As Joseph flagged, Frank hoisted the boy to his shoulders and jogged with him back to the house, where Anne was waiting.

While Frank was looking down on Belgate, his sister, Mary Hardman, was enjoying a rare day out in Durham city. She had ridden there in the bread van, for the house at the Scar was a good customer and the baker anxious to please its housekeeper. They sped along the country roads until the beautiful city came in sight; then they rattled over the cobbles, and came to a halt. The baker had business in the city until four o'clock: if Mary was standing in the Market Place then, under Lord Londonderry's statue, he would pick her up and convey her back to Belgate. Until then she was free to explore the shops. Such an expedition was a rare treat, and Mary had put on her best navy coat and hat for the occasion.

She wandered the narrow streets of the city, peering into the shops, enjoying the bustle of the crowd and the range of goods on offer, but by twelve o'clock her only purchase was a dozen caller herring, wrapped in newspaper and costing fivepence. She found herself then in Silver Street, with the cathedral and castle only a stone's throw away. If she went up there, she could sit in the quiet semi-darkness and rest her feet.

When she reached the Palace Green, the sun was shining, turning the surrounding stone buildings to a warm beige-colour that belied the crispness of the air. The towers of the cathedral soared before her, a delicate tracery against the blue sky. Behind her the squat solidity of the castle seemed to brood. Mary went forward, through the arched doorway, out of light into half-light, and made her way towards the altar and the great rose window. Halfway down the aisle she slipped into a pew and closed her eyes, praying first for her children and then for her brothers and sisters and their families. It was not a Catholic cathedral, but that was only because it had been stolen, from them centuries ago by that monster, Henry VIII. Mary knew the nuns who had taught her at school had come here every feast-day of St Cuthbert, for the saint's bones were under the altar, or some such place. If it was all right for the holy sisters, it was all right for her. Besides: there was only one God, and He was a Catholic, and the Prods would have to admit it sooner or later.

Poor Anne was pregnant again, and though she might be thanking God for it now, it would be different once it was in the world and dragging at her skirts. Mary prayed, too, for her employer, for his son and his feckless wife who had deigned to come back but who might as well live on the moon for all the presence she was in the house. Still, it was no business of hers which way the gentry lived, and if truth was told, a house with a disinterested mistress in it was easier to manage than one where the lady was breathing down your neck: Mary smiled wryly, remembering the vicar's wife who had dogged her early working-days. Then she took a sixpence from her purse for the offertory, and went out again into the cold, bright sunlight. She had three and a half hours before she could rejoin the baker, and suddenly it seemed a long time, with little to fill it.

She was walking back to the Market Square, hoping to find a pie shop and buy a bite to eat, when a drunken man reeled out from the door of a public house. Even in his half-crouching state there was something familiar about his figure. Mary slowed her step, anxious not to get involved, as the man clutched the windowsill of the inn and tried to straighten up. It was then that she recognized him: it was Dr Quinnell, the man who had delivered Frank's first child – and probably saved its life, into the bargain. She moved cautiously forward, her raffia bag dangling from her arm, her other hand holding her hat on her head, not so much against the wind as to bolster her own confidence.

'Dr Quinnell?'

The handsome face was even more ravaged now than it had been five – no, six – years ago. He peered at her.

'I'm sorry?' The words were slurred, but the tone was courteous. 'Do I know you?' He moved closer. 'Yes, I do.' Mary saw he was fumbling in the back of his mind for her identity, and decided to put him out of his discomfort.

'I'm Mary Hardman. Mr Lansky brought you to Belgate one night, six years or so ago, when my sister-in-law was in labour.

'And you helped me deliver the baby,' Quinnell said, his words slurred. 'I remember. It was a boy.' He looked suddenly doubtful. 'It was a boy, wasn't it?'

'It was,' Mary answered. 'They called him Joseph.'

'Called?' he said. 'He didn't die?'

'No.' She shook her head to reassure him. 'No, he's a fine little lad now. Six years old, and goes to the Board School.'

Dr Quinnell belched suddenly, and shook his head in apology. 'I'm sorry.' He moved forward and bent his head to confide in her, his breath reeking of drink. 'So many people die, you see. I never get used to it. Out like lights: a boom and they're dead. Or else the pox gets them – but we don't talk about that. They're still casualties of war .and their wives... but we don't mention it.'

Mary hadn't the faintest idea what he was talking about, and her eyes flicked past him towards the Market Square, seeking escape. Dr Quinnell saw it, and laughed. 'I've frightened you, I'm sorry. But it has to be faced, you know. Syphilis. There, I've said it. I saw a woman die today, because her man brought her back a present from France. Oh God, I wish the war was *over*.'

Mary wondered if he was mad rather than drunk; but the tears that trembled on his eyelids moved her to compassion. She left her hat to its own devices, and took a grip on Dr Quinnell's arm. 'Where are you going? I'll walk with you.' After all, she reasoned, as they stumbled along amid curious stares, he had saved her brother's child, and maybe his wife as well. To convey him safely home was little thanks enough.

He had left Brandon, he told her, and lived now in a house in Durham, near to the river. 'But you can't escape,' he said ruefully, drunkenly, half to himself. 'Go where you like, you can't escape.' When they reached the house, she had to take the key from his fumbling fingers and fit it into the lock.

Inside, the house smelled stale and dusty, but the furniture was good and there were nice pictures on the wall and books everywhere.

'Do you live alone?' Mary asked, suddenly anxious lest a wife might swoop from the back kitchen and ask what the hell a strange woman was doing in her hall.

'Yes,' Quinnell said. He chuckled suddenly. 'That's lucky, isn't it? No one to harm but myself.'

Mary sat him in a chair in a back room which overlooked the river and bore signs of occupation, then she went through to the kitchen and put on the kettle. There was little in the larder, but she found a packet of Symington's oxtail soup and crumbled it into a pan. There was stale bread in an enamel bin and butter in a dish. She toasted two wedges of the bread on the gas stove, for the kitchen range looked as though it had been neither cleaned nor lit for a twelvemonth, and spread them liberally with butter.

When she carried the soup and bread through to the living-room, Quinnell was snoring in the chair, but Mary shook him awake. 'Come on,' she said firmly, 'I haven't made this for nothing. Eat up.' She sat over him while he ate, and then fetched a stool for his feet; she had dealt with Stephen drunk more than once, and her brothers a score of times. She covered Quinnell with a plaid rug from the settee, and drew the curtains. 'There now,' she said. 'Go to sleep.'

Quinnell looked at her for a moment, bemused, then he closed his eyes and slept.

Mary went into the hall, and took off her hat and coat.

Then she went into the kitchen, cheered by the challenge of sorting it out in the two and a half hours left to her before she had to rejoin the van.

When she woke Quinnell just after three-thirty, with tea on a tray, a fire was glowing in the range, and another in the living-room hearth, and a pie made from corned-beef and onion was cooking in his oven. She cut short his apologies and gratitude with an upraised hand. 'You wouldn't take pay for what you did for our Frank. The old J –. Mr Lansky told us that. So this is by way of a thank-you.'

Quinnell put aside the tea and rose to his feet, and Mary saw that beneath the pall of dissipation there had once been a handsome young man. At first she had thought him fifty; now she reckoned he was probably no more than forty.

'I'll walk with you back to the Square,' he said, but Mary shook her head.

'If you want to please me, you'll drink that tea – and

then get a wash.' She blushed, alarmed at her own cheek, but feeling she might as well be hung for a sheep as a lamb. 'There's a pie in the oven for your supper: don't waste it.' She collected her bag, and skewered on her hat, and then hesitated in the doorway. 'And look after yourself.'

She had to run, then, because his clock had said quarter to four, but when she turned at the corner Dr Quinnell was still standing in the doorway. She raised her hand to his salute, and then pounded on, hoping she would take the right turnings, feeling an odd mixture of regret and satisfaction and amazement churning in her belly – for all the world like the runs.

Patrick Quinnell stood watching her until she had passed from his sight, rubbing sleep from his eyes, and trying to make sense of the day.

Quinnell had gone to war at its outset, having practised as a doctor for only seven months before he joined the Northumbrian Field Ambulance unit and crossed to France. He had known there would be blood and pain, but nothing had prepared him for the reality. He had arrived in Boulogne in the early hours of Wednesday 21 April 1915, and watched as the soldiers were herded into the railway wagons. The next day the Germans had launched the first poison-gas attack on the Ypres Salient. He was twenty-five miles away, but he could hear the preliminary bombardment.

The roads were full of old men and women and children on foot, some pulling handcarts, all trying to make their way to somewhere safer. Their numb expressions told Quinnell that they had been through all this before, and knew they would go through it again. And then reports of the gas attack came through, and he was ordered to report to a field-casualty station.

The full horror of war struck him then, together with his own inability to bring relief. He could cope with torn flesh and shattered bones, but could do nothing about the fear in the eyes of boys whose lives were ebbing away. 'Take this,' someone had said one night, thrusting a tot of whisky into his hand. And so it had begun.

Quinnell went with the Northumberland Fusiliers to Poperinge, and then back to Ypres. They marched through the ruined town, past the Cloth Hall and the cathedral, to the continuous sound of shells bursting all around. That night he had bought a half-bottle of whisky from a corporal and had lulled himself to sleep. By the time the brigade left Ypres and moved to St Julien, he was halfway to being a drunkard. On one occasion a salvo of shells had come over and knocked him flat against the side of a trench. He had lain there, winded, certain he was dead – and relief had flooded over him. But when another salvo landed ten yards away, fear galvanized him into action – he realized he was still alive, and cried at the pity of it.

Quinnell had carried on, doing what he could, closing his eyes to the blood, his nose to the stench of death, thinking only of the easement that would come with the bottle. It was early 1917, and he was on the Somme, when his condition became dangerous to the men who depended on him. He was called before an examining board and then sent home in disgrace. There had been official phrases to cover it up, but their meaning was plain. He had no need of official censure. Nothing could match the pain of his own remorse.

Now he had left the practice Lansky had found for him in Brandon, and was working in a Durham hospital where victims of venereal disease, caught in the war, were treated. He did what he could for the hopeless cases, he drank... and he prayed for death. And now a woman he hardly knew, in a prim hat, with a basket stinking of fish, had baked him a pie. There was no end to the extraordinariness of life.

*

Philip had told Esther to meet him outside the Picture House, and she was there promptly at four. The *Echo* boys were running up and down, waving their papers and shouting about the American economy crashing – but America was a long way away. Far more interesting to Esther were the pictures of film stars outside the cinema: glamorous women like Gloria Swanson and Norma Shearer and Greta Garbo: handsome men with neat moustaches, like H. B. Warner, and with gleaming, slicked-back hair, like Victor McLaglen and Ivor Novello.

The film tonight was *The Constant Nymph* with Mabel Poulton and Ivor Novello. When Philip arrived a moment later, he was carrying a box of glacé fruits and apologizing for keeping her waiting. She heard the usherettes giggle together as they passed through and up the stairs, but it didn't matter. She smiled at him as they settled into their seats, and then the lights dimmed and the wonderful music began.

Esther reached for Philip's hand in the darkness, loving the feel of his long, slender fingers entwined in hers, feeling, as she always did, the swamping tenderness that overtook her at the thought of him. *I'm happy,* she thought. *The world can think what it likes and it doesn't matter at all.*

When Philip had to withdraw his hand to subdue a cough, she opened the glacé fruits and handed one to him to ease his throat, but he was wheezing slightly now and whispered, 'No, thank you,' to the proffered sweetmeat.

The film was entrancing and Esther gave herself up to it, and to the trailer for the next week's attraction, Cecil B. de Mille's *The King of Kings* with Claudette Colbert. It was not until the lights went up that she realized Philip wasn't well, and then she was too preoccupied with helping him into the fresh air and asking the manager to call a cab, to think of anything that wasn't practical. It wasn't until they were in the cab rattling back to Valebrooke that she began to feel afraid. 'You'll be all right when you get home,' she said, reassuringly. Philip smiled, but his smile was one of regret rather than agreement. *Let him be all right,* Esther prayed desperately. *Let him be all right.*

She got Philip into the hall, but it was impossible to get him up the stairs. He was too weak, and breathing with too much difficulty. She telephoned first for the doctor, and then to his brother's house. Putting down the phone, she ran upstairs to strip off her good coat and hat, and to hide the glacé fruits and her leather handbag. It would never do for the Brodericks to know she and Philip had been out together.

'I'll get the blame of this,' she thought as she ran back downstairs to let in the doctor.

Between them they got Philip to his room, and she went onto the landing while the doctor carried out his examination. She had thought it was pneumonia again, the enemy of Philip's poor chest, but the doctor shook his head.

'Not this time, I'm afraid. His heart is failing.' He moved his hands to illustrate. 'His spine was infected with tuberculosis many years ago. We halted the disease, but the bones collapsed. As the spine foreshortened, the chest became constricted…' He brought his hands together in a crushing movement. 'The lungs were confined; the supply of oxygen diminished; and the heart has suffered.' He shrugged, but before Esther could scream alarm and bombard him with questions, there was a ring at the doorbell and she had with difficulty to compose her face and let in the Brodericks.

They swept past her to buttonhole the doctor. Esther would have liked to hear more of what he had to say, but she needed to speak to Philip, now, before the others came between them. She hurried up the stairs and opened his door, knowing, as she heard his breathing, that the doctor had not exaggerated.

She sat on the edge of his bed, smoothing his sheet, touching his hands and his brow, putting back the dark hair that had fallen towards his eyes. Without his spectacles his eyes were dark and liquid, an urgent gleam in them as he gestured towards his dressing-chest.

There was so much Esther wanted to say to him, but Philip was speaking and she had to bend to hear. 'In the top drawer, an envelope. Take it to Lansky. Hide it now, Esther.'

She touched her lips to his cheek. 'Sh.I'll get it later.'

He half-lifted himself, agonizingly, on the pillow. 'Don't you realize, they'll be through this house with a fine-tooth comb before I'm cold?'

Esther went to the drawer, then, and put the envelope into her pocket.

'There now, it's done. I have it safe,' she said, returning to the bed.

Something in Philip's face had changed: there was a slackening, an obliteration of lines. He looked relieved. 'I love you, Philip,' she said. 'I love you.'

He smiled and then he spoke again. 'Thank you, my dearest… I need you here…

Esther heard the door open, and then his brother was at the bedside, with the doctor in attendance, and Mrs Broderick was drawing Esther away. 'You can get on with your work,' she said. 'We'll call you, if you're needed.'

For a moment, in despair, Esther considered rebellion, but it would have been useless. She went on to the landing, closing the door behind her, and stood there for a long while before she summoned up the courage to go down, and get on with her duties.

Philip lingered for another night, and the most of a day. Whenever she could, Esther went to his room, touching his hand, smoothing his sheets, laying her cheek against his. At first he smiled at her presence, but at last he slept.

Occasionally she made tea and carried it upstairs to the sickroom where the Brodericks, husband or wife, were keeping watch. When darkness came, all three of them stood at the foot of the bed, looking down at the calm face of the sleeper.

'He won't last another day,' Mrs Broderick said. There was no grief in her tone: it was a statement of fact, no more. Esther offered to make a meal, and then sit with Philip while they ate it. To her delight they accepted, and she had one precious half-hour alone with the man who had taught her to love.

'My darling,' she said, stroking the hair from his brow. But Philip was slipping away from her, and she had to be content with placing her lips against his unresisting mouth, so that his last faint breaths should mingle with hers.

He died three hours later, while Esther crouched on the stairs outside his room, willing him to know that she was with him to the end.

'He's gone,' Mrs Broderick said, coming out of the bedroom. 'Quite peacefully in the end, which is a blessing. Put on a kettle for tea. There's a lot to be settled.'

Esther had been afraid she would cry, but the pain she felt was too bad for tears. She made tea stoically, warming the pot, putting in a spoonful for everyone and one over. She did not count herself; she knew she would not be included.

She carried the tray through to the dining-room, and then went back to the kitchen. Though she wanted to go upstairs again, she knew she must not. If she wanted to be allowed to stay in the house with Philip's body till the last moment, she must be careful not to show that it mattered. She was sitting at the kitchen table when Mrs Broderick at last came in search of her.

'You can clear the tray, Esther; then you can go. I'm sorry we kept you here so late.'

Esther had counted on being left alone with Philip, and it must have shown in her face. 'My husband is staying here tonight. I presume the spare bed is made? You'll want to go home now, but please come back as soon as you can. The undertaker will take my brother-in-law to his premises until the funeral, which we hope will be on Thursday. I'd better have your key, in case we need a spare. My husband will let you in when you come tomorrow.'

So that was how it was to be, Esther thought, as she mounted the stairs, ostensibly to check on the spare room where Mr Broderick was going to sleep, in reality to remove all traces of her presence and hide them in the landing cupboard. She could hear voices in the hall: the Brodericks were seeing out the doctor. She only had a few minutes, and plenty still to do, but first she must make her goodbyes.

Philip looked peaceful now, his eyes closed, his hands folded beneath the cover. She bent to kiss the cold brow and touch the unresponsive arms that had held her close so many times. 'Goodbye, my darling,' she said, and gently put back the sheet over his beloved face.

She felt strange as she went back downstairs. This house had been her sanctuary for six years, heaven for a few months, but soon she would no longer be allowed across its threshold. Suddenly she remembered the Dresden shepherd and shepherdess: they belonged to her, but it was useless to ask for them. She took them down from the mantelshelf and put them in her bag; then she went through to the drawing-room to say goodnight. She could only hope the items of clothing, the books and toiletries she had hidden in the landing cupboard would be safe until she could remove them. She didn't care now for the Brodericks' good opinion, but she did fear being banished from the house prematurely.

As she left Valebrooke, the gas lamps were still flaring in the deserted street. It was five o'clock in the morning. In an hour or two the street would resound to the rattle of the milk dray, and the postman's whistle as he delivered the mail. She had heard him the day before, whistling the song that was on everyone's lips: 'I lift up my finger and I say tweet tweet....' Esther started to laugh suddenly, an odd, discordant chuckle of a laugh. 'I lift up my finger and I say tweet tweet...' When she reached the park, she sat on a seat high above the town and stayed there till the dawn came, and the first day of her life without Philip began.

20

As soon as she had attended Max's wedding-reception, Diana went north, travelling with Howard. Loelia said goodbye with a hint of guilt in her demeanour and genuine regret in her words: 'I'll miss you, Di… but you'll be coming up to town soon, I'm sure. I'll take you somewhere wonderful and we'll get absolutely blotto together!' She paused. 'And it's for the best. Howard is so pleased about the baby. I'm glad for you both.'

Did she know it was her brother's child? If so, no hint of the knowledge showed on her face. They both knew that Diana would not return to London until after the birth; she must be seen to be with Howard if their circle was to believe he was the father of her child.

'I don't know,' Loelia said abstractedly, as they embraced. 'There are so many things to worry about at the moment.'

Diana knew she meant Max's punctured expectations of his wife's wealth. 'I expect we'll all survive,' she said coolly, and then turned away to Howard and the car that was waiting to take them to King's Cross.

Fox met them at the station, immaculate in his thick green cloth jacket with its high collar hooked at the throat, his green breeches and polished black leggings. The green cap with its shiny black peak was jammed beneath his arm, as he opened the door of Charles Brenton's Daimler.

'Good to see you back, ma'am,' he said and Diana felt a sudden lump in her throat.

'Thank you, Fox. I've really been away too long.' She thought she saw a gleam of sympathy in his eye, but when she looked again his face was as impassive as ever.

That first night at the Scar the conversation at the dinner-table was stilted. Things were a little easier when they went through to the drawing-room, and she played the song that every errand-boy was whistling: 'I lift up my finger, and I say tweet tweet'. That brought a smile to Howard's face, and on an impulse Diana left the piano and went to kneel at his feet.

'Oh Howard, I do mean to make things up to you.'

She had never looked lovelier, Howard thought, as he shook a deprecating head. Her face had softened with pregnancy, as it had done when she was carrying Rupert. Her dark hair was longer now and curled about her face; her arms and throat were white above the cerise satin evening-gown. A diamanté bracelet was clamped on her upper arm with an orange chiffon handkerchief floating from it.

'There's nothing to make up for,' he said. And then, anxious to assure her of his goodwill, he put a hand on her hair: 'We'll be all right, you'll see.'

'Yes,' Diana said. 'Yes, I think we will.' She bit her lip for a moment as if uncertain whether or not to speak. 'There's just one thing, Howard: please, *please* don't let your father force the Dragon Nurse upon me. That's the one thing I couldn't bear.'

'You must have someone to help you,' Howard objected. Privately, the thought of having Nurse Booth in his home for six months appalled him, too, but Diana would need attention of some kind.

'I'll find someone,' Diana said. 'There are plenty of people here. Look how well Susan has turned out: Rupert adores her. I'm going to get out and meet people – does your mother still help at that welfare affair? I could help there too, and I'd probably find some nice woman. Do you remember Esther, little Esther? She was a brick when Rupert was born. What's become of her?'

'She went to work in Sunderland, I believe – I haven't heard of her for years. Mary might know. There's some connection… Mary's brother is married to Esther's sister, at least I think that's it.'

'Well, then, nearer the time I'll speak to Mary,' Diana said. Howard turned away, wondering if Diana really had forgotten the circumstances of Esther's departure from Scar.

When dawn flooded the park, Esther walked to Lansky's house to break the news.

'Esther!' Lansky said. 'Not Philip?' He looked at her for a moment, and then he opened his arms. She came to the black coat-front, feeling the hair of Lansky's beard against her forehead, knowing that at last it was safe to cry. Sammy came running, then, and shook his head in disbelief, and Rachael brought herb tea and honey cake.

At last Esther remembered the letter, and fished in her pocket. 'He wanted you to have this.' Lansky knew what it was.

'Open it, Esther,' he said. 'It's for you.'

As she had suspected it was the will witnessed by the Lanskys, leaving Esther Gulliver everything of which Philip Blakeston Broderick should die possessed. Esther contemplated it for a moment, almost overcome by emotion, but knowing she must keep her head.

'I don't want it,' she said at last. 'They'll say I twisted it out of him. They'll say dreadful things….' She took the vellum in both hands to tear it across, but Lansky snatched it from her.

'Wait, Esther. Think!'

'I have thought. I've been thinking all night. I can't face

the things they'll think – the things they'll say. Not just about me, but about Philip, too. I want it destroyed.'

Lansky looked at Esther for a moment, and then he handed the will over without a word.

'Don't, Esther,' Sammy urged, anxiously. 'Philip wanted you to have it. It's not up to you.'

But it was up to her. Esther had made up her mind what she would do the day she had known of the will's existence. She tore it across, first one way and then another.

'I don't know whether you are a fool,' Lansky said, 'or the sanest woman I have known.'

'*I* know what she is,' Sammy said. 'She's *meshuge*: mad!'

When she arrived back at Philip's house in the afternoon, both the Brodericks were waiting for her. 'Can you come through to the morning-room?' Mrs Broderick said. Esther knew what was coming, and she was not going to lie, but she was not giving back the Dresden either.

The other woman pointed to the mantel. 'There used to be something there, didn't there? Two ornaments.'

'Yes, Ma'am,' Esther said. She spoke politely but her eyes were hard.

'Well?'

'They were mine.'

'Yours? I hardly think so.'

'Mr Philip said they were to come to me. He said it more than once.'

'And you couldn't wait to take them?'

Esther did not answer, but she did not flinch either, and after a moment the other woman's scornful eyes shifted, and she shrugged.

'Oh well, it's matterless. Now, the funeral is on Friday. The undertaker has been for the remains.' She might have been speaking of an unwanted commode. 'You'll be needed to dismantle the house. It'll be sold, of course. We'll pay you till then, and I'll give you a recommendation.' Her eyes flicked momentarily to the two spaces on the mantel, and then back again.

'Thank you,' Esther said, 'but that won't be necessary. I already have another position.' It was a small lie but a great satisfaction.

Until the day of the funeral, she swept and cleaned the rooms the Brodericks had picked over. They went at it like two children let loose in a sweetshop, going home at night burdened down with their booty. But Esther remembered the day the bailiffs had come to Belgate and she and Anne, with Frank's help, had salvaged something from their home. She flitted ahead of the Brodericks, retrieving Philip's favourite smoking jacket, the scrimshaw she had given him, several well-loved books and the second-best chess set, the one they had used each evening. She carried them boldly from the house in her shopping bag, and blessed the earlier misfortune that had taught her how to steal.

On the day of the funeral there was no place for Esther in the cortege. She rode with Lansky in his carriage and took her place at the back of the church, leaving before the interment so that she would be back at Valebrooke in time to serve the funeral eats. When they left the church she saw Sammy and Rachael standing vigil at the church door.

'Shalom, Esther,' Rachael said softly. And then: 'A *mentsh*. He was a *mentsh*.'

That evening Esther sat with the Lanskys, her tears stayed because she was with Philip's friends.

'What will you do now, Esther?' Sammy asked.

'You don't have to make decisions,' Lansky said gently, and his eyes were kind.

'I'll find another place, I suppose,' Esther answered. She felt heavy and weary, and her eyelids burned.

'Work with me,' Sammy said urgently. 'You work the market, I look for goods. Together we will prosper.'

There was a snort from Lansky's chair.

'We'll see,' Esther said, listlessly. 'Let me finish one job before I find another.'

That weekend Mrs Broderick gave her her wages, and a week's notice. 'We're moving out the things we want,' she told Esther. 'You can have what's left, if it's any use to you. But it must be out by Monday. What's here then will have to be broken up.'

'She knows that will make me take it,' Esther thought. 'She just doesn't want to pay for its shifting.'

The furniture the Brodericks left was large and old and unsuitable for most modern homes.

'Leave it to me,' Sammy said, when she carried her problem to him. 'Do you want any of it?'

Esther kept a chair with a brocade seat and a broken leg that had occupied a corner of Philip's bedroom. The rest was from rooms that had never been used. 'I'll find it a place,' Sammy said. And when she would have thanked him: 'No more *plaplen*.'

Life at the Scar was undisturbed by news of Philip Broderick's death. Anne mentioned to Mary that Esther had lost her place, and Mary sympathized, but she was preoccupied with a letter which had arrived for her at the Scar. *I got your address from my friend Lansky, I hope you don't mind.* She had not known the old Jew knew her whereabouts, but then again, people said he had eyes in the back of his head. She read on:

I want to apologize for my state the day we met, and explain if I can. I will meet you in the Market Square on any day you care to mention. I do hope you'll come. I need to make amends.
Yours sincerely,
Patrick Quinnell
P.S. The pie was delicious.

Mary deliberated for a day and then she replied. *I will be coming to Durham next Wednesday at two, if that's all right with you.* She wondered how she should sign it and then put, *Kindest regards, Mary Hardman*, and carried it to the post-box at the foot of the hill before she lost her nerve and changed her mind.

She rode into Durham on the bread van again, wearing her good coat and hat which were too flimsy for the winter, but the best she could do. She carried a beefsteak pie and some drop-scones in a wicker basket, but seriously considered leaving them behind the baker's seat on the grounds that they would (a) not be up to her usual standard, and (b) look as if she were pushing herself.

Quinnell was waiting in the Market Square by the Londonderry Statue, looking haggard but as sober as a judge.

'Mrs Hardman,' he said, taking off his hat.

'Doctor,' she answered, formally, and then spoiled it by breaking into a nervous laugh. They went into a tiny café behind the Maypole Dairy, and had tea and iced cakes at a table with a checked cloth and a spray of artificial daisies in a jar.

At first Mary spoke hardly at all, and Quinnell made conversation about trivial things. They moved on to the subject of children, then, and the baby he had delivered for Frank and Anne. 'She has three more now,' Mary said. 'And another's on the way. All easy births.' She grinned suddenly. 'Not according to her, but you know what I mean.'

Quinnell nodded, smiling, and then grew serious. 'About the last time we met. I'm sorry…'

Mary put out a hand and shook his arm. 'Hush. Think nothing of it. I've seen a man in drink before – more than one. My own man could sup his share.'

'What happened to your husband?' Patrick asked. 'I know you're a widow.'

It was easy to talk then: to tell him of Stephen, and the

move to the Scar, and her hopes for her children, and her worries about her brothers, dependent on the pit with unemployment rising by the hour.

When it was time for her to rejoin the van, Quinnell walked her back to the Square, and raised his hat in farewell.

'Next week?' he asked hopefully, and Mary lowered her voice in case the baker should hear.

'If you like,' she said.

'Same time, same place?'

She nodded and inclined her head, as the van began to move. Suddenly she remembered the pie and the drop-scones, still in the basket on her knee. 'Wait,' she said desperately, and opened the van door.

'These are for you,' she said, thrusting the basket at Quinnell. 'And for God's sake, watch what you drink.'

Her cheeks burned all the way back to the Scar at the thought of her own impudence, and her mood was not helped by the baker whistling 'You were meant for me' all the way home.

'Cheeky monkey,' she thought to herself, as she climbed out, and she slammed the door of his van with gusto.

Esther went to the cemetery on the first day of her new idleness. Philip's grave was still piled high with wreaths. She had brought her own tribute: a bunch of hothouse tulips. There should have been candles to light them, but she hoped that wherever he was there would be light in plenty, and that God would have restored him to the man he should have been. In her heart she did not believe in an after-life, but neither could she bear to disbelieve it. She bent and touched the newly turned earth before she left, and suddenly she knew that nothing died, nothing was wasted. Philip was in her memory, a distillation of his wisdom was in her brain. He would live on in Lansky, in

Sammy, in Rachael who thought him a *mentsh. While we remember him, he is,* she thought. As she walked away she wished suddenly that they had been brave enough to have a child – then Philip would have lived on in truth. Now it was too late.

'So,' Anne said, when Esther had greeted the children and turned out her handbag for sweets. 'You're out of a job, then?'

'Yes,' Esther said. 'But something'll turn up.'

'Don't go back to the Jew,' Anne urged. 'Make a clean break. If you've got to work, work where you'll be well thought of. I've told Mary, an' all. Her ladyship's come back to the Scar, full of her flighty ways; do this, do that. Turns up at the welfare clinic large as life. "Ooh," she says, "what lovely children." "No thanks to your lot," I said.' Anne grinned suddenly. 'Under me breath... but I said it. Anyroad, tell us about the funeral. Did he leave a will? I hope he's seen you all right after six years. Still, you're better off taking nowt – they'd only say he was funny with you. They've been saying as much round here, but Frank soon stopped them.'

So Philip was right, Esther thought sadly. Aloud she said: 'I don't expect to get anything, Anne. Why should I? I wasn't there that long, after all.'

'You never know,' Anne said. 'He might've taken a fancy to you, him being funny, an' all.'

If she doesn't stop, I'll scream, Esther thought desperately; and, as if Anne had heard, she changed the subject.

'By, that Estelle's an imp of Satan. If she'd been born in the Infirmary I'd've said they switched her. And wise! She's been here before, that one. I belted her this morning, but it did no good.' She shifted in her chair, plucking at the cloth of her dress where it strained across her bulging breasts. 'I'll be glad when me time's up, and no mistake.'

'How much longer is it now?' Esther asked.

'Five months. Never marry, our Esther – it's not worth

it. I used to think holy sisters were barmy; now I think they've got their heads screwed on.' Anne carried on, now complaining about her sister-in-law Mary lording it up at the Scar. 'It makes you think,' Anne said. 'That's where her man died. It beats me how she can forget.'

There was no getting away from bereavement, Esther thought, as she tried to look engrossed in her sister's words. It had come to Mary Hardman all those years ago, and she had seen it and not realized it would come to her one day. Mary had borne it, and carried on. Could she bear it as well?

21

Whenever she had been at the Scar before, Diana had fretted for London. Now she missed it not at all, except sometimes when a snatch of a song from a show came over the radio, or a newspaper showed a glittering gathering in a London venue. She made a conscious effort to enter into Howard's life, seeing how deeply troubled he was by rising unemployment, and the global unrest and misery that was evident.

In India, Ghandi was marshalling defiance to the salt-tax; in Russia, Stalin was wiping out the Kulaks; people were dying in unemployment protests in New York; and police were fighting with the out-of-work in London. There were millions unemployed in Britain now, in spite of Labour's coming to power. Trade-union leaders had denounced the total as showing 'the sickening effects of promises belied and hopes deferred'.

'Will it affect Belgate?' Diana asked, and Howard gave a despairing shrug. Charles had now given Fox and the new Daimler to Diana to go wherever she pleased; and on one of her first outings she asked him to stop outside the gates of her home. She got out then and walked to the brow of the hill to look down on Belgate.

She saw a village, consisting of four or five shops, a public house, a welfare hall, two churches and a huddle of dirty little houses, dwarfed by the black bulk of the pit and a heap that seemed to steam gently in the bleak winter sunshine. She had seen it many times before, but now she really took notice.

She saw the railway-lines that disfigured the landscape, the roofs dipping from subsidence, the closets at the back of each house, the fever hospital... then she looked down at her gloved hands, disfigured by the bulk of her rings. Was this the price of bedecking her: that the people of Belgate should live in squalor? She had lived off the profits of the coalfield for nearly a decade. What had she given back? Not even her presence there, most of the time.

'I shouldn't stand too long, ma'am,' Fox said, from behind her. 'The grass is damp.' He looked sympathetic, and Diana realized suddenly that he was young, and handsome into the bargain.

'Thank you, Fox,' she said. 'You're quite right.' He handed her into the car and she sank back into the leather upholstery, watching the hill fall away. As they sped through Belgate to the open countryside beyond, she was thinking that, for all her conviction that she was a woman of the world, she knew very little at all.

In the next few days and weeks Diana talked to Mary Hardman whenever she could, sometimes coming down to the huge kitchen or engaging Mary in conversation when she brought in tea.

At first Mary felt uneasy, even resentful, at this. But eventually she found herself feeling sorry for a woman so ill at ease in her own home, so patently lonely, and discontented with her own company. Talking of Belgate and their children, they came to understand one another a little better. Neither of them mentioned the death on the Scar, or the disastrous visit to console; neither of them forgot it, but each took pleasure in watching their children play together.

'Will you be with me when the time comes for my confinement?' Diana asked, and, when Mary agreed, she told Howard that she wanted only Mary and Dr Lauder to attend the birth. 'It's a second child, Howard: it won't be so difficult. Besides, it's what I want.'

Charles made a special trip to the Scar to change her mind, but Diana stood firm. If he insisted on employing Nurse Booth she, Diana, would pack her bags and go home to Barthorpe. The thought of a second grandson – for he was sure it would be a boy – being born under a Carteret roof was enough to change Charles's mind. He compromised by asking that a second, highly qualified doctor should be in attendance, and Diana agreed to this. 'We won't call either of them until the very last minute,' she told Mary, 'and by then we'll probably have managed it all on our own.'

She felt strangely healthy and serene, and eager to get on with the job of giving Howard a child. She seldom thought of the fact of its paternity. Her affair with Max seemed like some far-off, slightly embarrassing dream, which she would forget in time. Her serenity lasted through January and February, until she received a letter from Loelia with a cutting of a picture in the *Tatler*: Max and Laura at a party given by the rich and eccentric Duke of Westminster. That Max's Yankee wife should be there, in her place at Max's side, at such an enviable party was too much. Loelia's letter, telling of Laura's pregnancy and the glad news that most of her father's fortune had survived the Wall Street crash, was the last straw. Diana retired to her room and wept, until Mary bluntly told her to think of her unborn child.

Howard had watched Diana anxiously, afraid she would become bored and depressed in Durham. They dined with other couples, and went to the theatre in Sunderland, until Diana's pregnancy was too advanced for her to appear in public. Like Diana, he seldom thought of the child in her womb as a bastard. He had always detested Max Dunane, seeing in him everything he despised about the upper classes, so schooled himself to think of the baby as Diana's, and Diana's alone. Sometimes, thinking of Max's flaming red hair, he wondered whom the child would resemble, but he had many other things to preoccupy him and he did not dwell on it.

In the surrounding collieries, men had been laid idle year by year. Howard had managed to reduce manpower in the Brenton pits by natural wastage alone, and although this did not help the queue of youngsters looking for jobs, it meant that most houses in Belgate had one wage-earner at least – although at little more than seven shillings a shift, that did not mean much. Nevertheless, Howard was proud of what he had achieved, in spite of Gallagher and his father constantly reminding him of rising costs and the falling demand for coal.

He thought often of Trenchard, and the broken promise made to his friend – Lloyd George's promise that Britain should be a country fit for heroes to live in – and his own promise that he would help Trenchard to find a job. Anxious to save Rupert from similar remorse in later life, he took him on a tour of the Brenton empire, hoping to show him some realities of the working-man's world.

'You will own all this one day, and be good and kind to the men who work for you.' But the seven-year-old looked with something amounting to horror at the belching chimneys and the grimy faces of his workers. 'I'd much rather live in London, papa. I really don't like it here.'

Just after Christmas Edward Burton called on Howard in his office above the pit. 'I'll come to the point, Howard. All around the coalfield seats are falling to Labour; more with every succeeding election. Belgate is becoming a rarity, in that it has a Conservative MP. But John Conroy is a sick man, as you know. He can't stand again, and the way things are an election could come at any time. I've wanted you for Belgate for years. What do you say?'

'Why me?' Howard said, uncertainly.

'You're a new breed; the kind of man we need desperately if we're to retain a footing in the north. The Brenton name will carry weight with Conservative voters, but above all we need someone who represents what is best in

Conservatism – not some stuffed shirt from London who doesn't understand the Durham miner or have his welfare at heart.'

'I don't know,' Howard said. 'Would the people here want me?'

'I want you,' Burton said. 'I'm asking you to come forward. But I won't ask again. If you say no, or put me off, I must look elsewhere.'

'Give me time,' Howard said. 'A day or two: no more.'

When Edward Burton left, he brooded. He was critical of many Tory policies, but was it fair to criticize and then hang back?' He had always despised armchair critics. If he refused to stand, would that make him one himself? But if he stood for Parliament and won, what would happen to his marriage? Things had been so much better lately: could he put it at risk again?'

He carried the quandary to his wife, half expecting her to enthuse at the prospect of living in London, half expecting her to want him out of the way, as before, when she was ready to resume her former life. Her reaction touched him.

'What do *you* want, Howard? That's what I want. I've been too much taken up with my own affairs, but now I intend to be a better wife. If politics is what you want, I'll back you as much as I can. If you decide against it, I'll respect you for making the decision.'

Howard sat for a further few moments, and then he got to his feet. 'Thank you,' he said. 'I think you've helped me make up my mind.' He went to his study and telephoned Edward Burton.

'I'll do it,' he said. 'And God help us both to make it succeed.'

In the confusion of the past weeks or so, Esther had never thought about her period. When she realized it was long overdue she didn't worry at first. They could stop with shock; yes, the overwhelming grief she suffered would be the cause. She had been too careful for it to be anything else. And the tension in her breasts was due to the late period, no more.

It couldn't be a baby. Not only had she made sure she would not conceive, but she had cried herself to a standstill this past few weeks. The pain of life without Philip had been unbearable, the sense of loss an almost tangible thing. No baby could have survived that torrent of weeping, the nights pacing the floor, the days without food passing her lips.

But two months after Philip's death, Doctor Dix confirmed that Esther was pregnant. 'I can't be,' she said in bewilderment. 'I used suppositories and a douche.'

He shook his head. 'I'm afraid it didn't work, my dear. Have you someone to stand by you?'

Esther nodded, more out of a desire to get away than any conviction that anyone could help her now.

Outside in the street she walked like someone in a dream, oblivious of the rain that was falling. She moved towards the town, sometimes weeping; once, for a second, exulting; most of the time thinking furiously. What was she going to do? A passing carter swore at her when she almost stepped out in front of him, and several passers-by looked at her curiously. She wiped the rain and the tears from her face, tightened the belt of her black coat, and made up her mind. She must not think of what she wanted: that would be selfish. She must do what was right. She was sure of that, now – but how was she to accomplish it?

As usual she took her problem to Emmanuel Lansky. There was no easy way to tell him, so she simply spoke the truth. 'I'm going to have Philip's baby,' she said.

There was a long pause and then Lansky tugged at his beard. 'It is God's will,' he said, but he did not sound jubilant.

Esther had already decided what must be done: all she needed was his assistance.

'I must go away, Mr Lansky, right away. The baby will be born in summer, and I am going to give it up for adoption. I'll come back to Sunderland after that.'

'You will give the child away?' Now Lansky was shocked. Esther would have been moved by his disapproval if she had not remembered Philip's words: '*What would they say about a bastard with a cripple for a father?*' She knew what Philip would have wanted for his son or daughter: a good life.

'I want to go to Whitby, to the house where Philip stayed. I don't know what it'll cost, but I've got some money put by.'

'Hush,' Lanksy said. 'Money is not the problem, Esther. Knowing your mind is the problem. Once you give up the child there can be no going back.'

'There'll be no going back,' Esther said, and Lansky knew from the way she spoke that she would not be moved. Two weeks later she left Sunderland, ostensibly to keep house for an invalid cousin of the Lansky family.

'More Jews,' Anne said, when Esther went to say goodbye to her. 'You're a glutton for punishment, our Es, and no mistake.'

Esther's face was carefully schooled. The secret must be kept from Anne, of all people.

Lansky wanted to lend her money, but it was Sammy who came to her rescue with £30 – Esther's share of the profits – and a further £20. 'I got it for Philip's furniture, Esther. I sold it to that new boarding-house beyond the park. It was good solid stuff. They were pleased with it.'

Privately Esther doubted that the furniture would have fetched £20, but if it pleased Sammy to think he was fooling her… well, there would be ways of repaying him later.

She settled into the house at Whitby, hearing the sea roar at night, and a lone blackbird call before the wintry dawn.

She walked alone in the cold dusk and saw the ruined abbey on the hill, stark against the pale sky, the delicate tracery of a wheel window like a flower in the moonlight.

She wept very little, and smiled to herself a great deal, thinking that it was better to have loved wholeheartedly for a little while than to have half-loved for a lifetime. She sewed and knitted, so that her baby would not go from her unprovided for, and as the weather warmed with the spring she waited for the haar to roll in from the sea and remind her of the happiest three days of her life.

Sammy came to see her often, once plucking up courage to ask her whether she regretted destroying Philip's will. 'He's worth a packet, Esther, so they say. And he meant it all for you.'

There had been a moment, once, when Esther had thought that if she had had Philip's money she could have kept her child, but where would she have gone to hide its parentage? No, it was best as it was, and she told Sammy so.

'I'm learning to drive,' he said on his second visit. 'We need a van, Esther. When you come home we'll make things spin, you'll see.'

She was grateful to him, knowing he was trying to cheer her up. 'Yes,' she said, 'we'll make things spin, all right.' But in her heart she couldn't think beyond the day when her baby would come safely into the world, and would then go on to a good life. 'I want the best for him,' she told the doctor who was to attend her confinement, and he promised to make the proper arrangements.

The next time Sammy came he rattled up to her door ona noisy motor-bike with, wonder of wonders, his father upright in the side-car, goggles sitting oddly between his beard and his broad-brimmed hat, which was secured with a long woollen scarf tied beneath his chin.

'Only for you Esther,' Lansky said with a shudder, as he struggled free of the side-car. 'How are you, my child?'

She looked into his face and saw understanding there. He had lived for years without the woman he loved: he knew how she missed and yearned for Philip. Lansky put out his hand. 'You will cope, Esther. Don't be afraid.'

Later, when he had disrobed from the protective leather coat and gloves, she realized he had come on a mission. He sent Sammy out on an errand, and the speed of Sammy's exit told Esther it was pre-arranged.

'You have had time to think now, Esther; time to mull over the future. I want you to think about this child, the child of my good friend Philip and my equally good friend Esther. If you now want to keep the baby, it will be possible. I will help you.'

Esther shook her head. Behind Lansky's great head the window showed the sea, blue and clear, a white ship on the horizon sailing north. Oh, to be out there, and free! She licked her lips and knotted her hands in her lap, seeking the words that would convince him.

'I've thought it through, Mr Lansky. Please believe me. Philip and I talked... oh, we never thought there would be a child, we didn't intend there should be one. But we talked of the child we might have had.' Here her voice broke, and she bowed her head, lifting it when she heard a sob rattle in Lanksy's huge chest.

'Oh Esther, Esther, *let* me help you, for my friend's sake. To give away his child...'

She flashed at him then, her anger at the pain he was causing spicing her words. 'Do you think I don't want to keep it? My God, I think of it, I dream of it. I *feel* it, Mr Lansky, moving in me! But it's because I love it that I'm letting it go. Don't make it harder for me or I will surely die of the pain of it.'

When Lansky spoke again he spoke quietly. 'What do you want, Esther. Tell me.'

'The baby is going to go to a good home. That's what I want.'

Lansky raised his hands, palms downwards. 'We don't speak of it again.'

He paused and then he smiled. 'Now, show me this Whitby with its famous jet and its tales of Dracula. Make me forget I have to climb back into that infernal machine driven by my son, the madman.' His words were disparaging but Esther could tell he was secretly proud of Sammy's success. He did not any longer sound so anguished when he spoke of him. Thank God at least something was going right.

Mary Hardman went regularly now to meet Patrick Quinnell. Sometimes they took tea in the Maypole café. Sometimes she went back to his house, and cleaned and swept – discreetly, so as not to make him embarrassed. Sometimes he played his violin for her, Mendelssohn and Paganini, and pieces which made her smile like 'The Flight of the Bumble Bee'. And sometimes he talked of his work in the Durham hospital, where he treated victims of venereal disease. Mary had heard the dreaded words 'syphilis' and 'gonorrhoea', but they had seemed like some ancient plague, happening to people on another planet. Patrick made her see that they were diseases of the present day, and of the place in which she lived.

'They came back from France, Mary, one in three of them probably, carrying it to their wives and sweethearts. Now children have it; they are born into the world suffering from it. I thought I had seen the limit of suffering in Flanders, but this is worse. This is obscene.' Mary took Quinnell's hand, then, pointing out that he was helping them, that the war was long over, that sanity would come back to the world sooner or later.

She knew her visits were helping him. He still smelled of drink, but he was always in command of himself, and his appetite was returning. She began to look forward to her trips each week, as spring moved on towards summer, feeling her heart lift as the spires of the cathedral came into view. So it was with real regret that she wrote to Quinnell in May to say she could not come for a week or two.

Mrs Howard is near her time and can't be left, she wrote. *I'll write as soon as it's over and I can come to Durham again.*

Diana had taken to sitting in the window of a room that faced the sea. She was huge now, and her face was slightly bloated, but Mary found her much easier to get on with.

'It's started, Mary,' Diana said one morning, when Mary carried in her breakfast. 'Don't leave me yet… just sit beside me. I mean to do this myself if I can.'

Mary had helped at half a dozen births, and had endured two of her own. The idea of someone who had access to a doctor choosing to suffer labour without one seemed madness to her, but she sat obediently by Diana's bed, holding her hands when the contractions were intense, making her laugh in between with tales of the Belgate midwife and her penchant for a drop of stout. Howard brought Rupert to the bedside in the early stages, and kissed Diana's brow before he left the room.

'Not long now, my dear,' he said.

At last Diana's grip on Mary's knuckles grew painful and beads of sweat blossomed on her lip. 'I ought to tell someone,' Mary said. 'It'll be too late, if we don't watch out.'

'Five minutes,' Diana said. 'Five… more… minutes.'

She was panting now, trying to smile as she did so to keep Mary sweet and stop her from summoning help. 'If it's a girl I'm going to call it Pamela, but I can't think of a name for a boy. We used them all up on Rupert. What was your husband's name?'

'Stephen,' Mary said, thinking that in the circumstances Diana might have remembered a dead man's name.

'Stephen? I like that. Stephen Brenton? If it's a boy he

shall be Stephen...' There was an intake of breath, and then a squeal. Mary stood transfixed, realizing it was now too late to go for the doctor, but not wanting to bring the child into the world herself. Suddenly and inexplicably she remembered Frank's words when Stephen had died: *'It was her fault her pride and her greed and her need to have everything done yesterday.'* But as Diana moaned again, the words were forgotten. Mary rang the bell for hot water, and began to bring Diana Brenton's baby into the world.

'It's a girl,' she said joyfully as the child slithered into her hands, 'with a pair of lungs on her like Nellie Melba.'

'Let me see,' Diana said, struggling on to an elbow. Mary thought it was simply a mother's anxiety to see her newborn child, but in reality Diana was terrified that the baby might resemble Max. When she saw that her daughter had a mop of black hair instead of a ginger crown, she sighed with relief and sank back on her pillows.

'She's lovely,' Mary said admiringly, but Diana had closed her eyes to squeeze back tears of relief – and of regret that the man who had fathered her child had never once, in all the past months, enquired about her welfare.

A week later Sammy's bike rattled through Whitby again, but this time the side-car was occupied by a giggling blonde in a yellow tweed costume and a hat with a long feather in the band.

'She's a *shiksa*,' Esther whispered to Sam.

'So she's *shiksa*,' Sammy said. 'Who cares?' He had brought Esther two big white fivers – profits, he said, from a sale of corned beef – a jar of peach preserve from Rachael, and some papers and magazines. Later, after he had driven off, his passenger waving frantically from the side-car, Esther spread out one of the papers on her kitchen table. It said that unemployment was still rising. It also said that the will of Philip Blakeston Broderick had been passed for probate. He had left £14,000 12s 6d. She turned the page, trying not to think of what she had read, and saw that a daughter, Pamela Charlotte, had been born to Diana and Howard Brenton, and that mother and baby were doing well. By the next day's post Esther learned that Anne, too, had been delivered of a baby girl.

22

Diana was more at ease with her new baby daughter than she had ever felt with Rupert. For one thing, there was not the same restless urge to get away from Durham. She felt safe at the Scar, and in summer, as the hedgerows bloomed with cow parsley and dandelion, she grew to look forward to Fox collecting her and the children and taking them out to run free in the countryside. She and Susan would take turns with the pram, and Fox would walk ahead with Rupert and Catherine, falling back to help with the pram if the road was rough, or they encountered a bank.

Diana had come to rely on Fox. He was always courteous, good with the children, and helpful with Susan. She cherished a romantic notion of acting as Cupid between nursemaid and chauffeur, but when, walking in the woods once, he found a patch of wild orchids, it was Diana to whom he presented them. She was touched by the gesture, hiding her embarrassment in a shriek of dismay when she held them to her nose and, found they smelled of torn cats.

Howard was always pleased to hear of these outings, but seldom had time to accompany them. 'I must learn to drive myself,' Diana wailed. 'Loelia does it, and almost every other woman I know. And when I do learn I shall buy myself a Cadillac with synchro-mesh gears, and zoom around the countryside like an aeroplane.'

Privately Howard thought it would probably be better if Diana remained a passenger, but if she wanted to learn he would not stand in her way. He was preoccupied with his new role as candidate-in-waiting and by the increasingly shaky political scene in Westminster.

Unemployment was now becoming a public scandal.Ramsay MacDonald had appointed Sir Oswald Mosley, a magnetic orator and man of ideas, to deal with the problem, but he had stormed out of government in protest at the Cabinet's failure to implement his proposals. Clement Attlee had taken his place, but Howard felt he was too quiet and colourless an individual to heal such a long-standing and intractable sore. Lloyd George's support was vital to the minority Labour administration, and he was demanding electoral reform as the price of his continuing to bail out the government; but MacDonald would not commit himself to change in the lifetime of the present Parliament, and the Lib-Lab pact came to an end. If that were to bring a general election, Howard might find himself sitting in Parliament, 250 miles away from his roots and from the industries that produced his wealth.

Pamela's christening came as a joyful event in a sombre period. When Howard had first looked down at the newborn child, he had been afraid of his own reaction: would he feel hostility towards her? But he felt only pleasure at the sight of a life safely entered into the world. He was relieved that the child had been born in Diana's image, but it had seemed the baby peered at him, as if to establish kinship, and he had found himself bending forward and saying, 'Hello, Pamela.'

Charles, surprised to hear that the christening would not take place in London, immediately cast around for the most prestigious northern venue; but Diana had determined that the christening should take place in Belgate. She was grateful to Howard for the way he had stood by her after years in which she had not even attempted to fulfil her role as his wife. Now she meant to make amends by entering into the life of the coalfield.

The baby was christened on 8 June 1930, with Geoffrey, Caroline and Loelia as godparents, and a clutch of local gentry as guests. Diana had nothing in common with her sister-in-law, who was rapidly turning into a facsimile of her mother, but while they stayed at the Brenton home, she put herself out to be pleasant, enthusing over Caroline's children: Celia, now six, and Emily, three, and the new baby, Andrew. A splendid christening party with Champagne and a huge cake was held at the Scar; and while the Brentons feasted above, five mothers in the village below tried, with wet cloths and open windows, to bring down the fever afflicting their children. Diphtheria had come to Belgate. Before the epidemic ended seven children would be dead, among them Philomena Maguire. Not even the new baby, asleep in its crib, could assuage Anne Maguire's grief.

The Brentons knew nothing of the early days of the epidemic, but news of the goings-on at the big house spread through Belgate like a forest fire. When Anne Maguire knelt by her daughter's coffin, praying out loud for the forgiveness of sins, she thought in private of the biblical exhortation to extract an eye for an eye, a tooth for a tooth. She blamed her child's death upon the inequalities of life, and she blamed those inequalities on the Brentons and their ilk. When Esther had worked at the Scar, she had told tales of expense: of gowns that cost forty guineas, of silver backed brushes and kid gloves at £2 lOs a pair. In the coalfield, the minimum wage for a shift was 6s 61/2d. Since Anne had married Frank, she had seen his wages reduced by half, while his output and his working hours had increased.

But there was hope for the future. Manny Shinwell was the new Secretary for Mines; he understood pitmen and would see to their needs. Anne threaded her rosary through stiffening fingers, praying alternately for vengeance and for the sweet repose of her baby daughter's soul.

*

Esther's son was born on 28 August 1930, as England sweltered in a heatwave and temperatures in London soared to 94 degrees. The midwife sponged Esther's forehead with vinegar and water, but the sheets grew damp with sweat as the pain came and went, to no avail. The doctor held her hand between contractions and chatted about anything and everything, never waiting for her reply. 'Have you seen pictures of the new Sydney bridge?' he asked, and Esther felt a spasm of annoyance that he should expect her to be interested in events on the other side of the world.

Her anger must have done the trick. The pain began to escalate; sweat streaked down into her eyes, and then into her open mouth, as she screamed aloud in agony: 'Oh God, please, God!' Then there was a feeling of relief, and the midwife was holding up a blood-streaked bundle, slapping it until it cried aloud.

'Is it all right?' Esther asked weakly, anxiously, half afraid that some part of Philip's disability might have endured.

'It's fine,' the midwife said. 'And it's a boy, if you're interested.' The baby was crying and Esther held out her arms. After a quick whispered conversation between nurse and doctor, he approached the bed.

'Is it wise to hold the baby, my dear? Nurse can arrange for it to go to a good woman who will wet-nurse it along with her own child, until it goes to its new home. Why put yourself through further pain?'

'I want to hold him,' Esther said. 'For a few days, that's all… then I'll let him go.'

A few moments later the swaddled baby was placed in her arms and she looked down on a dark little face. 'He's like his father,' she said softly, joyfully.

The nurse's face registered surprise, and Esther heard the doctor whisper: 'He died.'

'Poor thing,' the nurse said, and when it was time to take the baby and put it in the crib her hands were gentle. 'You get some sleep,' she said to Esther. 'You've been a good girl. Now you need to rest.'

Esther kept the baby with her for two weeks, the lying-in period for a first-time mother. In the last two days she was well enough to dress and carry her baby out into the summer sunshine. There she crooned to him, and told the tight little face and the closed eyes that he had been conceived and born of love, and never to forget that fact as long as he lived.

On the fourteenth day, Sammy came, at her request, to take her home to Sunderland. He arrived in a green van bearing the legend *Lan-ver Products – Quality Assured*.

'That's our new name, Esther: Lansky and Gulliver. We're partners.' He was trying to cheer her up, she could tell. The name on the van had been painted in hastily, and Sammy's eyes were anxious. Esther was suddenly aware how mature he had become in the year since his nineteenth birthday. His slender frame had filled out, his chin had firmed, and he looked thoughtful, and concerned for her.

Esther walked to the crib and looked down on her sleeping child. She had experienced such pain over the last few months that now she felt numb, washed clean of grief and loss. But her determination had not wavered. 'Come here, Sammy,' she said and he came to her side. 'Look at him...'She moved the shawl from the baby's chin to give a clearer view. 'He's a lovely baby, and I want him to be happy. I want him to have a father and a mother, and a home somewhere where there will be no whispers, no cruel words.' She looked at Sammy, but his lips were trembling, and she saw that he could not bring himself to speak. She held out her arms and he clung to her.

'He is going to a good woman, someone the doctor knows who has tried for years to give her husband a child.

They are kind people; the father is a teacher. They will love this child.'

Sammy straightened up, looking shame-faced. 'Perhaps you're right, Esther. I'm sorry. I came to help, and…' He wiped his nose on the back of his hand, and Esther saw that he was not as grown-up as she had thought.

After that she dressed the baby carefully and packed his clothes in a Moses basket. When it was done she sat at the door of the cottage to await the doctor's arrival. She did not cry, but once she held the baby's face against her own and, feeling the fragility of his cheek, a little moan escaped her.

It was too much for Sammy. 'Don't do it, Esther,' he said. 'Don't do it… I can't bear it. Marry me, Esther, and I'll be a father to the poor little *boy t'shikl*.'

Esther smiled. 'I love you, Sammy Lansky, too much to say yes to anything so crazy.'

He would have argued but at that moment the doctor's car drew up at the gate, and Esther walked resolutely forward to give up her son.

It was Sammy who cried again on the way home through the lush green countryside, wiping his eyes on the sleeves of his linen jacket, sniffing furiously until Esther gave him a strong peppermint to clear his nose. She felt curiously empty and detached, but there was no pain. There was no feeling of any kind.

'I'm glad you're coming home,' Sammy said, when the mint was done. They were high in the Cleveland hills, seeing the landscape, majestic and deserted, to right and left, with the smoky blur of Middlesborough ahead of them. Behind her lay the seaside towns of Yorkshire. Somewhere, in the Victorian and Edwardian streets, at this moment, her son and Philip's was being cared for, cooed over, loved. *Please God, let him fare well*, she prayed. And she thought, too, of Anne, also mourning the loss of a child.

Sammy was once more trying to divert her with plans for the future. 'I see it all clearly now, Esther. Supplying the goods is one part of trading, and we do that already. But there's another part: making it possible for people to buy. That's where check-trading comes in. We go on selling surplus products, just like we do now, but we have a second business. We give people a voucher, to use at certain selected shops, shops with which we've made an agreement. For each pound of that voucher, we charge the customer £1 2s 6d, and for each pound spent the shopkeeper gives us one shilling. So we make 3s 6d on each pound.'

'But where do we get the money to give out in the first place?' Esther asked.

'The customers pay us back week by week, a shilling in the pound. You collect, I collect. And as we get the money back, we lend it out again... so it's working, working all the time. Trust me, Esther.'

'But what if it all goes wrong?' Esther said.

'*Folg mir a gang*,' Sammy said cheerfully. 'Or to a *shiksa* like you: no chance at all.'

'But is it fair on the customers: 2s 6d on each pound? It's a lot!'

'It's less than a money-lender charges,' Sammy said. 'And we'll play fair with them. We can help people, Esther, that's an important part of it.'

As the van began to come down from the hill, Esther tried hard to imagine the new and expanding business, hoping it would prosper and grow to fill the hole where her heart had once been.

As soon as Diana's confinement was safely over, Mary wrote to Patrick Quinnell to say she would come to Durham again with the bread van the following Wednesday. She arrived in the Market Square with her groaning basket, wearing her new straw hat with a navy and white ribbon, a printed artificial-silk dress with pleats from the knee in navy and white, and a plain navy edge-to-edge coat, with a navy and white buckle at the waist. She felt smart, if a bit over-dressed, when she stepped down and looked around for Quinnell. He wasn't there.

Mary waited by the Londonderry statue for half an hour, her spirits gradually sinking. She had been daft; that was the fact of it. She had believed that her visits meant something to him, when obviously they had not. She thought of the long day stretching ahead until the van returned – and her at a loose end with a basket full of baking to carry wherever she went.

At quarter-past one she made up her mind. She would take the basket to Quinnell's house and dump it, on the step if necessary. That would rid her of the burden and, she hoped, prick his conscience into the bargain. At least he could have shown up and made it clear he had had enough. She rapped on his door, to no avail, and was about to deposit the basket on the step when the brightly painted door of the next house opened and a head poked out.

'You'll be looking for Dr Quinnell?'

The man was old and crotchety, and inclining his head in the manner of the hard of hearing. Mary was about to say she only wanted to leave the basket, and ask if he could take it in, when the man continued: 'They took him away, a week ago – or may be two. Anyway, it was a Saturday. He'd got into a bad way: drink, of course. Someone came; I think it was one of the doctors from the hospital. I know where they've taken him, if that's any help?'

It was to a nursing-home in Cleveland. Mary copied the address and went on her way. What had made Patrick slip back when he had been doing so well? she wondered anxiously. The thought that it might have been her absence both pleased and horrified her. She shifted the basket to her other arm, jammed her hat further on her head, and went in search of a tea-room. She would have to think out what her next move should be.

Sitting over scones and tea, she pondered. Cleveland! She didn't know much about it, except that there were hills there, and it was the other side of Middlesborough, which, at this moment, seemed like the other side of the moon. By the time she left the tea-room, though, she had made up her mind to speak to Howard Brenton about it. He had been in the war; he would understand what it did to men. If anyone could help her, it would be her employer.

But when she returned to the Scar she learned that Howard Brenton was in Hull, on business. It was Diana who told her, and she was quick to notice Mary's disappointed face.

'What is it, Mary? You can tell me.' Though they had grown closer in the last few months, Mary was still reluctant to speak about personal things. 'Sit down,' Diana said suddenly and her tone was so sympathetic that Mary found herself subsiding into a chair. 'Now,' Diana said, 'tell me what is troubling you.' She spoke in the tone of one who is accustomed to being obeyed, and Mary resigned herself to confession.

'It's a friend. Well, a man – a doctor. The doctor who came to Belgate the night...' She almost said, 'The night all the doctors were fussing round you,' but she didn't. The story came tumbling out, then: the safe delivery of Anne's baby; the meeting in Durham; the drink; the despair of a man who could not face the pain of living.

'So I don't know what to do,' Mary said, desperately, when she'd finished her tale.

'Oh, it's simple,' Diana said. 'You must go to him now!' Within minutes Fox and the Daimler were at the door, and Diana had put in a forceful call to the nursing-home to say Mary was on her way.

The journey through the Cleveland hills seemed to take forever. Mary had thought she would ride in the front beside Fox, but he, face impassive, had opened the back door and, confused, she had climbed in. A glass partition separated passenger and driver, and Fox made no move to open it and speak to her. *I don't like him*, Mary thought, but then she settled herself in the deep leather seat, and tried to work out what she would say to Patrick Quinnell when they came face to face.

The nursing home was white-painted and rambling, set in large grounds, with weeping ash trees everywhere.

She found Patrick sitting in a chair on a verandah, his head supported on a shaking hand. He was dressed in striped pyjamas covered by a navy dressing-gown, and he was paying no attention to the other patients sitting nearby. He tried to smile at her, but she could see it was an effort. She put out a hand, but there was no response.

'Well, this is a nice state of affairs,' Mary said uncertainly. And then, determined to get a reaction: 'If I can't turn my back for five minutes…'

He did not speak but a tear formed in his eye.

'Come on, now,' she said, sitting down. 'Everything's going to be all right, you know. I'm here now.'

The day after Howard's return from Hull, Edward Burton telephoned to say that John Conroy, the sitting member for Belgate, had collapsed in a committee room at the House of Commons and had been admitted to hospital. 'It's serious, Howard. He's going to resign his seat as soon as we have a plan in place.'

That night Howard and Diana were dining with Howard's parents. 'Don't let your father start about the price of coal,' Diana begged, as they drove over. 'I can bear anything but that.'

'I'll try,' Howard said, 'but I'd sooner try to stem the incoming tide.'

News that Howard was a step nearer a seat in Parliament pleased Charles enormously, but he doubted that a by-election would take place. 'There'll have to be a general election before long. That idiot Mosley stormed out because the Cabinet wouldn't give them a free hand over unemployment and Attlee is his replacement. No doubt he'll want to go into debt to finance the loungers and ne'er-do-wells on the dole.'

'They have to do something,' Howard said. 'More are being laid idle every day.'

Charles grunted. 'We'll have to be laying men off soon. I've asked Gallagher to come up with some figures.'

Howard would have liked to argue against this, but he needed to keep his father in a good mood for something more vital even than men remaining in work.

'I see the last troops have left the Rhineland,' he said, hoping to distract him from home affairs.

'About time,' Charles grunted.

'I'm not too sure about that,' Diana said, forthrightly. 'I don't at all like the sound of Herr Hitler. I had a letter from Loelia the other day, and apparently everyone in London is saying he'll be Germany's saviour, but I don't like the man. I think Britain should stay on there, to make sure there's no trouble later.'

Charles chuckled at Diana's fear of Germany's revival, but Charlotte took little part in the conversation. She looked from one to another as they spoke, and cut her food into the precise, equal pieces she liked to raise to her mouth.

They talked of Europe, then, and holidays, and Rupert's graduation from pony to small bay gelding, until Howard cleared his throat.

'You've heard about the diphtheria, I suppose?'

'Yes,' Charles said. 'Damned bad luck.'

'I believe a child has died?' Charlotte asked.

'Three children have died,' Diana answered, 'and several more are terribly ill.'

'I hope you keep Rupert well away from them,' Charlotte said. 'I did warn you about his hob-nobbing with the little Hardman child.'

'Rupert is perfectly safe,' Howard said, 'unlike the vast majority of the children down there. It's not hob-nobbing that kills them, mother. It's lack of sanitation. Three of the children involved live in the Shacks. That's no coincidence.'

A spasm of annoyance crossed Charles's face and Diana hurried to repair the breach. 'Couldn't your men rebuild the houses there? They did such a good job at the Scar and if you need to cut back on coal-production anyway…?' She saw her mother-in-law's hand tighten on her napkin at Diana's daring to intervene.

Charles chewed on his beef for a moment.

'I suppose it could be done. We could look into it. I understand your feelings, Howard, but I hope you understand my caution. These things have to be costed. But, as Diana says, perhaps there are ways. We'll see.'

'I'd be grateful if you would consider it,' Howard said firmly. 'As for costings, they already exist. I've gone into it all carefully. I'm not suggesting we build mansions – just simple homes with modern amenities.'

'How exciting,' Diana said smoothly. 'I'm sure we'll all be pleased to see things work out.' She flashed a brilliant smile at her father-in-law. 'Now, tell me about your trip to the theatre last week. I hear you didn't enjoy the play?'

When they were driving away in the darkness, relieved to be going home, Howard reached for Diana's hand and squeezed it. 'Thank you for helping tonight. I think you might have just tilted the scales.' They were in sight of the pit now, the ever-lit pit that toiled for them by night and day.

'I hope I did help,' Diana said. 'I mean to.'

'Let's have a night-cap?' Howard suggested, when they were back at the Scar. They sat either side of his study fire, talking easily, laughing sometimes about the evening's conversation, or Rupert's latest exploit. At last they went up to the nursery and looked at the sleeping children. Pamela's tiny face was slack with sleep, the lips puckered, the dark hair damp on the pillow.

'She's a dear baby,' Howard said, and saw the flush of pleasure in his wife's face. Rupert was sprawled on his back, his arms thrown up on the pillow, a model van, a gift from Loelia, fallen from his hand.

'He's growing, isn't he?' Howard said. He wondered if he should tell Diana what Rupert had said about preferring to live in London, but something held back the words. Diana turned for a last look at the children, and then reached to kiss Howard's cheek.

'Goodnight,' she said.

Safe in her room she began to cast off the night's finery, thinking of Howard's face as he had looked down at the sleeping baby. There had been pleasure, and genuine affection there. She thought, too, of Max's face when she had told him she was pregnant: *'Grow up, Diana. You know the rules.'* And now he was awaiting the birth of another child waiting impatiently, if Loelia's letter was accurate. She was filled with remorse, not only for the way she had betrayed Howard, but for her lack of judgement when it came to men.

When she had changed into nightgown and wrapper, she sat down at her dressing-table and took up her hair-brush. She brushed for a while, and then she laid the brush aside and went along the landing to Howard's room. She knocked softly, so as not to rouse Susan or the other servants.

'Diana?' Howard, already in his pyjamas, the collar rumpled around his chin, was surprised to see her.

'I'm all right. May I come in for a moment?' When the

door was closed, she stood in the centre of the room, her chin tilted a little to give her courage, her arms at her sides.

'I want you to know that I'm sorry, Howard: for everything. And I'm wondering if we could possibly just... start again?' She saw his brows contract, and the tiny scar flicker almost imperceptibly; but she could not work out his reaction. Surely he wasn't going to make her wait?

To her relief, he came towards her, taking her in his arms, putting a hand up to the crown of her head and holding it against his chest. 'The honest answer is that I don't know, Diana. I want to; I want to very much – for the sake of the children, as well as for you and me. But I can't just wipe the past out in one second. Can we have time for both of us to think? We've been very happy here these last few months, and for the first time this house has been a home. I hope we'll go on from there...'

He paused, and Diana looked up into his face.

'But you can't just carry me to your bed?' She smiled, as he looked aghast at her frankness. 'Oh, Howard, however did I miss the fact that you are by far the nicest man I have ever known?'

When Diana had gone back to her room, Howard stood at the window and looked out into the darkness of the Scar. Above, in the summer-night sky, stars were twinkling. He thought of the Rhineland, the troops gone now, putting the final seal on peace. Perhaps it was time for him, too, to put aside old wounds. The 1920s had been a sad decade, at home and abroad. Perhaps the 1930s would be better? He went to bed, certain that his mind was too busy for sleep, but in the darkness he felt his lips curve in an involuntary smile, and then he knew no more until it was morning.

23

Anne had grown used to Frank poring over union papers and political tracts; they spread about the living-room, for all the world like mushrooms. She didn't altogether mind. She was proud of his status in Belgate, and even prouder of his regular trips to Durham, to meetings of the union at county level. But she drew the line at his interest in foreign affairs.

'Never mind India,' she told him when he spoke of Ghandi in reverent tones. 'See to your own back-yard, and let heathens take care of themselves.' When he worried aloud about the rise of the Nazis in Germany and Stalin's purges in Russia, she rolled her eyes heavenwards and begged the good Lord to send her a man with sense. But Frank had studied and read widely since he decided to try for a parliamentary nomination, and the more he read the more he understood that it was no good 'keeping your eye on your own business'. No one had said it better than Peter Lee, the miners' leader: 'Not only men but nations must realize that the human race is so constituted that it must learn to cooperate if civilization is to endure.' So he scoured the paper for news of the rise of the Fascists in Italy and Germany, of the civil war in China, and the unrest in Palestine.

But Frank's greatest joy lay in his home and family. No matter how sharp Anne's tongue, how rough the jab she would give him if he got in her way, he never for a second forgot how lucky he had been to get her. She had lost the slim figure that had been her pride, but the smooth, dark hair still crowned her brow and her eyes still tantalized him as they had done on the day he married her.

For their eighth wedding anniversary, he resolved to give her a treat. She had never been to a cinema, for in her girlhood the nearest one had been in Sunderland, and in the last few years there had been neither time nor money for him to take her. He knew she envied Esther her occasional trips to the cinema, and devoured any items in his paper that told of the American stars and their private lives. He recruited Mary to help him pick out a film, and to look after the children; and then he presented Anne with a fait accompli: two seats to see Marlene Dietrich in *The Blue Angel*, with a box of mint lumps and tea at Lockhart's café thrown in.

At first Anne flew into a paddy at the expense; then she declared the whole enterprise too complicated to succeed; but in the end she went, and sat like a wide-eyed mouse while Dietrich smouldered on the screen above them and brought about the ruin of her leading man. 'I love you, Annie,' Frank whispered in the interval, and received only the mildest of reproofs for his pains.

In fact a whole new world opened up for Anne Maguire – a world of romance, of heady excitement and glamour. On the way to catch the last bus hack to Belgate she did not resist when Frank took her arm, and that night, as she said her prayers, she included everyone, even Esther, who had turned flighty lately and was never home. She had missed Esther when she was working away in Whitby, and was glad that now she was back. She ended by asking for forgiveness for her sister-in-law, Mary, who was carrying on with a struck-off doctor, who would likely be hung for murder before he was finished. 'And God bless Frank,' she concluded, 'and let him get a nomination soon.'

*

Esther was conscious of Anne's pleasure in seeing her home again, and was grateful, though a trip to Belgate meant the pain of seeing Anne with her children. It meant the agony of holding Anne's youngest child in her arms, a reminder of that other tiny baby.

Sammy tried to divert her with work. They already had a barrow and an illicit pitch near the entrance to the market, and now they got a stall inside.

At first Sammy used his pocket as a till, keeping no books or proper stock records. If his pockets were bulging with cash – and if that cash was paper – they were prospering. Soon, in addition to the van, they had a two-ton Ford truck, which cost the unbelievable sum of £129. They also hired a cheery youngster with a smooth tongue to run the market stall.

'We need a bank account now,' Esther said firmly, and went out to buy a set of ledgers. By the time she had ruled them, they had a lease on a lock-up shop in Crowtree Road. 'Can't we stand still for a while?' Esther pleaded. 'We're going far too fast.'

'It can't be done, Esther,' Sammy said. 'Not in this business. Expand or die.' He took space in the Arcade in High Street, and turned the upper storey of the Crowtree Road shop into an office to house the check-trading operation, which had begun shakily but was now showing every sign of success. When Esther sat down to take stock of her own affairs, she found she was worth £325.

The following week Sammy bought a thousand cases of canned salmon at 26s the case. At the same time a scare-story about tinned salmon burst in a northern newspaper. Without space to keep the salmon until the public forgot, Sammy was forced to ship it south and sell it there for 12s 6d per case. The resultant loss was £675. Emmanuel Lansky was seen to have 'I told you so' trembling on his lips, though to his credit it was never uttered. Sammy recouped the loss over the next two months, but Esther could not bear the sight of canned salmon for a twelvemonth.

'It's time you bought a house,' Sammy said firmly, one day. 'Renting is for *shlemiels*.' Esther looked at her bank balance again, and saw the sense of it. She settled on a small terraced house in Carnforth Terrace, in Sunderland, close enough in for her to walk to work; far enough out of the centre for her not to hear the traffic.

'You can do better than that,' Sammy said. 'You can afford a semi, with a garden.' But Esther would not be budged. She liked having money in the bank: it was a new and comforting sensation, and she meant to go on enjoying it.

On the day after she moved into Carnforth Terrace she went alone to the cemetery. A black marble stone stood there now, bearing the words *Philip Blakeston Broderick, beloved son of Edward Stanley and Catherine Maude*. But Philip had been more than a son; he had been a beloved. As Esther's grief lost its first terrible edge, and she came to terms with the parting from her child, she rejoiced in the fact that for at least a part of his life Philip had been loved as a man should be loved: tenderly, passionately, and, in the end, productively.

Somewhere now there was a boy who might look and smile as Philip had smiled, who might have inherited Philip's fine brain or generosity of spirit. She did not yearn to possess the child, only to know that he was safe – but as to that, all she could do was hope. So she laid her flowers on Philip's grave, and asked him to watch over his son.

Some two weeks after Diana's plea for reconciliation, Howard heard that the health of the sitting member for Belgate had improved. There would be no by-election, and a general election, at which he would be required to stand, might be months away yet. It seemed a sign, a chance to take time out to repair his marriage.

The following month, Howard and Diana Brenton

crossed to France to stay at the George Cinq in Paris.

The streets had that heady smell that marks the city: food and wine and good cigars emanating from restaurants that hummed with chatter and laughter. It was in a high-ceilinged bedroom, its shuttered windows open onto the street, that they became lovers once more, without the eager excitement of their honeymoon days but with mutual joy that at last they had found a kind of peace.

'*Je t'aime, mon petit chou*,' Diana said teasingly in her schoolgirl French. Howard shook with laughter and stayed her words with a kiss.

They came back to the Scar, relaxed and happy, and nine months later, in August 1931, Diana gave birth to a son, Ralph Cecil James.

It was a time of turmoil. The Labour government had fallen and the nation was suffering its worst financial crisis yet. An all-party 'Government of Co-operation' had been formed, led by the outgoing Prime Minister, Ramsay MacDonald, whose aim was to halt the run on the pound.

'It won't last,' Edward Burton told Howard. 'His party regard him as a traitor, and we're on the verge of national bankruptcy. There'll be a general election within weeks.'

The election came, in fact, in October, 1931. The National Government under Ramsay MacDonald stayed in power with a massive landslide against the Labour party; and Howard Brenton was elected as member for the constituency of Belgate with a rise in the Tory majority there.

'I don't believe it,' Anne Maguire said sullenly, as she and Frank surveyed the wreck of all their hopes. He shrugged philosophically. 'There'll be other days, Annie. Other elections. Our time will come.'

Charles Brenton was elated by his son's election victory. 'Get yourself off to London and sort out this damned mess,' he told Howard. 'Leave the coalfield to me.'

Diana had stood by Howard throughout the campaign.

Now she reorganized the Mount Street house to give him working space, and travelled with him between his constituency and the House, making sure he saw as much as possible of the three children.

'I'm so glad we're back here,' Rupert told his mother, kneeling on the drawing-room window-seat to look out on the London street.

'But you like Durham,' Diana protested.

'Not really,' he said, a little shame-facedly. 'I love the stables, and fun with Catherine and that sort of thing, but I hate Belgate. It's so... *dirty*.' Diana thought of his heritage and shuddered. He was heir to an empire built on coal, and yet he showed little interest in the mining of it. She consoled herself with the thought that he was eight years old. Time enough for change.

Howard sat in the House of Commons, feeling a sense of utter frustration, listening to platitudes and insults thrown back and forth across the floor. It seemed the Coalition Government was succeeding in nothing. Oswald Mosley had left the Labour party and formed a party of his own, the New Party. It was dedicated to 'complete revision of Parliament to change it from a talk-shop to a workshop,' and although Howard despised Mosley, he felt a grudging sympathy with his aim of getting something done.

As he travelled up and down each week between Durham and London, he sought comfort from his newspapers; but there was little or none to be found. Spain had dethroned its king; Japan had marched into Manchuria; Stalin was purging anyone who disagreed with him; Ghandi was constantly agitating for India's independence; the Fascists were gaining power in Europe; and in Britain the curse of unemployment was stubbornly resistant to every proposed solution.

The Prince of Wales began a 'Buy British' campaign at home and abroad, but not even the nation's darling could halt the mass of cheap imports flooding into the country. By late 1932, riots and baton-wielding police were a common sight, and massed ranks of the unemployed were walking to London to plead their case.

London was the only place where there were signs of growth and plenty, Diana thought. Regent Street had been transformed, and a new store had replaced the last private houses in Oxford Street. Loelia twittered about 'economies', and went on spending as though money was water and fell from heaven.

In November 1932, as America swept Franklin Roosevelt into the White House, Diana gave birth to their fourth child, Noel Edward (for Edward Burton) Brenton. 'We have our family now,' Howard said, as he bent lovingly over Diana's bed. 'A girl and three boys.' Howard was devoted to all the children, but the time when Rupert had been his only source of affection had forged a deeper bond between them. It was Pamela, however, who, as soon as she could stagger on her own feet, had dogged Howard's footsteps. The first word she uttered was *Dada*; and when, with fat pink fingers, she picked her first daisy, she touched it briefly to her nose and then handed it to the man she knew as father.

Diana saw and marvelled; and the only antidote to her remorse was the happiness she saw in her husband's face. Like Howard, she was troubled about the state of the world. If Roosevelt was forging a New Deal for the Americans, Adolf Hitler was threatening havoc in Germany where his stormtroopers were roaring: 'Full powers or else…' and bringing violence to the streets. Children meant looking to the future, and Diana did not like what she saw.

For over a year Patrick Quinnell stayed in retreat, trying to beat his drink problem. Throughout this time, Mary Hardman visited him every week, travelling on the train to York when he was moved to a clinic there, keeping his home clean and aired in his absence. She was waiting for him when at last he came home; but when he asked her to marry him she refused. He was quality; she was a servant. A year later she took him for her lover, staying with him whenever she could snatch a night away from the Scar, holding him in her arms when he woke in the night and screamed his terror of a long-gone war. It was strange to have a man in her bed again, a halting lover at first, but a generous one, careful with her body, anxious to please, determined to give her pleasure.

'It's disgusting,' Anne told Frank more than once. 'Sits there like lamb and salad, and carrying on like a –.' She would have said 'whore', but something in the steely set of her husband's jaw made her say 'fast piece' instead. The truth was that she was envious now of Mary, who was no longer the widowed sister-in-law to be pitied and patronized. Instead, Mary seemed to Anne to live the life of Riley, riding here and there, in the Brenton car half the time, and on and off that bread van like a yo-yo.

Esther, too, seemed to be enjoying a charmed life: no money worries; her own boss, by all accounts – and a house of her own! 'If it ever comes off,' Anne had said to Frank sourly, when Esther first mentioned it. 'I don't see the Jews letting that much money out of the family.' When Esther announced that the house was indeed hers, it was a bitter pill, but Anne did her best to swallow it. 'We're sisters,' she told Frank. 'Esther's gain's my gain.' But privately she longed for the day when justice would be done, and she and Frank would take their rightful place in the world.

'That Mosley'll do it,' she said, warmed by what she read of Mosley's promise to mobilize the vitality and manhood of Britain to save the nation. But Frank had read further, and had seen the MP's threat to 'rely on the good old English fist'.

'I don't trust him – he's a troublemaker, if ever I saw one,' he told Anne warningly, not realizing for a moment how terrible was the truth contained in his words.

BOOK THREE

1935

24

As the Thirties progressed, there were disturbing tales from Germany. Dr Goebbels, the Minister of Public Enlightenment, was denouncing 'Jewish vampires', and Hitler's announcement that in future all people suffering from physical imperfections, such as blindness, deafness, deformity or epilepsy, would be compulsorily sterilized filled Diana with horror. The first news of concentration camps for Jews, surrounded by electrified barbed-wire and sentries who shot to kill, firmed her resolve to speak out. When Caroline and Geoffrey, visiting Sunderland, extolled Herr Hitler as 'a saviour', Diana told them she found their sentiments distasteful. And when Loelia said that Max was 'fearfully pro-Hitler', Diana reflected she had had a lucky escape.

Tales of violent anti-Semitism in Germany were one thing: meeting it in Britain was quite another. Crossing Piccadilly from the theatre to dine at the Athenaeum one night in 1935, Diana and Howard were caught up in a crowd protesting against black-clad Fascists who were reading anti-Semitic pamphlets.

'It's Mosley,' Howard said tersely as he hustled her into the safety of the club doorway. 'I think the man's gone mad!' Mosley had at last emerged as a Fascist, not only defending the boycott of Jewish traders in Germany, but advocating its establishment in Britain. His rallies were well-attended, and policed by black-shirted guards, some of them women trained in ju-jitsu. Outside the halls, flag-waving

Communists might protest; inside, the crowd listened in reverent silence to Mosley's mounting hymn of hate against the Jews.

Diana had never come face to face with Emmanuel Lansky, but she had seen the old Jew about his business in Belgate, and Howard spoke well of him. In London she occasionally met rich and well-born Jews; indeed Edwina Mountbatten was of Jewish descent, and she was the darling of society. If Diana was honest, she had to admit to a slight inhibition of her own where Jews were concerned – not enough to be called prejudice, but there, nevertheless. However, keeping Jews at arm's length in one's social life was one thing; hounding them was quite another. The old King had spoken of his 'beloved people' at the time of his Jubilee in May. *One people*, Diana thought, *whatever our differences... That's what we must be.*

The British Parliament was increasing its defence spending to counter Hitler's sweeping demands to re-arm Germany and repossess those areas lost under the Treaty of Versailles. 'There's going to be real trouble,' Howard told Diana sombrely. They were standing in the stableyard at the Scar, brought there in spite of a fine drizzle, to see Rupert's new mount.

'You can't mean war!' Diana said, but Howard did not give her the denial she hoped for.

Instead he looked to where Rupert bestrode his black mare, with a white blaze on the forehead and a fiery disposition. He was twelve now, and afraid of nothing. For the first time in years, watching his son, Howard remembered the trenches. A few years ago another war would have been unthinkable; now he could only pray that if it must come it would be over before his son was old enough to fight.

In Sunderland Rachael Schiffman had taken to her bed, with a goyah paid for by Sammy to care for her every need when he was not there. Lansky, too, hovered around Rachael's room, or sat by her chair on the odd occasion when she allowed Sammy to carry her downstairs. Sammy was in his twenties now, tall and broad with a mop of curly black hair on which he crammed his yarmulke only when likely to be observed by his father.

'I don't feel Jewish,' he told Esther, 'so don't go po-faced on me. As a Jew I'm a failure. But look how good I am at everything else.' This was accompanied by a self-deprecatory grin and a throwing up of hands.

'You don't improve,' Esther told him, but she loved him just the same. So she tolerated the stream of Gentile girl-friends, and he teased her about Stanley Jackson, the teacher from the grammar school who took her to the Empire occasionally, or for tea in Meng's café – the place where the cream of Sunderland society buzzed and chattered over the gold-rimmed china.

Emmanuel Lansky was deeply concerned about the ugly stories coming out of Germany, which he read in newspapers and in *The Jewish Chronicle*. Himmler had been appointed as overlord of concentration camps, where prisoners could be shot on the spot; and public places were displaying signs saying *Juden unerwünscht* ('Jews not wanted'). And if what was happening in Germany was fearful, what was he to make of Mosley's club-wielding Fascist thugs who were terrorizing Jewish parts of London? In Sunderland, he might sometimes be called a Sheeny or a Yid, or even occasionally a *Vad-je-van* – but at least there was no threat to his life.

As he broke his Sabbath *challah*, he vowed to give more to the Board of Guardians who were raising funds to help Jews driven to flee Germany. In the synagogue, when he intoned his Sabbath prayer, he prayed that Sammy would be forgiven for his misdeeds; and he prayed for Rachael to be well again, because he missed the sight of her going nimbly about the house. Most of all, though, he prayed for the eventual triumph of good because, for the first time in his life, he feared that evil might prevail.

Sammy was always home for the Sabbath, helping to lay the Sabbath table, covering the snow-white cloth with two *challahs* with their shiny plaited crusts sprinkled with poppy-seeds, with salt, bread-knife, wine and *bechers*, all lit by candles. Dishes of fruit, nuts and raisins stood about; and now, blessed innovation, a sheet of tin stood over the lighted jets of the gas stove which burned all through the Sabbath and heated the samovar, so that hot drinks were available the whole day through without anyone having to turn the gas taps.

Rachael would be carried down, and then the men would stand behind their chairs in absolute silence until it was time for Emmanuel to fill the largest wine-cup with golden wine, and softly make Kiddush, the blessing over the wine which was the introduction to the evening meal. Then the wine would be shared, hands washed and the *challah* cover lifted, so they could cut into the delicious loaves. Only after the first mouthful had been eaten could they speak, and then they would woo Rachael over the chopped fish or liver, letting her know how much her presence meant to the home. The meal would end with Russian tea and a *zemiroth* sung softly at the table, before the grace.

But when the Sabbath was over, Sammy was a different person: off in search of bright lights, racing around in his car, a *shiksa* by his side, leaving his father to fret by the fire. Esther watched, and was sad for Emmanuel; but Sammy was her friend, too, and she was coming to rely on him more and more.

Sammy was now urging her to move again, to a larger house in a better area; but Esther baulked at spending so much money on herself when, in Belgate, Frank and Anne were crammed into the Shacks with six growing children, some of them now almost adults. She suggested that she might make a down-payment on a bigger house for them, or help with the rent if they moved, and she saw a gleam come into Anne's eyes. But Frank's refusal was emphatic.

'Thank you, Es, but no, thank you. We'll get a bigger house afore long, the union'll see to that. And even if we didn't, we couldn't take hand-outs.'

'He's right,' Anne said grudgingly when the sisters were alone. 'It doesn't do to be beholden to anyone, even family. We'll just scrush on as we are till something gives.'

Privately Esther thought that the rampant over-crowding in Belgate would lead to an outbreak of tuberculosis before long. It had already swept through some of the colliery villages, and the sufferers had been carted off to Poole Sanatorium or Seaham Hall, the former home of Lord Londonderry which he had deeded to Durham as a hospital for chest diseases, so that people could die in stately surroundings. Esther had several attempts at changing Frank's mind, but she couldn't budge him. So she started to look at available houses for herself, hoping to find one and move into it in the spring.

All over Britain towns were spreading outwards. The Slum-Clearance Acts passed in the early Thirties had forced councils to build sprawling estates of subsidized housing. It was mandatory that these council houses should have bathrooms, which led to great hostility from private owners who had no hope of adding a bathroom to their two-down two-up homes. The council houses were often monotonous, identical and featureless, and finished in rough-cast; but most of the new owners, liberated from the slums, turned the pocket-hanky plots into veritable gardens of Eden. Even the bricks mellowed with time, and they became acceptable places to live.

Private estates sprang up, too, though a lot of them were jerry-built. 'A house is an investment, Esther,' Sammy said. 'You can't be too careful. And buy new: you don't want someone else's leftovers.'

Esther hid her smile. She was used to him talking to her like an indulgent uncle, though he was three years her junior. Besides, she had good reason to be grateful to him. Admittedly she worked hard and was conscientious, but Sammy was the business genius – and he had nerve. It was an unbeatable combination.

Now he drove her from house to house in his new Hillman Minx, the price of which had brought a tremor to Emmanuel Lansky's chin. They looked at houses which were mostly square boxes but disguised with unnecessary gables, pebble-dash, leaded panes (which were the height of fashion) or mock-Tudor timbering. Terraced houses were considered socially inferior, now, outside of London, and Esther could understand why.

Her present house, fond of it though she was, was narrow and poky, with a depressing and unproductive strip of earth in front, and a concrete yard behind. From the front door a long passage led to a dark, off-shot kitchen, and a small scullery which had the chill of death about it, winter or summer. Off the passage was a front room and a sitting-room. There was no bathroom, no electricity, and the WC was at the bottom of the yard.

The new houses might be less substantially built, but they were light and airy, square rather than narrow, with gardens back and front, and the blessing of electric light in every room. The front rooms were called lounges, and the kitchens, which were tiny, were called kitchenettes. However, the kitchenettes had fitted wooden furniture and gas stoves, and in the more expensive houses there was a hatch between kitchen and dining-room.

The house Esther chose had leaded windows, and because it was a corner site there was garden on three sides. It had two decent-sized bedrooms and one little more than a cupboard; and, to Esther's delight, a 'low-flush suite' instead of the old 'ball and chain'. There was a tram-stop at the end of the street, and a park around the corner. 'You can sit there and spoon with Stanley,' Sammy teased, but Esther had no intention of spooning with anyone ever again. Stanley was a nice man and deserved better than the friendly affection which was all she had to offer. Soon he would have to go! But first there was her new house to put in order.

Lansky gave her a set of cut-glass sherry glasses, and Sammy, ever practical, bought her one of the new Hoover vacuum-cleaners. 'No more dust up the nose, Esther. No more down on your knees. This is not an appliance I'm giving you – it's a liberation.'

She had the walls of her home painted in pale shades of distemper, with a toning paper frieze under the picture-rail, and the apple-green paintwork she had so much admired at the Scar years before. She splashed out on a three-piece suite and a standard lamp, and made deep-green curtains to match the tiles around the fireplace.

Sammy looked around when it was finished. 'There's only one thing missing,' he said. 'A *sim-cha*, that's what it needs.' So a celebration they had, with *lekach*, and wine, and a blessing from Emmanuel.

'Very nice,' Anne said, when she came over from Belgate to view the finished work. 'But it's a bit bare for my taste.'

Esther loved the spaciousness of her new home, where sunlight streamed in somewhere at every hour of the day. She loved her garden, and the feeling of being able to shut her door on the rest of the world when she chose. Still, it was always best to humour Anne.

'Yes,' she said, sounding rueful. 'But I'll be able to afford a few more things by and by.'

Anne, trying not to let her envy show, produced a host of questions designed to elicit any welcome faults the house might possess.

'The lavvy's inside? You'll need to be careful about smells. No range? Oh, I couldn't be doing with that – not that you do much cooking of course, being single.' Anne had pitied Esther, as the years went by and and all she did was drudge for others, with no man and no bairns, but now, inwardly, she was beginning to wonder. Still, she had a lad nearly up, and when he went into the pit things might improve. She went on mending, and patching, and sewing for other people, till her treadle leg ached and her lips were stiff with having to be polite to idiots who thought you could turn a 36-inch hip into a 42-inch, just by unpicking a seam.

'I'm on a treadmill,' she told Frank one night. 'Pedal, pedal and nothing to look forward to but me six foot of ground.' Her conscience pricked her, then, not for the stricken look on her husband's face but because she had ignored the one fact that mattered: Christ's promise to wipe away all tears. She tried to redeem herself in an orgy of sweeping and cleaning and boiling of whites, and was rewarded by finding a half-crown in the pocket of Estelle's navy drawers. She wondered where it had come from, but couldn't ask in case Estelle had some good reason to reclaim it. She bought a pound and a half of stewing-steak and four penn'orth of soup stuff with it, and still had change left over.

They had six children, now; seven if you counted poor dead little Philomena. 'And every one a saint,' Anne was heard to observe, 'except for that sour little bitch with the yellow hair.' Estelle, her second child was eleven years old and looked like a beautiful flaxen-haired doll. She scorned her home, and the monotonous diet, and talked constantly of the day when she would be rich and famous and could shake the dirt of Belgate from her feet. 'I don't know about rich,' Anne said once, in exasperation, 'but you have a good chance of being famous – because one of these days I'll throttle you. That'll make the papers.'

*

Estelle was not the only person discontented with Belgate. In spite of Diana's efforts on the night she and Howard had dined with his parents, the Shacks were still standing, and the same people living in them. To Howard's intense relief, young Stanley Gallagher had left Brenton employ. He had come to Howard one day, full of self-importance.

'I'm sorry to tell you, Mr Howard, that I will be leaving at the end of next month.' He had paused, obviously expecting Howard to break down and sob. When there was no reaction apart from a slight lift of Howard's brow he went on. 'I'm going to be a schoolmaster. It's all arranged. I start at college in September.'

Howard wished him well, and arranged for a leaving bonus, privately congratulating himself – and silently commiserating with the generations of children who would pass through young Gallagher's hands. But his father remained, a thorn in Howard's side. He was certain it was Gallagher who had blocked his plans for rebuilding the Shacks. There was no excusing his father, who could have ignored Gallagher's advice if he wished; but all the same, Gallagher was a constant obstacle to progress.

Howard longed to talk to Charles without fear of interruption. At the office, there was Gallagher, ears cocked; at home his mother, breathing disapproval. So he suggested they dine together while Diana was in London, and he baited the trap with a good claret. When the Daimler swept up to the Scar, Howard was waiting on the step.

They ate well: lobster bisque and a baron of beef, followed by peaches flamed in brandy – all favourites of Charles's. Howard was attentive to his father's glass and then, as they relaxed over port and cigars, he begged again for the Shacks to be rebuilt. 'It would mean so much, father. It would be a symbol, a testament of faith in the future.'

In his heart of hearts he had not expected to win, so

amazement seized him when his father leaned forward, a twinkle in his eye.

'Let it drop, my boy. I knew it would be coming when you issued the invitation – so I've seen to it. Those houses are coming down… and this time I'll keep my word.'

The sky was spangled with stars when they walked out onto the front step. 'I've enjoyed myself, my boy. It's nice to get away from the women now and again. But tell that minx of yours to get herself back here soon. We miss her.' Howard wondered if he could convey his gratitude and relief that the issue of the Shacks had been laid to rest, for he knew instinctively that his father meant to do it. In the end he contented himself with putting a hand on his father's shoulder and then standing, waving, until the car was lost to view.

25

The day following his dinner at the Scar with Howard Charles Brenton suffered a cerebral thrombosis. Howard was summoned from the cokeworks to Gallagher's office at Belgate, where he found Charles unconscious, purple in the face and breathing stertorously. Someone had loosened the tight collar at his neck, and put a rolled-up blanket beneath his head. A collier trained in first-aid knelt beside him, holding his wrist. The man's face was anxious. Howard knelt opposite him and gently touched his father's cheek. There was no reaction.

'Has someone sent for a doctor?'

'Straight away,' Gallagher said. 'I telephoned him before I spoke to you.'

The agent's thin face looked pinched, and his mouth was downcast. It was not until that moment that Howard realized the full implications of what was happening. If his father failed to recover, responsibility for the mines would fall on him… and that was what Gallagher feared. Conflicting emotions crowded Howard's brain. If he had the power to change things, so much would be possible. But what if he were not up to it? Fear struck him; then, as he remembered his father's face the night before, as he was leaving the Scar, remorse overtook every other emotion. How could he think of anything but his father's recovery?

The doctor came, unfolding his stethoscope, saying 'urm' and 'yes' as he listened and probed. 'I've been half-expecting this,' he said. 'But your father wouldn't be told.'

They carried Charles down to the colliery ambulance, and then drove him home. 'No point in taking him to the infirmary,' the doctor said. 'He'll do just as well in his own bed.'

Charlotte had been forewarned. She stood in the hall, hands folded at her waist, face calm. 'Take him upstairs,' she said. 'You can leave everything else to me.'

Howard held her arm as they followed the men upstairs, but Charlotte had no need of support. He had never seen her more in control. As she closed the bedroom door behind them when he left, Howard sensed that, in a sense, it was closing forever.

He and Diana would, he guessed, be allowed to enter to pay their respects, but his father's sickroom would be a walled city in which, for the first time, Charlotte's word would be law. Howard pitied his father, but there was nothing he could do about it. Life or death, and the area between, was something between husband and wife: too elemental to permit of outside interference. And besides, he had other work to do.

He turned on his heel and hurried downstairs.

Charles Brenton was unconscious for three days following his stroke. In that time Charlotte engaged a nurse: a fat, pathetic creature with an incipient moustache and hands like shovels. When Howard suggested they might do better if they looked further afield, Charlotte would have none of it.

'I need someone for the heavier part of the nursing; the rest I shall do myself. Nurse Garron will do very well.'

At first Gallagher hovered around the sickroom, full of solicitude. When the doctor finally announced that no further improvement could be expected, and that Charles was never likely to walk or talk again, Gallagher turned his attention to Charlotte. He knew it would be useless to woo Howard; there had been too much discord between them in the past. But Charlotte was another matter.

Charlotte had changed with Charles's illness, and part of that change was a new remoteness from her son. It was as though a curtain had come down between them. Howard had expected to take over the reins of the whole Brenton empire, but after ten days Charlotte pointed out that she was Charles's next of kin. In the circumstances, she had applied for power of attorney over her husband's affairs.

Once it was signed, she would assume Charles Brenton's role; until then, she would be grateful if Howard would keep her informed and make no major decisions without her approval.

'This was Gallagher's idea, wasn't it?' Howard asked.

'Not at all. I'm not entirely without a mind of my own, Howard.'

Howard looked from his mother to his father's immobile face, and saw his eyes darting agitatedly back and forth.

He knows, Howard thought. *He knows she is his master now.*

Diana tried to help in the sickroom but as soon as Nurse Garron arrived, Charlotte made it obvious that Diana would only be welcome to visit occasionally. When Diana, hurt, got up to leave the room, there was a small moan from the figure in the bed. Howard looked up and met his mother's eyes, and saw a dreadful satisfaction there.

Caroline and Geoffrey came, ostensibly to visit Charles, but in reality to size up the situation and see whether there were any pickings. It was a painful visit. Howard despised his sister and disliked her husband, and only Diana's hand on his arm prevented him from saying so. There was another bone of contention between them: Caroline and Geoffrey, also pro-German, were now rabidly pro-Hitler.

'We should let Germany get rid of the Reds,' Geoffrey said over the dinner-table, 'and put paid to French pretensions at the same time.' It was vain for Howard to argue about decency and democracy; only Diana could deal forthrightly with their folly.

'I can't stop you being foolish, Geoffrey, but if you must be on the wrong side, at least have the grace to shut up about it while you're here!'

In bed that night Howard told her he was proud of her for her outspokenness. 'That's all very well,' Diana said, curling against him. 'But lots of people agree with them. I'm not even sure about Loelia, and she's usually so sensible.'

'There's Churchill,' Howard said, seeking comfort.

'One man,' Diana said. 'And even if he were in charge, what could he do? Germany is strong, Howard: they've spent years re-arming while we enjoyed the Season, and America invented Mickey Mouse.' She turned over, and settled down. 'We might as well go to sleep, because there's nothing to cheer us up – if we lie and talk about it all night!'

Howard put out the light and slipped his arm around her. She smelled good and she felt good. He forgot about Herr Hitler and set about making love to his wife.

Frank Maguire was hoping to be included on the list of Labour Parliamentary candidates, but his inclusion did not come, much to Anne's chagrin. Frank did not waste time in regret; there were more important things to be done. He had revered Ramsay MacDonald, but the formation of a National Government had disillusioned him. MacDonald was MP for Seaham, a stone's throw from Belgate. The Seaham party had urged him to resign, since he was leader of a government 'without labour credentials', but MacDonald had refused; and in a subsequent election he had defeated the official Labour candidate.

Now as the 1935 election neared, Emmanuel Shinwell, something of a hero to the Durham miner, decided to stand against MacDonald. The Durham miners gave £100 to help his campaign, and Frank threw himself into supporting Shinwell. It was a tough contest. The former prime minister had a temporary landing-field built to enable aeroplanes full of his supporters to fly up from London to campaign. Shinwell had only the goodwill of the Durham miner.

By election day, Frank was exhausted and broke, having taken a week off work to canvass every house. Anne bit her lip, and served saveloys and dry bread to her children, for it was in a noble cause. Shinwell polled more than twice MacDonald's votes, and Frank stumbled home to Belgate and his bed feeling as though he had climbed Everest.

The following year, the Labour member for Spennymoor introduced a bill: 'To nationalise mines and minerals.' It was defeated at its second reading, but it fanned the flame of hope in the Durham miners, a flame that had started with the Sankey commission in 1919, and would not be extinguished.

There was pleasure and excitement for Esther in being able to choose things for her home, not needing to scrimp or pinch or take whatever came to hand. Sammy had opened two market stalls now, partially enclosed stands with goods displayed in pyramids. Groceries were still their mainstay, but the check-trading business was expanding every week, and now they gave out vouchers for furniture and shoe shops, as well as for drapers and outfitters. Sammy had opened a new store in Hendon, selling second-hand furnishings and smaller items of new, cheap furniture. 'Housing is booming, Esther,' he said. 'Everyone wants a home now. That's where the money is.'

According to Sammy there was always a financial tide to be taken at the flood. 'Wireless, Esther,' he said one day, bursting into the office. 'There's going to be an explosion of interest in broadcasting.' The following week they opened an electrical stall in the market, selling radios and allied goods, along with plugs and flex and adaptors. Each week Esther drew £12 in wages; more than enough for her needs. Each year they divided the profit, after taxes, into nine: two shares for Esther, three for Sammy and four for development.

Sammy next bought a shop and flat, just off the Sunderland town centre. The property cost £2,000, and Esther imagined the upper floor would be for storage or office space. Instead, Sammy turned it into an apartment, well-furnished and comfortable.

'Are you going to live in it?' Esther asked anxiously. Emmanuel's heart would break if Sammy left the family home, but Esther knew what restrictions life with his father placed upon Sammy's way of life.

He shook his head. 'I live at home, Esther. Here I play a little, that's all.' The latest playmate was a bottle-blonde who wore tight skirts and disturbingly high heels, and seemed in a permanent state of dizzy excitement.

Esther could only shrug. Sammy was Sammy, and could not be changed.

26

Charles Brenton's illness caused much speculation among his workers. At first, 'I hope the bugger suffers,' was the commonest remark, but as the old man hung grimly to life a certain grudging respect began to surface. Tales of Charles's intercessions when Gallagher had been too repressive were trotted out, and grew in the telling. That it was Howard who had been behind most of these merciful actions was not apparent. Men spoke sourly of 'young upstarts', forgetting that Howard was approaching forty and had worked for his father for nearly twenty years. 'Better the devil you know,' Anne said, on the subject of Howard as colliery owner. 'Remember our poor Esther! She had to run for her life .

Frank's contempt for the Brenton name and all it stood for had never wavered, but over the years he had come to understand Howard Brenton. He was a firm employer, but he was fair. Best of all, he was willing to admit when the management was in the wrong. When the nation's miners threatened to strike, demanding a flat-rate increase of eight shillings a day, he had looked sympathetic – unlike the rest of the coal-owners, who had huffed and puffed in their usual threatening fashion. In the end, the strike had been averted, and the men won sixpence a shift. 'It's little enough,' Howard had said to the union representatives; but when Frank told this to Anne she twisted her face. 'It's not sympathy we need, Frank. It's bread for our bairns.'

It would be the same, Frank reflected, until the mines

belonged to the men who worked them. Peter Lee had said it for years, but he had died without seeing his dream of nationalization realized. Other dreams, though, had come true. The Burnhope reservoir was Peter Lee's memorial, high on the lonely fells of the Pennines, gathering water from countless silver ribbons and piping it to the pit villages of Durham, so that death and disease would strike there no more. Frank had gone to the falls on a day when rain was driving like swords, and only the bleating of sheep could be heard. He had stood, cap in hand, to see Peter Lee's name set into the wall of the great reservoir, and had given thanks for one man who had kept a promise to the people.

As he shaved himself, now, in icy water, he reflected on Lee's words, imprinted as they were on his memory: '*We can never have true peace in the coal trade until we have nationalization.*' The owners said that would never happen, but they would have to eat their words one day, Frank thought, as he stooped to see his face in the cracked kitchen mirror. When it came to a showdown, the men would stand together, and this time there would be no going back. He cut a swathe of lather from his face and flicked it frexpertly into the sink.

Anne watched him from the fireside, trying to enjoy the scene. Normally she liked to sit comfortably and watch Frank shave; he was still a good-looking lad; better, now that he had broadened out and had a bit of authority about him. He was top dog in the Belgate union. One day it would be Durham, for them, and a posh union house. or even a seat in Parliament. God, she would lord it over a few folks then. In the meantime, though, she faced the thorny problem of finding out where Estelle was getting money.

She had tried, but getting to grips with Estelle was like holding water in a sieve. 'Where did you get these comics, sweets, sixpenny piece?' The blue eyes would roll heavenwards. 'What comics, sweets, sixpenny piece?' 'This comic, this sixpence – where the hell did they come from?'

Again the roll of the eyes, this time accompanied by a shrug of the shoulders. 'I dunno!'

The thought of Estelle and her new-found wealth brought on such unease that Anne got to her feet and moved to the back door. Where was the little bitch now? She stood on the doorstep and scanned the back street, but it was February, and not a soul about. She shivered, trying not to think of Estelle but concentrate instead on young Gerard, who had all the makings of a saint and would go into the priesthood and make her proud of him, but then the cold began to penetrate.

As she moved back she touched the lid of the rain butt, still bristling with frost in spite of a watery sun. It had been a hard winter. Anne's hands were red-raw with washing and wringing out and pegging out in harsh winter winds. Esther had bought her some hand cream in a pink jar. Anne had stuck it on the windowsill, but never found time to use it. Esther was stupid, sometimes, with her la-di-da ways.

On the wall the next-door cat, thin as a wraith, arched its back and spat defiance at her. 'Get off out of it,' she said and went back inside.

'Fancy a brew?' Frank asked.

Anne seated herself demurely. 'Fancy making one?'

'I will if you want,' he said half-heartedly, but he was already sinking into his chair and reaching for the *Daily Herald*. Anne sighed heavily, and took out her frustrations on the teapot and mugs.

'Heard how the gaffer is?' she said as she poured the tea.

'Just the same, apparently. They say his wife's got him like a little bairn. Serves the bugger right! All the same, it must be hard on a man like him, being at a woman's beck and call.' Realizing he might be giving offence, he changed the subject. 'Guess who was at the ward meeting last night?'

Anne took a sip of her tea and shook her head. 'Who?'

'Gallagher's lad.'

'*Our* Gallagher?' she said incredulously.

'He's no relation of mine,' Frank said. 'But if you mean Gallagher the colliery agent, yes. Well, his son, Stanley.'

'What did *he* want?'

'Membership,' Frank said. 'Apparently he's seen the light now that he's a student teacher. He says his dad's a class traitor. He's got the patter off nice, I'll give him that.'

'Do you think he means it?' Anne asked. She had suddenly glimpsed the wrapper of a chocolate bar at the back of the fire, half-burned. Where the hell had that come from? Fruit and Nut was twopence, and who had money like that to waste?

'He sounds as though he means it,' Frank said, oblivious of her sighing. 'But I think he has only converted because he wants to be on the right side. Next month's elections'll see thirty-two Labour candidates standing unopposed in this county: a third of the seats – and no one dare stand against them for fear of a thrashing. Anyone who wants to be anything in Durham had better see the light! But I'm marking his card, Annie. I remember the little swine when he was a Brenton pen-pusher: "It's the rules", "Do this or I'll tell my daddy". Stanley Gallagher will need to walk on broken glass before he convinces me he's not just jumping on the bandwagon.'

The death of George V in 1936 and the creation of a new king brought a brief surge of hope for everyone. Edward Prince of Wales had been the nation's darling for a long time. He seemed to understand his people; more, he seemed to care. Now he was in a position to translate caring to action.

The euphoria was short-lived. King George had died in the January. No one expected a sudden miracle, but the spring and summer rolled by with nothing changed for the better. October saw 7,000 black-shirted Mosleyites terrorizing the East End of London, with a Jewish tailor and his son thrown through a plate-glass window, and eight people injured.

In November 1936, Edward VIII visited the unemployment black-spot of South Wales. 'Something must be done,' he said, moved almost to tears. The nation waited with bated breath to see what the 'something' might be. But, if South Wales and desperate regions like it were to be saved, they would need some other saviour: the new king was too involved in his own problems to have energy for anything else.

Loelia long ago had told Diana all about the Prince's affair with Mrs Wallis Simpson, a protégée of their heroine, Lady Diana Cooper. 'She's ugly, Di! I mean, it makes one quite like one's own face,' she said, after her first encounter with the American divorcée. 'She's witty, and very sharp, and groomed to a T, but she looks like a – well, I was going to say a Pekingese, but that's not quite fair. Anyway, the Prince, poor fool, is besotted. Everyone's talking! At Emerald Cunard's, she slapped him on the wrist – *slapped* the future King of England! Max says she feeds him love potions, and I'm half-inclined to believe it. Although…' .Loelia leaned closer. 'They do say he's not frightfully sexy, and she knows *ways*. Enough said!'

Diana had seen a dozen lovelies come and go in the Prince's affections. She waited for Wallis Simpson to wane and exit, but it did not happen.

And then the Prince was catapulted into the role of monarch. 'That will be the end of the American lady,' Loelia said smugly – until Mrs Simpson's name appeared in the Court Circular.

In October, Mrs Simpson was discreetly divorced in an out of the way court in Ipswich. 'This is a crisis for all of us,' Loelia said dramatically, as though the whole future of the British aristocracy hung on the intimacy between king and courtesan.

But when Diana laughed, Howard shook a reproving head. 'We're losing prestige abroad, Diana, and confidence at home.'

As if unable to bear the suspense, the Crystal Palace burst into flames and burned to the ground on the night of 30 November 1936. Eleven days later the King was gone.

Esther listened to the king's halting words on the radio. '...You must believe me when I tell you that I have found it impossible to carry the heavy burden of responsibility, and to discharge my duties as king as I would wish to do, without the help and support of the woman I love... God bless you all. God save the King.' Esther wondered if even God could save the new king, with his reputed stammer and air of shyness – but it all seemed far away and remote from her own world.

In Sunderland, once the paper-boys had ceased to cry the special copies of the *Echo*, life went on as usual. Sammy continued to deal and prosper, and to pour money into Esther's account with almost unseemly frequency. 'I told you I'd make your fortune, Esther. See how I keep my word.'

Diana, on the other hand, found she was enjoying London once more. There was so much wonderful gossip at the moment that her head quite ached with trying to take it all in. The Prince – for she would never get used to thinking of him as Duke of Windsor – was rumoured to have made off with all Queen Alexandra's jewels: emeralds, and rubies as big as hen's eggs. Another source said there was a move afoot, led by Herr von Ribbentrop, to unseat the Duke of York before the Coronation and crown instead his younger and more glamorous brother, the Duke of Kent.

'Everyone is taking sides,' Loelia said 'and the Prince's crowd are terribly put out. They won't be having things their own way in future. There's a new Queen now, and it isn't Wallis Simpson.'

The new Queen, according to Loelia, who had met her several times, was tiny but very determined, with merry blue eyes which could freeze anyone who overstepped the mark. 'She doesn't go in for style, and she abhors make-up – well, when it's overdone,' Loelia said. The fashion in make-up, still of immense importance to women, was moving back again towards the natural. Diana found the new, muted make-up a little unexciting, but style was style and must be obeyed.

She sat with Loelia in the salon of the designer, Norman Hartnell, who was now designing for the glamorous actress Gertrude Lawrence. 'Isn't it heaven to be without the children?' Loelia breathed. She had four children now – two girls and two boys – and two nannies and a nursery-maid. Her children were, in Diana's opinion, demanding little horrors who ran rings round anyone given charge of them in order that they might torment their mother. They were often joined by Max's unruly brood of three boys. No wonder Loelia needed peace.

Diana concentrated on the gowns parading before them: wonderful creations, beaded and tucked, displayed on models so arrogant that they might just have descended from Mount Olympus. She wanted something to wear to an evening reception, and finally chose a chiffon and embroidered-lace evening gown, cut high in front and almost to the waist behind, with a matching turban that she might or might not dare to wear. She insisted on its being packed and loaded into Loelia's limousine, in case it was not delivered in time. The *vendeuse* went pale at the prospect of the House of Hartnell failing a client; but Diana went off with her dress box nevertheless, trying not to see a newspaper-vendor's board outside that proclaimed *Taxes rise to pay for re-armament*. Rupert was nearly fourteen. There couldn't, mustn't be a war.

Emmanuel Lansky worried endlessly about his son, but he worried almost more about the rise of Fascism. Spain was in ferment, now, and the tales from Germany even more horrific. In France there was a great deal of anger about English pacifism, and Sammy's maternal relatives had not been slow to express displeasure when Sammy visited them last. He read out to Esther a clipping from a Paris newspaper which ended: 'Does London imagine that Hitler has renounced any of the projects indicated in his book *Mein Kampf*? If so, the illusion of our friends across the Channel is complete.'

'This will end in tears and blood,' Lansky said. Esther thought of the stories she had heard from Frank, picked up from his union friends: perhaps tears of blood were already being shed in places like Dachau and Ravensbruck. As if he had read her thoughts, Lansky shook his head. 'Germany has become a *trefa medinneh*.' She knew enough Yiddish to know that *trefa* meant 'unholy'. He nodded again. 'Yes, a *trefa medinneh*, Esther: an unholy place.'

She put a hand on his arm, noticing how frail he was becoming, wanting desperately to comfort him as he had comforted her so many times over the years.

'Trust in God,' she said, but even as she spoke she knew her words were less than adequate.

Howard was coming to dread his visits to his father's sickbed. The anxious, pleading eyes in the steadily collapsing face, the fingers that occasionally plucked at the bedclothes, the inane laughter of the nurse as she babied the man who had once commanded a workforce – above all, the enigmatic face of his mother: they all chilled him. Sometimes, when he left the room, he would hear a half-squeak, half-scream from the bed, as though his father were imploring him not to abandon him. Yet when he raised the subject of further help for his father – a second opinion, or more expert nursing – his mother would not even listen.

'I am his wife, Howard: I know what's best.' Charlotte was his mother; could he override her wishes? Even Diana, still given to impulsive action, was unwilling to recommend a decision. 'Let's give it another day… a week.

The spring of 1937 came, and cherry blossom, and the horror of Guernica. Hitler's bombers, sent to help the Fascist Franco, pounded a city filled with women and children until, so Howard read, 'the smell of burning human flesh was nauseating'. As in every preceding year, Howard remembered Trenchard and how they had read A. E. Housman's 'The Cherry Tree' together in Flanders. Howard had been indecisive over Trenchard, and it had cost a life: was he making the same mistake again over his father? There was one thing he could do, however. He sent for Gallagher and told him to draw up plans for demolishing and rebuilding the Shacks.

'Is that wise, Mr Howard?' The agent's eyes were wary but there was a glint of defiance in them.

'I'm not prepared to discuss the wisdom of the decision,' Howard said. 'I want it done.'

Gallagher nodded. 'Of course.' He left the office and Howard sat still; ears cocked. He heard sounds from the adjoining office: Gallagher crossing the room, the creak of his chair as he sat down, and then a low murmur as he spoke into the telephone. A moment later his steps recrossed the room, and the door of his office opened, and closed behind him.

Howard stood up and crossed to the window, to see Gallagher emerge and get into his car in the yard below. He knew which direction the agent would take: not towards the cokeworks, or the other Brenton enterprises; not towards his own house on the outskirts of Belgate. He took the Sunderland road.

Howard went to the hat-stand and took down his black Homburg. If his assumption about Gallagher's journey was correct, he needed to assert his authority once and for all.

He found Gallagher in his mother's sitting-room, and the agent's look of dismay when he appeared drove the last sliver of doubt from Howard's mind.

'I won't beat about the bush, mother. I have just given this man an order, and I have reason to believe he's asked your permission to disobey me. Will you give it?'

Charlotte's face did not betray emotion of any kind. 'You're in charge of the day-to-day running of the collieries, Howard. However, matters outside of that operation are surely in the hands of the board.' It was a statement not a question.

'Call a meeting, then,' Howard said. He was glad that his mother made no attempt to plead a maternal bond. It allowed him to meet coldness with coldness, argument with argument. He turned to Gallagher: 'Call it for later in the week.' He inclined his head to his mother; said, 'Gallagher,' in clipped tones and went back to his car.

Howard did not want a fight at the moment. Increasingly he was beginning to see that he could not combine his duties as a Member of Parliament with the entire responsibility for Brenton affairs. But far more was involved in this question of the Shacks than the mere building of houses.

Back in his office, he sat at his desk, hearing the rather shame-faced return of Gallagher, smiling at his secretary as she carried in tea and biscuits on a tray. Eventually he telephoned to confide in Edward Burton, who knew of his dilemma and was sympathetic to it.

'Hold on, Howard,' Burton said at last. 'Don't desert us now, for God's sake. There's never been a greater need for good men in the House. Let's meet tomorrow, and see what's to be done, but don't act impulsively, I beg you.'

Howard felt comforted by his talk with Edward Burton. He would have to give up his seat, eventually, but this was no time to desert, with the Fascists rampant in Europe and an urgent need to rearm. There were siren voices in the House, speakers for peace at any price. He could not leave the field to them now.

At least Sunderland would benefit from increased defence spending, and so would Belgate. Britain's shipyards would have to build the much needed warships, and the spin-off from that work would affect every industry in the country.

Everywhere Howard went, people seemed to be whistling and singing, as though they had decided to ignore the dark horizon. The world had gone mad for music. 'I've got you under my skin' greeted him from every corner; every cycling errand-boy gave forth with 'one, two button your shoe'. And yet in London the previous week, the German ambassador had greeted the British king with a Nazi salute.

Howard took the problem of the Shacks to Diana and told her what his mother had decreed. 'She'll overrule me at the board meeting,' he said, pouring sherry and carrying a glass to his wife.

'When is it?' Diana asked.

'This week.'

'Well,' she said, 'I've never attended a board meeting, though your father made me a director when Noel was born. I shall come to this one – you can count on it!' She raised her glass in a mock salute. 'To victory,' she said.

The Maguires' regular paper was the *Herald*, but when he could afford it Frank bought the *Daily Sketch*. It was the

Sketch which told him in bold print: *You need not be frightened. Gas masks are comfy*. He might have believed it if he had not tried one at a lodge meeting and nearly choked. He was glad that his union was taking political action. Last year they had given to the anti-Fascists in Spain; there was talk afoot of helping other workers in Europe, and an increased feeling of political power among mineworkers.

Seats in local government fell to Labour at every election, and seats in national elections would surely follow. Until that moment when Labour had the power to see justice done, Frank would work, and wait, and do his best to keep Anne sweet. She had a gob on her now like a fire-eating dragon, but she was a good wife and mother, and that was all that mattered. So he filled in his Littlewood's coupon on Thursday nights, and sat with the children on Saturdays while Anne went to the local flea-pit and came home red-eyed with crying over Bette Davis or Louise Rainer or Edna Best.

Tonight she was getting ready to see Fred Astaire and Ginger Rogers in *Top Hat*, but Frank could tell there was something on her mind as she washed her face and neck at the kitchen sink, the collar of her blouse and cardigan carefully turned in, the sleeves pulled half-way up her forearms.

'Keep an eye on our Estelle,' Anne said as she dried her face and put herself to rights.

'What's the matter with her?' Frank asked.

'She's up to something,' Anne said tersely. 'She'll not have it, when I quiz her: innocent as a newborn babe, according to her. But she's spending, Frank – and she's not getting the money from me.'

'She likely runs errands,' Frank said, suddenly uneasy. He loved his eldest daughter, but she'd always been a handful.

'Who round here's got money for errands?' Anne said scornfully. 'What could she make at that, if she ran herself down to the stumps? No, I'm talking money: comics, sweets... I've found half-a-crown in her pocket more than once.'

'Where is Estelle now?' Frank asked, his mind seething suddenly with visions of Borstal and the stocks. He had seen bairns lift things in shops before – seen, and belted their lugs for them. But not *his* bairns: and especially not Estelle.

'Out,' Anne said. 'God knows where.'

A few moments later she went off with their next-door neighbour, and Frank settled to his reading, until he heard the back door go.

'Who's that?'

'Only me, dad.' Estelle stood in the doorway, pretty as a picture – and as innocent as a little angel. Frank was suddenly overcome with remorse; he'd been quick to think the worst of her, and no mistake. He tried to make up for it by chatting to her as she ate her supper of Fry's cocoa and bread and golden syrup, and put rags in her long blonde hair to ensure curls for the morning. She was thirteen years old, and if he had not known it, the swelling of her breasts, straining against the tight stuff of her cotton dress would have told him.

'Night-night pet,' Frank said, and kissed her clumsily as she went upstairs to the room she shared with the younger children, safely bedded by Anne before she went out. He looked at the clock: seven. Joseph, who at fourteen and earning, set his own times, was the only one yet to come home. He shook out his paper, and settled back into his chair.

He had just immersed himself in details of a proposed law to put a stop to Oswald Mosley's bunch when the tap came at the door. No one visited at night in Belgate, and Joseph would not knock. Frank put aside his paper and went to the door.

He knew the woman on the step by face but not by name. 'Mr Maguire?'

'Yes. I'm afraid the wife's not in...

She looked disappointed to hear Anne was out, but she

didn't budge. 'Can I come in? I've got something to tell you – something you ought to know.'

Frank let her go past him, wishing she'd had her man with her, or that Anne was there to buttress him. The woman turned, when she was into the room, and faced him.

'Do you know where your Estelle goes when she comes out of school?'

Frank hesitated, not liking the tone of the woman's voice. 'Round the doors, I suppose. Why?'

The woman sighed, as though wishing she hadn't come, and then she spoke. 'She's been going into Jimmy Carter's.'

'The fruit shop?'

'Aye. And if that wasn't bad enough, she's been taking other bairns in.'

'What do you mean? Have they been thieving?'

She shook her head impatiently. 'No, they've been going in the back shop…'

Frank understood suddenly, and in that moment knew that he could not bear to understand.

'What do you mean?' he said, to gain time.

'He's been up to things: mucking about with them. Your Estelle was the first, then she took other girls. He gave them money. I just found out; my little lass went today, the first time, and took fright, and ran home. I got it out of her easily enough. My man was going to the pollis, but I stopped him. We don't want the bairns being cross-questioned, and the less said the better. But I thought you ought to know, being as your lass was the…' She hesitated, seeking an acceptable word for 'ring-leader'.

'Yes,' Frank said dully. 'Yes, thank you.'

There was an awkward silence, and then the woman said, 'Well, that's all I wanted to say. I'd best be going.'

He showed her out and made his way to the foot of the stairs. 'Estelle? Get down here!'

One look at her face was enough to tell him she'd been

listening on the landing. She came halfway down the stairs and halted, clinging to the banister, and crying. The rag curls on top of her head shuddered with her sobs.

'I said down,' Frank said and held her eye until she came far enough down for him to grab her and drag her to the foot of the stairs.

'It wasn't me, dad. I didn't want to! He 'ticed us in. I never knew what he was doing. I didn't know it was wrong, dad. Don't tell me mam!' The words rattled out of Estelle until he fetched her a crack across the ear, and then stepped back, afraid of his own strength.

'Don't lie to me – don't make it worse!' Frank twisted her arm cruelly, thinking in one moment that he might break it and in the next that he didn't care. 'What did he do to you? Tell me!' A silence and then another twist and a squeal.

'All right, all right! He just looked... and touched me. I said no, I didn't want him...'

He shook her like a terrier shakes a rat. '*Did* you take along other bairns?' The sudden aversion of her head was answer enough.

He thrashed her back up the stairs, then he took his cap and muffler from the peg and let himself out into the yard.

There was still a light in Carter's shop, and he walked towards it, feeling the tears freezing on his cheeks as he went, feeling the food he had eaten an hour before lift in his chest. He let himself into the fruiterer's yard and walked towards the rectangle of light above the back door. It gave at his touch, and he stepped inside, seeing Carter in his blue overall, seeing his thin, ferret-like face, his curiously fleshy hands with their soil-ingrained fingernails, the hands that had defiled his child.

As Carter began to bluster, Frank held up an admonitory finger.

'I hope you've made your peace with your maker, Jimmy Carter, for by God I think I'm going to kill you now.'

He landed blows until he realized they were not being returned; until he heard the man sobbing, his hands held up to his eyes, half to protect them from blows, half to hide the shame in them. Frank left, then, and made for the dark bulk of the spoil-heap, where a man could weep to his heart's content and there was nothing but the occasional scurrying rat to overhear.

27

It was Edward Burton who found Howard a manager. Norman Stretton had been out in India, working for a rubber company, until ill health had recently forced him home. Like Howard, he had served in the war, and there was an openness about his face that inspired confidence. 'I know nothing at all about the mining industry – but I know men, and I'm not too proud to ask for answers.'

Howard promoted two of the overmen to deputy managers, and turned the colliery over to Stretton. With Howard on the end of a telephone, and with Gallagher's specialist knowledge, Stretton would be able to cope, at least long enough for the European situation to resolve itself. Satisfied, Howard went back to London, leaving Diana to follow him in a few days.

Diana travelled to London by train. Looking from the window of her first-class compartment, it was not the winter landscape she saw: it was Fox's face as he stood respectfully on the platform. At first his devotion to her had been amusing – and useful. When at last she had realized it was becoming obvious, and a potential embarrassment, she had made it clear that she expected him not only to know his place but to stay in it. Since then there had been an air of resentment about him, too indefinable to complain of, too distinct to ignore.

As the Cleveland hills came into view, Diana opened her *Tatler* and gave herself up to gossip. Later, as drowsiness overcame her, she closed her magazine, and swung her legs on to the opposite seat. A picture of her father-in-law's slumped figure came to mind: poor man, he was as good as dead. Indeed, he would be better off if he were dead.

Charlotte now reigned supreme, with Gallagher lurking in the wings like a poor man's Rasputin. As the train steamed south, Diana slept, waking at Doncaster to the uncomfortable thought that the next night she would have to dine with Max and Laura Dunane.

The Dunanes had set up home in Eaton Square, and the next day was Max's birthday. 'You must come, Diana,' Loelia had said on the phone, and Diana had realized that a refusal would be taken to mean she still cared; that Max still mattered. So she had packed her Schiaparelli jacket of pink silk brocade, with leaping acrobats in black and gold woven into the material and buttons fashioned like gold trapezes. She had a black grosgrain skirt to go with it, and a matching neckband. Schiaparelli was the wittiest of designers, and awfully good at keeping up one's spirits.

Max and Laura had just returned from America on board the *Normandie*, together with their three children and a retinue of five. As far as Diana could see, the marriage had worked out reasonably well, although Laura seemed remarkably susceptible to illness. 'She's taken to her bed again,' Loelia would say with increasing frequency. Laura had been a rich and pampered daughter, now she was a pampered wife who held the purse-strings. It was much the same thing.

She greeted Diana with affability, holding out a hand and inclining her cheek to be kissed. 'Lovely to see you, Diana. You must tell me all about the children.' Did Laura know that Diana's daughter was half-sister to her own children? If so, she carried it off well.

Max took Diana's hand and pulled her into a warm, whisky-scented embrace. 'Diana, you look ravishing, as usual. Where's old Howard? Such a pity he couldn't come, but I suppose the House is too great a pull.'

They ate *filet de boeuf* and delicious confections of spun sugar filled with syllabub, and afterwards the ladies left the gentlemen to their port and went up to Laura's bedroom to 'freshen up'. Loelia's nose wrinkled slightly at the phrase, but she went willingly enough; and Diana followed, half reluctant to enter the room Max shared with his wife, half curious about what it could tell of their life together.

To her relief, there was no sign of his presence. The room was a riot of bows and drapes, ruched curtains at the windows and around the four-poster bed. 'I sleep so badly,' Laura said, seeing Diana glance at the drapes. 'Poor Max has taken up residence next door because of my eternally burning lights.'

Through the mirror Diana could see Loelia's face, tight-lipped and secretive, just as it had been in the old days when she and Max had had something to hide. Was there a new secret? Some other foolish woman who would share Max's bed and then, 'knowing the rules', depart without making a fuss? Suddenly Diana longed to see Howard's dear, familiar *upright* face. She patted her forehead with a cologne-dipped tissue, and counted the hours to going home, trying all the while to enter into the other women's conversation.

Laura had just had her ears pierced, the latest fashion-craze in society circles. Until now it had been a custom of the middle-aged, but suddenly young married hostesses were flocking in droves to have it carried out. Trendsetters like Marina, the Duchess of Kent, and her sister-in-law the Duchess of Gloucester, had adopted a style that senior members of the royal family had always followed. 'The old Queen had hers done as a child, by a maid with a darning-needle,' Loelia said, with a shudder.

'How ghastly,' Laura murmured, complacently viewing her own lobes, still a little pink from the operation but boasting huge pearl drops. 'It's gruesome,' she said, 'but if one has expensive earrings, one's so much less likely to lose them. Max bought me these as a reward for being brave.'

Diana waited for it to hurt. Max had bought her pearl earrings once, laying them on her naked stomach as a surprise. She waited, but it did not hurt. Was it well and truly over, then?

The following day she lunched with Loelia, who was feeling hungover and depressed. 'The 0. M. used to say the world had gone mad, Di, and I thought it was just his usual moaning. Now I see he was right. All the great houses are going – not to woodworm or dry rot, but lack of staff, darling! No one wants to work in the pantry or the dining-room any more, oh no: that's beneath them. The kitchen or upstairs, that's out, too. They whistle in the corridor and smoke – *smoke!* – in their bedrooms! And if you dare to suggest they desist, they're off. Thelma Curtess says her maid shops at Selfridges. As for nannies, the less said about them the better. When I think what I'd give to have darling old Nanny Dunane here now… still, mustn't go on and on. I expect you have your problems in the frozen north. You are coming up to London for the grand affair, aren't you?'

The coronation was to be the grandest affair for years. For the first time film-cameras and BBC commentators were to be allowed into the abbey to see a reluctant but resolute King dedicate himself to the service of his people. Diana was not certain that Howard wanted to be in London for the occasion. 'I don't know,' she told Loelia. 'We haven't decided yet. Belgate is going quite mad over it, so perhaps we'll be needed there.'

They talked of Loelia's dress for the abbey, which was being made by Norman Hartnell: 'But only because I'm a regular client. He's getting too exclusive for words.' And then of the coming summer. 'Will you get away?' Loelia asked anxiously. 'It must be difficult with the Brenton *père* at death's door.'

'Howard wouldn't want to leave Britain. I suppose we could go to Scotland, or the Lakes.'

Loelia pulled a sympathetic face. 'It's not the same, is it? There's something about the Continental platform at Victoria... well, they call it the gateway to the world, don't they? We're going to Rome and Naples in the autumn, and we're at the Lido for the whole of July. It would be so nice if you and Howard could bring the children. I've got some darling Vera Borea beachwear. Think about it: lying in the sun all morning, eating figs and gossiping; afternoons of bridge and more sun, and then delicious cocktails and food at Harry's Bar in the evening. Heaven!'

'I don't think Howard would contemplate Italy at the moment,' Diana said. 'He's so worried about the Fascists.'

'You can't blame poor Italy for one silly little upstart,' Loelia said. 'Henry says it will all settle down soon. Once we get the new King crowned the government can concentrate on the international situation.'

In Belgate the coronation provided a wonderful excuse for merrymaking. Bunting was dug out from cupboards and lofts, and the jazz band which Frank and Anne had started in the strike, to amuse the children, polished up its kazoos for the big parade. Each child was to have a mug from its school, and a collection was organized in the pub and at the Welfare to lay on a street party.

'I still wish it'd been the Prince of Wales,' Frank said, remembering the visit to South Wales and the demand for something to be done. But Anne had crossed the Prince of Wales and his fancy-piece from her list. When bits about them appeared in the paper she cut them out and threw them on the back of the fire.

It was an empty gesture, but it gave Anne enormous satisfaction – and there had been little enough of that since her discovery that her daughter had been defiled. Since then, every curtain in Belgate had twitched when any of the players in the drama went by. Carter had ventured into the pub one night, and the father of one of the other children had found him there and thrashed him while men stood round and watched. The village bobby, who knew every leaf that stirred in Belgate, came in, took in the circumstances, and turned on his heel, leaving justice to be done. No one shopped at Carter's any more, and the windows were growing sparser with every day that passed. 'He'll be driven out,' Anne said with satisfaction. 'And wherever he goes, we'll make sure they know.'

She would sit at the table, twisting her hands and brooding bitterly. 'Where did I go wrong, Frank? That's what I ask myself over and over again. I've asked the priest: he says we're all born sinful, but that's not much consolation.' She sniffed and avoided Frank's eyes. 'I've asked myself if it's my side, Frank. My father drank, you know that – and I've never been quite sure about our Esther: you know what Jews are like, never mind cripples. On the other hand, there's your Mary: flagrant about it! How many years has that gone on, living over the brush, or as good as? And don't put on that "I don't know what you're talking about" face. You know Mary sleeps with that doctor, and so do I.' She wept again. 'Our poor Estelle, mebbe it's bred in her from both sides.'

In the end Frank was glad to slip out to the pub for a half of bitter, using the pretext of having coronation plans to sort out. As he entered the warm, friendly atmosphere of the Half Moon he felt a greater kindliness to the new King than he would have believed possible an hour or two ago. At least *he* had got him out of the house.

Mary Hardman would have been shocked to hear herself described as 'living above the brush'. She thought that she and Patrick were unbelievably discreet, never appearing to spend a night under the same roof, never holding hands or touching in public. In the café where they took tea on her day off, in their walks in the park or around the shops in Durham, they walked erect and separate. Even in the darkness of the cinema the most she would allow was a discreet hand-holding under the cover of his folded mac in winter, or her handbag in summer.

When they were alone, it was sweet for both of them. There was an unhurried quality about their lovemaking that Mary did not remember from her time with Stephen. That had been urgent, even savage, always accompanied by a desire to conceive or a terror of conception. Now Patrick took responsibility for contraception, and she felt safe with him – although his fervid desire not to reproduce was strange to her.

'This is not a world to bring children into,' Patrick said once, as they lay comfortably, their need for one another stirring but not yet demanding release. 'I love you, Mary. I love you so much.' He buried his face in her neck, then began to take the kirby-grips from her hair. 'I never thought I'd love anyone: I only wanted to forget the pain and the confusion and the utter pointlessness of it all. You've drawn me back into life, and I'm grateful… But I'm afraid, too. Afraid of it all happening again. I saw a man today, still heaving and gasping from gas. "Got a family?" I asked him, just to make conversation. "Yes," he said proudly. He was *proud* to say he had a son in the DLI – the infantry, the first line in! The boy is twenty. If there's another war he'll go in like his father did – and the cloud will come over the front line, and the boy will go down, and he'll be left gasping for life, like his father.' Suddenly Patrick moved away from her, and Mary knew there would be no lovemaking, that day at least.

'Lie still awhile,' she said, patting his arm, 'and in a little while I'll make a nice cup of tea.'

While they drank their tea, Mary confided her new worry to Patrick, pleased that it took the shadows from his eyes and allowed his face to relax into the softer lines she was used to now. 'It's Fox,' she said. 'You know he works for Mr Howard now? Well, he's always taken Mrs Howard here and there, and kept the cars at the Scar right: he gets what's needed, and I pay him, and put his bills in with mine. For years we've done that, ever since I went up there. Anyway, this last year it's changed: he's putting bills in for this and that… not little sums: big amounts. And there's no way I can say yea or nay. What do I know about cars?'

'So you think he's cheating?' Patrick asked.

Mary was reluctant to say it outright, but she shrugged.

'Well,' Patrick went on, thoughtfully. 'You'll just have to find out.'

Sammy insisted on a celebration for the coronation. Rachael was carried down to the sitting-room to a groaning table. 'Champagne, Schiffy,' Sammy said. 'What else for such a day?' He kept up his usual patter of jokes and teasing, but Rachael was very quiet.

'Are you tired?' Esther asked her sympathetically. The old woman looked across to Emmanuel to make sure she was not overheard.

'A little tired, yes,' she said. 'But very much afraid.' She saw surprise in Esther's eyes and smiled. 'Not for myself, Esther – I've had my life, and God be thanked, I have a blessed old age. It's the boy I fear for.'

Esther patted the wrinkled hand. 'He'll be all right. I know he's a bit wild sometimes, but –' She meant to say Sammy was settling down but Rachael shook her head.

'Not that. So he's a little wild, so who cares? A good girl will come along and see to that. It's war I fear, and the hatred. This Hitler! Everywhere the Jews are threatened.

Emmanuel, the *mentsh*, keeps it from me, but I know. I see, I hear, I *read*. Now, not even the land we were promised is safe: Jew fighting Arab in Palestine, and both of them fighting the British.'

Esther had read in the paper of the 'irreconcilable conflict' between Jews and Arabs in Palestine, and the plan to put the holy cities like Bethlehem and Jerusalem under British protection. And she had read, too, of the concentration camps for Jews all over Germany: Buchenwald and Sachsenhausen, and Dachau. No wonder Rachael was afraid.

And then suddenly the radio was on, and the awed voice of the commentator was telling of the golden coach leaving Buckingham Palace, drawn by eight greys with four postillions and six footmen, eight grooms and four Yeomen of the Guard walking alongside, and a King with an anxious face, wearing deep red and snow-white ermine, with the Cap of Maintenance on his head. Of the Queen, relaxed and smiling in ivory satin, embroidered in pure gold thread with the emblems of the British Isles and the Dominions, and a train of purple velvet, dropping a curtsey to the old Queen who had broken with tradition to attend the coronation because her son was in need of her support.

'It'll be all right,' Esther whispered as the music rolled and the Vivats rang out. 'There's a new King, and a new order. It'll all work out, you'll see.'

In Belgate, the street party was in full swing. The men congregated in the Half Moon, clustering around the wireless specially brought in for the event, while in the street the women toiled after the children, and carried laden plates in to the men. The bunting fluttered on the lamp standards, and every window sported a Union Jack. Rain clouds gathered to watch. 'Don't you dare,' Anne Maguire said, scowling heavenwards; and the clouds obeyed, holding in their rain until the eats were over, the favours handed out, and replete fathers were ejected from the pub to carry their offspring home, shoulder-high.

'It's been a grand day,' Frank Maguire said; and then, letting his allegiance to the 'People's Prince' go once and for all: 'God save the King.'

Diana and Howard Brenton had meant to visit the celebrations, bearing gifts. Instead they gathered downstairs in the Brenton house, half-heartedly listening to the radio while Charles's life ebbed away upstairs.

Charlotte would allow no one in the room except the doctor and nurse. 'I'll call you when the time comes,' she said. But when the yellow eyes made their final plea for a sight of his son, she folded her hands on her pleated and pin-tucked breast, and smiled down at her husband as he took his last, slow breath.

'He's gone,' the doctor said, relieved that he could get away from such a conflict.

'Poor thing,' the nurse said, and closed the staring eyes before anyone else could see reproach in them.

Downstairs Cosmo Lang, Archbishop of Canterbury, presented 'King George, your undoubted King' and the huge congregation shouted in unison: 'God save King George.' As the new King knelt at the altar to take the oath, Diana Brenton took her husband's hand and led him upstairs to pay his final respects to his father.

Howard was genuinely grief-sticken, but it was Diana who felt the death most keenly. Charles had always been her ally, someone she could rely on to take her part. His championing of her cause had helped to hold her marriage together, when, if it had not been for the gift of the London house and his constant deferring to her whims, she might have done something foolish. She was happy, now, with a husband she liked and respected, and for that she was deeply grateful to her father-in-law.

Loelia wrote to sympathize and also to relay details of the coronation.

I can't tell you how moving it was, Di. I am so sorry you missed it all. The old Queen said the Yorks would do very well, and on this showing she's right. I must admit it was an ordeal, going on for hours as it did and not a lavatory in sight. Henry swears some of the older peers had 'contraptions' under their robes. Still, to the important things: no one put a foot wrong, although it was horribly complicated. The King looked very spiritual, quite exalted really, and when the trumpets blew the Vivats my hair actually stood up on my head. When the Queen was crowned, all the peeresses lifted their arms to put on their coronets, and the white kid gloves going up together looked just like Swan Lake. You have never seen such jewels.... I was splattered with the Colvile gems, and looked positively dull by comparison.

London is still en fête. We were at Hampden House last night for the Sutherlands' ball, and it was dazzling. The new Queen, in a divine Hartnell gown of tulle and lace, looked like a Winterhalter portrait. Every royal in the universe was there... there'll be no holding the Sutherlands now!

It must be awful for you being in mourning at such a time. If we weren't so tied, Henry and I would come north for the funeral: I quite liked the old ogre, and you need moral support. Still, I will make it up to you when I see you.

Much love, Loelia.

Charles Brenton's funeral service, in Durham Cathedral, was attended by dignitaries from far and wide. But Diana was more touched by the sight of his colliers, lining the road to the Bishopwearmouth cemetery. They did not show great grief or sense of loss, but their heads were bowed in respect, their caps twisted in their clasped hands. 'Look,' Howard said as the cortège slowed. 'There's old Lansky.' Diana, seeing Howard was moved by the sight, inclined her head to the sombre, bearded figure.

At the graveside Howard stood between Diana and his mother, but it was Gallagher's arm Charlotte took as they walked back to the car, leaving Howard to escort a weeping Caroline.

She wept even more profusely when the will was read. She had done well, but Howard and Diana had done better. Charlotte was provided for most adequately, but her reign over the Brenton business empire was over. The old King was dead and the crown had passed to his son.

28

Mary Hardman felt better as soon as she had confided her suspicions of Fox to Patrick Quinnell. 'It's only fair to make sure that what you suspect is true,' he said. So she kept the bills Fox submitted for payment and, where she could, she checked whether or not the work specified had been carried out. The result was staggering. Fox was taking at least £5 a week by false pretences – doubling his wage. There were four cars in the Brenton garages now, and he distributed the bills cleverly between them, but after eight weeks Mary had ample evidence that for every £10 genuinely spent, £15 was being claimed.

There was no chance of either of the Brentons detecting the fraud; Mary controlled the bills for a household of seventeen: herself, a cook, a kitchenmaid, an upstairs maid, a parlourmaid, a houseman, two gardeners who lived out, Fox, Susan, the nanny, a nurserymaid, and the family. Nothing was skimped or counted, and £5 more was neither here nor there. Nevertheless, it was theft.

When at last she was sure, Mary carried her suspicions to Diana. If Fox had been a different man, she might have confronted him herself but he had always considered himself a cut above the other staff. There was only one thing Mary could do.

Diana had spent a happy afternoon contemplating the refurbishment of the Scar. At Christmas she would have lived here for fifteen years. In that time there had been a constant scheme of redecoration and purchase of new items of furniture, but never, since that first time, had she done the house from top to bottom. Throughout the Thirties, taste in decor had veered from the traditional to the ultra-modern. Tubular steel and glass, black-and-white kidskin chairs, Lalique wall lights against Venetian red walls... she had seen all these things in the houses of her friends, along with the obligatory Constance Spry flower-arrangement of dead grass and poppy-heads. Lady Milchett's bedroom had gold-lacquered pilasters and shiny blue walls; Lady Drogheda's dining-room was black glass; and Noël Coward preferred zebra stripes of brown and off-white. None of that would do for the Scar, but Diana meant to be the tiniest bit daring and had sent for fabric samples from every avant-garde designer in London. She was contemplating a design of black and white fish swimming in an apricot sea when Mary knocked at the door.

'Sit down,' Diana said, sweeping pattern-books off a chair and putting aside her samples. Mary made the house run on oiled wheels and was not to be treated lightly.

The news about Fox came as a blow. 'Are you sure?' Diana asked, and then again, 'Doubly sure?'

But there was no arguing with the evidence Mary placed before her. One car had had three exhausts in a year; another its brakes re-lined twice in eight weeks. It was fraud on a grand scale for a provincial chauffeur, and it could not be allowed to continue. She and Mary drank tea together, and then Diana went alone in search of Fox.

She found him in his cubby-hole above the garage, shiny booted legs on a chair, hands folded across his shirt front, a wireless blaring out dance tunes. He was surprised to see her there, and swung his feet to the floor. 'Ma'am?' he said, as he stood up.

Diana sighed. There was no easy way to say what must be said. 'You're cheating my husband, Fox. Please don't deny it, because I know it's true. I'm hurt, rather than angry. I trusted you.'

She saw denial forming on his lips and then die away. 'What happens now?' he said, and Diana was taken aback both by his words and the insolent way he said them.

'I expect my husband will dismiss you, Fox. I don't see that he has much alternative.'

Fox moved forward until he towered over Diana. She could smell sweat, and see hair at the unbuttoned neck of his shirt. 'Not if he doesn't know,' he said. 'Not if you don't tell him.' He was smiling, and poking the inside of his cheek with his tongue. 'After all, I've kept a few secrets for you. Years ago, mebbe. Still...' He let the words die away suggestively.

Diana was puzzled for a second, and then she remembered the times he had taken her to meet Max, or driven her to the station and overheard her telephone calls.

'How dare you?' she said with dignity, and turned on her heel.

Esther walked to Belgate on her afternoon off. She was having driving lessons from Sammy now, and he had offered to accompany her while she drove the car; but then he might have been subjected to Anne's spite, and Esther couldn't bear the thought of that. Besides, it was a lovely day, and she liked to walk between the banks of wild flowers and hawthorn that lined the road. She called in at the cemetery on the way, slipping out of her silk knitted cardigan and folding it over her arm.

She was growing to like her own company, too. She felt stronger now, independent and unafraid. *I've grown up,* she thought ruefully, snapping at a foxglove as she passed. Perhaps she had grown up too far? She was certainly cautious with money, now.

'You're *meshuggener*,' Sammy said ruefully. 'You're buying a car more like a toy, to save pennies.'

Esther was buying, much to Sammy's disgust, a seven horsepower Baby Austin, only a fraction higher in price than a motorcycle and side-car. She would soon pass her driving test, and Sammy was urging her to buy a Lagonda Tourer, or even, if she wouldn't spend £375, a Ford Popular – but Esther meant to stand firm. A dark-blue Baby Austin was what she wanted, and what she was going to have.

Am I turning into a lone wolf? she wondered now. Certainly she had dispensed with Stanley, her tame schoolmaster, not simply because he was quiet and colourless but because she did not want a man in her life.

Esther was approaching the Shacks now. She had heard that the houses were to be demolished soon and replaced by nice-looking houses with casement windows and brick walls, three or four bedrooms, and an offshot kitchen. Perhaps Frank and Anne would get one, and relieve their overcrowding, Esther thought hopefully; but when she suggested this to Anne it met with a hollow laugh.

'The Brentons give *us* a house? Pigs'll fly before that happens. Besides...' she looked around her, 'when I get out of here, our Esther, I want to do it in style. A big house, like the Durham officials have – or a house in London, mebbe, when Brenton loses the seat.' She cocked an eye at her sister. 'Don't look like that: Frank stands a good chance of a nomination when old Willy Coxon snuffs it. The old sod'll never retire, that's certain, but we all go some time, and when he's out Frank'll be in. I'll be Lady Muck of Vinegar Hill then – you'll need to pay for an audience.' She grinned. 'My God, not to have to worry, Esther! If I had that, I'd be laughing. Anyroad, I'll put the kettle on and then let's have the news.'

They talked of the death of poor Jean Harlow – who had only got what she'd been asking for, according to Anne – and then moved on to Anne's other scarlet woman, Wallis Simpson.

'They got wed, then. Disgraceful! Married by a vicar, an' all. I've always said the Church of England's corrupt.'

'It was very a quiet and private wedding,' Esther said.

'It can't be private enough for me,' said Anne. 'All his fine promises, and then he goes off with a whore!' She was launched into fervour now, regurgitating the opinions Frank had brought home from lodge and party meetings, berating any and every public figure, but saving her best for Hitler, whom she called 'that Adolf' and accused of trying to wipe out not only Jews and gypsies, but Catholics as well. Lansky had already drawn Esther's attention to reports of Catholics clashing with the Nazis in Munich, and the closure of some Catholic schools in Germany, so she was able to give proper sympathy, and Anne was duly mollified.

'Take care of yourself, our Es,' she said when they parted. She stroked her hair from her forehead, and Esther saw that her hands were wrinkled and sore from constant immersion in the washtub.

Walking home as the first tones of dusk crept over hedgerow and field, Esther thought about how sharply her path had diverged from that of her sister. She had hung on Anne's every word when she was a child; now she felt affection for her sister, but, if she was honest, she also felt pity. She laughed aloud at this admission, thinking of Anne who, at this very moment, was probably full of pity for her own spinster and childless state. And Anne would never know: the secret of Philip's child must be kept forever. Esther felt tears prick her eyes and tried to divert herself by picking an armful of meadowsweet and ragwort to take home for Schiffy.

But it was too late to put flowers in a jar for Rachael. She had died quietly that afternoon, in the chair by the window where Sammy had placed her.

*

Howard sensed the tension as soon as he left the train at Durham. Fox met him at the station without his usual smile and 'Good journey, sir?' When he reached the house, Diana did not come out to the step to greet him. Instead she was waiting in the hall, her face unusually grave.

'I've asked for some tea,' she said and led the way into the morning-room. The tea came almost immediately, and Diana poured solemnly before she spoke. 'I'm afraid I've something awful to tell you, Howard. Fox has been robbing us – quite systematically and over an extended period.' She told him of Mary's evidence, and her own confrontation with the chauffeur. 'And then he said that if I told you he would tell you certain things about me: things that happened long ago.'

'Things which I already knew of?'

'Yes,' Diana said. 'I didn't tell Fox that, because that would have been to admit that what he implied was true but there is nothing he could tell you of which you're unaware.' She knew she did not need to give that assurance but she gave it just the same.

'There's only one thing I fear,' she went on, and Howard nodded, knowing what she was about to say.

'That was the first thing that occurred to me, and is the only thing that worries me: that he might be able to damage Pamela.'

'What can be done?' she asked. She had often felt remorse over her affair with Max, but usually because of its effect on Howard. Now she was afraid for her child, and the pain was even greater.

'There's only one option,' Howard said. 'If Fox stayed we'd be completely in his power. He has to go.'

He gave Fox an hour to quit the Scar, and when Fox would have argued he raised a hand. 'Greed I could have forgiven – you've been a great help to us all in the past few years. But you threatened my wife. How shortsighted of you to think there might be a secret we kept from one another! I can't forgive you that.'

As he walked back to the house Howard tried to remember Fox's background circumstances. For such a long time he had been just Fox, a Brenton possession to be retained or dispensed with at will. 'He robbed me,' Howard told himself. And then again, 'The man lied.' But as always it filled him with unease to have such power over other people's lives.

29

Rachael's death had had a profound effect on Sammy Lansky. If anything, he was more pious in his devotion during the mourning period than Emmanuel. Esther took over the running of their business, glad to discover that she could cope with, and understand, the many facets of their dealings; gladder still to think she could pay her respects to Rachael by giving service, as Rachael had done all her life.

It was November before she went to Belgate again, this time behind the wheel of her own car and in response to an urgent plea for help from Anne. *We're being moved out of the Shacks,* her letter had said. *They say it's temporary and we'll move back when the place is rebuilt but I don't believe it. They'll dump us somewhere and leave us, just because we're Maguires. Come if you can, I could do with a hand.*

Esther took with her a copy of a new women's magazine, *Woman*, and a bag of groceries from the market, carefully damaging the packets and denting the tins so that they could be casually handed over as rejects.

'Come in,' Anne said in tones of doom and Esther's heart sank. 'You'll have to make your own tea if you want it, Es. And don't say I'll be glad about the move eventually. I probably will, but right at the moment I want to feel put out.'

Esther set aside her hat and scarf and moleskin swagger coat, and set about assembling the tea while Anne bemoaned her own fate and talked ominously of the gasmask drills taking place in every Belgate school. 'I won't let our Joseph go to war, Es, I'll tell you that. They'll have to shoot me first.'

Together the sisters packed and crated and prepared for the Maguires' move to an old colliery house in a nearby street. 'I'll miss this house,' Anne said, when they were done. And then, fearing she had been over-sentimental: 'I must be mad.'

Six weeks later, as crowds stood and gawped, the Shacks fell to the demolisher's iron ball. 'I never thought I'd see the day,' Frank Maguire said, spitting stone-dust from his tongue and watching Belgate's second most famous landmark disappear. The pit wheel remained, presiding over the destruction, and Frank could almost have sworn he heard the creaking mechanism express its regret at the passing. As he looked at the rubble he wondered if there would be war. War from the air. Destruction. And if Joe went to fight, what would become of Anne? He thought of how she had described her last pregnancy: 'Nine months of purgatory, Frank, and then it's heaven on earth for a year or two, till they start giving you lip.' Frank smiled at this, knowing that not one of his children, with the exception of Estelle, would dare to defy their mother. 'You know what's funny?' he said now, his voice thick with emotion. 'The older and dafter you get, Anne Maguire, the more I love you.' That night in bed he drew her close and stroked her cheek. 'Things'll get easier, lass, you'll see. We've got holidays with pay now: it'll be nationalization next, and no more twopence looking down on a penny-halfpenny.'

'Will there be a war?' Anne asked, for once uncertain. 'I worry about our Joe. It's guns and marching all the time with him, and you preaching gloom and doom.'

'Don't pay attention to me,' Frank said. 'I've always been too big in the gob, you know me. As for our Joe, if it has to be the army, it's as good a life as any other. Better than going down the hole.'

'Mining has done all right by us,' Anne said. She had food in the cupboard now that she had two working colliers in the house, and a good outfit in the wardrobe from Marks and Spencer. Estelle would be working soon and that would help further. She was paying a shilling a week off the sitting-room carpet, a red and beige wool square that would do for the rebuilt Shacks if they ever got there; and she had put a deposit on the first of a set of wheel-backed, solid-oak kitchen chairs at 6s 11d each. Given a year or two, and if they did get a move, she would have a home to be proud of. Joe had a job as a datal hand, which could lead to hewing if he stuck it. But Anne would have to have a long think about what to do with Estelle: she was not to be shipped out into service. Anne had not forgotten her shame when Esther had skivvied – and if she had come out of it all right, it was more by good luck than good management. Estelle could get into trouble without encouragement: putting her into service would be asking for it.

'You know what,' she said, as they snuggled down for sleep. 'We ought to find our Esther a man, before it's too late. She's thirty-one.'

'Plenty of time,' Frank said equably. He was thirty-seven and he knew that his life was just beginning. He began to kiss his wife and felt her arms twine about him. Too late, they both realized it was the wrong time of the month.

Diana spent January 1938 at Barthorpe. Her mother took ill just after Christmas, and Diana was with her when she died a week later. Howard came for the funeral, and stayed for a day or two to console his father-in-law. Sir Neville was full of gloom, not only about his own life, which he saw as drawing to a close, but about the future. 'I approved of Herr Hitler in the beginning: saw him as a Saviour, if I'm truthful. Let him sort out the damn Germans, I thought. And then that damn fool Mussolini… I began to listen to him instead of laughing at him. "War puts the stamp of nobility on a people," he said, and I began to think of my son lost in France. Not much stamp of nobility there: a life snuffed out before it started. The Fascists are glorifying war, Howard, offering it as a rational alternative to humanity's problems. The real trouble is, they're not gentlemen. Men of standing never seek to rule – it's something they accept if they must, but they do not seek to dictate. That's why Mosley has never had followers of consequence – only idiots in the drawing-room: he's plenty of those. But the people who back him on the street, his black-shirts, are riff-raff. Englishmen will sacrifice themselves for their side, or for England, or for honour – but not for power. That's why only cads become dictators, and dictators are always cads.'

It was said with all the authority of a man trained from birth to be superior, and yet there was a kernel of truth in it. Howard went back to London strangely comforted. He had been back only three weeks when news came that Diana's father had also died, in his sleep. Barthorpe had passed to a distant cousin, and Diana was arranging the transfer of her personal possessions to Mount Street and the Scar.

She was subdued when Howard brought her back to London after the second funeral. 'She needs taking out of herself,' Loelia said, and arranged a dizzy round of visits to theatres and restaurants. They went to the Palladium to see the Crazy Gang and then to Quaglino's for oysters mornay; they saw *Going Greek* at the Gaiety, with Leslie Henson and Fred Emney, and went on to the Casino, where diners ate in private boxes while watching lavish, American-style floor-shows. 'Not quite my thing,' Howard said in the cab afterwards, and Diana, laying a sleepy head on his shoulder, agreed.

The following day Howard sat in the House while a member spoke of children of thirteen and younger, armed with brushes and paint, marching along the Frankfurterallee in a Jewish neighbourhood in Berlin, daubing the Star of David on shops pointed out to them by adults. According to the speaker, German children were now forbidden to play with or speak to Jewish children; and Howard saw Anthony Eden nod, as though in confirmation. He thought of his own children, Rupert away at Stowe, the others safe at the Scar. Rupert was almost fifteen now, desperate for the time when he could leave school and join the Flying Corps. If there were war with Germany, and if it dragged on, he could lose his son.

That night he sat late at the House, not wanting to miss a word of the debate; aware that in his pocket was a letter from his sister praising the Nazis for the way in which they were revitalizing the German nation and for their annexation of Austria.

> *It was such a privilege to be in Vienna when Adolf Hitler arrived* [Caroline wrote]. *You've never seen such tremendous crowds, all wild with delight. It made the Coronation look positively tame. Hitler stood upright in his car, wearing a brown uniform and saluting the crowds, and young girls were going wild and throwing flowers. Now that Germany and Austria are re-united, Geoffrey is sure Europe will settle down and we can all sort out our problems. The Austrians are overjoyed to have Hitler as their leader. The Archbishop of Vienna, leader of all the Austrian Catholics, gave the Hitler salute as he entered and left the referendum polling-booth, which shows all these dreadful lies about anti-Catholicism and Jew-baiting for what they are.*

Far from adoring the Nazis, the Austrian Chancellor had said: 'We have yielded to brute force… God save Austria.' But Howard had long since abandoned attempts to make Caroline and Geoffrey see facts. They were not alone in their folly. The Windsors had visited Hitler; Lady Astor had been heard to say there was nothing worth fighting Hitler about; and the Astor seat at Cliveden was the meeting-place for a coterie who at worst were campaigning on behalf of Fascism, at best were sympathetic to it.

People like his sister and brother-in-law were closing their eyes to the truth, although it could be seen all around them, even in the personal columns of *The Times*, where there were increasingly frequent advertisements: '*Viennese lady, university educated, Jewess, kind manners, fond of children seeks post or au pair, help household. Reply Anna Marie Hauser, Vienna.*' Or '*Young man, German, orthodox Jew, seeks research, cataloguing in similar household. Need is urgent. Please help.*' Soon England would sink beneath the weight of frightened people seeking sanctuary from the great and wonderful revitalization of his sister's hero.

That night, while Howard was at the House, Diana was dining with Loelia. Max was there, too, alone because Laura had taken to her bed with one of her imaginary illnesses. It was quite like old times when they adjourned to the drawing-room, and Diana was persuaded to play the tunes they had danced to fifteen years before. They turned back the carpet as they'd done in the old days, and Loelia and Henry circled the floor amiably, like the old married couple they were. Max leaned on the piano, sometimes watching Diana, sometimes humming along to the music.

'I've missed you,' he said to her, as she paused for a moment between tunes. And then: 'Kiss me, little piece of ice… Mon Dieu!' Diana remembered the line from *The Sheikh*, seen so long ago, and fluttered her eyelashes as she gave the reply: 'The vile climate of my detestable country has frozen me so thoroughly that nothing can melt me!'

They both laughed, then, and for a moment the old magic flared: Max's eyes on her, his body a tantalizing arm's reach away. He had been such fun! Diana's resentment almost melted – but only for a moment. She began to play Howard's favourite song, 'It's a sin to tell a lie,' and the danger was past.

*

At the beginning of June, Emmanuel Lansky closed the door of his Belgate shop for the last time. He had sold it to a cobbler, more use to the community than a pawnbroker now that there was more money about. Besides, Lansky was getting tired – and, if he was truthful, he was afraid. He had relatives all round Europe, and his wife's family in France. In every letter they told of fresh horrors. A pogrom was being carried out in Austria, obscenely called 'the great spring-cleaning' by Nazi newspapers. Jews were being excluded from their professions, Jewish judges dismissed, Jewish shops forced to admit their origins, or even close. Richard Tauber, the singer, had been driven from Vienna, and a German pastor called Niemöller sent to the Sachsenhausen concentration camp for daring to protest about the pogrom.

Air-raid shelters were being built in British town centres, and Lansky had received pamphlets on civil defence through his door. The government was expecting war, and yet his son still skylarked as though there were all the time in the world for fun. After Rachael's death, he and the boy came close for a brief period, but when Sammy's first terrible grief wore off, he went back to his old wild ways, coming home often in the early morning, eyes on his cheeks, the smell of cheap perfume on his clothes.

Emmanuel tried to concentrate on his prayers, but a new and dreadful litany kept threading through his mind: Dachau-Buchenwald... Sachsenhausen... Lichtenburg: the camps where Hitler was seeking a solution to his Jewish problem. German courts were taking children away from parents who did not toe the party line. Not only Jews: Christian pacifists and Catholics were equally at risk if they did not agree to rear their children 'physically, intellectually and morally in the spirit of National-socialism'.

When Lansky met with his fellow Jewish elders, they spoke of the need to provide homes for children from Germany and Austria. His own inability to take in any refugees grieved him. If Sammy were married, it would be different. If Rachael were here still, they could have filled the house. Lansky knew Esther would help him, but she was busy working most of the week. He sought solace in prayer, and in his books, but it was becoming impossible to shut out the outside world, however hard he might try.

Norman Stretton was a godsend to Howard Brenton. Now, whenever he came back to Durham, he found everything in order at the colliery: men going cheerfully about their work, productivity rising, and improvements in living accommodation taking place slowly but surely. Gallagher had never accepted Stretton's coming in above him. At first, he had tried subtly to sabotage Stretton's efforts. Then, when he found the other man too clever for him, he became openly obstructive. Howard itched to dismiss Gallagher, but Stretton stayed his hand. 'Let it go, please. For the time being at least.' Howard could only agree, but when Gallagher asked to see him on one of his brief visits to the Belgate pit, he was apprehensive.

There was a sneer on the agent's face when Howard entered the room, a sneer that filled him with foreboding. In fact, Gallagher was the bearer of good news.

'I want to leave,' he said shortly. 'But I want it made worth my while. After all...

He began to bluster, and Howard realized that he was expecting an argument. He held up a hand.

'How much do you want?' he said peremptorily, and when Gallagher named the figure of £400 he doubled it and wrote out a cheque on the spot. He longed to say, 'Cheap at the price,' but it would have been a vulgar gesture, and he limited himself to a curt: 'Thank you for your help over the years.'

When the agent quitted the office, Howard felt a sensation of almost physical relief, as though a brooding unpleasantness had vanished from the building. It was only afterwards that it occurred to him to wonder what Gallagher was going to do with his time in the future.

30

As the summer drew to a close, tension mounted, not only in London but everywhere. People who had never contemplated owning a wireless scraped up the money to buy one. Frank bought a large set second-hand in the Sunderland market and carried it home on the bus. 'Nice,' Anne said sourly. 'I've tried to persuade you to get one for ten years. Hitler can do it in ten minutes.'

'It's you I bought it for,' Frank said, and showed her how to manipulate the knobs.

Patrick Quinnell had two sets. He offered one to Mary for her sitting-room in the flat at the Scar, but she turned it down. 'Bad news travels fast enough,' she said. Nevertheless, on lazy summer afternoons when they could be together, she sat with him in his sitting-room listening to the music, the plays, the talks that streamed from the fumed-oak cabinet.

The only intrusion was the news broadcasts, with their talk of Czechoslovakia. Mary knew that Patrick was troubled, but Czechoslovakia seemed to her too far off to be threatening – until the day that Anne confided her worries about Joseph and his ambitions to join the army. Then Mary was struck by the dreadful thought that she, too, had a son of military age.

John was twenty now, and an aspiring farm-manager, apprenticed to a friend of Howard Brenton in the west of Durham county. How would he fare if there were a war?

And what of Catherine, seventeen and ready to embark on nurse-training at the Royal Infirmary?

'Hitler wants war,' Patrick said to Mary. 'He needs it, and he means to have it. He's purged the German army: men of honour have gone, and been replaced by thugs. The officer corps would have stood up to him, but he sacked two of their leaders on the grounds that one married a prostitute and the other is a homosexual. Now he's the Supreme Commander, and there will be no more opposition.'

Mary had blushed at the mention of homosexuality. It was one of the two great unmentionables, the other being venereal disease. Patrick talked of both freely but Mary still had her inhibitions. He did not notice her discomfort, however. He had something else on his mind.

'I've been thinking again,' he said. 'I'm forty-seven. You,' He smiled, 'are twenty-one. It really is time we settled down.'

'I *am* settled,' Mary said. She was thirty-nine and very content. Outside, Patrick's garden was ablaze with flowers. It could have been Eden as far as she was concerned.

'I'm serious.' Patrick reached for her and held her close against him, seeing the faint lines that had come to her face with the years, the way her hair was fading so that it was deep gold at the nape of the neck, but pale gold around her face. She was growing older, and it made him love her more. 'I think there's going to be a war, Mary. It won't be a war like the last one; this war will come out of the trenches and into the towns and villages. It will be war from the sky. I want you to be my wife; I want to have a right to your children if anything happens to you. No, don't scoff – it could. And I want you to have what's mine in such a way that there can be no argument.'

'I'll think about it,' Mary said uneasily. But he was not to be put off.

'We've both thought long enough and you've said me nay more than once,' he said. 'Now, let's name a day?'

But Mary thought of her son and daughter, of her dead

husband, and most of all of the gob of her sister-in-law, Anne.

'Not yet,' she said. 'I expect this talk of war'll blow over. If it doesn't, we'll see.'

Emmanuel Lansky had seen some of the refugee children brought into Britain by volunteers. His friend, Eli Cohen, had shown him the children's passports with the letter J stamped on the front page in red, and told him of parents' pathetic attempts to smuggle out funds: ten-mark notes wrapped up in a sandwich; gemstones sewn into hems. Nothing could be hidden in toys, for the German guards smashed those in the hope of finding hidden booty. Only the tags were left, tied to the children's clothes, proclaiming them to be Dorli or Liesl or Jakob.

Emmanuel and Sammy had both given generously to the Central British Fund for German Jewry set up by Lionel de Rothschild and Simon Marks. The British government had said that no child admitted to Britain must be 'a charge on public funds'. Money Emmanuel could give, and he was happy to do so; but the tales of children decanted from ships at Harwich crying '*Mutti, Mutti*', or worse still, '*Hilfe* (help)' made his heart ache.

He read the small-ads in the *Jewish Chronicle*: *Please help me bring out of Berlin two children, boy and girl – ten years – best family. Very urgent case; Which family would like to take over a Jewish boy, fifteen years, from first-class orthodox Viennese family, and give him a chance to be taught a trade? Father was in jewellery trade, now penniless. Very urgent*.'

Could he perhaps take on a boy who was almost a man? Could he face once more the agonies he had gone through with Sammy?

The crisis kept Howard in London when he would have liked be at the Scar. Rupert was on holiday from school, driving Diana mad with his pleas for flying lessons 'as soon, as very, very soon as possible, darling mother. I have to be a hero.' Diana conveyed her worries to Howard via the telephone.

'Don't tell me he's joking, Howard; he means it. He's positively lusting after a heroic death. It just needs Pamela to tell me she wants to be a VAD and I'll throw myself, screaming, from the nearest cliff. Catherine Hardman went off to the Infirmary today, so noble and dedicated, and I wish you'd seen Pamela's little face.'

Anne Maguire's eldest son, Joseph, born on the same day as Rupert Brenton, had had none of Rupert's advantages, but he had turned out a credit to her. Although she tried to hide it, he was her favourite child. She had never got over the scandal of Estelle and the fruiterer; and, unlike poor dead little Philomena, who was with the saints, the others were bloody little varmints. By comparison Joseph had been an easy child to rear. Until now.

'I can enlist when I'm sixteen if you and me dad agree. Don't stop me, ma! I'll send money home, and you won't have to feed me.' Anne couldn't bring herself to tell him that pounds, shillings and pence didn't enter into her calculations for once. She had never shown tenderness to her children. How could she clutch a boy who was almost a man and tell him she couldn't bear to let him go? He would only think she was after his pay-packet – which might have been true once, but wasn't in this case.

She was heavily pregnant now, and had hardly enough energy to cook and clean. Estelle was old enough to help her, but she spent all her time reading magazines or peering at her face in the mirror until Anne turned it to the wall. 'I won't have vanity in this house,' she said. 'That's one thing I will not have. You're pretty enough; primping won't improve you.' She didn't add that Estelle was too pretty by half, but it was true. And too pretty for safety, which was even worse. But the thing that most tortured Anne was Estelle's complete lack of conscience or compunction. She had never heard the word amoral, but she understood the concept and knew it applied to her eldest daughter.

'That's just in case,' she would say, cracking Estelle across the ear as she came through the door. Just in case of what was never explained: Anne didn't feel the need to enlighten Estelle, not after what had happened with Carter. As for the others, they were better left ignorant. Estelle would try to duck the blow, would wince if it landed; but would not appear to care much either way. At last Anne left her to her own devices as much as she could.

Anne was peeling apples on the doorstep in the warm summer sunshine when Esther appeared one day, stepping from her little blue car for all the world like Lady Muck.

'This is for Estelle,' she said, handing over a good cloth coat with an astrakhan collar.

'That's right,' Anne said, 'ruin her. Don't mind me.'

But when Estelle put the coat on, clutching the collar to her neck and twirling to show off her prize, Anne had to acknowledge that her daughter was as bonny a girl as you were ever likely to see.

Howard knew there could be no compromise with Hitler, now that the truth about his intentions was known. He knew it from his own instincts, and from the writings of correspondents such as G. E. R. Gedge of the *Daily Telegraph*, who had been proclaiming the truth for what seemed like a lifetime to a population who seemed not to want to hear.

You will shrug your comfortable shoulders in England, you'll say 'bogey tales' when I tell you of Viennese women whose husbands were arrested without charge receiving a small parcel from the postman with the curt intimation; 'To pay, 150 marks for the cremation of your husband – ashes enclosed, from Dachau'.

Howard watched the anxious faces on the Government benches, and pitied the men who had to carry such a huge burden. Sir John Simon, the Chancellor of the Exchequer, was listened to in hushed silence as he restated the Prime Minister's warning that a country devoted to the ideals of democratic liberty could not stand idly by if Czechoslovakia was attacked. 'That declaration,' said Sir John, 'holds good today.'

Howard did not doubt that Hitler would march on the Czechs, which meant there would be war. Whatever the horror of war, it would be preferable to submission. He travelled north the next day to see to matters in his constituency, and to perform an important ceremony.

The rebuilding of the Shacks was at last complete. A neat row of eight brick houses stood where fifteen rubble-walled dwellings had been. Each had a kitchen with a shining range, a bathroom, and wide casement windows to let in light and air. In the old days, when Gallagher had ruled, houses had been allocated according to status and a man's willingness to suck up to the agent. Now houses were given out according to need; and the Maguires, with the large family, were first on the list.

'I don't believe it,' Anne said when Frank told her. 'You're not a boss's man!'

'It's not like that now,' Frank said, trying hard not to let too much pleasure show. 'Well, so they say.' He found it hard to believe they were really leaving the temporary house with its cockroaches and its privy and its general air of decay. All the same it was true, and he had a harrow laid on for the shifting.

They stood in the crowd that Saturday morning, as Howard mounted the small dais, formed from a plank supported by bricks, his hair ruffled by a slight breeze, his hat in one hand, the other hand, thrust into the pocket of his grey jacket, holding the few notes he had made for his speech.

He looked around at the crowd, mostly people who had been allocated houses like Frank Maguire, who was a troublemaker but a likeable one. Mary Hardman was there, too, to see the rebirth of the street where she had once lived. There was a thin, dark man by her side, who looked studious and slightly seedy, and Howard wondered if he was the mystery man-friend. He turned to whisper to Diana, but saw that she had noticed for herself and was smiling indulgently at Mary. Norman Stretton, his manager, was at his side. 'Ready?' he asked. Howard nodded and Norman called for silence as Howard stepped forward.

'We come here today at a time of great turmoil, not only for our country but for the whole of Europe and beyond. Those of us who remember the war…' His eyes met the eyes of Mary Hardman's companion, and he realized that the man was intent on what he was saying. '…those of us who remember the senseless waste of the trenches pray that there will be no further conflict. But if the need to defend freedom arises, I know the men of this country will not be found wanting.' Impossible to guess from their faces whether or not the crowd agreed with him. Howard cleared his throat and went on.

'War is a time of pain. It is also a time of comradeship. That is why this development, which I hope is the first of many, will be known by the name of a friend of mine, a man I had the honour to serve with in France, a man who was a casualty of that war.' He looked across to where Stretton now stood, ready to remove the tarpaulin screen. 'This street is to be known as Trenchard Street. I hope the people who live here will have many happy years in their homes.'

There was sporadic clapping and then Howard was stepping down, and Diana was squeezing his hand.

'Well done.'

But Howard suddenly saw young Stanley Gallagher, standing before him, hands in pockets, a badge in his lapel proclaiming *Peace*.

'Good morning, Mr Howard – oh, of course, it's Mr Brenton now, isn't it.'

'Good morning Mr Gallagher,' Howard said civilly. 'I hope you and your father are both well?'

'Very well,' the man said. The words were polite enough, but the tone was a sneer. 'In spite of everything, we bear up.'

'Good,' Howard said shortly, and moved on. The elder Gallagher, he now knew, was working as temporary land-sale agent for Lord Londonderry in the east of the county. It couldn't be far enough away for Howard.

He and Diana were almost at the car now, and he turned to look for Mary, wanting to meet her companion. As if she read his thoughts, Diana plucked at his arm. 'Leave them alone, Howard. There's something going on. Mary had hold of his hand at one stage, I'm sure of it.'

There was indeed 'something going on'. As Howard had spoken Mary had sensed a quiver in Patrick Quinnell, as though he were vibrating to Howard's words. She looked at him, and saw how mention of the war had upset him. She had woken him from too many nightmares not to understand his pain. 'I've been thinking,' she said quickly. 'Not that there'll be a war – still, if you meant what you said, we might as well get wed.' She had lain awake all night, deliberating, and she had not meant to tell him yet but the impulse to comfort him proved too strong.

That night, as Mary and Patrick talked of an October

wedding, Howard drove into Sunderland to see his mother. He went alone, for Diana visited Charlotte every few days. 'She'll enjoy having you to herself,' she said now. 'I'll be waiting when you come back.'

Howard found Charlotte in the drawing-room. It smelled of dust and polish, and he realized that the windows had not been opened for a very long time. 'Mother.' He kissed her cheek, his nose wrinkling involuntarily at the faint odour of urine under the scent of lavender water.

Charlotte did not ask him to sit down, or move from her chair. Her beige dress was immaculate, and her pearls still swung from her cliff-like bosom, but there was a change in her. The parlourmaid who had admitted Howard hovered near the door. 'Would you like some tea, sir?'

He looked at his mother. 'I'd like a drink, if I may.' In his father's day there had always been brandy on the sideboard, and wines and spirits in the cellarette underneath.

His mother spoke. 'Bring sherry, Sarah.' She did not say another word while they waited for the maid to return. Then Howard poured two glasses, and resumed his seat. He felt uncomfortable, like a small boy summoned to see the Head.

'Well, mother.' He raised his glass. 'To your health. How are you?'

'I'm well.' She was giving him nothing: no peg on which to hang a conversation, no sign of any bond between them.

'Is there anything you need? I know Diana sees to things...'

'There's no point in her coming so often. I have everything I need. I have good servants.' Charlotte raised her glass and sipped her sherry. 'If I'm honest, I find Diana's visits quite disturbing.'

'I'm sure she means well,' Howard said, stung.

'I'm not concerned with her intentions, Howard. If she has meant well over the years, by you, by her children, or by me, then she has signally failed in her intentions.'

'I'm sorry you feel like that.' Howard tried to keep his

voice steady. 'And even sorrier to see how deeply mistaken you are. Diana is a great comfort to me and a wonderful mother…'

'Is she, Howard? Is she really such a paragon? I seem to remember a different state of affairs.'

He felt old suddenly, as though he had never been this woman's child. He had not realized his mother had known of Diana's affair with Max, but there was no mistaking what she meant. He drained his glass and stood up.

'It's always a mistake to dwell on the past, mother. Let me know if there's anything you need.' Suddenly he remembered that she was his responsibility. 'I'm arranging for an air-raid shelter to be built in the garden here, so please work out where you want it to be. It may be just a precaution, but I don't want you to be unprotected in the event of war.'

'If you think it's necessary,' Charlotte said, distantly. 'Close the door as you go.' She did not ask about her grandchildren. She did not wish him goodbye.

Howard stood a moment, looking at her. Then he closed the door of the drawing-room as requested, and let himself out into the cool evening air.

In mid-September, in Nuremberg, Hitler demanded that 'the oppression of three and a half million Germans in Czechoslovakia shall cease'. It was a prelude to his marching into that country, and the whole world knew it. France and England warned that, in the event of German aggression against Czechoslovakia, neither would stand aside. Two days later Neville Chamberlain, the Prime Minister of Great Britain, flew to Berchtesgaden in a 'last-hour attempt to preserve European peace…

The Times reported that the Führer responded 'at once and cordially'. As the crisis developed, *The Times* grew more and more placatory until it declared: 'There is nothing sacrosanct about the present frontiers of Czechoslovakia. They were drawn twenty years ago and they were drawn wrongly in the opinion of many qualified to judge.'

Neville Chamberlain flew to Germany for a second meeting with Hitler, and while he was boarding the plane Mary Hardman was paying for her wedding dress: a beige crêpe confection from the Guinea Gown shop, with puff sleeves and a beaded basque.

'I don't know how she dares,' Anne said. 'Off-white, after her goings-on!'

Frank was to give Mary away; Catherine, her daughter, would attend her, dressed in pink and carrying a smaller version of her mother's carnation bouquet.

'Am I doing right?' Mary asked herself again and again, until Anne informed her tartly that she was doing the only possible thing to save herself from an eternity in purgatory. 'And we both know what I'm talking about, Mary, so there's no need to spell it out.'

But Catherine and John were pleased with her decision, and Frank was relieved to see her making it legal at last. Who else mattered?

Everyone was invited to the wedding: the family and staff at the Scar, Patrick's friends from his practice in Durham; the Maguire family, including Esther. The church hall was booked, and the Belgate undertaker was laying on cars for the bridal party – and for Anne, who Patrick confidently expected would give birth as he made his vows.

'Well,' Mary said, matter-of-factly, 'she likes to be the centre of attention, so I couldn't rule it out.'

Only Howard would be absent, for he could not leave London at such a time of crisis. He wrote to Mary to explain, and to tell her of his pleasure at her news: *I simply can't find words to tell you how pleased I am, how much I have wanted your happiness, even though the idea of the Scar without you after all these years is almost unthinkable, and is only made bearable for us all by the thought of pleasant trips to Durham to see you in your new home.*

Mary folded the letter and put it carefully away, thinking all the time of the diffident young man who had stooped through her doorway that dreadful day so many years ago. She thought, too, of Stephen, wondering what he would have made of her remarriage, thinking of the stone sink, still filled with heartsease, lovingly replanted every year. It would accompany her to Durham to be placed carefully outside her new door. Could you blend old and new? Mary knew you could love twice, for she loved Patrick fervently without diminishing her love for Stephen in the least. In the end she put away the imponderables, and got on with the satisfying job of embroidering butterflies on the satin petticoat she would wear on her wedding day.

Mary revelled in preparing her trousseau, casting out her pink brocade corsets with their lacings and buying the new elastic underpinnings that allowed room for expansion; discarding the last of her old-fashioned camisoles, and buying petticoats and knickers in wonderful artificial silk that gave the soft feel of silk and satin, and a flattering cling. 'I must be mad,' she told herself more than once, but she bought just the same.

'Of course,' Diana had said, too firmly to brook argument, 'the reception will be held here at the Scar.' Mary would have preferred the smoky fug of the Half Moon, but that was where they had celebrated her wedding to Stephen – and if the Half Moon was out, there was nowhere else big enough to accommodate all the people who wanted to wish them well. 'Thank you,' she said to Diana, diffidently. The thought of that first day on the Scar did not affect her, for its ghost had long since been laid to rest. When she went to her wedding she would pass through the gates Stephen had made, and she saw that as a blessing.

Diana had given a great deal of thought to a suitable gift for Mary, something that would show how much her work with the family had been appreciated. In the end she settled for two gifts: one from herself and Howard, and one from the children, to be presented by Rupert who was looking forward with gusto to his first wedding. The Brentons' gift to Mary was a Crown Derby tea and dinner service: delicate china, with garlands of tiny roses linked by gold swags.

The children's gift was presented early, and was designed to be used on the honeymoon trip. It was a short jacket of Indian lamb, close-curling fur with a snug collar. 'You're getting married on 1 October,' Diana said. 'With luck it'll be cold enough to wear this when you leave, so we wanted you to have it now.'

Mary's going-away outfit was green wool crêpe, with a matching felt hat. 'Perfect,' Diana said when it was shown to her. On an impulse she leaned to kiss Mary's cheek. 'We'll miss you,' she said – and was amazed when Mary's arms came round her in an uncharacteristic hug.

In the Lansky household Neville Chamberlain's trips to Europe were watched with mounting gloom. The Prime Minister had asked for 'immediate German demobilization', but even Sammy in his most optimistic moments did not expect Hitler to agree to this. One day he went with Emmanuel to see some of the refugee children. He tried to make them laugh, but the solemn little faces did not move. He talked to them in French, his mother's language, but it meant nothing to them; when he tried Yiddish he could see they understood, but still they did not respond.

'It's a *she'alah*,' Sammy said to Esther as they drank their mid-morning coffee above the town-centre shop. 'If there's a war, I'll have to join up. You'll need to see to things here.' He looked at her with a twinkle in his eyes, though Esther knew he was in a serious mood. 'I've been thinking, Esther; we get on together, don't we?' He didn't wait for an answer. 'If things get any worse... well, I think I'm asking you to marry me. We could make a home...' He didn't say 'for the children', but Esther knew it was in his mind.

'You're not on about that again,' she said, unable to work out whether or not he was joking. 'Oh, not that I'm not flattered...'

'I wouldn't misbehave,' Sammy said, 'if that's what's holding you back? And I'm quite a catch!' He rolled his eyes. 'And I'd be better than Stanley at you-know-what!' He winked as Esther laughed out loud.

'No one could say you don't have *chutzpah*, Sammy. Now, remember time's money: drink that coffee and cut out the *plaplen* – and not a word to your poor father about this. He's got enough to bear at the moment.'

But as Sammy went breezily down the stairs, Esther let herself think about what he had said. She always had fun with Sammy, no doubt about that. And she owed him so much. She had no definite religion of her own now, only a belief in God. Conversion to the Jewish faith would be possible – except that she had not been born a Jew and that meant a great deal. She sighed and put aside major decisions as the telephone shrilled out the real business of the day.

In Belgate Frank was getting ready to go down the pit. It was Thursday, and on Friday he had a day off, to prepare for his sister's wedding on the Saturday. He was looking forward to getting bathed in their posh new bathroom, and to laying out his new suit for the wedding morn. They'd be paying for the bugger forever, so he meant to enjoy the wearing of it. He decided not to think about the goings-on in Europe; if he could get Anne through the next two days, he could certainly cope with war. He had never loved his wife more than the day she had produced the deposit for his suit. 'You can't let your Mary down on her big day,' Anne had said, and Frank had cried like a baby. He had a spanking new house and a wonderful wife, and a new suit into the bargain.

As he walked to the pit, he whistled 'I like a nice cup of tea in the morning' – whistled, because he only knew that one line of the words. As he went, he checked over his tasks for the wedding-day in his head. Seeing to Anne in her state would be a full-time job, but he must also stand by Mary, who was relying on him. He was still whistling as he entered the cage, and he felt an elbow jog him sharply in the ribs. 'That's enough of that, marrer. There's nowt to chirp about, working in the Red Star.'

The Red Star seam was notoriously unpredictable but Frank was in no mood to be serious. He leaned towards the speaker. 'You recovered, then, Alec?'

Even in the semi-darkness as the cage descended he could see the man blush. A week ago he had come home drunk and had fallen asleep with his arm over the back of a bentwood chair. When he woke in the morning he found he had lost the use of his arm, and ran screaming to Dr Lauder. But the doctor had seen 'Saturday-night palsy' before: a nerve deadened by pressure while a man lay in a drunken stupor over the back of a chair. He sent the patient off with a flea in his ear, and the whole waiting-room had heard it.

'Good,' Frank said when no reply came. 'Well, here we are, lad... the pit bottom. Red Star here I come!'

31

Howard watched the mounting preparations for war with a heavy heart. Thirty-four London hospitals were cleared for casualties, and the unemployed found some relief as to dig slit trenches in London's parks. Searchlights were mounted, gas-masks doled out, and a pathetically small number of anti-aircraft guns were fixed in emplacements. Shops ran out of electric torches, and sandbags sprang up everywhere like weeds in the cracks of pavements.

Diana had bought sticky strips to protect the Mount Street house windows, all the while proclaiming that the situation was unreal. She adorned one window with them, before declaring the effect too ghastly for words, and departing for the Scar and the greater pleasure of the final preparations for Mary's wedding. It was the autumn now and the world was holding its breath.

The Queen went to Clydebank to take her husband's place at the launch of the ocean liner Queen Elizabeth. The King had to stay in London to sign a State of Emergency act. In Parliament they talked of the monarch's offer to send a personal letter to Hitler 'as one ex-serviceman to another', but there was almost universal disapproval of such a gesture. If anyone was to be humiliated by Herr Hitler, it must not be the King. As Chamberlain asked the House to release him 'to go and see what I can make of this last effort', they rose to cheer and wave order-papers. Howard was one of the few who stayed in his seat. Winston

Churchill, Anthony Eden and Leo Amery stalked from the chamber.

The next day the Prime Minister, famous for his rolled umbrella, flew off again, and that night Flanagan and Allen took to the stage of the Palladium to sing the song that was to echo around the country within the week: 'Any umbrellas, any umbrellas to mend today?'

Mussolini, Daladier, Hitler and Chamberlain were closeted together for hour after hour. Business in the House went on as usual, but Howard found it difficult to concentrate. If Chamberlain *could* secure peace with honour, a generation would be saved – but Howard was certain he could only compromise.

He was crossing the lobby of the House when he heard the low murmur of conversation around him suddenly increase in intensity. It was quarter to two in the morning, and the four-party conference had been in session for twelve hours or more.

'Has something happened?' The member he addressed was a crony of Sir John Simon, and the relieved look on the man's face told Howard the news before he spoke.

'It's peace!' the man said. 'A negotiated settlement. Thank God!'

Howard felt an involuntary lightening of spirit. There would be no war! But a moment later the reality swept over him; Hitler had won. There could be no other meaning to 'a settlement'. Hitler would never have backed down, therefore Chamberlain and Daladier must have given way.

Howard was moving in search of colleagues whose opinions he respected when an attendant approached him.

'Mr Brenton, sir, I've a message from your wife. There's been a bad accident at the pit. The Bellfield, is it? I think that's what she said.'

'Belgate,' Howard said dully. This was what he had feared all his life: a disaster. 'It would be Belgate. Is my wife still on the line?' His voice sounded strange, and his leg was paining him, as it always did at times of crisis.

'No sir. She said to tell you she's there herself, and to come when you can.'

Howard found a telephone in the attendant's office, and rang the colliery office at once, his heart pounding. But the only person there was a workman, who was out of his depth. 'They're all at the pit-head, sir. I'm only here to mind the phone. I don't know much… but it's bad, sir. It caught the shift changeover, that's what makes it worse.'

Howard caught a train in the early hours, not stopping even to pack a bag. If only there were no deaths! As the train sped through the sleeping towns he prayed that no act of neglect on his part, or under his jurisdiction, was to blame. Sometimes he dozed, or tried to read something from his briefcase. At one point he found himself whistling the new Cole Porter hit, 'In the still of the night, as the world is in slumber…'He closed the briefcase, then, and leaned his forehead against the glass.

The faces of men he knew at Belgate flashed through his mind: Cornforth, Dodds, Maguire, Lomas ... Lomas had lost three fingers on his hand to a conveyor belt. Let it not be Lomas! And then the new chauffeur was opening the car door, and Howard saw Durham cathedral silhouetted against the lightening sky as they took the Belgate road.

When Frank came to, his first sensation was of flour on his tongue. Somebody had filled his mouth with flour… but as he tasted and tried to put the alien substance from his tongue, he realized it was not flour but coal-dust. He could see it swimming in the light that came from his overturned lamp. He tried to move his legs but they were held fast, so he edged his trunk forward until he could curve his fingers around the lamp's base, and pull it towards him. He lifted it high, glad of its rays – until he saw what they disclosed. He was trapped in a space about four feet square and four feet high. Access to the shaft was obliterated by a fall of rubble, clay and small stones.

Frank lay still for a moment, taking in the horror of what he saw, and then he heard a faint buzzing near his ear. It was a fly: a fat bluebottle, trapped like him a thousand feet underground.

'Hello, marrer,' he said seriously, and then, as the fly buzzed aimlessly from wall to wall, he wept. When his tears ceased to make furrows on his dirty face, he cursed quietly, blaming the cavils for his plight. He had always scorned the old customs on cavilling day: the day when lots were drawn for the best places to work. Some men turned the fireside fender upside-down; others put the cat in the cold oven; still others put chairs on the bed upside-down. Frank had done none of those things, leaving everything to chance. And here he was, flat on his back, with pee or blood oozing down the inside of his leg.

He didn't feel brave, which perturbed him. If someone broke through to him now he would bawl like a baby – and that would make a nice tale in the Half Moon! Frank pictured them gathering next day for a drink. If he were dead by then, what would their verdict on him be? Suddenly it occurred to him that they might not mention him at all: he could be gone, and the earth closed over him, as if he had never been. By God, he wasn't having that! Frank pulled himself to a sitting position and began to pick the rocks and shale off his legs laboriously, piece by piece.

When he tired, and had to lean back for breath, he wondered what time it was? Was it daylight up above, and the church bells ringing for peace – or maybe for war? He started picking again, at rocks this time, feeling his nails splinter and tear as he went.

Eventually he slept, dreaming of his mother and the poke of sweets she had given him after his first day in the pit. He had thought it was to be a daily reward for being a man, but it had finished at the end of the first week. He had been scared then, in that noisy hell of the Neptune seam, with tubs jerking and crashing, and the rumble as layers of coal buckled and shifted. When he woke he was still scared, the dream persisting so that he could not be sure he was really awake. And the pain in his legs was intensifying.

Thirsty, he felt around for his snap tin with its bread and cold bacon and colder tea in a bottle. In parts of the pit the walls bled water, but there was none here. He shouted suddenly: 'I want to go out – bye. Out – bye! *Out – bye!*' But it only filled his mouth with more dust, that tickled his throat and caused him to gag. Frank closed his eyes on a vision of the earth above, the landscape scarred by generations of coal-gatherers but beautiful still. An image of dark fields newly ploughed came into his mind, with white birds rising from the fresh furrows. And then he thought of Lemon, the most intelligent galloway in the pit who could back into the timbers without being led. 'Ha'd up,' he said to the outer darkness. 'Gee-ba.' Galloways never wanted to do what you wanted them to do. When they felt your hands on the limbers they would back. Many a man had broken his fingers that way.

If he died, he thought, they would blow the buzzer for half an hour, and lay the pit idle for a day. The crake man would go round to make sure it was known, and they would release pigeons at the grave – up and up, into the wide sky.

Years ago he had got a watch from the Jew: a good watch, sold long ago. Anne had bought him one in the Durham Market, but the bugger had never worked. Never would now. Tick-tock. He would never get to Ruskin College and make his mark in the world. More important, there would be no one to stop Annie forcing Gerard into the priesthood. Poor little bugger! He could do with a priest now, though. 'Forgive me father, for I have sinned.' Frank closed his eyes, too weary to remember all his shortcomings, the light of the lamp seemingly imprinted on the inside of his eyelids, so that it glowed there like the doorway to Hell.

Esther lay, her heart thudding, trying to identify the banging which seemed to be coming from all around. It was still dark; who would batter on her door in the middle of the night? But when she crossed to the window she saw Sammy's car under the lamp before she saw the gleam of his dark head below. 'I'm coming,' she called, and ran downstairs, praying that if Emmanuel Lansky were dying he would live long enough for her to say thank you to him.

'What is it?' she said anxiously when Sammy tumbled into the hall.

'It's the pit – I heard from a policeman as I came home. A bad accident, they say. The copper was a Belgate lad, and he says Frank Maguire is one of the missing men… they all know Frank, because of the union. I thought you'd want to know.'

Esther was already running upstairs, unfastening her nightgown as she went, reaching for the first clothes that came to hand.

She drove to Belgate in the little blue car, seeing the sun come up in the east, seeing the anxious women trekking towards the pit, singly or in pairs. 'That's where I'll find our Anne,' Esther thought, and swung in the direction of the colliery gates.

They had woken Anne at three in the morning. 'No one knows anything yet,' the caller had said, but Anne could see from his shifty eyes that he knew more than he was letting on. 'Trapped in the pit': after the Montague disaster they had closed the pit with the bodies still inside. She wanted Frank back, dead or alive. If they wouldn't reach him and bring him up, she would cause such a stir in the colliery yard that they would have to go down again. She woke Joe to accompany her, and Estelle, to see to the rest of the family.

'Dad'll be all right,' Joe said calmly. 'He knows the pit, me da. It'll not best him.'

Anne felt comforted then, remembering a day when they had slung Frank's pit-boots in at the door and said he was in the Infirmary. She had gone off like a headless hen, to find him sitting up in bed, drinking soup, large as life.

'He can't die,' she said as they walked to the pit. 'He's giving your Auntie Mary away the morn.'

By the time the dawn broke, a hundred or more people were gathered in the pit yard. Hastily erected barricades kept them back from the shaft, but nothing would have kept them outside the yard. Twelve men were unaccounted for, and two boys. Some women were weeping quietly, but most stood stony-faced, the only sign of agitation being fingers that plucked ceaselessly at cuffs or buttons or hair. Esther came to stand with Anne. Then Patrick Quinnell arrived, anxious to help the Belgate doctor if he could. Mary had been there all along, having been roused first when Diana was told, and having come with her mistress to see which of the Belgate men were lost.

A fine rain was falling now, so that every face was misted as though with tears. People shivered and moved their feet, but no one wanted to break away and leave. At last Esther sent Joe off to see what needed to be done at the Maguire home, where there were little children to be got to school. 'Why don't you go too, Anne?' she urged. 'You're due in three days' time – you can't stand here for long!'

'I can stand here as long as it takes,' Anne said, and that was that.

A watery sun came out, but somehow it made matters worse. Police and firemen came and went, and somebody said. 'The Sally Army'll be here before long. They always send a tea-wagon.' Then suddenly the wheel high above them began to turn, and a sigh went through the crowd.

Three men were in the cage, when it arrived at the surface, lying inert on stretchers, but still alive; three others stood beside them. Women peeled off from the group, and went wailing their joy into the ambulances. 'My God, I'm cold,' Anne said, listlessly.

There was a sudden stir as a van nosed its way through the crowd. 'It's the doctor,' someone said, but another woman shook her head: 'No, it's not. It's the Jew. It's old Lansky.' It was Lansky, strangely dishevelled, and Sammy, still dressed like a toff from his evening out. They climbed from the van and opened up the rear door to reveal bakers' trays and two steaming urns.

'Right,' shouted Sammy, 'bread and beef dripping this way.' He was handing out wedges right and left, and his father was pouring tea into cardboard cups that bore the legend 'Dorsella milk food'. Esther went to help him, a lump in her throat. 'I love you, Sammy Lansky,' she said as she was jostled by people clustering round after hope in the shape of a cuppa and a wedge.

Lansky was presiding over blue bags of sugar, solemnly asking, 'One spoon or two?' His hat was tipped as far back on his head as anyone in Belgate had ever seen it, and a tartan muffler around his neck hardly concealed the fact that for once he was wearing his shirt open at the neck.

'He'll want paying next,' young Stanley Gallagher said, as he moved away with his cup. 'Trust a Jew-boy.'

But a woman who had greeted Lansky like the regular customer she had been for years, turned on Stanley, wiping breadcrumbs from her mouth to spit her reply.

'You shut your scabbing mouth, Gallagher. And make yourself useful or scram.'

'Heard about Munich?' Sammy asked, when there was a lull in demand. 'It's peace! For the time being at least.'

'Thank God,' Esther said, but somehow war in Europe

seemed remote at this moment, and peace equally unimportant. Joe had come back, and was now half-supporting his mother. 'Our Anne can't stand much longer,' Esther said. 'But she won't leave until Frank's up.'

'How many children will this be?' Sammy asked.

'Seven,' Esther said, 'and one that died with diphtheria.'

Sammy slipped away then, bending to whisper in Anne's ear. Esther's breath caught, fearing her sister's tongue might get carried away with itself. But Joe was bending too, his freckled face earnest, and Anne was rising to waddle between the two men to the van, where Sammy cleared space for her to sit, moving the urn so as not to restrict her view of the shaft.

From a window in the manager's office above the yard Diana Brenton watched the scene below, waiting for the wheel to turn again and signal hope. It was sixteen years almost to the day since that other death on the Scar: sixteen years! She would have liked to be down there, doing something to help, but she didn't know what to do. And besides, she feared she might not be welcome there.

She could see Rupert down below, his school scarf slung round his neck, hands thrust in pockets, earnestly trying to hold the bridge for his father, but looking oddly out of place. 'He's like me,' Diana thought ruefully. 'He doesn't belong here.' Eight-year-old Pamela had begged to come too, and the anxiety in her eyes for the Belgate men had been genuine. And yet she had no Brenton blood, no heritage of the coalfield. Diana sighed and leaned her forehead on the glass, wishing Howard would come. This was his place. He belonged here.

The wheel began to move again, and the crowd inched forward. Diana knew, suddenly, that some of the men in the cage were dead. She felt helpless and then, as she looked down at her well-shod feet and silk-stockinged legs, she felt guilty. This was the price of coal: premature death for the men and bereavement for the women.

I've been selfish, she thought and knew, as she thought it, that there was no real chance of her changing, however she might have seen the error of her ways. If there had been a war after all, she might have been brave, have found something worthwhile to do, paid some of her debts to her fellows. But there was going to be peace, and the same old social round would continue – even in Durham where she gave or attended dinner-parties just as she had done in London. *God forgive me*, Diana thought, and then, as the wheel stopped: *And God help them*. There were two stretchers and two men in the cage, and two rescuers. They shook their heads to the waiting officials, and Diana knew that meant there were no men left alive down below. She groped in her pocket for her cigarette-case and took a consoling puff, as she watched Rupert hold out his hand to help one of the men to a stretcher.

Frank Maguire was the last one out of the cage.

'Oh God,' Anne said, lumbering from the van to push her way to his side. 'Oh God, Frank, I've been praying for this.'

'Not half as hard as me, our lass,' Frank said through teeth gritted against the pain of two broken legs and multiple lacerations. When they had finally broken through to him, he had been unconscious and gradually succumbing to the foul air. Then there had been a rush of cool wind on his face, and voices urging him to open his eyes. He had seen the clustered lamps and thought for a moment that he was in heaven – until they had moved his legs and he screamed aloud that he was in hell.

Now he grinned feebly at his wife, hoping she would bend to kiss him. But Anne, after her joy at the first sight of him alive, was determined to recover her composure.

'You've done this to get a bed before I do,' she said sharply. But the tears were still streaming down her face, and Frank smiled to show he understood.

'Is old Chamberpot back yet?' he asked, as someone stuck a Woodbine between his lips.

'It's peace, mate,' the stretcherbearer said. 'Now let's get you fixed up.'

The Sally Army came, efficient and cheerful in their bow-tied bonnets and navy uniforms, setting the Lanskys free. The Lanskys took Anne home in the van, and once there they persuaded her into a chair. Lansky waited for them to settle her as he'd waited while her first child came into the world, and received as gracious a nod as she could manage for his pains. Joe was carrying the youngest child, David, in his arms, and tear-stains on his cheeks gave the lie to his grin.

'I like your new house, Mrs Maguire,' Sammy said, winking at Esther. 'She might be my sister-in-law soon,' he added in a whisper, 'if you see sense.'

'Hush,' Esther said, not daring to look to see if Emmanuel or Anne was listening. 'You'll be locked up one day.'

'The offer stands,' Sammy said, as they followed Lansky back to the van. 'But you can't kiss me right this moment. I've been up all night.'

As they drove past the pit, back to where Esther had parked her car, they saw Howard Brenton's Daimler turn in at the pit gates.

'Poor devil,' Sammy said. 'He'll have some sad homes to visit before he sees his own home today.'

The rain grew heavier as Esther drove wearily back into Sunderland. It was raining all over England, drenching the Cabinet who waited on the Heston tarmac for Chamberlain's return. As he left the plane he waved a piece of paper promising *Peace in our time*, and received, in return, a letter of congratulations from the King.

By the time Howard Brenton had finished the sad round of visits and was back home at the Scar, the Premier was waving to the crowd from the balcony at Buckingham Palace, flanked by a relieved King and Queen. When he had left for Munich he had said: 'When I come back I hope I will be able to say, as Hotspur said in *Henry IV*: "Out of this nettle danger, we pluck this flower, safety." *Would* they all be safe now, Howard wondered, as Freddy Grisewood's familiar tones described the scene.

'It's a mess, isn't it?' he said, as Diana handed him a whisky and soda.

'Munich?'

'That… and today. Four men dead, and one seriously ill in hospital, along with two others. The price of coal.'

Howard had looked into the faces of the men in hospital and had wanted to point out that, like them, he was a son of the coalfield. But there had been a gulf between them and he had not known how to bridge it – not even with Maguire, with whom he had believed, in spite of everything, he had an affinity. But he would find out why the accident had happened. That, at least, he could do for them.

'Come and have some dinner,' Diana said. 'But first I have to ask you this: one of the men in hospital is Mary's brother, who was going to give her away. They're going ahead with the wedding, but they need someone to propose the toast and make a speech. She wants you to do it.' She moved to put her arms around him. 'Do you mind?'

'No,' Howard said wearily. 'I think that's the first nice thing to happen in a long while.'

Candles were burning in the church for the men who had died, but the wedding party felt a quiet joy as they assembled, for Frank was alive and this was Mary's day.

'Do I look all right?' she asked, and Anne tucked in a stray bit of hair and flicked a bit of imaginary fluff from her sister-in-law's lapel.

'You'll do,' she said.

'By gum, I must look me best,' Mary whispered to Catherine, her bridesmaid, as she put her hand on her son John's arm and began the long walk to the altar. And then she could see Patrick, smiling today as he had smiled when he lifted the first-born Maguire into the world.

'All right?' he asked, as Mary came to stand at his side.

She nodded, too full to speak, remembering another wedding day when she had believed that happiness was a right and something that endured forever. Now she was aware that it endured only for a little while – which made it doubly precious.

She turned to smile at her children, and then back to face the man at her side. He was grey now, and the lines of weariness would never leave his face, but there was light in his eyes again, thank God – and with His help she would make sure it did not go out.

As he stood in St Benedict's church, Howard was thinking of Stephen Hardman's funeral, and of his death on the Scar – the moment when Howard's own life had begun in earnest. He had been a boy until then, even after France. But on that hillside he had become a man.

When the service was over, in an orgy of confetti and rice, they trooped up to the Scar, to the long dining-room where the best of the Brenton china and silver was laid out to honour Mary's guests.

'My God,' Anne whispered to Joseph as she looked around, for once over-awed. 'They've pulled out all the stops and no mistake.'

She had often imagined this house but never, ever grasped how magnificent it was – too splendid, even, for envy. She could never aspire to this, and in a funny way that made it more bearable. Her eyes sought out Esther in the crowd: her sister looked smart, in navy blue, with a white lining to the brim of her hat. She had been a servant here once – and look at her now! Truly, the world was changing, and about time, too.

The meal was excellent but simple, for Diana had wanted to please rather than impress. There were good wines, but not so fine as to confuse unaccustomed palates. 'Very nice,' Anne said, forgetting for once to be grudging in her praise.

When the meal was over the speeches began.

Howard proposed the health of the bride and groom, and was eloquent in Mary's praise. Patrick, replying, spoke of his unbelievable good fortune, and raised his glass to the bridesmaid. Joe Maguire thanked Howard and Diana on his father's behalf, haltingly at first, and then proudly; and Anne, head modestly bowed and hands folded on her swollen belly, asked God to forgive her for loving her first-born best, and then thanked Him for saving that first-born from war.

Diana also gave silent thanks for a peace she could scarcely believe in, but for which she, too, was grateful beyond words, since it had spared her son. Across the table Rupert was flirting with Catherine Hardman, who, as usual was looking at him with adoring eyes. It would be better if that fizzled out, Diana thought – but she was not going to worry about it today.

Afterwards, as they all waited for the bride to put on hergoing-away outfit, Diana sought out Esther Gulliver. They had spoken briefly earlier but only across heads. 'It's been a long time,' Diana said, and held out a hand. They turned to look at Rupert, each of them remembering how they had held hands on the day of his birth.

'He's a fine boy,' Esther said. 'You must be proud of him.'

'You've never married?' Diana asked, taking in Esther's expensive suit, her well-cut hair and immaculate fingernails, curled now around an alligator bag that must have cost a small fortune.

'No,' Esther smiled. 'I have a job instead. One I enjoy very much.'

'Esther.' Howard was there too, bowing to her, acknowledging the years since she had served at the Scar. 'It's.– my goodness – fifteen years. You look… quite wonderful.' His eyes held admiration. 'Do you have a family?' He was looking round, expecting her to point out husband and children.

'No,' she said again, hoping her eyes did not reveal her pain. 'I'm afraid not.'

'But you live here still?' He was remembering that night at the Scar, the night he had learned of Trenchard's death. She had been a child then. Now she was a woman, and a handsome one into the bargain.

'I live in Sunderland. I'm in business there.' Esther was suddenly proud she could say that, and aware of how far she had come. Aware, too, that Howard was still the handsomest man she had ever met. 'Well,' she said in a little confusion, and thankfully, seeing Mary descend the stairs, 'I think the bride's about ready.'

They saw the bridal pair off in a haze of good wishes, the younger ones running after the black Morris until it was out of sight, although the sound of the rattling cans tied to its bumper was audible for another full minute.

At the wheel of the car, Patrick turned to look at his new wife. 'I can't believe we've done it. Right up to the last minute, I never thought you'd turn up.'

Mary smiled, taking off her wide-brimmed hat so that she could lay her cheek against his shoulder.

'I had to turn up,' she said. 'Seeing as I'm two months gone.'

'So it's peace,' Frank said. He was clean and comfortable now in the high hospital bed, his wife at his side, huge on the bentwood chair, full of news about the disaster and the wedding and the end of the threat of war.

'Thank God,' Anne said. 'At least our Joe's safe. Mind you, our Estelle's downright disappointed – it would've been exciting, according to her! She doesn't get her ways from my side, Frank.'

Frank knew better than to argue. 'She'll change,' he said. 'When she grows up.'

'It was a very nice wedding,' Anne said grudgingly. 'Nothing spared, I can tell you. You would've been proud. And Brenton did all right with his speech. Not that I don't still live for the day when we're the masters. There'll be no deaths in the pit then.'

'Four gone,' Frank said. 'There'll need to be an enquiry.' He was thinking ahead to the moment when he must enter the cage poised above the dark mine shaft again, and wondering if he would be up to it.

'That's what she said: Lady Muck. At the wedding she said, "We have to find out why." She stayed around in the office while we were waiting, I'll give her that. Her and the old Jew.'

'What was *he* doing there?' Frank asked.

'They were both there, father and son, doling out stotties and tea like they were going out of style. They're not tight, I'll give them that.' A sudden spasm crossed Anne's face and she gripped the chair. 'My God, Frank, that's what you get for being nice about Jews! Me waters've broken.'

Emmanuel Lansky felt very old that night as the Sabbath drew to a close – not just because of loss of sleep, but because of what he felt in his heart. He watched Sammy, who, thoughtful for him, was leafing through the *Jewish Chronicle*: what would become of the boy? He thought of the coming feast of Rosh Hashanah, New Year, a fresh start. But evil which was not rooted out would grow. *I am afraid*, Emmanuel Lansky thought, and climbed the stairs to his room to pray.

He was praying when a knock came at the door, and his son entered. 'I've been thinking, father, about the children.'

Sammy waved the *Chronicle*. 'There are two boys mentioned here, only twelve. We could take two boys – bring in a woman to care for them, set them up – send them to *yeshiva*, if it makes you happy!'

Lansky could not answer. Joy had swelled up in his chest and cut off his words, for his unruly and wayward son was a *mentsh* after all, and all was safe in the hands of God.

In the house at the Scar they drank Champagne, a good Laurent-Perrier chilled for the occasion. 'Once we're sure it's peace, I'm going to resign my seat,' Howard said. 'I'm needed here in Belgate.'

'If that's what you want to do,' Diana answered.

'Will you miss London? We'll still be able to go there, but I know how fond you are of Loelia.' There was so much more in Howard's question that Diana put down her glass and came to sit at his feet.

'We're grown up now, Loelia and I. Both of us have other things to do with our lives, other loyalties. Besides, we can use the telephone since we have incredibly rich husbands, which is probably just as well! Loelia sees the long-distance operator as an extension of herself.' Diana paused. 'And there's nothing in London I hanker for, Howard. Everything I want is here.'

There was silence, then, for awhile. *I mean it*, Diana told herself. *I must, must make it the truth*.

'Esther Gulliver has grown up, too,' Howard said at last. 'It seems only yesterday she was a child. I used to feel the most dreadful guilt about employing her when she looked as though she should be at school.'

'She's a tycoon now,' Diana said, 'according to that sister of hers. She's in partnership with the Lanskys; has her own house and a car. I'm glad. She was a nice little thing, and I was a less-than-wonderful employer.' She smiled up at him. 'There, I've confessed my sins. Now, pour me another glass of Champagne and take me to bed. Tomorrow the news may be bad again, and we'll all be steeped in gloom. Tonight, at least, let's celebrate.'

Howard poured the drinks and sat back in his chair. Was there peace at last? He could hardly believe it but he fervently hoped it was true. The nation had suffered enough in the last few years. He remembered the old King George V, broadcasting on the occasion of his Jubilee in 1935. The message had gone round the world, in the voice of a sick old man, touching hearts wherever it was heard. Especially the final words which had turned out to be his farewell: *'From my heart I thank you, my beloved people…'*

Within eight months the King was dead and the beloved people had plunged from one crisis into another. First the Mrs Simpson affair, then the abdication. The nightmare of unemployment and after that the mounting threat of war. And now there had been a compromise. Or a defeat? 'Let there be peace,' Howard thought. 'Let the beloved people be spared another war.'

Alone in her neat house, Esther leaned back in her chair, wiggling toes now mercifully free of her patent court shoes. She poured herself a glass of sherry from the table at her side and took an appreciative sip. It had been a nice wedding, but it was good to be home and a relief that Munich had turned out so well. Philip's son could grow up in an England free from the threat of war. She closed her eyes, trying to imagine what the boy would be like now, but it was too painful. Instead she took another drink and thought of the coming week. Anne would need help, with the baby almost due and Mary away. She could treat the youngest four –. well, maybe not the little one – to *Snow White* at the Regal. They'd all enjoy that. And she'd take cakes from Meng's when she went. Esther smiled, thinking of their faces when she arrived bearing gifts.

It had been a long day. She picked up the bottle and topped up her glass. 'No more after this,' she thought. But there must be a toast, Sammy's favourite. She raised her glass and spoke aloud: '*Lechayim*,' she said. 'To life.'

At that moment the youngest Maguire came roaring into the world; and, while England enjoyed a relieved and peaceful sleep, German troops crossed quietly into Czechoslovakia.

It is 1939 and the threat of war looms ever closer as Hitler unleashes terror across Europe. In the Durham mining village of Belgate, the inhabitants brace themselves for the conflict ahead.

While Howard Brenton, conservative MP and colliery owner, attempts to pacify the miners, his beautiful wife Diana is drawn once again to the lover who abandoned her. Meanwhile, Frank Maguire, chairman of the miners' union, struggles with his wife Anne to make ends meet and to control Estelle, their daughter, who is fatefully drawn to Rupert Brenton. And as the Lansky family copes with the arrival of two young Jewish refugees from Germany, Sammy Lansky enlists, leaving the care of his thriving business to the increasingly sophisticated Esther Gulliver.

As the crisis of war deepens, the people of Belgate are swept up in the struggle for survival that will eclipse personal differences and draw rich and poor together...

Coming soon from Little Books,
the story continues in:
Strength for the Morning

'A super story – the sort of book you simply do not want to finish'
Sunderland Echo

'Once again, Denise Robertson has created a world of real people, with a warmth that brings them to life... Will a third volume be enough?'
Northern Echo